Squire Throwleigh's Heir

Also by Michael Jecks

MICHAEL JECKS

Squire Throwleigh's Heir

**SIMON &
SCHUSTER**

London · New York · Sydney · Toronto · New Delhi

A CBS COMPANY

First published in 1999 by Headline Book Publishing

This edition published in Great Britain in 2013 by Simon & Schuster UK Ltd
A CBS COMPANY

1 3 5 7 9 10 8 6 4 2

Simon & Schuster UK Ltd
1st Floor
222 Gray's Inn Road
London
WC1X 8HB

www.simonandschuster.co.uk

Simon & Schuster Australia, Sydney

Simon & Schuster India, New Delhi

A CIP catalogue copy for this book is available
from the British Library.

ISBN: 978-1-47112-635-2
eBook ISBN: 978-1-47112-636-9

Typeset by Hewer Text UK Ltd, Edinburgh
Printed and bound in Great Britain by CPI Group (UK) Ltd, Croydon, CR0 4YY

In memory of Dick.
A kind father and generous father-in-law.
He is missed.

CAST OF CHARACTERS

Sir Baldwin of Furnshill   The Keeper of the King's Peace of Crediton in Devon, Sir Baldwin was once a Knight Templar, but when his Order was destroyed by the Pope and the French King, he managed to escape back to his ancestral home. Now he is known as an astute investigator of violent crimes.

Lady Jeanne   Baldwin met his lady while staying in Tavistock, and they became handfast soon after.

Edgar   Now Baldwin's servant, before Edgar was the knight's man-at-arms in the Knights Templar.

	He is a professional, trained fighter, but now enjoys the quieter existence of country life.
Bailiff Simon Puttock	An old friend of Sir Baldwin's, Simon is bailiff to the Warden of the Stannaries, the mining areas of Dartmoor. As such Simon has legal authority over those who live on the moors, and had often helped Baldwin in his enquiries.
Margaret Puttock	Simon's wife, daughter of a local farmer and mother of his child, Edith.
Hugh	Simon and Margaret's devoted servant.
Roger of Throwleigh	The local squire, who has died.
Herbert	Only son of the squire, and therefore his heir.
Lady Katharine	Squire Roger's wife, and mother of Herbert.
Daniel	The steward of Throwleigh manor and head servant to the squire's family.
Brother Stephen of York	An educated cleric who has served Squire Roger's lord, Sir Reginald of Hatherleigh, and who now tutors Herbert.
Petronilla	A young maid who works at the manor.

Anney	Personal maid to Lady Katharine, who has held this position since the death of one of her sons, poor young Tom.
Thomas of Exeter	A grabbing merchant, now down on his luck, who is the brother of Squire Roger.
Nicholas	This thuggish man is the senior servant in Thomas's household.
Sir James van Relenghes	Squire Roger had served in the King's army and Sir James claims comradeship with him when he visits the manor a short time after the squire's death.
Godfrey	In these troubled times, Godfrey, a retired mercenary soldier, earns his money from training people to protect themselves. Sir James brought him as his personal guard.
Edmund	A local villein who is being evicted from his rented lands.
Christiana	Edmund's wife.
Jordan	Edmund and Christiana's son, and Herbert's playmate.
Alan	Anney's son and Jordan's and Herbert's friend.

AUTHOR'S NOTE

Historical novels present some unique problems for the author. A plot may form with great clarity and precision in the author's head – books often more or less write themselves once the characters have been fleshed out – but what sort of vocabulary should one use to tell a story, set like this one, in the 1300s?

English is an astonishingly rich language, with a fabulous bank of old or ancient words upon which an enterprising novelist can draw to add authenticity. By throwing in references to, for example, a 'misericord' – the dagger used by knights to put an enemy out of his misery, or a 'falchion' – a heavy-bladed, single-edged sword used by some men-at-arms, and by mentioning trailbastons and shavaldours, crucks and cob . . . one can delight those readers who enjoy discovering medieval terms.

And yet no one could write an entire story using the same vocabulary which was current in the 1300s.

English in those far-off days was a mixture of Latin, Norman French, German, Saxon, and even some Arabic – utterly incomprehensible to most of us in the late twentieth century. Any person doubting this should get hold of a copy of Chaucer's *Canterbury Tales* in its original form, unedited and untranslated; I defy anyone to understand a single line.

Even apparently familiar words can fool the casual reader; our modern interpretation will often be completely different from that understood in centuries gone by. For an easy example, look at the word 'nice': its meaning has altered from 'foolish' or 'stupid', 'extravagant in dress', and 'slothful' in the 1300s, through 'particular' and 'precise' in the 1600s, to its present meaning of 'agreeable'.

Many writers try to get around this problem by giving a spurious patina of authenticity to their work. They throw in the odd 'Gadzooks' in the hope that it will lull the reader into believing that they have researched their subject carefully. Reader, beware! 'Gadzooks', for example, was first recorded in the late 1600s, so would be completely out of place in one of my novels. Most people recognise words of this nature because they were used by Shakespeare, and link that later medieval period with earlier times, but people in England and their language changed massively between 1300 and 1500.

I have deliberately chosen to write my stories in the language of today, having made the simple assumption that if an English reader were to buy a copy of *War and Peace* by Tolstoy, or even *The Three Musketeers* by Dumas, he or she would expect the Russian and French texts to have been translated; likewise the work of Geoffrey Chaucer.

But there is another problem, of course. If one writes in the language of today, one may be tempted to use words that couldn't have been in common parlance in the historical period in question. I recently received a letter of complaint on exactly that point: the lady was irritated that I had used words like 'posse' and 'gang', along with 'thug' and 'lynch'. She said that these words were too modern for her taste and dragged her back from the 1300s to the present, distracting her from the main story.

It is a difficult charge to answer, because it shows precisely the double-sided problem confronting a writer of historical novels.

Take 'posse'. Most people associate this word with cheap extras playing a band of grubby cowboys in a Hollywood Western; in reality, it is a very ancient word; 'posse comitatus' was a legal term defining a group of armed men or an armed force, and 'posse' was certainly in use in 1300; at the same time 'gang' was being used as a collective term for a group of things or people. Thus these two words were actually *correct* for the period, and the fact that they are still in use today is hardly my fault! In the case of 'thug' and 'lynch', 'thug' has been known in English only since the 1600s, and 'lynch' since the 1780s; if a writer were to exclude any words which have come into use over the last two hundred years – or, worse, four hundred – he or she would find it next to impossible to write anything!

Writing an historical novel is therefore fraught with dangers; one faces upsetting some folk by using archaic, incomprehensible terms, and alienating others by employing words which are simply too contemporary. All I can do is plead the best of intentions and try to steer a middle road in

7

the hope that people will enjoy my books for what they are: lively medieval mysteries that spring from my own over-heated imagination!

It is time now to apologise to those readers who expect to find an accurate local history within these pages. In *Squire Throwleigh's Heir* I have shamefully misused north-eastern Dartmoor. There *was* no manor west of Throwleigh towards Shilstone to the best of my knowledge; its existence was invented by me for the benefit of the story.

Nor was there ever a Squire Roger with a son called Herbert. I am not aware of the existence of a real James van Relenghes, nor his guard Godfrey, Thomas of Exeter, Stephen of York, or of any of the other characters.

However, similar incidents to those portrayed in this novel *did* happen. Men and women who had been freed from their serfdom were sometimes appallingly badly treated, their status as freemen being denied by avaricious lords and ladies. For one real-life example of sheer greed, look to Countess Margaret of Norfolk, who challenged poor Alice Comyn, accusing her of not being a freewoman. Alice's father had been made free by Earl Thomas, the Countess's father, but the Countess found a loophole: Earl Thomas's estate was under an entail such that the Earl couldn't alienate property except during his lifetime. Thus, the Countess argued, Alice couldn't be free. On the Earl's death, Alice's father's rights to freedom were automatically revoked, as were those of all his children.

This was sharp practice of the worst kind, but it wasn't the only example. Other cases abound.

In the same way, I have not invented 'Conventionary Tenure'. This unpleasant form of tenancy came into existence during the early 1300s in the earldom of Cornwall, and appears to have been used around the western borders of Devon too. Under its terms, people could be thrown from the land they and their forefathers had held for decades simply because another person offered a higher rent. Fortunately, not all landlords took part in this.

One last word is important, I feel.

In this novel, I have made some comments on the English martial arts. Some may doubt that there were expert English fighters because over the years we have happily forgotten these predecessors of modern boxing.

However, although now it is considered wrong for people to learn to use weapons, and the police control all access to firearms for even target purposes, this is an extremely recent development. In previous decades the British have led the world in methods of self-defence because we have tradition-ally believed in the right to 'keep and bear arms' to protect ourselves from foreign invasion or against overbearing governments in London. In both world wars this century, it was the rifle and pistol shooters of Great Britain who were first to join the Army. The proof of this lies in the archives of clubs such as my own; over half its members were wiped out during one day on the Somme.

Throughout Britain's long history, skills and techniques have been passed down that have enabled our fighting men to win battles all over the world. For instance, our sailors were still learning sword-fighting with sabres up until very recent times – skills which were recorded before the Conquest.

For those who wish to learn more about ancient English fighting techniques, I heartily recommend Terry Brown's

MICHAEL JECKS

English Martial Arts, published by Anglo-Saxon Books. This fascinating book tracks the development of the 'Master of Defence' through history, and because Terry himself is a modern martial arts expert, he can bring to life some of the methods of fighting with broadsword, sword and buckler, sword and dagger, and especially quarter- and half-staff.

Even so, in *Squire Throwleigh's Heir* the way in which fights are presented, the types of weapons used and the methods of using them, are all drawn from my imagination, and any errors are entirely my own responsibility.

Michael Jecks
Dartmoor
October 1998

CHAPTER ONE

If he'd known that this was the day he was going to die, Squire Roger of Throwleigh would have behaved more coolly, but lacking this prescience, he lost his temper instead.

It wasn't his little son Herbert's sullenness so much as his denial of any knowledge of the matter that made Roger's blood boil. Playing with friends in the orchard was so petty an offence that the squire wouldn't usually have bothered to get to the bottom of it, but he knew Herbert had been there – he had seen him! – and even as the squire bellowed for the boys to stop, he had seen his own lad turn, the fear transforming his face.

By then it was already too late. Had the squire's horse been to hand, he might have been able to head them off before they could reach the concealment of the bushes, but his horse was in the yard with the rest of his hunting party, and so the miscreants had escaped, scurrying away through the long undergrowth and pelting for the riverbank.

When the squire demanded the identities of the culprits, it wasn't with a view to exacting punishment. He was a sporting man, and knew that he should long ago have secured this gap in the hedge. The hole would have to be plugged, and for now he had only a casual interest in which of the vill's youngsters had dared trespass on his land.

'I don't know.'

At first the squire had been amused. The response was the instinctive answer of a small child to an enquiry by Authority, and Roger had almost been inclined to shrug it off, but when he followed up his query by promising not to mete out retribution, he became irritated by Herbert's refusal to cooperate. It was honourable of him to try to protect his friends, but his refusal to admit to any knowledge of the crime was plain foolish – and intolerable.

'Do you mean to say you will not tell me who the others were?' he thundered.

'I don't know them, sir,' Master Herbert stated stoutly, his small round face pale, his eyes downcast in trepidation.

His father seized his arm. 'Don't lie to me! I saw you with them! I saw you there, shoving them out – do you think I'm blind and stupid? Now tell me who they were!'

The boy shook his head stubbornly, and his father felt the familiar tension in his chest, like a band tightening around his heart. 'You deny you were with them?' he grated, all patience flown. 'Then I'll tell you who they were: Jordan and Alan! That's who you're protecting, isn't it?'

'Father, please don't have them punished . . . It was my idea, not Alan's; and Jordan gets such a dreadful beating when his father is angry.'

The wan complexion and tone of near-desperation in the five-year-old's voice almost made Squire Roger relent, but if he didn't carry out his threat, his son might feel he would always back down in the face of a plea. 'No. You lied. If you'd told me yourself who they were, I wouldn't bother, but you lied to me. Now you'll see what harvest your deceit yields. *Brother Stephen!*'

'Father, please, I . . .'

The squire strode towards the house, pulling his son after him. He had crossed half the distance when the priest came hurrying.

'Brother, my son has lied to me: you'll thrash him to teach him never to do it again,' said the squire curtly. The tall, thin priest took Master Herbert's arm, nodded silently, and took the boy away.

Squire Roger watched his son being dragged from the court. The lad stared up at the priest with a look of sullen fear, and not for the first time the squire felt near-contempt for his boy. He'd been found in the wrong, and should accept his punishment, yet he always exhibited this feeble-spirited horror of any form of retribution.

He had no idea it was the last time he would ever see his son.

In Exeter, Godfrey of London finished the last of his hundred press-ups on his clenched fists and sprang lightly to his feet, breathing easily.

It was essential to keep fit, and Godfrey despaired of those clients who ignored this, the single most vital element of one's training. All too often youngsters professing a desire to learn his skills would swear to follow his strict regime, but they'd then go feasting and whoring, indulging their gluttonous whims. Their bellies would grow flabby, they'd develop double or – God's blood! – treble chins, and all the time they'd say they were obeying his orders. It was pathetic.

Godfrey was not sanguine about their prospects: they would suffer or die as a result of their shortsightedness. He was paid, and paid well, to teach them – and if they wished to learn he could instruct them in techniques which should, all things being equal, keep them alive. If they wanted him as their tutor without bothering to pick up anything from him, it was their loss. He got his money and that was all that mattered.

He walked to the rack and selected a pair of cudgels, a man of middle height, with a square face and grizzled hair. His arms were not heavily muscled, nor were his shoulders over-wide, but he had a loose, controlled way of walking which to another fighter would be enough warning. His features held the proof of his history: one long scar cut across his nose, under his left eye, and then down below his cheekbone; a second swept from temple to beneath his thinning scalp; a third followed the line of his right jawbone. But those who had inflicted these injuries had all paid in kind.

Hefting the clubs, he stood in the outside guard, his right hand forward, the club's tip pointing up to protect his right flank, while holding the left one low to cover his belly. Slowly he began the measured sequence he rehearsed each morning. His right hand moved back to block an imaginary attack, his left advanced to parry a second; his right twisted and lunged forward for the opponent's head. Retreating slowly, he twisted his torso to swing in hard with his left, then thrust with his right before reverting to the outside guard again.

As he swung them in his slow dance of defence, his mind wandered, and he reviewed the potential of his clients – especially his most recent, and strangest, Sir James van Relenghes.

It was common enough for Godfrey to be hired to show how different weapons could be used, but he was sure that in this case there was more to it than mere anxiety about felons. The mention of a single man's name had made his client mad. Never before had Godfrey seen such powerful loathing on someone's face.

They had been walking in the court before Exeter Cathedral, and had stood aside to allow a priest to pass. The fellow had nodded politely to them in gratitude, but then, noticing another man ahead, about to duck into an alleyway, the cleric had called out, increasing his pace to overtake him, lifting his robe for greater speed: 'Is that you, Master? Master Thomas Throwleigh!'

Van Relenghes started as if he recognised the name, and swore in a venomous undertone. He spoke in Flemish, but Godfrey had fought in the Low Countries and understood the hoarse-sounding, guttural language.

'Damn you, Squire Roger of Throwleigh, damn you, your poxy brother Thomas, and all your line. May you all burn in hellfire for eternity!'

Squire Roger watched his son being dragged away with mixed feelings of guilt and irritation.

It was high time Herbert grew up. He was five, old enough to be sent to a household to learn the twin crafts of courtesy and war. A place for him had been confirmed at the home of Sir Reginald of Hatherleigh, and there, Squire Roger was sure, the lad would mature well. Sir Reginald was known to be a firm disciplinarian.

The squire strolled to his horse. His pack of harriers were ready, milling round the yard and making the horses whisk their tails irritably. His berner, the master of hounds, and his whipper-in were mounted and waiting. Squire Roger hesitated; when he'd seen the boys in the orchard he'd been about to set off hunting, yet now he must delay his sport to seek the culprits. It was frustrating: for a moment he was tempted to forget the whole thing.

His horse gave a skittish dance, and the squire bit back a curse, hauling the reins to cow the beast. The cause was his son's shriek, coming from the chapel's open shutters high overhead. In the court the cries were pitiable, each interspersed with the solid crack of a stiffened leather strap.

Squire Roger peered up indecisively. Herbert's suffering appeared to make further retribution unnecessary. He'd almost decided to leave the matter and ride for the chase when he caught a glimpse of a figure hurrying towards him and gave an inward groan. It was his wife, and he knew the line she would take.

'Husband, the priest is beating Herbert again!' she cried.

'My dear, I told him to. Our boy lied to me.'

Lady Katharine listened as he explained what had happened. 'But he is so young still,' she protested. 'He's only five.'

'If he's old enough to lie, he's old enough to feel the strap.'

'When all he did was try to protect others?'

Her words made his doubts return. 'What would you have me do, Lady? Ignore his lies?' he demanded gruffly.

'You could at least catch the boys who were with him, and make sure that every welt on our son's backside is felt by those whom he defended,' she pointed out.

Squire Roger glanced at his berner, who studiously avoided meeting his look, and finally gave an exasperated grunt. 'Oh, very well, woman! I'll go to the vill and chastise the brats, but you realise this will ruin my morning? Why I should have to waste my time on trivial issues like this, I hardly know, but since you demand it, I suppose I must comply.'

He mounted, cocking an eye at the open window as another cry burst out, and whirled his horse round. His wife called to him, and he hesitated for a fraction of a moment, long enough to acknowledge her raised hand. Then, slowly, her mouth widened in a broad smile and over his irritation he felt his heart beat faster with love for her.

He grinned in return, then trotted over to her, took her by the shoulder, and kissed her. Bowing from the waist, he made her a mock salute before pointing his horse's head to the gate and setting off to the little vill.

Alan stopped panting, swallowing hard as he tried to listen over his thudding heart. 'Shut up!'

His accomplice, Jordan, gave him a hurt look. 'How can I stop breathing? You get me to run as fast as I can, it's only *normal* to want to breathe afterwards.'

'Shut up, or I'll make you!' Alan threatened, the light of battle shining in his eyes.

Seeing his clenched fists, Jordan subsided, scuffing his bare toes in the dirt beside the road, mumbling to himself.

He didn't see why Alan should always try to lord it over him. There might be two years between them, but Jordan knew he was just as mature as his friend.

'Shut up, I said!' Alan hissed.

Jordan would never forget this day, nor the terror of being chased by the squire. As soon as they'd heard his voice they'd taken to their heels. Squire Roger was a figure of immense awe. He owned the land and the people on it. Fabulously wealthy, he needed three shelves on his sideboard just to show all his plates and jugs. Whenever Jordan thought of the man, that was the first thing that sprang to mind, the stunning amount of money Squire Roger must have in order to acquire so many beautiful pieces. He'd heard it rumoured that some were silver as well – real, solid silver!

He could just see the manor from here – a massive grey block on the side of the hill above them. Glancing towards it, Jordan felt a shudder pass down his back. It'd been very close that time. He'd been so sure he could hear the squire's horse pounding after them as he pelted along behind Alan; he could imagine the rider, his arm raised, the whip in his hand, ready to bring it down on their heads.

It was all Alan's fault, Jordan thought moodily. Just because he was that little bit older, he thought he could get away with anything. Sometimes Jordan felt that although he was only nine, he was quicker to recognise potential danger than his friend. And now they were both in for a thrashing, thanks to Alan's stupidity – Jordan had never wanted to see the lambs in the orchard in the first place.

'I don't think they're following,' Alan said hopefully.

Jordan snorted in derision. 'You reckon he didn't see us? What – when he bellowed like that?'

'He may not've realised who we were.'

'How many boys are there in the village?' Jordan asked scathingly.

'Well, I don't hear his horses, do you?' Alan challenged.

Jordan scowled with disgust, and he pointed. Alan spun around and saw the squire's men leaving the gate. He gave a small sigh of resignation. 'Oh. That's that, then!'

Anney, maidservant to Lady Katharine, quietly closed the door to the chapel and made her way down the spiral staircase. She had seen it all, the boy being dragged inside, his stubborn refusal to bend over the priest's knee, the sudden slap Brother Stephen had aimed at his face to make him obey, the ripping of his shirt and hose while his hands were firmly gripped by the man of God, who stared at his altar with a kind of wondering fervour before wielding the heavy strap on the child's bare buttocks.

It was with the greatest difficulty that she managed to keep the grin of delight from her face.

Any pain inflicted on the boy who had killed her son was welcome.

CHAPTER TWO

The ride to Throwleigh was only short, but the squire was of a mind to dawdle. Although it was a trivial little incident, the recent scene had brought his son to the forefront of his mind, and the squire was growing anxious on his boy's behalf.

It wasn't the lie in particular: his son was only young, and children had a different view of the world. No, Herbert was cause for concern because of the squire himself. He was old – almost fifty – and soon must be dead. Many heirs met with fatal accidents while still young, when those around them could sniff a potential profit from their death, and Roger knew there were several who might consider their lives enhanced by Herbert's absence.

The priest should be able to help defend the boy but there, too, was a problem. Stephen was reliable, and Sir Reginald's letter introducing him had been glowing: Sir Reginald had used the tall, pale, ascetic priest as tutor for his own sons, and the cleric's firm discipline had been enough even for that strict knight. In any case, once Sir Reginald had recommended Stephen, it was impossible for his squire to refuse the honour of being granted the same teacher who had taught the knight's own sons.

And yet there was a worrying enthusiasm in the way Stephen set about 'chastising' his charge; he seemed to take delight in beating any disobedience or misbehaviour out of Herbert and his friends. There was that story Roger had heard about him . . .

With that Squire Roger shook his head. It must be a rumour. If it were true, someone would have proof. Rumours were always rife about men who wore the cloth; nobody believed a man could renounce the pleasures of the flesh. Ignorant peasants were prepared to believe the most lurid stories about the libidinous exploits of priests, rather than accept that they might be able to stick to their oaths of chastity. No, it had to be a rumour, and the squire wouldn't give it any credence.

Clattering into the village, he felt the pain clamping around his heart again, increasing with the prospect of the imminent confrontation. The tightness had been getting worse for some weeks now. He had known it when he was still a young man, back in the days of the French and Welsh wars, when he had boldly followed Sir Reginald behind the King's banner. Then, excitement had led to a similar tautness within his breast as he spurred his horse on to battle.

Of course, that was all many years ago now. King Edward was dead and in his grave, and his lacklustre son, Edward II, had taken the throne. The squire hawked and spat with contempt. Cocking his leg over his horse's withers, he rested his elbow on his knee and cupped his chin as he considered his King with a sour revulsion.

All the auguries were good for King Edward II's reign: he had inherited subjects who were at peace with each other, a well-filled Exchequer and a contented kingdom – and yet since 1307 when he became King he had squandered them all. His men he had slaughtered in the ruinous battles with the Scots, especially at Bannockburn; his money had been frittered away piecemeal in foolish company with actors, singers and labourers; and the contentment of his kingdom was destroyed by stories of his fondness for the men in his court.

More rumours, Roger noted heavily. Lazy fools with nothing better to do would often slander their betters, and yet Roger himself didn't doubt that much said about the King was true. He recalled how Edward had rewarded his very close friend Gaveston, creating him Earl of Cornwall, and since Gaveston's death at the hand of the Earl of Warwick, the King had transferred his affections to young Hugh Despenser, another man whom Roger viewed askance. The Despenser family was keen to expand its influence and gain more land and power, and the ruthless, acquisitive young Hugh was even now imposing his will on the Welsh lords in an attempt to win for himself the title of Earl.

This was the world his son had to survive in, Roger reflected sadly. If he could stay alive, perhaps he could protect his boy: employ a good master of weapons to show him how to physically defend himself; find a politically aware scholar to teach him how to keep himself safe from barons like the Despensers, who would otherwise steal his lands and property.

But the squire knew he wouldn't be around for much longer. All he could do was try to ensure that his son was shielded from some of the most obvious dangers.

At least his wife would be able to advise their boy, he reminded himself. Katharine was capable of protecting herself *and* Herbert. Thinking of her brought a smile to his face. To him, their marriage still seemed little short of a miracle. His sole regret was knowing that he must leave her alone to fend for herself and their son. The certainty of their separation, until they could meet again in Heaven, made his spirits fall whenever his thoughts turned that way.

Reaching the vill, he forced himself to throw off his dejection. The church stood alone under the looming height of the hills, while the houses and cottages huddled below it as if seeking some warmth from each other, like a pack of hounds curling up together against the cold. Some of the places had drifts of smoke wisping from them, all magically swept away with each fresh gust of wind. The road was thick with mud and dung from horse and cattle, and the squire swore as a gobbet of green-brown cow's muck splattered on his tunic. He brought his leg back down to his stirrup and spurred to a slow canter.

The first of the houses he must visit was out at the northern edge, and he knew his way there only too well. He had been there often enough before.

It was little more than a shack. The whitewash had worn away from the walls, exposing the cob to the elements, and the mud mixture had been washed off it in large runnels. Without a man, it was hard for her to keep the cottage maintained, Roger reflected. He could see the dilapidation all around. The thatch was thin, sunken, moss-covered and holed by nesting birds; the door was crooked, and dragged on the ground, scraping an arc in the dirt; one shutter was almost off its hinges. Anney, the serf who lived here, was fortunate in having work at the squire's hall, for without it, since her man's dereliction, she would be reliant solely on the generosity of her neighbours.

'Alan,' he bellowed as he stopped outside her door, 'where are you, boy? Alan!' There was no reply, and the squire scowled. 'Where is the little devil?'

The berner gave a quiet cough. 'I think he's in the fields, scaring the birds.'

'Well, Berner, you go and find the bastard and give him four lashes from your whip, all right? We'll go and see the other lad.'

The squire jerked his horse's head round and set off unwillingly to Edmund's farm. He didn't want to see Edmund; not now he'd told the fellow he was to be thrown off his land.

Edmund was drunk. There was nothing new in that, but today he was less bitter in his cups than usual; today he was maudlin, more keen on bemoaning his fate than blaming others for it. His wife was relieved because it meant she was less likely to suffer a beating, but their problems weren't going to go away.

Edmund sat on his three-legged stool at the door, his pot in his hand, drinking slowly. There was much to consider, for Edmund was about to be evicted from his home and his lands. Another man had offered money for the tenancy of his little parcel of land, and Edmund couldn't better the offer, not after the last few years.

If he had been a philosopher, Edmund would have blamed fate, but as it was he had no doubt about who was responsible for this disaster: his lord, Squire Roger.

Hearing yelping, he stared down the road in a lacklustre manner. Soon he realised it must be a large pack of hounds – and there was only one man in many miles who could have such a number of beasts for hunting. Suddenly Edmund's mouth went dry: the squire must be coming already to throw him from the land!

He stood, spilling ale, and gazed up the road with a quick fear, expecting to see an army of retainers, but a moment's reflection made him calm down, and he shakily set his pot on the ground. It wasn't the quarter day, that wasn't for two more weeks, and Steward Daniel had promised he had until then to find the money. Still, as the noise came closer, he was convinced that this must be his squire. Braced with a new resolution, Edmund stepped forward until he was in the roadway. He would beg.

He had no choice. There was no way he could find the extra money. He had nothing to sell, neither produce from his land nor goods he had made, and any money he had saved had already gone on essentials. The squire was a kindly man – Edmund's father had often said so – so surely Squire Roger would look favourably on him, the son of his favourite man-at-arms?

Licking his lips nervously, Edmund glanced longingly at his pot, but before he could fill it, Squire Roger cantered into view, his hounds at his horse's hooves.

'Where's your boy, Edmund?'

Edmund blinked. 'Jordan? He's off playing somewhere, I think – with Alan, I expect. Squire, may I speak to you? I have a favour to beg, and—'

25

'Silence! Just tell me where he is,' Roger snapped. 'He was in my orchard this morning and I want him punished.'

'I will see to it, sir, but first can I ask you about my tenancy?'

'What?' The squire cast him an irritable look. 'You need to speak to Daniel about that.'

'But he says I must go if I can't pay, sir! Where can we go if you throw us off our land?'

The squire looked meaningfully at the pot by the stool. 'Perhaps if you worked harder, you'd earn enough to keep the place, Edmund. Why should I help a family of trespassers? If you can't keep your damned son under control, don't expect me to help you!'

'But, sir, think of my father and the service he gave you!' Edmund had dropped to his knees, and now he touched the squire's stirrup. 'Please, sir, give me a little longer to pay.'

Squire Roger glowered down at his tenant with contempt. 'Get up, man! Your father wouldn't have begged like a leper.'

The squire was struck with a sudden anger. This feeble-minded dolt was behaving like a fool, pleading while his son was no doubt laughing behind the squire's back, knowing he could go and play in the orchard any time the squire's own son gave him warning. Herbert was proved to be a liar; his berner was God knew where, seeking the other brat, so Squire Roger couldn't go hunting as he wanted – and now this wretch was clinging to his stirrup like a lovesick woman stopping her lover from riding to war.

'Get up, I said!' Tension was gripping his whole chest now as his rage built. Around his heart he could feel the growing tightness.

'Please, Squire.'

'Let go of my foot, you bastard!'

His whipper-in came forward and idly, with as little emotion as if he were flicking a fly away, brought the heavy stock of his whip down on Edmund's head. The farmer collapsed, calling, 'Squire, please!'

A sharp pain suddenly exploded in the squire's head, and there was a simultaneous bursting in his chest. He couldn't breathe: his mouth opened once, twice, but he could make no sound. There was a chill sweat springing from his forehead, and he wanted to wipe it away, but his hand was numb, while his arm was full of shooting agony; pain stabbing up and down like raking thrusts from a heavy knife. Through the horror of his sudden paralysis, he saw Edmund fall back, a gash on his forehead welling thick blood. The squire wanted to tell the whipper-in to stop, even as he saw the stock rise a second time.

For Edmund, lying stunned as the horses danced around, the sight of the weighted whip's handle looked like the instrument of his death. A hoof caught his forehead a glancing blow, and he felt nausea rising, but before he lost consciousness, he saw Squire Roger.

The squire had gone an ashen colour – the colour of a corpse. His eyes were walled and blank, his lips blue. As Edmund watched, the squire gave a short gasp, as of infinite suffering, and toppled slowly from the saddle.

He was dead before his head struck the roadway.

'He's *what*?' Thomas cried, and dropped his goblet. His brother, Squire Roger of Throwleigh – *dead*! Blood-red wine spread out in a puddle by his foot, while the gaudy gilt cup rolled off the dais and came to rest against the messenger's foot.

'Sir, Daniel the steward sent me to warn you. The funeral will be . . .'

'Yes, yes, I heard you the first time,' Thomas broke in impatiently, his face serious, demonstrating the correct sadness on hearing of his sibling's death. 'It's awful! Poor Roger, dying like that – the manor must be in a turmoil. Well, it's plain I must go back. You'll need wine and food: there's plenty in my kitchen. See my cook and get yourself vittles. I shall speak to you again before you leave. Poor Roger!'

He dismissed the man with a wave of his hand, and sat staring at the door for several minutes, hardly moving. '*Dead!*' he exclaimed once, shaking his head, but then slapped his thigh and gave a low, wheezing laugh. 'Dead!'

Standing, he retrieved his goblet, filled it, and held it up in a silent toast. Drinking deeply, he smacked his lips, and laughed again. 'Oh, and here's to my brother's poor grieving widow, dear little Katharine, lady of the hall – but not for much longer!' Pausing, he bellowed, '*Nick!*'

'Sir?'

The voice of his steward came from the screens passage, and Thomas jerked his head. 'Come in here!'

Nicholas was a little older than his master. Short, with a leather jack stretched tightly over his broad shoulders and a face marked heavily with the pox, he looked more a man-at-arms than a bottler, which was the case. He had been a soldier for a period, until his master had taken him on as a servant, and ever since he had served Thomas loyally. He glanced at his master curiously from shrewd brown eyes.

'Tomorrow we leave for my brother's house in Dartmoor. Pack clothing and essentials for four weeks,' Thomas instructed self-importantly.

'Your brother's? But I thought you and he hated each other,' Nick said, his spirits falling. In his mind's eye he could see the moors again – cold, bleak lands in which a man could die without anyone realising.

'Ah, but my brother, the skinflint with the heart of frozen lead, has died, Nicholas. That means we may have a solution to our problems – for a nice, fat, juicy inheritance may well be flying our way. Now make haste and pack, and with any luck when we return it'll be with my brother's money in our purses.'

CHAPTER THREE

Godfrey swore under his breath and let the point of his rebated sword drop an inch or two. 'I said hold your hand *here*, at the belly.'

His student, a sulky youth brought up in Italy, sneered at him: 'It's hardly an elegant posture, is it? My teacher in Venice told me to hold my arm out behind because it balances the body. It puts the attacker at a disadvantage, too, because he can't see so much of the body to hit.'

'Really? Show me, then. I'm not too old to learn.'

Godfrey returned to the outside guard, his sword hand well out to his right, blade angled upwards, so that he was peering just under the middle of the blade at his opponent, while he held his left hand out flat, low before his belly. The young man, little more than a boy, smirked happily, danced on the balls of his feet for a moment or two to ease his calves, then sprang into his imitation of the outside guard, his arm held out behind him.

It was a pose Godfrey had seen often enough with those who had stayed a while on the continent. There men preferred to look fashionable rather than fight effectively. Godfrey's attitude was entirely pragmatic and English: if he was forced into a fight, he had one aim, and that was to *win*! If his left hand was dangling out behind his body, it might well give some benefit in terms of balance, but that advantage was outweighed by the fact that it left his whole left side unprotected. While he concentrated on the lad before him, Godfrey decided how to teach this simple lesson.

There was a flash. Godfrey saw the attack not so much in the movement of the blade itself, but in the sudden narrowing of the lad's eyes as he moved his sword arm, lunging forwards with his whole body. Godfrey gave an inward sigh as he saw his pupil shift foot, hand and body in one united movement, and brought his own blade down to block it easily. He made no other move, unsure whether the stabbing manoeuvre could be a part of a feint, but his attacker pulled back, a slight frown wrinkling his forehead, and Godfrey had to suppress a groan. He had hoped that there might be a second blow concealed beneath the obvious one.

When the second stamp, lunge, stab came, Godfrey blocked the sword, then stepped quickly to his left, grabbing his opponent's sword arm as he went. He put his foot on the boy's forward boot and pulled. The lad was already off-balance, and this dragged him over. As he fell, Godfrey held his blade at his belly.

'That's not fair! You shouldn't hold a man's arm!' the student spluttered angrily once he had managed to rise to a sitting position.

Godfrey hauled him up by his shirt and held him close, staring into the suddenly scared face while the point of his blunted sword tickled the boy's throat. 'You think an outlaw could give a bollock about what's fair or not?' he hissed through clenched teeth. 'You reckon a drawlatch would think, "Oh, I mustn't kick the poor master in the coddes because he's got a sword, and it wouldn't be fair"?' He dropped the mincing tone he had adopted and shook his pupil with contempt. 'If you want to stay alive, assume your enemy will be devious and unfair – and make sure you're nastier than *him*. Now pick up your sword and try again.'

They had three more bouts. In the second, Godfrey scornfully knocked the lad's sword aside and grabbed his shirt, kicking away his legs and shoving him over. Next his student tried a half-decent left attack followed by a right slash that almost surprised Godfrey, but he blocked both, knocked the fellow's arm and spun him around before drawing his sword along the length of his opponent's back and kicking him down. Their last combat involved a short flurry of blades, a hit, then a second and a third, before Godfrey had come close enough to punch the boy, not too hard, on the jaw while his blade pressed unrelentingly on his belly.

It was while he was wiping his face with his shirt that he heard the door shut, and turned to see his newest client standing in the doorway, a faint smile on his face as he perused the scene. On the floor before Godfrey, his student was gazing up with fury in his eyes while he felt his jaw, but Godfrey also saw the beginnings of respect. He kicked his opponent's sword away before reaching down and helping him to his feet. 'Right! You've tried your Venetian ways, and you'll agree there's merit in mine. Next week we'll practise techniques which won't look elegant, but which'll save your life.'

'Not next week, Godfrey.'

The master of arms glanced at his client. He was leaning on the wall, a broad grin on his face.

'No, next week you will come with me to a little manor out on the moors, where we will visit the house of an old friend of mine. A squire who has, very sadly, died. You will be my guard.'

It was three days later that Simon Puttock and Sir Baldwin Furnshill made their journey to the little village of Throwleigh. They had left the knight's home in Cadbury early in the morning, and after taking two halts to rest their horses and take refreshment from their wineskins, they had not made particularly good time, but were at least reasonably fresh as they breasted a hill and could at last see Dartmoor ahead through the trees.

For Simon, as they jogged slowly down the muddy, rutted track, it was a return to his new home. As one of the bailiffs to the Warden of the Stannaries he had been living at Lydford for five years now, riding out over the wild lands to settle arguments or arrest criminals. Seeing the bleak landscape ahead was almost welcome. At the sight of the awesome bulk of Cosdon Hill to their right, Simon felt his heart give a leap before their view was obliterated once more and the travellers had to duck beneath another spread of low beech branches.

Baldwin couldn't feel the same pleasure. To him the land-scape of Dartmoor was barren, infertile. It was as if a race of giants had fought a pitched battle here and blasted the whole area until nothing remained, not even a tree. To him it felt threatening and unwholesome.

It wasn't only the moors, either. Even here, in the lush woodland immediately north there were very few people; wherever Baldwin saw evidence of habitation, it looked long deserted. Every so often he would notice a weed-strewn track leading into the trees, proof of a long-disused assart, where someone had hacked down trees to build his cabin or to feed his fires. These woods had been cleared for coppices and farming; men had burned out the roots of old trees, gradually beating back the frontier of the woodland until enough bare soil existed to graze a cow. This was the way the land had been brought to heel over decades – but now the land had won.

The assarts looked as if they had lain deserted for ages. Since the appalling famines of 1315 and 1316, many of the smaller farms and homesteads even this far west had been evacuated, and where men had once worked, burning and sawing, now the brambles and nettles had taken over. Wherever the trees allowed a sprinkle of sun to strike the ground, the ubiquitous foxglove had colonised and erased almost all evidence of man's occupation.

It all suited his mood, for Sir Baldwin Furnshill, the Keeper of the King's Peace in Crediton, was joining his friend to witness the funeral of Squire Roger of Throwleigh, representing the Sheriff, who had been called away to meet the King's procurers, while Simon was there to represent the Warden himself.

The knight, a tall man in his middle forties with the build of a swordsman, broad-shouldered with a heavily muscled right arm and still slim-waisted, rode easily, as befitted someone who had travelled extensively. His face was keen and sharp, with a neatly trimmed beard of the same dark colour as his hair, but his features had been marked with pain over the years: lines lay etched deeply into his forehead and at either side of his mouth.

His companion, a close friend, was more than ten years younger, yet did not look it. Simon Puttock's hair was richly peppered with grey, and his figure was beginning to run to fat.

'You are putting on weight, Simon.'

'Bollocks!'

Baldwin gave him a look of haughty disdain.

'If you want to distract yourself, think again about your fiancée,' Simon laughed. 'Don't try getting at me.'

'It is a shame that Squire Roger chose this moment to die,' Baldwin admitted.

'Why, because it's only a short while to your wedding, you mean? Ah, I'm sure he'd be sorry to have dragged you from your home when you're in the middle of the preparations.'

That was why Simon had been with his friend. Simon's wife was helping Lady Jeanne, Baldwin's fiancée, to prepare for their wedding, and Simon had been diverting Baldwin, trying to keep his mind from the myriad details of the celebration – and preventing the knight from getting in Jeanne's and Margaret's way. For once it was a relief to Simon that his daughter was not with him, for Edith had elected to stay at Lydford with a friend rather than make the gruelling journey to Furnshill. If she had also been there, Simon was sure she would have been under the feet of the bride-to-be at every opportunity.

'You think *I* have any say about the arrangements?' Baldwin protested. 'God's bones! I had thought that Jeanne would have had little time to organise *me*, especially now she's lost her maidservant.' It was a never-ending source of pleasure to him that she had, too, he reflected secretly. Jeanne's 'maid' had been a large, coarse, brutal figure, an ungainly, peevish, froward woman who put the fear of God – or the Devil – into all she met – especially Baldwin. He shuddered at the memory. 'But no! What with inviting the guests and telling me where they must sleep, and Edgar taking over all the other preparations . . .'

He stopped himself. The delight he was giving his friend was almost painful to observe, and he had no desire to increase Simon's pleasure. It was curiously unsettling to reflect on the matter, too. Soon his whole life would be altered, he knew. The absence of his servant, Edgar, was a proof of that. Formerly Edgar had never let the knight out of his sight, and yet where was he now? Baldwin and he had been together for many years; Edgar had served as his man-at-arms when they were both warriors, and without him Baldwin felt strangely naked.

But Edgar refused to let anyone else take over the supervision of the wedding. In any case, while the bailiff was at his side, Baldwin was content. It would be a very hardy outlaw who would dare attack a knight and a sturdy fighter like Simon, especially seeing the quality of their weapons. Baldwin touched the hilt of his new riding sword with a feeling of smugness.

It was short, the blade only twenty-one inches long, but it was made of the most beautiful, bright, peacock-blue steel he had ever seen, with grey steel quillons that curved gently from the leather-covered hilt, and a pommel that balanced the whole weapon perfectly. When he first picked it up, it felt almost alive in his hand.

Sir Baldwin had bought it only a month before, and it was so much lighter than his old war sword that he hardly felt it at his hip, but that wasn't the only reason why he was already so fond of it; he liked the writing – and the motif on the reverse. Baldwin had found a good jeweller who had used a burin to carve the four letters carefully into the long fuller of the blade, filling each with silver wire and hammering it tight: *BOAC*. They stood for *Beati Omnipotensque Angeli Christi* – Blessed and Omnipotent are the Angels of Christ. But on the other side of the blade was a simple sign: the cross of the Knights Templar, his old Order.

Baldwin felt his mood lighten as the trackway narrowed, went into a dip. Soon they were out from under the trees and paused at a ford. The two men rested their horses again, letting the beasts dip their heads thankfully into the brackish brown water that ran from the moors.

'Not far now,' Simon commented as his horse puffed and snorted, shaking its mane, before stooping for more.

Baldwin patted his rounsey's neck. 'You knew the squire, didn't you?'

'A little. I had some dealings with him. The usual petty stuff: he had his villeins run away and declare themselves miners. And miners dammed his streams and diverted his water for their leats. Didn't you know him?'

'Yes,' said Baldwin. He had a recollection of a heavy-set man with a red face and hoarse, bellowing laugh. 'He was invited to the wedding with his wife. Poor devil!'

'He had a good life,' Simon said disinterestedly. 'Fought many battles, won his lord's thanks and respect – and a pleasant estate.'

'True.' The knight knew as well as any that the easiest way for a man-at-arms to make money was to capture an enemy knight or lord and sell him. Squire Roger had been thoroughly successful at this, taking prisoners of such importance that he had been able to sell them, for a share in their profits, to his King. Without the cost of keeping them, but with a significant share of their worth, he had become wealthy. 'He always struck me as a generous, capable man,' Baldwin continued. 'How did you find him?'

Simon considered a moment. 'A gentleman: always courteous, keen to avoid disputes. It's not often you meet someone like him. His wife was much the same – bright and intelligent. She and my wife got on well.'

'I suppose the funeral will be in the village?' Baldwin asked, his mind moving on to the sombre event they must witness the next day.

'Yes. The church lies west of the hamlet. It's a lovely place, the Church of St Mary the Virgin, very peaceful. His body will rest there happily enough.'

Baldwin nodded, and they clattered along together.

'I believe the priest was the squire's own man,' Baldwin observed as he kicked his horse on. 'Doesn't he live at the hall?'

'Yes, I think so. The squire employed him as a tutor. I can't imagine too many priests who would be prepared to come to a quiet backwater like this.'

'Godforsaken little vill would be nearer the mark, wouldn't it?' Baldwin said lightly. 'Still, some like the desolation.'

'Some of us do, yes,' Simon chuckled. 'But you don't have to search for motives here, Baldwin. There's nothing suspicious about Roger's death.'

'No,' Baldwin agreed, grinning. He and Simon had investigated many murders together, but he had no concerns about the sudden death of the squire. There was no suggestion of violence: he'd simply fallen dead from his horse. It was sad, but there was not much to regret in a swift and painless death.

The only issue that could cause difficulties was the will, but Baldwin felt sure that a man like Squire Throwleigh would have ensured all was in order. No doubt his wife would control the estate until the heir was of age.

A slow smile broke out over his features as he considered that word 'wife'. It was a curious title. A woman who was prepared to become the possession of another. Not that Baldwin would ever think of his Jeanne as a chattel. She was too precious to him.

'Are you thinking of her *again*?'

'Well? What of it?'

'Nothing, Baldwin,' Simon laughed, 'but try to keep your feelings away from your face, all right? Don't forget we're here to witness a burial. If you keep that inane grin on your face, Roger's widow will be within her rights to have you flogged around the churchyard!'

Baldwin hurriedly brought his mind back to the present. There was one topic which he knew Simon would treat seriously.

'What is the name of the heir?'

'Herbert. He'll inherit his third.'

'Until his mother does the decent thing,' Baldwin observed.

'That'll be a long time,' Simon said shortly.

'She won't give her son her share?'

'Not for some time. The boy's only five or six – I expect she'll stay and protect it, and him, until he is old enough to look after himself.'

Baldwin nodded. A man's will divided his possessions into three, after paying off debts. One third, the dower, would go to his wife; a second third would go to good causes so that his soul would be well received; only the last of the three parts would go to his heir. In cases where the heir was too young to look after himself, his mother would remain at home and act as guardian, but normally she would leave as soon as her son was old enough to fend for himself, retiring to a convent, or taking the vows and living as a recluse in a small property and not interfering in her son's life, giving him her dower to protect the estate, and living on whatever portion her son chose to send to her.

As the knight mused, their road took them due east. Here they were sheltered under great trees forming an avenue. It was like the road up to Cadbury, and Baldwin found himself comparing this remote manor to his own lush demesne. Looking about him, he felt that if he possessed so barren a site he would feel guilty asking a woman to marry him. He could never have brought Jeanne here. It would be cruel to ask a woman to live so far from a city or civilised people. The thought made his face twist in a sardonic grin, for Jeanne's old home wasn't far from here.

It led Baldwin to wonder how the squire's heir would survive. Lads of that age were resilient, he knew, but losing a father was a traumatic experience at any age. He could still recall the feeling of emptiness when his own father had died, even though he was almost a man by then, being eleven years old. His mother had died five years before, giving birth to his fourth brother who, like the third, had not survived a single year. Now Baldwin could hardly remember what she looked like. All he was sure of was her auburn hair. At least the squire's lad still has his mother, he thought.

The trees thinned and suddenly fell away as they came closer to the vill. Now they could see its extent: a few houses on the left, a pound on the right where stray cattle and sheep could be collected, and ahead lay the church, an imposing building in heavy grey stone. Beyond, on the northern road, was a small cluster of additional houses, but Simon took the other track, heading round the southernmost point of the church grounds, and then trotting off towards the moors.

'That's Cosdon,' the bailiff said, pointing to the massive hill to their right. 'From the top you can see for miles. Wonderful views all around. I was up there once, and could swear I could see the sea both to the north-west and south-east. I wouldn't be surprised if you could see your house from up there.'

Baldwin said nothing. Simon adored the moors, but to his mind the hill felt threatening, like a monstrous creature that was even now preparing to spring down and crush them. On its rounded back a heavy-looking grey cloud hung as if tethered there. He gave a shudder. It was something to do with this place, he was sure. There was an aura of cruelty – or perhaps just a simple lack of compassion – here, in this landscape. He had a sense of the unforgiving nature of the moors. The land gave the impression that it was aware of the beings who strove and struggled in the small village at the hill's feet, but watched them without sympathy or tolerance. It

41

would destroy them with as little feeling as a child stamping on a beetle.

The road began to rise, and when they had travelled another half-mile from the vill, they came to long strips of fields, a meadow, and at last an orchard with a stream bounding its easternmost edge. Simon pointed with his chin. 'There it is. Welcome to Throwleigh Manor.'

It was a great, low, squat building – long, and to Baldwin's eye, gloomy. There was no curtain wall; the outer defence consisted merely of a hedge of thorny bushes, closely planted and layered. Behind the house was the rising mass of yet another hill, its flanks smothered in heather, while to his left Baldwin saw a broad expanse of marshland. On his right, a clitter of heavy grey stones lay haphazardly, like rubble from a ruined building.

Simon spurred his horse and they rode on over a wide verge to the house itself. The sun had disappeared behind the moor before them, and the day had taken on the dingy hues of twilight. In this aspect the house took on an alarming appearance: dark and menacing.

Baldwin had to remind himself that it was Simon, not he, who was prone to superstitious fears, but as they trotted towards the buildings he felt a powerful sense of sadness which was almost palpable about this house of mourning.

CHAPTER FOUR

The serving girl covered her face again as soon as the priest left the chapel, and she went back to the security of her kitchen. Shoulders heaving, she crossed to the little three-legged stool near the fire, and collapsed on it in a fit of powerless misery.

'Petronilla? Come on, foolish chit, this'll never do!' Daniel, the household's steward, patted her shoulder. Her paroxysms of grief began to fade, and he fetched her a pint of wine, holding it under her nose until she wiped her eyes one last time, and looked up at him with bleary-eyed gratitude. 'Come on, drink up. You can't go to serve your mistress looking like this. You don't want to make her feel even worse, do you?'

'I'm sorry, sir, but it was, was . . .'

'I know. We all loved him. He was kind and generous. The squire can never be replaced for us, Petronilla. He can't be.'

She saw that his eyes were becoming misty too. Daniel, she recalled, had been a footsoldier alongside the old squire in many battles in France and Wales, and suddenly she realised that he was trying to cope with his own grief while ensuring that all the servants of the hall performed their duties. His courage in the face of his own loss was enough to make her feel almost ashamed.

'Daniel, I am so sorry, I never thought about you.'

He replied with an unsteady smile, but then gave a loud sniff and glanced through the open door. 'Don't worry about me, dear. I am old enough to have buried almost all my friends and, although I don't like it, I'm at least used to it. Save your sympathy for the squire's widow. And for his son,' he added heavily, with an emphasis that made the girl look up.

'Herbert? Why do you sound so sad when you mention him, Daniel?'

'Because he's the squire now, girl. He has the full weight of the manor resting on his young shoulders, whether he wishes it or no. And there are many who'd like to deprive him of his inheritance.'

With this gloomy observation, he saw Simon and Baldwin entering the yard. Muttering a curse, he shouted for grooms and ran out. Had he looked back, he would have seen Petronilla's eyes fill with tears again.

She bit her lip as she placed a hand on her belly, touching the new life beginning there, before sobbing afresh.

Baldwin and Simon dropped thankfully from their horses, rubbing sore buttocks and stretching their aching thighs. It was a relief to see the steward hurrying towards them.

Daniel was a tall, cadaverous man with thinning, grizzled hair. His eyes were dark and shrewd, with laughter-lines to prove that he was a happy enough fellow normally, but today their gleam was muted in deference to the occasion.

'Bailiff, I am glad to see you again. If you and Sir Baldwin would follow me?' They were led over the threshold into the screens. Here Daniel stood aside and motioned them into the hall.

Simon was struck by the cheerful atmosphere. If he had not known that they were met here to bury a man, he would have thought a celebration was in full flow. There was a thick crowd, all well-to-do, standing away from the great fireplace, talking loudly, all grasping drinking cups. As he entered, the noise was deafening.

He glanced over the group, but it was the woman he noticed almost immediately.

She sat on a small chair at the fireside, a sombre young boy whom Simon took to be the heir standing near to hand, his head downcast. Lady Katharine of Throwleigh was a slender woman in her middle twenties, tall and elegant in her green velvet and linen coif. She watched the men as they entered, with an intense stillness.

Where she sat the room was in comparative darkness. The candles and sconces were all set away from the fire, and here the only light came from the burning logs themselves. When Simon was some few feet from her, he could see the immensity of her despair and sadness in her drawn features and red-rimmed grey eyes. The boy didn't raise his head to look at the guests; he appeared to be absorbed in his own private misery. Behind him, almost hidden in the shadows, was a quiet maidservant, but Simon had no interest in her. He had eyes only for the lady of the house.

He bowed, offering his respects on his own behalf as well as his master, the Warden of the Stannaries. Baldwin stepped to his side and bowed in his turn.

'My Lady. I have come, as you asked, to witness the funeral of your husband, not only so that I can pay my own respects to him, but also in order that I can represent the Sheriff, for your husband was a good and loyal subject to the King's father. I can only say how deeply sorry I am.'

'Thank you, Sir Baldwin. It is kind of you to come, and I am grateful to you for your words.' She was stiffly formal, but her voice, although hoarse with crying, was warm, and her manner courteous as she thanked him and Simon. 'Of course I remember your last visit, Bailiff.'

'Yes, my Lady,' smiled Simon. 'I helped your husband with the peat-cutters.'

It was a common enough dispute on the moors, and boringly familiar to Simon. A group of men had wandered onto Squire Roger's land, cutting turves for their fires, and when he had demanded that they should stop, they said they were miners. A tin miner had the right to fuel for his workings, but these men were nothing to do with the mines, and Simon had evicted them.

'My husband was always grateful to you for your help,' she said, and suddenly her eyes brimmed with tears, and Simon had to lean forward to catch her words. 'He would have been pleased that you had time enough to come and make your farewell, Bailiff.'

A short while afterwards, Lady Katharine pleaded a headache and left her guests to go up to her room, calling her maidservant Anney to join her. The men in the hall appeared to think that her departure was a signal for merry-making, calling for more wine or ale, one or two demanding food, and many shouting for 'Petronilla!'

Soon she came in, a tall, attractive, fair-haired girl of some twenty summers. It was obvious that she, like her mistress, was deeply sorrowful. Although she served those who called to her, as soon as she could she put her tray down and went to the young boy, putting her arms around him.

Baldwin cocked an eye at his friend, and the two took their place by the fire, a little away from the others, where they could talk without interruption. They weren't to be left alone for long, however.

A priest entered and, noticing the young servant, he called to her. She regretfully left the child, who slipped out through the door to the solar. The priest spoke to the maidservant quietly, and she took on a still more sombre mien before hurrying out in her turn. When she had gone, the cleric gazed distastefully at the rowdier of the guests, before crossing the room to Baldwin and Simon.

'Bailiff? Surely I remember you from when you were last here?'

'Of course, Brother Stephen,' Simon said, raising a smile as the cleric joined them.

Baldwin was struck not only by the man's strong, flat-sounding accent, but also by his effeminacy. He was tall and slim, with an oval face of pale complexion, and curiously full and fleshy lips. His looks would have suited a woman, and Baldwin was reminded of some of the rumours about the clergy, which suggested that priests were often caught in compromising situations with women. There were always stories in circulation of how priests broke their vows. At least, Baldwin thought privately, women would be safe from this man!

'You are to conduct the funeral tomorrow?' the knight asked.

'Yes, not that the other guests seem to realise that is why we are all here.'

'You must forgive them, Brother – they're celebrating their own lives. It's not that they intend to demean Squire Roger's memory, just that they are making merry while they still can,' Simon said.

'It is disrespectful to a man who was uniformly loved and honoured,' said the priest primly.

Simon sought to distract him from the behaviour of the other guests. 'The service will be tomorrow?'

'We performed the *Placebo* this afternoon, and the body is lying in the church tonight with the parish poor standing vigil over him,' Stephen agreed. 'Tomorrow morning we shall sing the *Dirige* and celebrate the *Requiem* Mass, then inter the body.'

'And then I hope Lady Katharine will be able to get over her pain,' said Simon.

'Oh, I doubt it!' said a voice behind him.

Simon turned to meet the alcohol-bleared smile of a man in his late thirties. He had a short, thickset body, with a barrel of a chest and almost non-existent neck, on top of which sat a large, square face. He looked as though he would be happier wielding a weapon than a jug and drinking horn, but for now his expression was one of drunken vacuity, and he waved his wine in a broad gesture that splashed red droplets against the wall.

'There's many of us won't forget the squire in a hurry, eh, Stephen?' he said. The words came out playfully, and the man prodded the monk with his jug, splashing a quantity of wine on Stephen's robe, but Simon, looking into the drunk's eyes, saw the anger and jealousy burning there. 'No, poor Lady Katharine will never be able to get over her shock, I expect. My brother was too kindly and generous for her to forget him, so I fear *you'll* not be able to wed her for her money, sir!'

Baldwin drew in his breath at this insult to his friend, and Simon stiffened, but the man gave a rasping laugh, drank a little more, and almost in an instant was serious. 'Your pardon – I jest. My brother was good to the villeins on his land, as well as to his friends. No one will be able to forget him quickly. And his wife won't want to wed again, I expect, not after living with my poor brother.'

'You are Thomas of Exeter?'

Baldwin's question made the man shoot him a glance. 'Yes, Thomas of Exeter, they call me now. Surprising how speedily you lose your name when you live away for a short while, isn't it, eh? In the city I'm always Thomas of Throwleigh, son of the Knight of Throwleigh, younger brother of Roger – but here I'm only Thomas of Exeter, like a damned serf, or a plain barber. There was a time when I could have been a knight, you know!'

'I am sorry your brother has died,' Baldwin said quietly. 'But it is good that you are here to comfort the squire's widow, and help her execute her duties towards their child.'

The man had raised his horn to his lips, but now he let it fall away, staring with open-mouthed astonishment at the knight. He gave a half-giggle, as if absorbing a joke. 'Me? Here to help her and *him*?'

'Sir, be silent!' The priest's words were uttered in so menacing a tone that the room fell quiet for a moment, all the guests glancing towards them. Thomas curled his lip but said no more, turning and stumbling from the room.

Stephen sighed and shook his head. 'My apologies for that, Sir Baldwin, Bailiff. I deemed it better to silence him rather than allow him the opportunity to disgrace himself in front of so many people. The trouble is, gentlemen, Thomas and the squire were never comfortable in each other's company, and I fear . . . That is, I am sad to say that Thomas of Exeter came rushing here as soon as he was told of his brother's death less from affection or a desire to help his sister-in-law than from the keen anticipation of his own advancement.'

'Ah!' Baldwin said, his eyes going to the doorway once more.

Simon stared from one to the other. 'What?'

Stephen gave him a long, sad look. 'Thomas had no idea that his brother had an heir, Bailiff. He thought he was about to inherit the Throwleigh estates.'

The next day was cold and drear: suitable weather for a miserable occasion like this, thought Baldwin. He stood pensively, his cloak wrapped warmly about him, watching as the body was lifted from the hearse before the altar and carried, draped in its magnificent pall of cloth of gold, out to the graveyard.

At other funerals Baldwin had been aware of sadness, regret, even occasionally happiness in the knowledge that a loved one was on his or her way to Heaven, but never had he experienced one where there appeared to be so many undercurrents.

The widow, Lady Katharine, stood with her glorious hair and face covered by a veil and hood, her hands fidgeting with the enamelled brooch at the neck of her cloak, while her frame shook with sobs. At her side was the tall and lugubrious Daniel, her steward, who leaned on his staff, keeping his distance from his mistress, and whose face was wrenched with grief. Baldwin noticed on two occasions that he lifted a hand as if to touch his Lady's shoulder to offer her comfort – although both times he thought better of his presumption.

Before her was the child – a small and rather feeble-looking boy, with tow-coloured hair and livid features in which the dark eyes seemed to glow with an unnatural fire. His eyes were fixed upon the grave, and while he uttered no sound and his body exhibited only the most subtle signs of grief, the tears poured down his cheeks in an unending stream. Yet Baldwin noticed that there was no contact between mother and son, and he wondered at that. It was surely only natural that she should provide her son with, and receive in return, a little comfort at such a harrowing time, but both stood alone, close to each other, but utterly apart.

Simon and he waited with the mourning guests on one side while the priest intoned the prayers and scattered earth on the face of the shrouded corpse at the bottom of the grave. Only then did the boy give a loud gulp, but his mother snapped at him to be silent.

Stephen appeared to be labouring under a great emotion. Although he was the kind of man who would always have a pasty complexion, today Baldwin thought he looked positively ill, with an unhealthy waxen sheen. His voice was hushed, less with apparent grief for the departed squire, more with a kind of nervous anxiety. Baldwin wondered fleetingly whether there was any justification for that impression: perhaps the cleric had been told he was no longer needed now that the squire was dead.

The only time Stephen's face softened and he appeared to think of anyone other than himself was when he glanced at the fatherless boy. Baldwin thought at first that it was proof of compassion for the child, but then he began to wonder. Baldwin would have expected sympathy, but Stephen had an odd, wistful look about him. It made Baldwin wonder what the priest was thinking.

Thomas stood with his eyes downcast, but never on the body, only on the ground at his feet. His cheeks were flushed, his eyes bloodshot and sore-looking. Baldwin thought he looked like a man who has spent the whole night in prayer, a man who has begged God for the forgiveness of any sins his brother might have committed ... and yet the knight reminded himself that the symptoms exhibited by the dead man's brother were identical to those of an oaf who has over-indulged himself with wine the previous night.

The service over, the mourning group walked slowly to the church gate and prepared to ride back to the house. Simon and Baldwin went to the widow's side and made their farewells.

'You are going so soon?' she asked, her face still shrouded by her hood. 'We have food and drink waiting at the hall, gentlemen.'

'We have far to go; I fear we must return,' said Baldwin. 'And although I am sorry to have met you under these circumstances, I hope you will consider me a friend. If there is anything I can do for you while you suffer from your loss, please send me a message.'

'Thank you for your kindness, Sir Baldwin. And of course you must go – I had forgotten your happiness in the midst of my despair. I had the best husband in the world: a good friend, a gentle husband, an honourable soldier and a noble and honest man. Perhaps I should consider myself fortunate to have had him for my own . . . yet I can only feel grief, and no gratitude. Our time together was all too short. But you must go back to your lady, Sir Baldwin, and my blessings go with you. I hope your marriage will bring you as much joy as mine did me.'

'I am grateful, Lady Katharine. I need hardly say that my thoughts and prayers will be with you.'

'Thank you again, and Godspeed.'

Taking their leave, Baldwin and Simon mounted their horses and set off back the way they had come the day before, riding up the slope to return to Crediton. Before they passed into the trees once more, Baldwin turned in his saddle to wave, and caught a glimpse of the widow. She was standing straight and still, an honourable lady refusing to bend to her despair in her loneliness. As Baldwin gestured in farewell, he saw Herbert walk falteringly to his mother and take her hand. She glanced down, as if surprised at the touch, but when she saw it was her child, she snatched her hand away.

Baldwin shook his head as the trees cut off his view. In all the world there was nothing he wished for more fervently than a son of his own, a lad to inherit his demesne and who could protect his villeins, and yet Herbert, Master of Throwleigh, appeared to have lost the love of his own mother. There were some women, Baldwin knew, who were unable to give affection to their children, who as speedily as they gave birth handed their offspring to wetnurses and then to tutors, but he was surprised that Lady Katharine should feel that way towards her son. She looked to him the sort of woman who would delight in children.

He put the matter from his mind with the thought that it must have been caused by her mourning. It was surely only a transient state, and her love for the boy to whom she had given life would be bound to return when she had recovered from the shock of her loss. No doubt then it would be reinforced by their mutual dependence.

With that conviction to comfort him, Baldwin spurred his horse. No mother could hate her own flesh and blood – not for long. He knew he himself would adore any child he fathered, and he was confident that his new wife would too. Jeanne had a special, soft smile for children. It was plain to Baldwin that she would feel a keen delight in giving him a son, and the sense of wholeness, of belonging, which he had felt on taking her hand when they had become engaged returned to his memory and made him smile. There could surely be nothing so wonderful as creating another life. It was his own most fervent desire. No, he put the widow's behaviour down to depression. All considerations other than his wife-to-be's pleasure on seeing him home once more fell from his mind, and he was taken up with happy musings about her.

Later, when he recalled that scene, he would blame himself for what happened.

CHAPTER FIVE

Edmund entered the hall nervously, his old felt hat gripped submissively in his hand. It was a relief to see that, although the steward Daniel was standing beside the table and the priest was seated behind him with a great ledger resting on his lap, the squire's widow was also present, in her chair on the dais near the fire. At least she would champion the son of her husband's most loyal retainer, he thought with relief.

'Edmund . . .' the steward began, and glanced at his mistress as if for support. She gave an irritable flap of her hand, and he hurriedly carried on. 'Edmund, it has been brought to the attention of my Lady of Throwleigh that you have been talking in the village about hiring a lawyer to work for you.'

'I don't want to, Mistress,' Edmund blurted. 'It's only that . . .'

'Your mistress would like to point out that as a villein, you have no rights in any court other than her own.'

Edmund stood gaping. At last he found his voice again, and ducking his head respectfully, he spoke directly to her. 'I'm sorry, Mistress, but there must be some mistake. Your husband granted my father his freedom, gave him his paper to show he was free. That means I'm no villein, I'm free as well. Otherwise I'd not have been able to inherit Father's lands.'

'That was an error. You have to pay the heriot now,' the steward said, and swallowed loudly.

Edmund ignored him. The heriot was the fine paid by a serf in order that the oldest son could take over his father's duties, but Edmund was free, so he owed no heriot. He ducked his head again to Lady Katharine, who sat listening carefully. 'Mistress? There *must* be a mistake. I still have the bit of paper back at my house, and—'

She cut him off with a graceful wave of her hand. 'It is possible *you* made a mistake, yes. Your father was given a certificate of manumission from serfdom by my husband, but that was only to last for my husband's life.'

'No, Mistress,' Edmund said firmly. 'It proved that he was free, and so were all his children and his children's children for ever. I am free, Mistress.'

She gave him a long, cold stare, then nodded to Stephen.

The priest sighed and slowly opened his ledger. 'This confirms the entail under which the manor was held by Squire Roger, God bless him.' He tapped the page, avoiding Edmund's stare. 'Under the terms of the entail, the squire could not alienate any property except for his lifetime. His lifetime having expired, any property he gave away must be returned.' He slammed the covers together and bowed his head.

'You understand?' Lady Katharine snapped and gave Edmund an unpleasant smile. 'It is very easy, villein: your father was born a serf. My husband gave him his freedom, but any papers my husband signed which gave away anything from the manor became null and void as soon as he died. Your freedom is ended with the death of Squire Throwleigh. As soon as he died, you became a villein again.'

'Mistress, that can't be right!'

'It is the law.'

'I'll get a lawyer.'

Daniel shook his head sadly. 'You can't. You are stated to be a villein, Edmund. The only court you can appeal to is the manor's, and Mistress Katharine will not allow you to waste the court's time on such a silly matter.'

'I'll go to the King's court. I'll fight you!'

'You can't,' said Lady Katharine, and she stood up. To Edmund she radiated an unwholesome, evil power, and as she walked slowly towards him he felt himself recoil, his bowels turning to water in his sudden fear.

'You can do nothing, Edmund Villein. *Nothing!* If you go to court I will declare you "unfree" and your case will fail. You are to lose your lands already, and I believe it was in part because of you that my husband died, so if you make it hard for me, I will see to it that you and your family have the harshest duties of all the villeins in Throwleigh. Think yourself lucky, Edmund. You were to lose everything. Now I will let you stay in a toft, a cottage without land, on my demesne – but I will keep my eye on you.'

James van Relenghes considered the doorway with a soldier's eye. It wasn't particularly strong, but the squire had had few enemies to fear. The buildings were constructed with a view to defence against bands of outlaws, and men of that type would have been deterred by the thorn hedge. If they had won their way through to the court, the house, with its thick walls of solid, grey moorstone, would have been proof against them. For there to have been any expectation of success, an attacker would have required artillery, beating at the walls with missiles, or mining beneath them until the walls above collapsed. Nothing less could force the occupants to surrender. No incompetent vagrants armed with sticks and daggers would be able to take the place.

He carried on towards it, Godfrey riding behind him on a pony.

Van Relenghes had explained nothing of his reasons for visiting Throwleigh Manor. The Fleming had merely said that he was forced to visit this place because his old friend had recently died, and wished to have his bodyguard with him. It had been surprisingly easy to persuade Godfrey to accompany him. Van Relenghes thought it was the lure of the money he offered, yet in truth that had little to do with it; Godfrey earned enough already. His willingness was due to his interest in the Fleming. Ever since van Relenghes's outburst in the Cathedral grounds, Godfrey had wanted to find out more about his strange client.

While waiting for the Fleming to ready himself for the journey to Dartmoor, Godfrey had asked questions of his usual sources, but no one knew anything much about van Relenghes. He was staying at an inn near the Cathedral grounds, he was known to be foreign, and could have an evil, short temper – a description that covered half the men within the city's walls.

On the other hand, Godfrey had picked up quite a bit about the man who had occasioned van Relenghes's outburst of swearing. He was Thomas of Throwleigh, brother to the squire who had so recently died. A merchant, Thomas had fallen on hard times of late – in part due to his habit of gambling at the bearpit. His fortunes had not prospered, and now he was in sore straits. There was no need for Godfrey to ask anyone about the squire himself. Godfrey was a fighting man – he knew of Squire Roger.

The ride to Throwleigh had not given Godfrey any more information about his employer. The tall Fleming rode in silence, grunting when a question was directed to him, like a man deep in his own thoughts. By the time they reached the moors, van Relenghes was in a foul humour. It was lucky, Godfrey thought, that he had seen the lad before he could fire his sling at the two of them, for there was no telling how his employer would have reacted.

The boy had been sitting in a tree near the river, idly spinning his sling. As soon as he caught sight of the two men, his eyes had narrowed, he had lowered himself on his branch, and the sling had begun to whirl faster and faster. It was common enough for brats to shoot at passing horses, trying to unseat their riders, or better, to see how well they could ride at speed, but fortunately Godfrey had spotted him, on the lookout as he was for ambush from outlaws. The master of arms had reached behind him and pulled his crossbow free from its retaining strap, not bothering to cock it, but letting it point casually at the tree. The boy had grinned, ducking his head, his sling slowing, sitting back to wait for the next, less observant, traveller.

Godfrey could smile now, knowing that he had averted at least one attack, if only that of a child, and that they were here, safe at Throwleigh Manor.

They waited at the entrance to the stable block. A groom was not long in arriving.

'What's the matter with you?' van Relenghes asked the groom, a rheumy old man of almost fifty, who moved slowly, and with apparent misery.

'My master is dead, sir. He died three days ago, and we only buried him this morning.'

'You show him the proper respect, then. But this is terrible news. Surely you don't mean that the good Squire Roger, famous throughout Christendom for his courage and his exploits on the battlefield . . . You don't mean he has died?'

Godfrey nonchalantly dismounted and leaned against the gatepost, listening with the greatest interest as his client lied.

'Oh, sir! Did you know him?' the groom exclaimed.

'I fought with him in France under good King Edward, the King's father. He was my friend.'

'Then, sir, Squire Roger's wife will be most happy to see you.'

So saying, the ageing groom shouted for the steward, and in a few moments Daniel arrived. He bowed deeply, and led van Relenghes and his guard into the hall.

Godfrey was not certain what lay behind this sudden conversion from a man who had apparently loathed the squire, but he intended to find out.

*   *   *

Just inside the stables, Nicholas, Thomas of Exeter's steward, sat stitching at a new leather sheath for his knife. He had been safe enough so far. Even Daniel hadn't recognised him with his beard, and he'd managed to avoid seeing Anney. Now he watched the two men as they crossed the courtyard to the hall, and as Godfrey walked inside behind the Fleming, Nick narrowed his eyes thoughtfully.

The steward turned to the man at his side, another member of Thomas's retinue. 'Those two – did you see the one at the rear, the shorter one?' he asked.

'Yes – what about him?'

Nicholas wasn't sure. The light was pretty bad here in the yard, and he hadn't been able to study the man in detail. 'He just reminded me of someone,' he said, and went back to his work, but every so often he glanced at the hall as if troubled.

It was a week later that the boy Alan scurried through the undergrowth. He only halted when he could hear voices close at hand, his every sense strained to breaking point while he scrutinised the land ahead, panting and wiping the sweat from his eyes.

He was at the edge of the roadway, concealed by the bracken at the verge, and before him the land dropped away to the woods at the side of the stream. Four riders were conversing, or rather two were talking while their servants sat on their horses on either side.

Alan knew who they were. The two chatting were the Fleming and the brother of the dead squire. The Fleming and his servant rode over this way often enough; there was nothing new in their being here, and Alan paid them little attention. Far off in the distance he could spy a wagon, but that meant nothing to him. He needed to know who was nearer to hand.

His blood was up, and in his hand he gripped a small switch, which was now, in the eleven-year-old's mind, a keen sword.

Looking eastwards, back towards the manor, he studied the road carefully. There was no sign of the enemy there, and he peered westwards thoughtfully. They might have taken the longer route and tried to cut him off. He meditatively chewed a thumbnail while reviewing his options, then squirmed away, back up the hill until he was far enough distant from the riders for them not to be able to hear him.

His heart was pounding with excitement. Their games tended to be unpredictable. Sometimes Jordan and Herbert would spring out at him from their hiding-places, and there was little he could do to defend himself. If he was pretending to be Scottish, and was bored, he might surrender in the most cowardly fashion, but on other occasions, when he was pretending to be an outlaw, he would snarl and rage, fighting to the last. He always enjoyed those encounters. Today he was a bear, hunted by the others.

Hearing a new voice, he peeped through the furze back towards the road. It was a woman. Intrigued, he crawled down the slope a short way. From his new vantage he could see her: it was only Petronilla, the maid from the manor, talking to the riders, laughing and joking. There were only two men now, he saw; Thomas and his man had left. Alan shrugged and turned to continue on his way. Once he felt adequately concealed by the bushes of furze and clumps of heather, he ran back up the hill. Here, he knew, was a sheep track that led up to the immense pool and mire of Raybarrow. If he were to take that route, he would be safe from ambush . . .

Suddenly a hand gripped his shoulder fiercely. He was yanked backwards, and a voice hissed in his ear: 'What are you doing up here, boy? Spying?'

Alan cried out with quick fear and surprise, for the sound of that particular voice warned him of punishment to come. He wriggled ineffectually, and gradually stilled, but even as he allowed his shoulders to sag, he gave a sudden, convulsive leap to the side. His assailant cursed, but his grip was broken, and he couldn't reach round to capture the lad again. Alan made off at full pelt, up the hill away from the road, before dropping in among the bracken and hiding, panting with fear.

In mid-sentence, Petronilla stopped and stared.

Van Relenghes followed the line of her gaze. From here at the side of the rushing water, the hill rose to the moors. The stream had cut a steep-sided valley to the right. Near this the bemused van Relenghes saw Stephen of York slashing and stabbing with a stick at the bushes and heather all about him.

With a muttered curse, Petronilla gathered up her skirts and ran to him. The Fleming was tempted to follow. 'Do you think she might need our help?' he asked his bodyguard.

Godfrey shook his head. 'I reckon she knows what she's doing. If she wants help, she'll call.'

'But she might get lost. It wouldn't make me look very good in her mistress's eyes if I left her here and she got hurt,' said van Relenghes doubtfully.

His concern made Godfrey smile to himself. 'How would her mistress look upon you chasing after a young maidservant, sir?'

'You are quite right, old fellow! While I have designs on the beautiful widow, I shouldn't allow myself to appear too interested in her maid, should I?' And van Relenghes laughed.

Further up the slope, Herbert and Jordan had witnessed Alan's capture and escape. They stared at each other wide-eyed. Both recognised the priest, and both feared for their own safety. Down the hill they could see him slashing at the bracken where Alan had dropped into hiding. Without speaking, both crawled away, back up the hill towards the mire at the top.

Thinking that Herbert was right behind him, Jordan scrabbled as fast as he could, anxious lest he should be grabbed and given a thrashing. There were few men who could instil such terror in him, but the priest was one such. As soon as he felt it was safe enough, he scrambled to his feet. There was no sign of Stephen now. He had disappeared, to Jordan's relief.

But then he realised that Herbert was no longer with him. Jordan felt chilled with fear. He knew what Brother Stephen was like. Sighing to himself, he turned, and slowly, with infinite care, he made his way back.

The thick bracken muted the chattering of the stream, and deadened all sounds, for which Jordan was very grateful. Soon he came upon a foot protruding from the heather in front of him, and he grinned and touched it.

Alan jerked round fearfully, breathing a gasp of relief when he saw who it was. He and Jordan remained in a good humour for some time. It was only later, when they heard Stephen roar, giving a bellow like that of an enraged bear, that their mood changed.

And a few moments afterwards, they heard Herbert's shrill scream.

CHAPTER SIX

When the messenger arrived, Sir Baldwin and Simon were in Baldwin's hall, pulling off their boots after a hot and dusty day's hunting intended to take the knight's mind off his coming nuptials. Baldwin was bellowing for Edgar to get drinks for them when the cattleman's son Wat came in nervously, saying that Edgar had gone to Crediton to order more food.

'Very well, then,' Baldwin muttered irritably. 'Fetch us wine, and be quick! We have had nothing to drink since before lunch.'

The lad rushed off, his cheap boots slapping on the flagged passage, and Simon raised an eyebrow to his friend. 'Do you really think it's a good idea to let him serve us? You know what he's like with drinks – if Edgar hears you let Wat loose in his buttery, he'll leave your service!'

Baldwin threw his overtunic on the ground and sat in his chair. 'I don't know what to do with the boy,' he said wearily.

'He is perfectly well-behaved when he's sober, but if there's a broached barrel of ale in the same room as him, he will empty it and fill himself. I dare not leave him alone with drink until he learns to moderate his thirst.'

The two men were seated when the messenger was brought in. Baldwin recognised him as one of the servants from Throwleigh Manor, although it was not the same man who had brought the news of Squire Roger's death, and the knight stood abruptly.

The messenger's legs looked as though they could hardly support him, he had ridden so far, so quickly.

'I'm sorry, Sir Baldwin,' he gasped, 'but I have been sent at utmost speed to ask you and the bailiff if you can help a poor widow in sore distress.'

'Is it your mistress who asks this?' asked Simon sharply. 'Has she suffered some new calamity?'

Even as his friend posed the question, Baldwin felt as if a steel fist was clenching around his belly and squeezing.

'Bailiff, Sir Baldwin . . . my master, the mistress's son Herbert, is dead.'

It took little time to prepare for their departure the next day. It was appalling to hear of the Lady of Throwleigh's terrible misfortune, losing her only son so short a time after the death of her husband, and Simon's horror lent haste to his preparations.

The bailiff was surprised at how his friend had taken the news of the lad's death. From the moment the messenger had delivered his solemn request, the knight had sat quietly, deep in thought. He had left the table shortly after the meal the night before and gone out for a long walk, refusing any company, and this morning he had said little to anyone before they mounted their horses. Now he pressed Simon to greater speeds whenever the other man slowed.

When they came to Hittisleigh, Simon spurred on to ride at his side. 'Baldwin, what is it?'

The knight did not turn his gaze from the horizon ahead. 'It is my fault that the boy has died, Simon.'

His friend blinked in surprise. 'How can it be your fault? You weren't there.'

'I was too tied up in my own prospects, in my own happiness, to recognise the misery on that poor child's face.'

'Rubbish! I was there too, and I saw only grief for his father; a very proper sadness.'

'I saw more, Simon. I saw an uncle who wanted to inherit his nephew's lands and a mother who apparently had no love for her son. Two dangers to the child, and I ignored them both, being too bound up with my own delight.'

'Even if you're right and one of them truly did hold an evil design on young Herbert, there was nothing you could have done.'

'At the very least I could have spoken to them and made my suspicions plain so that they would never have dared attack him. He was only a *child*, Simon. Just think of it, a little lad of only five years, snuffed out like a candle. How could someone do that?'

Simon shrugged. 'You know as well as I do that children die every day. They get lockjaw, they catch chills, they contract diarrhoea . . .' His voice trembled as he recalled the death of his own infant son, Peterkin, from a fever two years ago.

'Forgive me, old friend. I do not wish to cause you pain,' Baldwin said gently, his face softening in compassion for Simon and Margaret's loss. 'However, those are natural deaths. They are different from deliberately ending a child's life for reasons of personal greed, or . . .' Baldwin recalled the expression on Stephen's face at the graveside, '. . . or some darker motive.'

'If you'd let me finish, I was also going to mention the girls who are allowed to die because their parents can't afford to feed them.'

'That is wrong, but one can comprehend the motives which might lead a parent to allow a girl to die,' Baldwin said, with a troubled expression.

Simon threw him a quick look. 'Really? I could never leave my own little Edith out to die of cold on a winter's night; nor can I understand how any other parent could.'

'Simon, I am sorry if I have upset you again. All I was trying to say was, it seems understandable to me that a man who already suffers from the most terrible hardship because of his poverty, one who has little food because the harvest has been poor, who has other mouths to feed, who has no money because his lord takes all he can earn, who has too many daughters already and cannot even think of ever having enough money to dower them all – well, in that position I *can* understand someone allowing a baby to die. In that example it is not someone killing for cruelty or personal benefit, it is a patriarch taking action for the better safety and security of the other members of his family. I find that easier to swallow than the murder of a young lad simply to satisfy a man's avarice.'

'I fail to see the distinction. And what is more, I still fail to see how you can blame yourself in any way for Herbert's death. Are you seriously saying that you would have gone to Lady Katharine and accused her of planning her son's murder?'

'Simon, I don't *know*,' Baldwin said despairingly. He sighed, head bowed for a moment. 'And yet I feel quite certain that if I had not been so tied up with my own pleasure and thoughts of my marriage, that young fellow would still be running around over the moors now. I cannot help it; I am convinced that if I had been more vigilant and thoughtful, Herbert, the heir of Squire Throwleigh, would still be alive.'

Night was falling as Baldwin and Simon clattered into the yard behind the house. The knight dropped from his horse as soon as he entered under the low gateway, shouting for a groom. When his horse was taken, Sir Baldwin impatiently tapped his foot until his friend joined him, and the two men made their way to the door.

Daniel, the steward, appeared in the doorway as they approached, and servants saw to their baggage.

The hall looked just as he recalled it from their previous visit, only a few days before, but now Baldwin was struck by how few were present. Whereas many of the local magnates and lesser nobles had turned out for the dead squire, only those from Throwleigh itself, Stephen of York, the servants, and van Relenghes – whom Baldwin did not recognise – were present. The knight felt outraged that so few had come to witness the burial of the boy. Perhaps it was because there was still a day to pass before the interment, but that was hardly an excuse! There was one other face he recognised, that of Thomas, the boy's uncle. Thomas raised his glass in a vaguely convivial gesture that disgusted Baldwin, and he turned from him quickly, hoping that Lady Katharine hadn't noticed.

Anger, frustration and a sense of his own guilt made his voice harsh as he bowed to the lady of the manor, saying, 'I am sorry to be here again, my Lady, so soon after your other dreadful loss.'

Lady Katharine lifted her eyes to him. In her hand was a swatch of pale linen, with which she wiped at the constant tears. 'I could have wished a happier occasion for your visit, too, Sir Baldwin.'

Her maid patted her back as she dropped her head in misery, sobbing silently. Lady Katharine's whole body shuddered with her grief, and the maid looked at Baldwin with a quick frown and shake of her head. He nodded curtly and gestured to Daniel. While the lady wept, Simon and Baldwin went out to see the body.

The maid left her mistress and fetched wine. She poured a goodly portion and passed it to Lady Katharine, watching with a kind of weary disinterest as she sipped. To the maid's mind there was no cure which could ease the loss of a much-loved son. She, Anney, knew that only too well.

Perhaps now her mistress would understand it, too.

Simon and Baldwin marched with the steward to the storehouse beneath the hall. Thomas followed them, overtaking the group as they arrived at the door.

'Here, Sir Baldwin,' Daniel said sadly, throwing open the door.

'Fetch lights, man. I can't see my hand before my face in this gloom,' Baldwin snarled, and Daniel hurried out, shocked, as if he had never been bellowed at before.

Baldwin strode to the little table on which the boy's body lay. He could just make out the features of the child, and his own face hardened. 'If I find your murderer, child, I shall see him or her hanged,' he swore.

'You think the boy was murdered?' Thomas asked. He had a stupid, befuddled look, and Baldwin ignored him. The steward finally returned with a pair of stands in which thick, yellow candles gave off a good light, but a foul odour as well, reeking of tallow and burning animal flesh as they guttered in the draught.

'Here!' Baldwin commanded, and the steward immediately complied, setting the candles on either side of the knight.

The boy was covered in a shroud, and before the knight could put out his hand to pull the cloth aside, Simon was already turning away, wincing. It wasn't only the thought of the wounds he was about to witness, it was the smell – the poor lad had clearly been stored in the coolest undercroft, but decomposition had set in swiftly.

Baldwin hardly noticed his movement. He snatched the shroud away with a determined air, as if fearing what he might discover, and studied the tiny figure. 'Gracious God! This is awful – he has great wounds, as if he has been beaten and crushed,' he said, his voice dropping in awed horror.

'Yes, and we still don't know who did it,' said Thomas, staring down at the little figure.

'Then you should have acted more damned swiftly to find the killer!' Baldwin snapped.

Thomas gave him a faintly baffled look. 'It isn't easy. That road's busy, Sir Baldwin.'

The knight opened his mouth to roar at him, but then stopped and peered down at the child, his face filled with a kind of relieved wonder. 'You mean he was killed on the road?'

'I thought you knew, sir. Yes, the Coroner has been here and confirmed it. Poor Herbert was run down on the road above the house. It's quite likely the killer didn't even realise he'd hit the child.'

Out in the yard, Nicholas brushed Sir Baldwin's horse and saw it had hay and water. When he was sure it was well catered for, he went back to the door and lounged against the post.

His master Thomas was a crooked bastard, as Nicholas knew only too well, but he hadn't expected such cold cunning from him. Thomas's appalled shock on discovering that he was five years too late to take over the manor, that he had a nephew who was already in possession, would have been hilarious if the news wasn't so dire. If their master was bankrupted, then they would all be in the same boat. There weren't many places for men like them to go. Each had his own problems. Especially Nicholas; especially here; especially since the death of Anney's first child. So far he had managed to avoid seeing her, and his master knew why he had to skulk in the stables and not take his place at Thomas's side like any other steward. It was the only sure way to avoid a disastrous meeting.

Still, their business here would soon be over, Nicholas thought to himself as he watched the knight and the bailiff stroll back from the storeroom towards the lighted door of the hall, and then they could leave Throwleigh for ever, take their money and get back to Exeter, where they belonged.

He glanced behind him, towards the moors, and shivered. There was no way he wanted to live out here.

Not again.

Sir Baldwin felt as if a great weight had been lifted from his shoulders. Since hearing of Herbert's death he had tormented himself with the thought that the lad had been murdered; thank God his assumption was plainly wrong. In his relief he overruled the quiet voice at the back of his mind which questioned how a lively, healthy boy could have been run down by a cart. Perhaps he had fallen; maybe Herbert had already been unconscious. All Baldwin knew was that the lad must surely have had an accident, and with that thought the sense of guilt, almost of complicity, had sloughed from his body, leaving him feeling fresh and clean.

As soon as he entered the hall again and saw Lady Katharine, Baldwin strode over and took her hand, offering her his sincerest and most heartfelt condolences.

The woman seemed comforted by his words and sympathy, and asked him: 'Will you remain for the funeral, Sir Baldwin? It will take place in four days' time.'

'I am sorry, but I fear I must return home. My wedding is the day after tomorrow.'

'I remember,' she murmured. 'We were to have been there. I can only hope that you will bring your wife to visit me here when you can. It would be a great pleasure to meet your lady.'

'Lady Katharine, you are very kind. I swear I shall bring her here as soon as I can – when you are over the worst of your grief.'

When Baldwin joined Simon near the fire, the knight couldn't help but sigh with relief.

'Oh, I thank God! I had expected a murder, and instead I find a simple – although tragic – accident,' he murmured, his attention returning to the grieving woman sitting on her chair while the servants moved about her. 'It's awful. I can hardly believe I was prepared to accuse even *her*, if I found evidence that her boy had been murdered.'

Simon nodded. 'And there's no doubt?'

'Oh, the lad met with an awful accident. His ribs are broken, and there is the track of an iron-shod wheel over his breast, as well as what look like hoofmarks. There are several scars, all probably caused by a scared horse. You know how beasts react when they are startled – and any but a warhorse will avoid a dead or injured body. The poor devil probably ran out into the path of a carter and was struck before the horse could stop; perhaps the animal tried to, but the weight of the cart forced it on. The boy was knocked over, and maybe the horse reared, hitting him again. Anyway, a wheel definitely went over him. He would probably have known little if anything about it; unconscious as soon as the hoof struck his head, and the life crushed from his frail little body as he was run over. Poor fellow! But I was foolish. Who would want to kill a lad like him?'

And on his journey home the next day he was able to smile and whistle, all thoughts of Herbert driven from his mind by the prospect of his wedding.

Daniel walked slowly from the hall and out to the sanctuary of his buttery, where he sank down on a stool, gripping his staff in both hands as an old man might clasp a prop.

It was deeply upsetting to see how the lady had taken the death of her son. Daniel was confused. His mistress had appeared so cold towards her boy when the squire had died, Daniel had half-expected her to show little emotion on hearing of Herbert's death – and yet she had been distraught to the point of losing her mind.

The steward gazed unseeing at the far wall. Jugs lay on the shelf, pots above, with taps and spiles jumbled among them ready for the next barrel to be broached. The Coroner had come in here to pocket his fee before viewing the body out in the storeroom and riding off again. He had recorded the death as an accident but that still left the question of how it could have happened. How could someone have killed the boy and made off without leaving evidence? It seemed too remarkable for it to have been an accident.

Daniel shook his head. It was hard to conceive of anyone knowingly committing such a hideous crime. It wasn't only evil, it was cowardly. Suddenly the steward's face stiffened as he recalled an interview.

It was at the last assessment of the manor's men, when he had stood before all the villeins in the hall, Stephen noting all the details down in his great roll at the table behind him. Despite the clean rushes strewn everywhere by Petronilla, the atmosphere had been foul, which was why the squire himself had left it to Daniel. There was a sour smell of unwashed bodies, which mingled unpleasantly with that of the ill-cured skins brought by the warrener.

The meeting was much like any other, except this time there was a piece of unwelcome news for the tenant named Edmund. Throwleigh was never profitable, and the squire had chosen to take on some of the newer ideas being tried in the Cornish estates. He had made his villeins *conventionary* tenants. No more did they have the right to remain on their land by virtue of paying their taxes; now they must agree to better any other offers. And this year a baker from Oakhampton had offered to take up the seven-year tenancy on Edmund's property, promising more than the other man could hope to.

Poor Edmund had appeared unable to comprehend the blow. He had stood shaking his head, refusing to accept that he could be forced to lose his whole property, a broken man.

Daniel could easily recall the second meeting, at which his lady had pushed Edmund still further, denying that he was free, rejecting his right to take his case to the King's court. At the time Daniel had thought she was pushing the man too far, but she was determined. In her mind the death of her husband was linked to the man in whose yard he had died. She held some kind of vindictive grudge against him. But Daniel had seen Edmund's face harden during that meeting, as if he felt he had nothing to lose.

An insidious thought crept into his mind: Daniel had seen him the day Herbert died. Edmund had been there, on his cart.

CHAPTER SEVEN

When Sir Baldwin de Furnshill walked from his house, he
didn't even notice the bright spring sunshine. The Keeper of
the King's Peace was an intrepid fighter, a man who had
survived wars and persecution, yet he had to pause on his
threshold, staring at the throng before him with nervous trepidation, quelling the cowardly urge to turn and flee indoors.
Only when his friend Simon joined him could he take a deep
breath and set off.

The road to the church was packed. All his servants were
there at either side of the path: the men grinning and bowing,
one or two still holding the tools they had been using that
morning, one man with a billhook dangling from his belt,
another resting on his fork, a shepherd leaning on his crook,
his dogs panting at his feet as if they too were laughing at the
knight's expense.

All the womenfolk chattered and giggled to themselves as
they kept up a lewd commentary on Sir Baldwin from behind

their hands. Urchins and beggar-children scampered along in his wake, calling out for alms and catching at the money tossed by Simon, who walked at his side.

'Why in God's name did I agree to go through with this?' Baldwin muttered to his friend.

Simon struggled to keep his face blank, but failed. 'It was your choice, old friend.'

'*My* choice? She forced me into it.'

'Aha! Do you mean that? A frank confession would add zest to the betting.'

Baldwin stopped dead and stared at Simon, his pale features reddening. 'You mean they are betting on whether I have already . . . already . . .'

'No,' said Simon gravely.

Baldwin breathed a sigh of relief.

'They are gambling on the sex of the child, that's all. They're sure it'll be born in July or August.'

Baldwin groaned, 'The *bastards*!' and eyed his tenants with a fresh suspicion. It felt as if he was seeing them all for the first time. On any other day they would treat him with respect – and a degree of caution – but today the normal rule of law had been inverted: today he was a figure of fun, a source of amusement to even the lowest of his serfs. They lined his route from his house at Furnshill all along the track to the church at Cadbury, and there, he knew, they would all stand about to witness his betrothal, chuckling or giggling at every stumble he made. He murmured gloomily, 'I wish I were a mere serf. Then Jeanne and I could exchange vows without the need for all this.'

Simon laughed aloud. If Baldwin truly believed that, he also knew it was surely the only advantage in a life of utter poverty. For a marriage to be recognised it was necessary that a man and woman should be seen to give their promises, but there was no legal requirement for them to be made in the church's grounds – that was merely a custom that had grown up. Often poorer people would swear their oaths in the presence of friends, and only at some later stage, when the wedding had long been consummated, would they go to the priest for his blessing. But the rich felt the urge to go to the church door, even if only on the practical ground that all their servants should be able to see their new mistress.

'And miss out on your feast? How would Jeanne feel about that?'

'Have you seen how many people she has invited?'

Simon clapped his friend on the back. It was many years since his own marriage, but he hadn't forgotten the gut-churning embarrassment of standing before all his contemporaries and other hecklers at the church door. He knew how his friend felt – and took a cynical pleasure in maximising his suffering.

'All your good money going to waste on wine and ale for comparative strangers, eh?'

'I grudge no one my drink. If anyone will regret his thirst, it will be the drinker himself, tomorrow morning,' Baldwin retaliated, casting a sidelong look at his friend. Simon had more than once been seen looking faintly green about the face, quiet and introspective, the morning after an evening of Baldwin's hospitality.

The knight secretly studied his friend as they approached the church. The bailiff's grey eyes gazed out at the world with a calm self-confidence, and Baldwin knew that in part his strength of spirit came from his wife, Margaret. Theirs had not been a marriage of estates, a contract between wealthy families designed to seal a business transaction or guarantee an inheritance; their vows had been willingly exchanged.

Baldwin was pleased that his own wedding had likewise sprung from mutual affection and friendship, but it was the other aspect of the ceremony which gave him a strong sense of unease, for Baldwin had been a Poor Fellow Soldier of Christ and the Temple of Solomon, a Knight Templar, and ever since the destruction of the Order by an avaricious French King and his lackey, the Pope at Avignon, Baldwin had held the Church and its organisation in contempt. For that reason Baldwin had chosen to wear a tunic of white today, in memory of the Order he had served and the men with whom he had lived, at whose side he had fought, and whose lives had been betrayed and ended in persecution ordered by the French King.

It was also why he wore his new riding sword. He wanted to have the symbol of his Order with him at his marriage: perhaps for sentimental reasons, perhaps because he felt the need to affirm his comrades at such an important ceremony. He was no philosopher, and did not seek to understand his own motives, but was happy that the new sword weighed heavily at his hip with the little carved Templar cross nearest his person.

He had friends within the Church, it was true, men such as Peter Clifford, the Dean of Crediton Church, but for Baldwin, a knight who had taken the three-fold oaths of poverty, chastity and obedience, the organisation led by the Pope, a man who had cynically discarded the Templars purely for his own profit, must itself be corrupt.

Still, he reflected, approaching the grey block of the old church on the hill, at least today it wouldn't be that damned fool Alfred, the priest who usually held the services at Cadbury; Peter Clifford himself had agreed to officiate.

'Come on, Baldwin, stop dawdling!' Simon chuckled and led the way up the last few hundred yards to St Michael's Church.

Here the crowd was thicker, with many friends from Crediton where Baldwin was the Keeper of the King's Peace. The gravedigger was shamefacedly trying to conceal his spade behind him, thinking it looked out of place today. Mingled among the crowd were others: squires, knights and a banneret. Even the local Coroner had made the journey from Exeter. Their horses stood at the edge of the church-yard, held by grooms while their riders mingled and chattered, waiting for Baldwin and his bride. Near the entrance were parked Baldwin's own wagons, filled with barrels of his latest brew of ale, and his servants and guests were all making free of it.

For once the abstemious knight felt jealous of drinkers.

Lady Katharine was in her hall. Outside the sun was high in the sky and it illuminated the room with long shafts of light in which dust-motes and insects danced. Occasionally a swallow entered and circled above, then darted out through the window again.

If this was a normal time, she would be outside, sitting in her small garden, listening to the birds singing, while sewing or working with Daniel to ensure the manor produced a profit. If her husband were still alive, she might go hunting with him, her falcon on her wrist.

But this was not a normal time. Her man was dead, and so was her son.

She could remember when she first met her husband. It was seven years ago now, when the King had been in St Albans, and Katharine's father, a knight banneret, had been in attendance.

It had been wretched. Famine was striking all in the kingdom, for rain had killed off much of the harvest, and what remained had to be dried in great ovens before it could be used for anything. Although the King tried to control prices by issuing Ordinances which regulated the cost of all foodstuffs, these only strengthened the black market. Floods were widespread, and Katharine could remember the despair of farmers who couldn't sow their crops. In St Albans there was no bread to be had, not even for the King himself.

And in the midst of this gloom, she had been the target of every fool in parti-coloured hose. Youths so callow she had no wish to give them a second glance, had circled about her like dogs around a bitch. Some tried to amuse her with jokes; she ignored them. Others flattered her and tried to tempt her with gifts; she rejected them. But her success in ridding herself of these popinjays only led to others trying to attract her with lewd words; one even suggested she should let him visit her in her room. Him she had stared at coldly, and left.

All the time she was pestered by these fools, Squire Roger had avoided her gaze. She had looked to him often, where he stood at the other side of the room, hoping that he might recognise her plight and come to rescue her, but he had nobly smiled and moved on. Only later did she realise that he had thought her content with men of her own age. Yet she had not desired them. She only ever wanted a strong husband, a real man. Someone like him.

And it had been a real delight, a wonderful, ecstatic recognition, when she had seen the love in his eyes. She had thought him cold, but that was a mask to conceal his true feelings. When she confessed how she felt, she found him as passionate as herself, and that same day she and he had become handfast, engaged to be married.

Her father had *not* been over the moon about it. He'd been hoping for a good local marriage to strengthen his lands, but he was too kindly a man to ignore the obvious adoration that Squire Roger felt for his daughter, and which was so clearly reciprocated. And, he might well have reflected, there could be advantage in being allied to the squire of Sir Reginald of Hatherleigh.

But their time together had been too short, Katharine thought as the breath caught in her throat and she felt another bout of sobbing threaten her composure. And now their only child was gone as well.

Her husband had fallen from his horse, and it must have been God's will that he should have died there and then, but Katharine couldn't rid herself of the conviction that Edmund had contributed to his end.

A murdered man might be gathered up to God because He had ordained the fellow should die, but his killer should still be punished. That was why she had a personal determination to see Edmund pay, forcing him to revert to servile status. He had angered Squire Roger and possibly increased the heat of his blood, making him burst his heart.

She clenched a fist and pounded the arm of her seat:
Edmund would suffer for taking her husband from her!

Baldwin took a deep breath and strode on, glancing neither
to right nor left as he went up to the door where Peter Clifford
stood waiting.

'Sir Baldwin, good morning! The sun has favoured you
on this happy day; God must be smiling on you.'

'I didn't expect it from the look of the weather yesterday.
I was convinced we would get washed out,' Baldwin admitted gruffly, his eyes darting hither and thither as he sought
out his wife-to-be. 'There's still time,' he added gloomily,
glancing up at the thin, white clouds hanging peacefully in
the almost clear sky.

Peter laughed and continued chatting inconsequentially.
He had conducted many such ceremonies, and knew the
torment Baldwin was going through, if only at second-
hand. In his experience, grooms were always nervous and
stiff until after the formal service. Baldwin was true to
form.

The knight was pale and, although Peter would never have
said so, he was sure that Sir Baldwin was viewing the ceremony with the utmost trepidation. No matter, Peter thought
to himself: once the food and wine began to flow, the most
terrified groom always recovered.

They were still waiting in the porch when Simon heard a
murmur in the crowd, and he walked to the churchyard gate.
There he found his wife standing in attendance to another
woman.

'Jeanne, you look wonderful,' he said simply.

*   *   *

85

Looking about her, Anney thought that Lady Katharine's hall had the atmosphere of a prison. It was a place of doom and misery. There was nothing in it to lighten the spirit. If she could, she would have left long ago, but that was impossible, even though it contained almost every painful memory of her life: not only the trial of her man, but the inquest of her son.

The husband she had sworn to cleave to had been accused here, in this very room, by his true brother-in-law, the brother of his first wife, the man who had come to expose his bigamy.

There was no doubt of the validity of the charge. He had no choice but to confess, and although he protested that his first wife had trapped him, that he had never wanted to wed her, he had been forced from Throwleigh. Anney had been left alone with her children who, she learned, were legally bastards. She was ruined. No matter that she had given her vows in good faith; the men of the vill regarded her as tainted, and as they made clear to her from that day on, she should be grateful for any attention they might choose to offer.

It had been hard. She had been abused by everyone. The women ignored her, or joked at her expense; the men were worse. A woman needed a protector. Without one, whether father or husband, grown-up son or brother, there was no security, no safety.

This was brought home forcibly the first time she was raped on her way back from the hall. The man responsible was drunk and had seen her approach. She'd known him all her life – that was what really offended Anney more than anything, the fact that he was as old as her father before he died. The fellow had made advances and thrust her into the hedge before lifting her skirts and . . .

It wasn't the only time, either. The men of the village looked on her as fair game. She had given herself to a biga-mist, so she was contaminated – a mere common stale. After a few weeks, Anney had taken to carrying her dagger as she walked, and that afforded her some little protection; once she wounded a man trying to molest her.

And then, when her little boy Tom, Alan's younger brother, died in that futile, stupid manner, the light had blown out from her life, like a rushlight caught in a gusting breeze. Once more she had been brought in here to this damned hall, to receive the terrible news, and when the Coroner arrived two days later, it was in here that he came, to undress the little body of her Tom.

At first she had felt quite calm as they removed his clothes, which were still damp from when he drowned, but when the Coroner had pulled his arms and legs apart before the greedy gaze of the audience, all of the jury staring with rapacious eyes, she had felt her control slipping. Was it just that they were hungry to see another's death because that made their own somehow less fearsome to contemplate? She didn't care; she had loathed them all from that moment.

That was why she had carried on working at the manor. She couldn't face labouring in the fields with the other villag-ers after seeing their hideous excitement as the Coroner turned her boy's body over, showing them in turn the back, the head, the neck, the arms, the legs, his belly, and his strangely sad little shrivelled penis. She could never work alongside those who had enjoyed her son's humiliation, even after his death.

This room would always be loathsome to her. Hateful. The officers were different, but the hall's atmosphere was unchanged. She despised it and everyone in it.

Especially the hypocrite – the priest who was supposed to be above worldly things, and who was no better than any of the other men in the village: he was a degenerate.

Hadn't she seen the proof?

CHAPTER EIGHT

Lady Jeanne de Liddinstone smiled at the bailiff and gave him a low curtsey. She was dressed in the gown of bright red velvet that Baldwin had bought for her at Tavistock Fair, but now it was trimmed with grey fur, and she wore a narrow girdle of red with a harness of silver. A linen wimple covered her red-gold hair, and the white of the head-gear made her cornflower-blue eyes stand out still more brightly in comparison.

Simon opened the gate for her, and she and his wife entered, Jeanne walking at his side, his wife Margaret following a couple of steps behind, leaving the place of honour to the bride.

'How is he?' Jeanne whispered.

'As twitchy as a deer at bay!' Simon whispered back, and was rewarded by her throaty chuckle. He continued, 'I doubt he'll be able to remember the words. He won't be happy until he's out of here and back at his manor.'

As he spoke, the enthusiastic chatter all around them died away, to be replaced by a contemplative quietness. Baldwin's workers eyed the bride-to-be speculatively, wondering how far they might dare to try the patience of their new lady without causing her to lose her temper. The wealthier women in the crowd compared her cloth with their own, assessing the value of her tunic, rings and necklace, while their menfolk watched her movements lasciviously, gauging the line of her figure and nudging each other as they exchanged lecherous comments on her ability to tire her new husband during the coming night.

'My Lady?' Simon asked, holding out his arm. Lady Jeanne had asked him to act as her nuptial father, giving her away at the wedding, for she was orphaned, and her only living relatives dwelt in the English possessions in Bordeaux. She slipped her hand through his elbow, and together they walked slowly to the waiting knight.

Peter Clifford smiled broadly, straightening his back as the two came near. Baldwin, he saw, had gone quite pale, but the priest wasn't worried: he knew most grooms looked close to fainting. And that was only right, because they were about to take part in one of the most important ceremonies of their lives.

When Jeanne reached Baldwin's side, her hand still through Simon's arm, the priest made the sign of the cross, scowled at one merchant who chose that moment to give a loud guffaw, and called out in a carrying voice: 'We are here to witness the marriage of Sir Baldwin de Furnshill to Lady Jeanne de Liddinstone. Is there anybody here who knows any reason why these two might not be legitimately wedded in the eyes of God?' He paused, his gaze sternly flitting over the people gathered all about before resting on Baldwin. 'Sir Baldwin, please make your oath.'

Baldwin swallowed. On a sudden his mouth felt dry, and there was a flickering in his belly which, matched with his lightheadedness, made him feel disorientated, nearly sick. Licking his lips, he faced Jeanne. Touching the cross of the hilt of his sheathed sword with his left hand, and taking Jeanne's hand in his right, he repeated the words he had heard so often before. 'My Lady, let all those present witness that I here take you as my wife, for better or worse, in health and sickness, to have and to hold from now until the end of my life, and there I give you my oath.'

She smiled as he spoke, and he saw the sunlight dance in her eyes as she made her own vow to him.

There was a stillness as Jeanne confirmed her dower, her whole estate of Liddinstone. The silence continued while Baldwin handed Peter Clifford a purse of coins for the poor. Peter took the ring from Simon and blessed it, before passing it to Baldwin. The knight lifted Jeanne's right hand and slipped the ring over her index, middle and third fingers, while Peter solemnly intoned, 'In the name of the Father, the Son, and the Holy Ghost,' before he finally set it on the third finger of her left hand.

And then suddenly all was bustle. While the ceremony at the church's door would always remain crystal clear in Baldwin's mind, the rest of the day went by in a whirl. While he stood, smiling proudly at his wife, a garland of fresh flowers was thrust between them, and Baldwin was prompted by the priest to kiss his wife through it, seeing her through the mixed yellow and red flowers as if for the first time. A moment before his lips met hers, he saw her eyes close.

He marvelled at his good fortune; it took an effort of will not to laugh with sheer joy.

Thomas could hear the sobbing in the hall even as he left the stables, and he screwed up his face in disgust. Rather than enter the scene of such melancholy, he took a seat near the gate on a lump of moorstone and surveyed the view with satisfaction. At last his financial embarrassments were coming to an end.

It was the famine which had started his decline, but knowing that was no comfort. So many had left the city then, back in 1315 and during the following two years, and Thomas had speculated happily, sure that his fortunes would build nicely once the food began to flow again, but all at once he discovered that he had accumulated too much property, and couldn't cover his debts with ready cash.

There hadn't been any great concern at first, because Thomas had loads of friends in the city, and knew he could rely on them to help him. He'd met some at a tavern one night, and had confessed to a slight difficulty, nothing more. Thomas knew he wasn't stupid, and could remember most of that night quite distinctly – even though one of his mates had insisted on mixing him several drinks, which must have been strong, for Thomas's head the next day was God-awful – but still, Thomas knew he was far too shrewd and cautious to have made any stupid comments in a place like an inn near the docks.

And yet the curious thing was, that was the last time he had been able to discuss his troubles with those friends.

Someone else must have been listening while he spoke, Thomas thought. That was why his credit with suppliers had been frozen.

But now all was well; and all because his brother had fallen dead from his horse and his nephew had died.

When you looked at it, life was quite a joke really, he thought, and now, while he was facing away from the hall and was quite alone, he allowed himself to smile broadly at last.

There was no need to conceal his very real joy.

Peter bellowed for quiet as the guests cheered, rowdier elements calling out crude suggestions to help Baldwin and his wife during the coming night. The priest offered up prayers for them, giving them blessings in God's name. He led them into the church and, while they knelt in the nave, he gave more prayers in their favour, and then handed them each a small, lighted candle before celebrating Mass with them.

Unseen as the knight and his lady had entered the church, two men at the back of the crowd had glanced at each other meaningfully. While the press outside thinned, all joining the bride and groom in the church, these two strolled unhurriedly to the wagons.

Edgar, man-at-arms to Sir Baldwin, and more recently the knight's bottler and steward, a tall, straight man, serious by nature and assured of his own importance, went straight to the largest wagon, on which two great casks were set. He rummaged under its seat until he found a small sack which he opened. Inside were two drinking pots, which he passed to his accomplice, Simon's servant Hugh.

Hugh, a taciturn, narrow-featured man with the slim build of a moorman, took them and filled both, holding one to Baldwin's man. 'To your master.'

'To Sir Baldwin de Furnshill and his lady, Jeanne,' Edgar nodded, and they drained their pots.

'What now, then?' Hugh asked after their second drink.

Edgar shrugged while Hugh bent to fill them again. There had been a time when he hadn't wished to talk to Hugh, when he had thought the bailiff's servant was too common for a man like him, who had, while a sergeant in the Order of the Poor Fellow Soldiers of Christ and the Temple of Solomon – the Knights Templar – dined with princes and lords. More recently, having been thrown together with Hugh over the last four years whenever their masters had met, he had grown to enjoy the moorman's company.

'Everyone is to go to Furnshill for the banquet. You know the way of these things. It's lucky the kitchen was designed on generous proportions,' Edgar said, eyeing the waiting horses and carts. 'There'll be no work finished today on Sir Baldwin's estate.'

It was a subject he felt strongly about. He was the knight's steward, and was responsible for the profits from the lands around Cadbury. To be steward was an honour, but it was a heavy responsibility as well. All looked to him when anything went wrong: if there wasn't sufficient grain stored through the winter to sow in the fields, if there wasn't enough food for guests at a feast, if the harvest failed and provisions must be acquired, it was the steward who was to blame.

As steward, he was always on the lookout for the next potential problem, and today he found it while Hugh was passing up his fourth large cup of ale. Edgar took it, but his eyes narrowed. 'What's that noise?'

Hugh listened, an expression of vague perplexity on his face. Sure enough, there was a quiet buzzing sound. He cocked his head, staring all around at the churchyard, but could see nothing. Then Edgar gave a muttered, 'Oh, Hell's teeth!' and sprang down from the wagon. He peered beneath the cart parked alongside and groaned: 'God's blood, but you can't keep him off it.'

Underneath was young Wat, the Furnshill cattleman's son, all of thirteen years old, and as drunk as a blacksmith on St Clem's Day. He didn't waken when they grabbed his booted feet and hauled him out onto the grass, nor when they called to him, or pinched him; he only grunted and rolled over. Hugh experimentally tipped half a cup of ale over his head, but the lad merely smiled happily and licked his lips in his sleep.

'Come on, Hugh,' Edgar said resignedly. 'We can't leave him here.'

The two servants each took an arm and hoisted the youngster to his feet. His legs wouldn't support him, unfortunately, and it was hard work to keep him upright. In the end, Edgar clambered onto the wagon, and was just taking hold of Wat's arms to lift him into it when he realised that the guests had begun to leave the church. He swiftly dropped to the ground again as Baldwin appeared in the church's doorway.

'Quick, prop him,' Hugh hissed, and the two supported the slumping figure between them as the knight and his lady walked out.

Baldwin felt curiously lightheaded as he paused in the porch. His whole life had undergone a transformation, he knew, and yet he himself hadn't changed. The sky looked wonderful, with a few tiny, fluffy clouds hanging motionless in the azure blue, and from here he could see the verdant countryside stretching away for miles. The scent of flowers came to him, and their strong, sweet odour made him feel quite drunk.

It was a day he had anticipated with keen delight for five months, ever since he and Jeanne had become hand-fast, shaking hands on their engagement in the presence of Simon and his wife. Now he had almost completed the Church's rituals. There was only the blessing of the bridal chamber to come. Then he and his wife could dispense with any further nonsense and get on with their lives together.

As he thought this, he caught sight of Jeanne's face. She was just leaving the shade of the building, and as the spring sun caught her features she was suffused in a golden glow. He felt his heart lurch. He had been a soldier, a Templar, then a wandering outcast, almost an outlaw, before returning home to his lonely bachelor existence, and to know that this wonderful, attractive and intelligent woman had accepted him as her husband gave him an intense pang, almost of pain.

With that thought he stepped into the sun, and felt a thrill of pure pleasure as he saw her gasp with delight. This was a touch of his own. That morning he had made sure that Edgar sent the children to his garden. Now there was a soft rain of rose petals thrown by four of his workers' cleaner children. Seeing his wife's expression, Baldwin knew his efforts had been well-spent. He fumbled for coins and tossed them as the shower began to falter.

'My Lady?'

Jeanne accepted his hand and they made their stately way down the church's yard. At the cart, Baldwin saw his servant. He gave Edgar a smile, and nodded towards the gate. To his surprise, Edgar appeared to ignore him. Baldwin assumed the man had missed his instruction. 'Edgar, open the gate for Lady Jeanne.'

'Sir.'

Edgar sprang quickly from the cart, marching before Baldwin and his wife. The knight followed, he and Jeanne walking more sedately, but when they were almost at the gate there was a sudden uproar as people began to guffaw, and Baldwin spun round glaring, thinking they were laughing at him or his wife.

Instead he found himself confronted with the sight of Hugh trying to support Wat. The servant gave a weak smile, hitching Wat's arm over the wagon's wheel and leaning back nonchalantly, but even as he looked away casually, as if unaware that anything was amiss, his arm had to shoot out to catch the sliding Wat, hauling him back upright by the scruff of his neck.

Baldwin pursed his lips. The boy's drunkenness was an insult to his wife. He opened his mouth to bellow, but before he could, he felt Jeanne's hand on his arm.

'Edgar,' she said sweetly, 'perhaps you could help the cattleman's boy? He seems to have some form of food poisoning.'

'Yes, madam.'

'And ensure that he is given a good wash at the church trough while everyone is still here, would you? I'd not like to think he might be dirty when he joined our celebration. See to his washing yourself, would you?'

Edgar clenched his jaw. Her meaning was all too clear: he was the steward, so he was responsible for the cattleman's lad and he must join in the indignity of publicly washing the brat. He rejoined Hugh and the two half-dragged, half-carried Wat to the trough, while guests and villeins bellowed their delight.

Baldwin took his wife's arm and they walked through the gate. Here his present stood waiting. For a second Jeanne didn't notice, but then she gasped.

The pure white Arab mare stood quietly under the tree, the new saddle and harness gleaming. Her coat shone like snow under bright sunlight, and the gold chasing on the leatherwork was almost painful to look at, it was so bright. As she moved, bells fixed to stirrups and bridle tinkled musically.

'Baldwin, your mare . . .'

'Not mine any longer, my love. It is customary to give one's leman a gift on the day of marriage. I give you this horse. I hope you will find her as much of a pleasure to ride as I have myself.'

Jeanne smiled, her hand already on the bridle. For a moment her eyes filled with tears, she was so happy, and she had to blink them away. Then she touched her husband's cheek and kissed him again while the guests roared and cheered behind them. She accepted his aid to mount the mare, and sat proudly in the saddle, her tunic awry, her skirts rucked up, while Baldwin took the reins and walked his bride back to his manor.

It was quite alarming how Petronilla had altered since the squire's death, Daniel thought.

He was standing in the screens, leaving his poor mistress in the hands of Anney, much though it grieved him to quit her side in her present state. When the poor woman was so desolate, Daniel felt he should be with her.

Petronilla kept on weeping when she was alone. The silly chit appeared to have been dreadfully affected by the way that the squire had so suddenly been taken from them, and quite often when Daniel saw her in the dairy or buttery, he noted her raw, red eyes. Of course it was only right and proper that a serf should miss her master and that she should mourn his loss, but Daniel found himself wondering; Petronilla had looked so bonny just before the squire's death, with her glowing cheeks and fresh complexion.

He sighed and walked to the door, standing on the threshold. Outside in the yard he saw Petronilla herself, talking to the priest. Even as Daniel appeared in the doorway, she bent and kissed Stephen's ringed finger while he made the sign of the cross over her head.

That was another thing. The girl had taken to speaking to Stephen regularly since the master had gone. She always appeared to be near him, confessing sins or some such – surely she didn't have *that* many guilty secrets?

But Daniel had other matters to concern him. It had occurred to him that the bailiff couldn't have known about Edmund's imminent eviction or his return to servile status.

Daniel realised perfectly well how the bailiff would have viewed the whole affair: a man falling from his horse and his son dying shortly afterwards. The first was all too common with men of the squire's age; the second was surely only a sad accident. But Daniel knew something that the bailiff didn't: he knew about Edmund.

CHAPTER NINE

Sir Baldwin eyed the plates on the table before him with mistrust. He had long ago given up eating rich foods, preferring simpler fare, but now, at his wedding feast, he had been presented with as complex a mix of pounded, mashed, coloured and spiced dishes as could be found in any palace to satisfy the jaded palate of a royal courtier.

Before him, bowls brimmed with concoctions of the wildest colours: purples, reds, oranges, greens, and some with different mixtures, like the odd-looking dish near his left hand that was quartered white, yellow, green and black. The sight made Baldwin swallow nervously, aware that he would probably have a troubled stomach the next morning.

It was a relief to be able to recognise common foods. To the side of his salt was a dish of roasted thrushes, and beside that, some 'mawmenny' – ground mutton in a wine-based gravy, thickened with the minced meat of a fowl and almonds, flavoured with cloves and sugar, and coloured with red dye.

There was a plate of blancmange, too: an appetising mixture of veal, pounded and minced, boiled with sweetened almond milk and seasoned with sugar, salt and pepper.

The custard pies were more complex. He had seen them being made: tiny shreds of veal boiled in wine, with sage, savory, hyssop, pepper, cinnamon, cloves, mace, and other strong spices and herbs, the whole thickened with eggs before having dates, ginger and verjuice added. The final operation involved pouring the mixture into the small pastry cases, somewhat inelegantly called 'coffins', and cooking it.

It sometimes seemed to the knight that the whole basis of the art of cooking for a feast was to disguise even the simplest of foods by adulterating it with so many herbs or spices that the taste buds rebelled. He watched the stuffed capons being marched to his table with a sense of relief. At least there was little the greasy, rotund tyrant of the kitchen could do to a good, plain fowl, he thought.

The cook had been Edgar's idea. Sir Baldwin would have been happy to have used his own man, who was perfectly capable of turning a spit or filling a pastry case, but his servant wouldn't hear of it. 'Not on your wedding day, Sir Baldwin! You can't let Jack cook for you on your wedding day.'

'Why not, in God's name?' the astonished knight had demanded.

'You must aim to impress everyone,' Edgar had protested before seeing the blankness creeping into his master's eye. If there were any arguments guaranteed to fail with the knight, they were those of the responsibilities of modern fashion. Edgar quickly changed tack. 'And how would your cook feel, being the only senior member of your household who wouldn't be able to eat with you in your hall on the day of your marriage?'

Baldwin's refusal had frozen on his lips. He wanted to enjoy his nuptials, but he also wanted all his people to celebrate with him. It was an ancient tradition, no doubt, yet he agreed with many of the old customs, especially that which demanded that a lord should hold festivities in his own hall with all his retainers about him. The same custom would have dictated that the cook should have performed his duties in the kitchen, of course, but Baldwin was secretly swayed by the logic of allowing his own man a few hours' relief. If Baldwin was truly honest with himself, he was also of the same mind as Edgar: Jack was undoubtedly competent at manufacturing large numbers of simple pies or roasting whole beasts over the kitchen fire, but when it came to making his new wife feel at home, Baldwin wasn't so confident.

His eye drifted over towards his temporarily unemployed cook, who sat at the bottom of one of the tables, a fixed glower on his face. Jack *hadn't* wanted to be relieved of his duties. When Edgar had informed him that he was to be saved the responsibility of feeding so many people, he had shoved the seneschal out of his way and marched straight to his master. It had taken all of Baldwin's powers of persuasion to ensure that the new cook didn't end up stuffed on the table with all the other roasted meats.

Now Jack fixed him with an eye so accusing that Sir Baldwin shifted guiltily in his seat. He smiled at his wife.

'My Lady, would you like some blancmange?'

She shook her head ruefully. 'Not now, sir. I've already eaten more than I usually do in a whole week!'

Baldwin felt the same. King Edward II had proclaimed in the ninth year of his reign that his subjects should have only two courses of meat, and Baldwin surreptitiously felt his tightening belt and restrained a groan and a belch. This was already the third course, and he was aware of an unpleasant rumbling deep in his bowels. Too many sweetly flavoured foods; too many rich, spiced meats; too much good wine.

Sitting further along the table, Simon Puttock cocked an eyebrow at his wife and jerked his head at Baldwin. 'I think our abstemious friend is suffering!'

Margaret Puttock smiled at her husband. Simon and Baldwin had been friends for so long now that she could hardly recall the time before Baldwin had arrived in the area, when she and her husband still lived in the small village of Sandford, before Simon was given the awesome responsibility of becoming the Warden's Bailiff at Lydford.

Glancing up at the knight, she saw him studying a stuffed fowl with an expression that bordered on alarm. He had sliced off a piece of golden, slightly dry meat from the breast, and beneath it had found a thick layer of stuffing, which glowed bright orange in the candlelight. He had the look of a man who, rich beyond all dreams, has only gold in his house, yet who has found that proximity leads to aversion and now seeks to find something – *anything*! – made of a different material.

Margaret looked away before she burst out laughing, and took another spoonful of the paste on her trencher. It was good to see Baldwin married at last. She had tried to help, introducing the knight to all the most eligible widows and young women in the area, but had failed to find one who fired him with enthusiasm. It was only when he met the tall, red-haired woman from Liddinstone that he had at last succumbed. Margaret did not grudge him her wasted effort; she held only an abiding gratitude that he had finally selected a woman whom she could be pleased to call a friend. It would have been very difficult if Baldwin had chosen someone Margaret had loathed.

'I only hope he doesn't fill himself too full of this wine,' Simon said, taking a long pull from his drink and gesturing to Edgar for more.

'I imagine his wife will be hoping the same, Simon,' she said meaningfully, giving his drinking horn a hard stare as Baldwin's servant refilled it.

Simon laughed and took another good draught. He laughed again as he caught sight of the pale features of the cattleman's son Wat, who was staring at the food on the table with an expression akin to horror.

The bailiff was in excellent spirits, delighted for his friend, who was happier than at any time since they had met, and filled with the hope that soon his own wife might become pregnant again. He winked at Margaret and set the horn aside for a moment while he concentrated on his food. Simon didn't suffer from Baldwin's scruples about food. The bailiff had been brought up on simple fare, and when he was offered special dishes he tended to try everything. Although he could feel his belly beginning to rebel, there were several bowls he had not yet investigated and he was determined to remedy that deficiency. When his friend caught his eye, Simon waved happily, still chewing, and saw Baldwin raise an eyebrow in sardonic amusement.

Baldwin shook his head, and turned back to his plate, but after a while he stopped chewing and frowned slightly.

Jeanne noticed his altered mood. 'What is it, my love? Is the food not to your taste?'

'The food is wonderful,' he lied smilingly. 'It is only my appetite. I am replete.'

In truth, Baldwin had recalled the face of Lady Katharine of Throwleigh, and it was the vision of the weeping woman which had destroyed his appetite. And yet, as he reminded himself, there were no suspicious circumstances. The father had died naturally, the son had been run down. And that was that.

Wasn't it?

The next day dawned clear and sunny, a perfect spring morning.

Simon stared from his window in the guest room. From here he could see over a swathe of southern Devonshire almost to the sea. The sun shone brightly from a cloudless sky, and the scene was perfectly framed by the lines of trees at either side. His wife was still asleep, and the bailiff dressed and walked down to the hall. Here he found the servants at work clearing the mess of the night before, sweeping around the odd recumbent figure slumped on the table or lying amid the soiled rushes.

The bailiff nodded happily to Edgar. It was some surprise, after the amount he had drunk the previous day, but his head and guts felt fine. He had only a minor pain in his head and the feeling that a walk outside would be kinder to those who breathed the same air as him.

He stepped into the buttery and filled a wineskin, tut-tutting as he surveyed the slumped figure of Wat, snoring gently at the side of one of Baldwin's great barrels of ale, a happy smile on his face. Slipping the thong over his neck, Simon walked out to the southern-facing wall. An old tree-trunk stood there, on which Baldwin's men split logs, and he sat on it, taking a good swallow of wine, then leaning back and gazing over the view with a contented sigh.

Thus it was that Simon saw the messenger before anyone else.

'He sent this man to ride through the night?' Baldwin exclaimed.

Simon nodded. The stableman was the same who had been sent with news of Herbert's death, a bedraggled, exhausted lad of almost eighteen. 'Daniel must have thought it was important.'

'Of course,' said Baldwin, peering at the messenger once more. His words had been few, the meaning clear. 'Daniel thinks his master, the boy Herbert, was murdered, and asks that you go to the manor to investigate.'

'I have to go,' Simon said heavily. 'Although I'm not sure what this Daniel thinks I can do . . .'

'I'm coming with you.'

'You've just got married. You can't go to an enquiry on the day after your wedding!'

'Be damned to that!' Baldwin declared hotly. The sense of languorous fatigue with which he had awoken, the thrill of seeing his wife's face at his side, now pricked at his conscience, as if he was himself guilty of complicity in the child's death. 'I always had the conviction that the boy had been murdered, but I allowed myself to be gulled by that avaricious bastard Thomas. Well, I'll not make the same mistake again!'

'Baldwin, we don't know that he wasn't killed by accident.'

The knight carried on as if he had not heard his friend. 'How could I have been so stupid? I must have been born a cretin! All right, the boy was run down – but how often does that happen?'

'My friend,' Simon said calmingly, 'we don't know that he was murdered, all we know is that Daniel *thinks* he might have been. That isn't reason enough for you to desert your wife. You stay here, and I'll go and look into it. Boys and men get run down and killed every day of the week.'

'Rubbish, Simon! Those who get run over are drunk, or fall accidentally. They die outside alehouses, or just outside their own doors. But young Herbert died out on the moors – and he wasn't drunk. He would have jumped from the path of a wagon.'

'Pure supposition!'

'Logic!'

'Baldwin, you cannot leave your wife the day after your wedding; it's not right.'

'Leave me? What makes you think he would be leaving me, Bailiff?'

Simon's heart sank. He had wanted to keep this from Lady Jeanne, but now there was no way to conceal it. 'I am truly sorry, Lady, I wouldn't want to be cause of dispute between you and your husband. I shall leave you so he can explain.'

Jeanne lifted her eyebrow, then gave a low chuckle. 'Bailiff, if you think that I don't realise what's going on here, you have no understanding of the loudness of your voice.'

'But you asked . . .' Simon stammered.

'Why you thought he would be leaving me here. Of course he won't. I will be joining you both to see Lady Katharine and help soothe the poor woman.'

CHAPTER TEN

The two men set off long before the sun had reached its
zenith, this time with their wives and servants in their train.
The exhausted messenger was remounted on one of
Baldwin's own stallions, but even so they made slow
progress.

Wat had been told to pack a few clothes and join them.
Although his head hurt horribly and his stomach felt like
a seething cauldron of acid, he was nothing loath: this
was an adventure. He had never gone further than
Cadbury before, except once when he had travelled to
Crediton, and his father had never been so far as
Dartmoor, so this would be a feather in Wat's hat. What's
more, he would be avoiding the hard work that was about
to start: the planting of the Lenten seeds, the barley and
oats, rye and vetches, upon which the manor depended,
and with which he would have been expected to help. If
their visit lasted long enough, he might even be absent

for some of the long, dull days sitting out for hours on end with his pouch of pebbles and slingshot, ready to frighten off any birds or rabbits that tried to steal from the manor's fields.

Baldwin kept an eye on the lad, conscious of his responsibility. Wat pattered along cheerily enough at his side, but the knight was concerned that he shouldn't overtire himself. Baldwin was riding his favourite rounsey, a good, steady bay which could eat up the miles comfortably, while Jeanne followed, chatting quietly with Simon's wife, on her new Arab. Simon was on his ageing hackney, Margaret on a palfrey which ambled along gently.

'I still can't believe that Herbert was murdered,' Simon said now. 'Sure, it's a pity the lad died, but these things happen.'

'You make it sound like a simple accident. Daniel suspects the same as me, yet you speak as calmly as if you saw it happen.'

'Well, I almost feel as if I *did*. I've seen so many similar deaths: drunken workers who've fallen into the road; infants and toddlers who strayed – remember, the boy was only five years old. You've seen them just as I have. And often the driver of the cart doesn't dare stop and report the accident. At the least they might be faced with the expense of a heavy fine, while if they ride on as if nothing had happened, they may remain safe.

'And there's another thing, Baldwin,' the bailiff added. 'The victim in this case was the son of the squire, and was himself the heir. Who'd dare admit he'd run down his own master?'

'Yes, that much is true,' Baldwin agreed, but even as he pronounced the last word, Simon saw his mind was racing along a new track.

'Now what is it?'

'Hmm? Oh, I am sorry, I was merely considering the implications of what you had said. That the driver of the cart could be one of the manor's own villeins.'

That reflection made the knight quiet for the rest of their journey.

Jeanne studied Throwleigh Manor as they approached, and couldn't restrain a shudder. It was so grey, too exposed and rugged, merely a space in which people could exist, not somewhere she could ever consider as a home. Dropping from her horse, she put her hand through Baldwin's arm. She was aware of a feeling of gloom sinking into her spirit, as if the buildings were sucking the pleasure of her marriage out of her. Daniel the steward appeared at the door and walked down to greet them. He went first to Simon, and thanked him fulsomely for making the journey again. Then: 'Ladies, perhaps I could show you into the hall to meet Lady Katharine, while I speak to your husbands?'

He led the two women away and Baldwin glanced about him while the grooms took their mounts. 'Edgar, Wat is in your charge,' he said. 'See to it that the little brat doesn't make a nuisance of himself.'

At a nod from Simon, Hugh went off with them, and the two men waited for Daniel. The place was sunk in a gloomy light, for the sun had fallen behind the hill to the west, and only a dim twilight lay over the yard. It was a relief when Daniel reappeared at the door and crossed the yard to them. 'Gentlemen, perhaps you wouldn't mind if we were to take a little walk, away from curious ears, you understand?'

The steward took them through the gates to the clitter outside. 'I am most grateful to both of you – to you, Bailiff, and especially you, Sir Baldwin. It must have been a sore wrench to come all this way.'

'I assume you had good reason to demand our return,' Simon said.

Daniel made a weak, fluttering gesture with his hands. He felt spent after the worry of sending the messenger to ask Simon to return. It wasn't something he was used to, acting on his own initiative, especially since he hadn't been able to confide in anyone else. In the service of his squire, he had only needed to follow Roger's commands, and had looked upon his job as a position almost of sacred trust. Now he had gone out on a limb, and he wasn't sure whether he was about to fall or not. He took a deep breath.

'The manor has lost two masters in a matter of days, and I have a duty to their memories. I am certain that someone murdered the young master, and I ask that you bring his murderer to justice.'

Simon sat on a rock. 'Explain yourself!'

'Sir, whoever was driving that cart must have known who the master was, and yet they didn't come to report their deed to the Lady. They *must* have intended to kill him.'

Simon shook his head. 'My friend, if you were a local peasant on your way home, half-asleep at the reins, it's quite possible that you'd fail to notice a boy running out in front of you.'

'Have you never run over an animal?' Daniel inter-rupted desperately. 'Even a small animal, a rabbit or a cat, makes the wheel jolt. If it does that for a little creature, how much more will the wagon jump when it rides over a five-year-old boy? The man *knew* he had run someone down.'

'That doesn't make him a murderer,' Baldwin pointed out gently. 'It could have been an accident: if your master ran out without thinking, it was hardly the fault of the carter.'

'If it was an accident, why didn't the man come and confess?'

'He might well have feared the response of the Lady Katharine,' Simon said frankly. 'There's no evidence to suggest that the lad's death was anything other than a sad misfortune. Accidents happen.'

'Sir, shouldn't we try to find out who was responsible?'

Simon gave an unwilling nod. Apart from anything else, he had a duty to help the Coroner collect the *deodand*. A chattel which had caused a man's death was forfeit, theoreti-cally to be given to God in expiation – although in reality the *deodand* was a fine imposed on the owner, the value then put to pious uses. In this case the *deodand* must be the horse and cart, a goodly fine.

Daniel continued, 'Sir, that road is usually busy, and so it was on the day the poor boy died. I know because I was outside buying fish – it was a fast day – and while I haggled with the fish-seller, I could see the traffic.'

'So we're unlikely to find the culprit.' Simon shrugged.

'Sir, after the seller left, I remained outside a while longer, getting men to roll the fish barrels to the storeroom. I heard one more wagon, and saw it turn away in front of the house, heading down the road to Throwleigh.'

'What time would this have been?' Baldwin demanded. There was a nervous, almost scared look to the steward now, and Baldwin was sure he was at last coming to the meat of his story. The knight could feel his belly tense with expectation.

'Sir, it was in the afternoon – after nones.'

Baldwin nodded. 'You say men were with you to get the barrels moved. Was anyone missing from the house?'

The suddenness of the question made the steward blink confusedly. 'It was a fine day, sir. Only Lady Katharine herself and I were here. She was still deep in mourning, after all.'

'Who was in with you? Her maidservant?' Baldwin probed.

'No, Anney was out. So was Petronilla. Most of the servants were: two grooms had gone to Chagford for stores, and the berner was exercising his harriers with his whipper-in. Is this important?'

'Very well. Were the guests all out as well?'

'Yes, I think so. Does it matter?' Daniel became irritable. 'I'm trying to tell you about a man who had good reason to hate the master, and you ask about all these others!'

'My apologies, but we need to know to whom we can speak to corroborate your evidence. Were the other guests here on that day?'

'Sir James van Relenghes was out riding, sir, with his servant, Godfrey. They had come to visit the squire, and stayed to show their respect when they heard of the master's death.'

Simon glanced at him sharply. There had been a curious emphasis on the word 'respect'. 'You doubted their sincerity?'

'Bailiff, I've been here for as long as the squire, since 1306. Before that I served with him in many battles, and I never heard him speak of this Fleming – and yet here he is, claiming great friendship with my master. I can't help but doubt him.'

'What of the priest?' Simon asked.

'Stephen? He was probably at the church in Throwleigh . . . I didn't notice him.'

'I see. Let's return to this cart – did you recognise the man on it?'

'Yes, sir, I did,' said Daniel, pleased to be able to return to the point. 'It was a villein called Edmund.' As he spoke the name he felt as if he was betraying a member of his own family. It was the curse of a steward to have to bear witness sometimes against the serfs of the demesne, and he never enjoyed doing it. He had known Edmund all his life, and his father Richard before him. If only the latter were still here, he – but there was no point wishing for the impossible. They were both dead and gone: the master whom Daniel had loved and honoured and the servant Richard, who had sired Edmund – a fellow who had very good reason to hate the squire's widow and son.

Simon folded his arms. 'Have you told your mistress any of this?'

'God's blood, sir, I couldn't!' Daniel burst out. 'Edmund was the man who made the squire so angry that he died, and the mistress has been furious with him ever since. What would she do if I told her I thought this man killed her son, too?'

'But if you're convinced that this man was responsible?'

'I am, sir. There were no carts after his. If a previous vehicle had struck Herbert down, Edmund must have seen his body, yet he didn't report it. No, his was the wagon that crushed poor Master Herbert. But I wouldn't have the man killed on the spot without a chance to defend himself in court.'

Baldwin eyed him dubiously. It appeared strange that a family servant should withhold such important information. 'If you are certain, you have a duty nonetheless, so why do you save it up to tell us, Daniel?'

'So that you can question Edmund and have him arrested if you find evidence against him. All I ask is that you question the man. Come with me now, speak with him and see what you think.'

Simon rose and stretched. 'Get back in the saddle now, you mean? No, I don't think that's necessary. The man's unlikely to run off if he hasn't already.'

'But you will talk to him?' Daniel insisted.

The knight grunted his agreement. 'Wake us in the morning, and we will go with you.'

Daniel beamed with gratitude, as if for the first time in days he felt he had achieved something. He bowed, and walked off with something of his old pride.

Simon shook his head. 'You know what's occurred to me, don't you?'

'Yes – that Daniel has carefully pointed the finger at the only poor fellow who has no prospect of a lawyer or any other help,' Baldwin sighed. 'And of course he was most willing to divert our attention from all the other people who could have been involved.'

'Cynic! You're assuming someone *was* guilty,' Simon reminded him. 'My thought was, he's forcing us to conduct an enquiry whether we like it or not. Daniel must have believed we would let the matter lie. And so he called us back to find out that the carter might have run over the boy. Why should he do that?'

When they re-entered the hall, they found it already well-filled. Thomas was there, drinking cheerfully from a large goblet, and he welcomed them effusively.

'So good of you both to return to witness the funeral. Sir Baldwin, have you met Sir James?'

Baldwin found himself looking into the darkly handsome face of a tall man in his late thirties. He had strong features, with a high brow, and serious, keen brown eyes which watched the knight with a strangely focused stare. His concentration was easily explained when he opened his mouth to utter a courteous welcome.

'You are a Fleming?'

The man gave a short bow. 'You are quick to recognise an accent, Sir Baldwin. Yes, I am called James van Relenghes, but I have lived here in England for some years now.'

'You speak our tongue very well,' said Simon.

'It is kind of you to say so. I was lucky enough to serve your last King as a mercenary during his wars in France, and picked up much of your language.'

'Ah, of course. And that was where you became a friend of Squire Roger?' Baldwin asked.

'Yes, sir. He and I served in the same battles, and often shared in the rewards.' Van Relenghes sighed dramatically, shaking his head in sorrow. 'I was so sad to hear of my friend's death, and now this: his only son struck down.'

While Baldwin spoke with the man, Hugh went past carrying a jug of wine. Simon waved to his servant, who came over and filled his pot, then went to offer wine to Baldwin. To reach the knight he had to pass behind van Relenghes, but before Hugh could come close to the Fleming, Godfrey quickly stepped forward from the shadow of a pillar and halted between them, making as if to take the jug. Scowling fiercely, Hugh snatched it away. In his turn, Godfrey set his jaw and flexed his legs, rising onto the balls of his feet, ready to spring. It was his duty to protect van Relenghes from any strange or dangerous men, and he included in that category men who walked up behind his master.

'Is there a problem?' Baldwin enquired.

Van Relenghes heard the surprise in his voice and turned to see what had caught his interest. 'Oh, Godfrey, I think the servant is safe enough,' he said in a condescending tone that turned Hugh's scowl to a malignant glare that could have melted iron.

'Very well, sir,' said Godfrey, mockingly waving Hugh forward, and the fuming servant poured for Baldwin, his eyes fixed all the while on the weapons master.

'My apologies, sir,' van Relenghes said as his own pot was refilled. 'My guard doesn't always know when it is safe to relax.'

Baldwin nodded understandingly, but did not speak to the Fleming again, and watched him warily when he walked away, Godfrey a few feet behind him. Simon almost smiled at Baldwin's face, but then he caught sight of Daniel, whose eyes were fixed on van Relenghes. The steward's expression made Simon's grin fade.

It was one of utter loathing and hatred.

CHAPTER ELEVEN

Baldwin and his wife were honoured by having their own room in the solar. When Jeanne pleaded exhaustion after her long journey, Daniel called the young maid Petronilla to show them the way to their quarters. Baldwin recognised the girl from his first visit to the manor: she was pretty, he thought, and eager enough to please, if a little vacuous. She took them up to a room next to the solar block, beside the chapel, that had its own large bed. Edgar had already been there and had set out the room as Baldwin expected: there was a jug of weakened wine by the bed, and a bowl of water and towel had been set out on a large chest so that he and Jeanne could rinse away some of the dirt and grime from their journey.

When Petronilla had gone, Jeanne sat on the bed and hesitantly held out her hand to Baldwin. Even as she saw him smile, she felt his reluctance to come to her.

It wasn't that he was a man like the King, who preferred men to women, and she knew full well that he was not one of those misogynistical knights who disliked women purely because of their sex, considering them devious and untrust-worthy; no, she was certain that it was simply that he had spent so many years alone and without the comfort of a woman's company that made him shy in her presence, a shyness made all the more poignant for him when they were alone. That he should feel this way, and that he should revere her and respect her and her body, made her want to embrace him all the more strongly.

There was another reason for his slowness in going to her, but Baldwin was not sure he could confess it even to her: he had been a Poor Fellow Soldier of Christ and the Temple of Solomon, a Knight Templar, and while a Brother he had taken the three-fold vows of poverty, obedience – and chastity. Although he adored Jeanne, although he longed for her and thought that the sight of her seated on their bed was a picture designed to tempt an angel, he was nonetheless aware of a reticence to touch her, as if by so doing he was repeating the denial of an oath already sworn.

But his honour was not tainted, he had to remind himself. He had sworn obedience to the Pope as God's own vicar on earth, but the Pope had resiled; he had not protected those who had sworn loyalty to him, and had instead thrown them to their enemies in return for money. And that meant that all his vows could be thought of as retracted, as Baldwin knew. And yet he also knew that his vows had been made to God, not the Pope, and he wasn't certain that even the Pope's lack of honour could pardon his own lack of constancy.

Jeanne smiled at him, her blue eyes sparkling more than in the brightest sunshine. She lifted her hands to him, and he forgot his torment for another evening. With a groan, he crossed the room and took her in his arms.

Next morning, Edmund threw the last of the bundles of wood onto the growing pile under the eaves of his shed and stood straight, hunching his shoulders to ease the strain, before leaning down to pick up the next log. Hefting the axe, he was about to swing when he heard the horses. The sound was not unusual. This road was not very busy, but travellers were not uncommon, and yet today Edmund paused, axe ready, while he waited to see who might be riding towards him. He hadn't forgotten the last encounter with the squire.

His wife, Christiana, was in the yard collecting eggs, and she saw him waiting there expectantly. The attitude of attention was sufficient to make her stop her work and walk to the fence to see what had caught his interest.

The road curved and twisted beneath the trees this far from the vill itself and, although she too could hear the noise of many hooves, she could not see the riders. She set the eggs down by the gate and walked out to her husband's side.

Seeing that she had left her work, his face fell into a frown.

'What are you doing here?' he grumbled.

'I wanted to see who it—'

'Shut up, woman! Hell's fires! Haven't you enough things to do?' He lifted his fist threateningly.

Christiana quailed, and retreated towards the house. It was hard enough being married to a feckless man like him without having to endure his beatings whenever he was confused or disturbed.

She risked a glance over her shoulder and, seeing he was looking away again, she spat in his direction. Theirs had been a marriage of love at first. She and he had made their vows, without the knowledge or consent of her parents and she had joined his family immediately the priest had confirmed their right to remain together. They had needed to see him because her parents refused to believe that Edmund and she had made valid wedding vows; so, standing before the priest, they had repeated their oaths. On hearing what they said, he had declared that these had been spoken 'in words of present consent' and, although it was wrong for the two not to have had a nuptial Mass, their marriage was valid.

But they had both been young, not yet sixteen, and now she regretted her reckless decision. Edmund was weak, vacillating over any decision, and whenever he was upset about something he took it out on her. Touching the tender spots at her jaw and cheek, she mumbled a curse at her husband. That was where he had clouted her on the day he had taken the cart over to Oakhampton. The pottage she had cooked wasn't ready yet, that was his excuse – yet why should it have been? He hadn't told her when to expect him home, and their son wasn't back yet, either. How could she be expected to know when he would return?

It was so unfair! She had welcomed him when he walked through the door, but when she had asked him why he was back so early, purely to make conversation, her words seemed to send him into a rage. He shouted at her for being a stupid, interfering bitch, and punched her, saying he didn't know why he had ever agreed to take her off her father's hands. Leaving her sobbing on the floor, he had stalked from the room, saying he would eat at the alehouse.

It wasn't the first time he had hit her, and it wouldn't be the last, she knew. Blinking tears away, she caught a glimpse of movement and shortly afterwards saw five men on horse-back trotting round the bend in the road. Although she recognised Daniel, the manor's steward, out in front, the other four were unknown to Christiana.

However, the men all had that grave, stern appearance which boded ill to a poor serf, and she felt her heart lurch within her breast. Her feelings toward Edmund would never return to the old level of affection, but if he was in trouble, she would be alone and unprotected: she would not be able to look after Molly and Jordan on her own. Slowly, she crept outside into the yard again, moving cautiously so as not to alert Edmund to her disobedience.

Baldwin motioned with his hand, and at his signal Edgar and Hugh stopped their horses while he approached the house with Simon and Daniel.

'Godspeed, sirs,' Edmund offered tentatively as the men reined in, lowering his axe.

The knight studied him. Edmund was one of a type he had found in towns and villages all over Christendom. He was a hard man, formed by the climate of the moors, weathered and beaten like the moorstone itself. His face was prematurely old, with cracks tracing paths all over it, each etched deeply by sun, wind and rain. His back was bowed with the struggle to produce food in a harsh, inclement land. Sparse brown hair framed his saturnine features, and although his beard was thick, dappled with reddish patches, his pate was bald, the flesh showing oddly pale compared with his face.

But it was not only his outward appearance that was so familiar to the knight. The man's face held a kind of unfocused anger and bitterness. It was as if he knew that anyone he might meet was naturally formed to be an enemy, and that enemy would in the end destroy him. It was a look Baldwin had seen on the faces of men and women all over the world when confronted with their lords and rightful masters. His appearance was not improved by his flushed cheeks and bloodshot eyes – proof, if Baldwin had needed any, that the man was drunk.

The knight looked about him at the little yard where this farmer tried to make his living. Before the house was a small plot, criss-crossed with narrow paths, where Edmund grew a sparse collection of weedy vegetables. This early in the year there was not much to show; only a few young bean and pea plants dared raise their heads above the soil, and a couple of cabbages, survivors of the previous year, with the inevitable worm-holes drilled through. The garlic had thrived during the freezing winter, and frail little stems were poking through the mud. His attention moved on. He could recognise the herbs set out further on: hyssop, marjoram, thyme, camomile and rue among others, and all appeared to be growing well in the fresh spring sun.

At the side of the house was a well, with a barn behind, and Baldwin could see the rails which had once contained a pig. Now there was neither sight nor sound of an animal, and the knight was struck with a sense of dilapidation and decay. It made him frown. If this had been one of his own tenants, he would have seen to it that Edgar had spoken to the man, telling him to pull himself together. People who suffered from misfortune were the responsibility of the parish, and the congregation would often look after them, but the village could only be expected to help those who tried their best. There was no reason for people to put themselves out and give up their own hard-earned food for the indolent or foolish.

There was a muted clucking from the opposite end of the house, and Baldwin saw the woman. She was standing under the eaves, her frightened gaze flying from one man to another, and then back to her husband. Baldwin had never seen her before, but her pinched, grey features and scrawny figure told him much. The large bruise at her chin told him even more – and any sympathy for the serf in front of him dissipated. The recently married knight had no time for a man who beat his wife.

'Why do you keep on at me, Daniel?' the farmer was whining. 'What am I supposed to have done now?'

Baldwin saw Simon kick his horse forward. The bailiff cleared his throat. 'You know your master, Squire Herbert, has died?'

'Of course I do! Everyone knows he's dead – the poor lad.'

'And do you know how he died?'

Edmund shrugged. 'I heard he was found at the side of the road. I suppose he was hit by a man on a horse or something.'

'And what if he was hit by a man on a cart?'

'It's all the same, sir,' the farmer said, but he looked pale, as if the blood had fled from his face. Baldwin wasn't sure if Simon noticed, but the woman gave a start as if from fear.

Meanwhile Simon continued, his voice level and grave, his face impassive. 'Where were you on that day?'

'Me, sir? I was here.'

'That's a lie!' snapped Daniel. 'I saw you on your cart that afternoon. Where had you been?'

'I didn't kill the lad.'

'I didn't say you did – but the fact you make that connection is suspicious in its own right,' the steward stated deliberately.

Baldwin watched the farmer. He was obviously very scared, but who wouldn't be? Daniel was the sole representative of the power of the man's master. The knight raised his hand to silence the steward, and dropped from his horse. 'Can you fetch me a little ale or something else to drink?'

Edmund looked surprised, but nodded and shouted over his shoulder to Christiana before ungraciously motioning towards the log. 'You wish to sit?' he asked, letting his axe fall to the ground.

Looking at the mossy lump, Baldwin gave a thin smile and shook his head. 'No, I am happy to stand, thank you.'

Christiana soon came out with an ale jug, a cheap pottery drinking horn and a stack of pots resting on a wooden plank. Lifting her makeshift tray, she offered Baldwin the horn.

The ale was good, he noted with relief. He had regretted his demand almost as soon as he had opened his mouth. Sometimes the ales brewed by poorer wives were utterly undrinkable; the dreadful quality of the grains and the rank herbs they used to try to stop the brew going off conspired to produce a sour beverage which only a fool or a man half-dead from thirst could have desired. This was a good, sweet ale with a malty flavour. 'It is excellent,' he congratulated her, and saw the nervous duck of her head at his appreciative comment. With an anxious glance at her husband, she darted off to offer drinks to Simon and Daniel.

'So it should be,' the farmer grunted. 'I don't see why I should have to drink an unhealthy brew.'

Baldwin nodded coldly. As she poured his ale, he had been close enough to observe the bruise on Christiana's chin, and noted that it was only one of several marks and blemishes on her face. Her husband had taken to beating her regularly – the proof of a bully. The knight was disgusted by the man.

He returned to the subject. 'When the young Squire Herbert died, you were out on your cart. He died late in the afternoon, and you were seen at about that time, riding along the road where his body was found. Where had you been?'

To Simon, still on his horse, it looked as though the farmer was going to deny that he had been out, but Baldwin lifted his hand, and the farmer looked into his eyes. All at once, his gaze dropped, as if in shame, and he nodded.

'I was out to Oakhampton, selling some stuff at the market.'

Simon drained his pot and lifted himself from his saddle. As Christiana passed, he touched her shoulder and refilled his pot from her jug before leaning on his horse's withers.

His friend was watching the farmer intently. 'You had ale when your business was done?'

'Of course I did! It was a warm day. I only had the two quarts.'

'Why were you there?' Simon interrupted.

'Our pig escaped during the floods last autumn, and the stupid animal drowned, so I was trying to sell what I could to buy a new one. Not that I got much, since what little I had wasn't first quality.' He waved a hand at his decrepit farmyard. 'Our produce hasn't been good, not since the famine. So afterwards, I went to the inn to have a quick drink. But I came straight back.'

'You took the direct road?' asked Simon.

'Yes, sir.'

'No, you didn't,' Daniel interrupted. 'If you'd wanted to go home directly, you'd not have turned up towards the manor.' He looked at Simon. 'Bailiff, there is a fork in the road from Oakhampton. One branch leads here, but the other goes straight to Throwleigh itself.'

'I fancied going past the manor,' Edmund protested.

'Why?' pressed Baldwin.

'It was . . .'

'And don't forget that if you're not careful, you might be arrested for killing your master,' Daniel added pointedly.

Edmund glowered, and for a moment Baldwin thought he would be silent, but then the farmer lifted his head defiantly. 'Sir, I'd seen a dead rabbit in the road. It'd only just been killed – maybe by a sling or something. I picked it up, and then I thought I'd better take it to the manor, so I rode on, but there was no one there.'

'Liar! I was at the gateway and saw you ride straight past. You never made any attempt to leave a rabbit or anything else.'

'I was going to leave the rabbit, but I dozed, and the pony found the road home.'

'You poached the manor's rabbits!' Daniel asserted.

'I never poached anything – someone else killed it. I was going to take it in . . . Anyway, if I hadn't, it'd only have been stolen by a dog or a fox,' Edmund protested sulkily.

Seeing the scandalised steward taking breath, Baldwin swiftly said, 'I think we can forget about rabbits, Daniel. Let us draw a veil over such matters; in trying to hide them, people may be forced to conceal other facts which could help us. Now, Edmund, you stopped your wagon and collected up this tiny cony-corpse. You then rode on towards the manor, is that right?'

'Yes, sir.'

'And saw what?'

'Nothing, sir. I was tired: I rode back dozing, and saw nothing else until I turned off to go back to the village.'

Baldwin shook his head. 'What of other carts?'

Edmund stared confusedly. 'Oh, there was only the one, the fishman's cart. I saw him on the road heading north, some while before I got to the fork and noticed the rabbit.'

'So if he had knocked the boy down, you would have seen the body on the road?'

'I . . . Yes, I suppose . . .'

'So he hadn't, had he?'

Edmund was silent, his nervous gaze going from one to another.

Simon finished his pot and gave him a not-unfriendly look. 'We're not here to arrest you, farmer. All we want to do is clear up what actually happened to the lad.'

'But I don't know!'

'Did you see anyone else up there?' Baldwin asked after a moment.

Edmund was alive to the possibilities and dangers of his situation. If he admitted whom he had seen, he could be dealt with severely; yet if he held his tongue, he would surely be at risk of losing his life. He took a cautious glance at Daniel. The old steward was frowning fixedly at him, as if daring him to make any comment about the people he had seen up on the moors that day. Edmund swallowed quickly.

'Sir, I did see some folks. I saw the girl, Petronilla, the young maid from the hall. And I saw Anney, Lady Katharine's maid, walking further up on the moors. No one else.'

And as he told the lie, Edmund stared guiltily at his feet.

CHAPTER TWELVE

While James van Relenghes supped his wine by the fire, Godfrey slipped out through the screens and left the hall by the great door to the yard.

Striding quickly, he crossed the court and paused a moment at the wide-open stable. People were always bustling about in here, shouting to each other, oiling and polishing saddles and bridles, gentling the horses, grooming them, taking the great animals from their stalls to be set into harnesses to go to the fields, or preparing them for exercise. One idle weapons master went more or less unnoticed.

He saw the man he wanted, and moved around the room, always keeping his target in view. As he came closer, he reached under his jack and eased his concealed knife in its sheath before covering the last few yards at speed. He gripped Nicholas's arm and beamed into his face.

'Well, now, old son! Isn't this a nice thing, eh? Christ's wounds, but it's been ages. Last time we met was in France, wasn't it?' he babbled, pulling the startled servant towards the doors. 'How long has it been – what, seven years? No, must be more than that – say about ten. Still . . .'

By now he'd brought his quarry out to the open air, and his wide eyes lent his smile a somewhat manic air as he brought his face close to Thomas of Exeter's right-hand man.

'. . . it's never too late to renew an old acquaintance, is it, Nicky boy?'

'He was lying,' said Daniel bitterly.

The steward was peevish. He'd hoped for greater things from the famous knight of Furnshill; Sir Baldwin was supposed to be almost omniscient, and yet to the steward's mind the knight had just had the wool pulled over his eyes by an unscrupulous serf. He could have got more from Edmund himself if he'd been left alone to question the sod, without the supposed benefit of the knight's presence.

Baldwin sighed. 'The man's mere appearance on the same road as that on which the boy died is no proof that he was present at Herbert's death, let alone that he had an active part in it. What of your own fish-seller?'

'Sir Baldwin, you yourself pointed out that if the fish-seller had run Herbert down, Edmund would have seen the body.'

'Very well, then. Let us suppose that Herbert *was* run down by Edmund,' Baldwin said. 'But was the man awake? He admits going to the inn, admits to returning after a few ales – how often have you seen a man in that condition? If the boy ran out from the side of the road and fell under his wheels, despite the bump he might not know anything about it.'

'His wagon was empty, and he's only got a light one. If he ran down the boy, he'd know *all* about it,' Daniel asserted.

Baldwin was even more convinced that the steward was determined to implicate the villein for some unknown reason, and the knight wasn't prepared to be a willing accomplice in the destruction of Edmund for a crime of which he might well be innocent. 'There is no evidence to suggest that he was guilty of anything,' he said strongly. 'Even if, as you say, he was aware of riding over a child, you couldn't expect him to run straight to the manor, where people like you would assume he was guilty of murder.'

'Of course we would! Who else had a wish to attack my Lady Katharine's family!'

Baldwin stopped his horse and stared.

Simon looked as baffled as he felt. 'Why on earth would a nonentity like him want to hurt the likes of her?'

'Because she's reclaimed him as a villein!' Daniel burst out. While the two men stared, he explained the legal loophole by which Lady Katharine had trapped Edmund back into her service.

'But that's outrageous!' Simon cried. 'She is taking advantage of her position – and doing so to overrule her husband's express wishes.'

Daniel suddenly felt very old, and almost regretted calling the bailiff back. He had no choice: he must explain how the manor he served could unfairly treat its tenants.

'We're trying a new system here – just like the Earldom of Cornwall,' he began defensively. 'If someone else offers more money than the existing tenants, the highest bidder wins the land.'

'You mean serfs are evicted when their lord is offered a good sum?' Simon asked.

'Um . . . not only then. This is for free tenants as well. The tenants on our lands have a lease for only seven years, and when it is due for renewal, anyone who can offer more money may have it.'

Baldwin and Simon exchanged shocked glances. Tenants were either freemen or serfs. The former paid fixed rents, while the latter had the burden of labour owed to their lords as well as the expense of the feudal taxes: the *merchet*, paid by women when they wished to be married, *chevage*, paid by serfs who wished permission to live away from the demesne, plus a range of other arbitrary charges that could be imposed by a greedy lord. But this very arbitrariness only affected those who were servile, not the free.

Daniel pointedly avoided their eyes while he explained how the system worked. Every seven years the existing leases were terminated and the plots thrown open to the highest bidder. First refusal was given to the existing tenant, but if another offered a better price, that person won.

'You mean that even loyal tenants of a magnate could be thrown off their land just because someone who isn't even local decides to offer money?' Simon asked.

'Well – yes, sir.'

'It should be illegal! How can men have any faith in their masters when they're treated so shabbily?'

Baldwin too was frowning. 'The old way is for all retainers to be safe while they stay loyal to their liege-lord. If this sort of idea were to take hold, where would the kingdom be? If no man can trust his lord's integrity and commitment, no one would be safe. The King himself could decide to impose the same tenancies on his lords!'

'Hardly, sir. He wouldn't dare rouse all the nation in that way,' Daniel said.

'But has this Edmund been disloyal?'

'Well, not that I know of, but he is a very inefficient farmer, and he can't afford . . .'

'You think that because of this dispute, Edmund could have caused his master's death?'

'He angered Squire Roger by begging, reminding him of the service his father Richard had given.'

'Loyal and faithful service?' Simon asked.

'Yes. That was why his father was freed.'

'And this is his reward!'

Daniel glanced mournfully at the bailiff. 'Sir, I don't invent the laws, I only obey my commands.'

'As you should,' Baldwin agreed. 'Yet for the squire's accidental death – there is no suggestion that Edmund struck the squire – for that, Lady Katharine is determined to punish Edmund. I suppose you think that as a result of her actions, Edmund saw a means to hurt her even more cruelly, and rode down her son? I have heard of such cases, but you want me to believe that a weakly bully like Edmund could do such a thing? I doubt whether he would have the guts or strength of purpose to attempt so horrific a revenge.'

'Sir, Edmund was the last man to pass. If the master was run over, *who else* could it have been? It must have been Edmund!'

'You keep repeating that!' Simon snapped. 'So what? In God's name! Even if that bastard Edmund *did* run down the child, it's probably only because the fool was asleep and the death an accident. Accidents *will* sometimes happen, and no one is responsible when they do!'

'But, Bailiff, he must—'

'*Enough!*' Simon rasped. 'I will hear no more! You've got some kind of fascination with this poor man, and it's unreasonable and foolish. God's teeth, do you really think that a miserable serf like him could dream of harming the heir to Throwleigh? Wake up, man, you're dreaming.'

Daniel held his angry stare for a moment, but then his head dropped, and Simon saw a tear fall from his nose. The bailiff was strangely shocked to realise that the steward was weeping.

Jeanne was waiting for them in front of the house, Wat at her side in case she needed an errand run. She smiled and walked to meet the men as they approached but, before she had covered a few yards, she realised that their mood was not good. Simon rode with his face as black as a moorland thundercloud, while Baldwin kept his distance, staring up thoughtfully at the hill behind the house; Daniel brought up the rear with the two servants. She instantly decided to make use of the customary cure for such moods, and sent Wat to fetch wine.

'My lord?' she asked tentatively as they came close, and her husband broke into a smile of sheer delight.

'Jeanne! Where is Margaret, and Lady Katharine?'

'They are walking out in the garden behind the stables,' she said. 'Was your journey worthwhile?'

He saw her glance behind him at the scowling steward. 'No,' he admitted. 'I think the only thing we achieved was upsetting Lady Katharine's man.'

She listened seriously as he spoke of their visit to Edmund's house. As he finished, she gave him a grave look. 'Are you really so sure that he is wrong?'

'As things stand now, yes,' he said. 'The boy was certainly run over by a wagon of some sort, but I see no reason why this man should be responsible. And as for murder . . .'

'You don't think Daniel could be right and this fellow wanted to kill the boy in revenge for losing his land – and his freedom, of course?'

Wat returned with the wine, and Baldwin took a sip, watching as the youngster filled pots for the other men. Why should someone want a child dead? he wondered.

'What's that?'

Hearing the cheery call, Baldwin winced. The last man he wished to speak to at this moment was Thomas, Squire Roger's brother. Jeanne saw his look, gave her husband a fleeting smile, and walked away, apologetically telling Thomas that she must prepare for breakfast. Recollecting his manners, the knight fitted a suitably polite smile to his lips before turning to greet the man from Exeter. 'Good morning, Master Thomas. I didn't hear you approach. We have been over to Throwleigh to speak to some of the men and find out whether anyone could shed any light on the death of your nephew.'

'Oh, of course,' said Thomas, shaking his head dejectedly and taking Wat's remaining wine pot. 'So sad to see a young whipper-snapper like him cut down in so meaningless a manner. Did you – er – find out anything?'

There was an odd look in his eye, and Baldwin hesitated before answering. 'No,' he said eventually. 'We spoke to some villeins, but there was nothing to be learned from them.'

'Very sad. Still,' continued Thomas, glancing along the road towards Throwleigh, 'I daresay I shall be able to clear it all up when I begin to make my own enquiries. As lord of the manor, it is my responsibility.'

'Lord of the manor?' Simon echoed. He had tethered his horse to a large ring in the courtyard wall, and now stood near Baldwin.

'Well, of course, Bailiff – but I suppose you didn't know. The manor is entailed, and may only be passed to a male member of the family.' He smiled smugly up at the building behind them. 'This all belongs to me now.'

It was in order to leave the presence of the gloating man that Baldwin announced his wish to visit the chapel. The knight was revolted by the self-satisfied smile Thomas of Exeter wore as he surveyed what was now his property. Baldwin felt only disgust for him, and his leave-taking was so short that his rudeness penetrated even Thomas's thick skin, and he stood staring after Baldwin with a degree of surprise as the knight stalked away.

Baldwin stomped along the yard, through the hall, and into the peace of the little room. He stared at the altar for a moment, then genuflected automatically and walked to sit on a bench by the wall.

The naked greed in Thomas's eyes was repellent. It was as if the knight had been granted an insight to the man's soul, and he shuddered at the sheer avarice that flamed there. Herbert's death meant nothing to him: oh, he would make the right sad noises, he would declare himself desolated, he would offer every sympathy to the poor mother left alone to survive her husband and only child, but that was the limit of his compassion. His true feelings were limited to a desire to get his hands on the house and demesne of Throwleigh.

Hearing steps, Baldwin sighed to himself. It seemed there was nowhere to gain a few moments' peace in this household. The door opened, and Baldwin saw the slightly flushed features of Stephen.

'I am sorry, Brother,' he said immediately, 'if I am intruding on you . . .'

'Not at all, my son. Can I help you, or are you seeking solitude?'

Baldwin looked away. Setting aside Herbert's death, he did have that other, private, concern: his feelings towards his wife. He loved her, but he always felt the restraint of the vows he had given as a Templar monk: poverty, obedience, and *chastity*. It was wrong, he was sure, that he should feel guilty about making love to his wife, but the sense that by doing so he was breaking his oath was too strong to ignore. It was not a matter he could discuss with anyone who knew him well, but he would be enormously comforted to share his anxiety, even though he could not explain the full details. He licked his lips in sudden indecision.

'Brother,' he began tentatively, 'could I speak to you about a matter . . . It is rather embarrassing . . . er . . . in the strictest confidence?'

The form of words was a matter of politeness, and no more. Both men knew that the confessional was sacrosanct, but Baldwin also knew that, if ordered, a worldly monk could be prevailed upon to divulge his secrets to a senior monk or bishop. Even as Stephen nodded silently and sat at his side, Baldwin was considering how best to ask the question he needed answered.

'Brother, I am afraid that in my life I have sinned.'

'We all sin.'

Baldwin gave a faint smile. 'Yes – but I mean intentionally. Brother, if a man takes an oath and then is betrayed, does that mean the oath itself is null and void?'

Stephen looked at him, surprised. 'What do you mean?'

Baldwin took a deep breath. He couldn't confess to his membership of the Knights Templar, for since their destruction many priests would look askance on one of that fraternity – especially bearing in mind the nature of some of the accusations. 'Well, suppose I were a man of the cloth, and had taken the vow of chastity, and yet was tempted into . . . um . . . into lust for . . .'

He stopped. The priest had gone as white as the plaster on the whitewashed wall, then as red as Baldwin's crimson tunic. Standing, he stared down at the knight with an expression of sheer fury. 'You dare to try and trick me into . . . You *bastard*! You try to accuse me – no, don't! Don't touch me!'

CHAPTER THIRTEEN

Alan saw another pigeon, a tempting, plump target. It swooped over the tree high above him, flew across the field and on, but even as he held his breath, it made a wide circle, and returned in a leisurely manner. At last it dropped down towards the field.

His decoy, a live pigeon tethered by the leg to a stick, which kept flapping and cooing, showing that there was food here, was working well. Alan pursed his lips as the new bird came down, beating its wings wildly as it landed, and as it ruffled its feathers and tucked its wings away, Alan was already whirling his long-stringed sling over his head, behind the cover of his hedge. Still spinning, he let go of the cord.

The bullet was released. It slipped from the leather patch and flew true. The boy stood, eyes glued to the bird, motionless, and saw the pebble strike the wing, feathers flying. Instantly he was up and over his hedge, haring towards the pigeon, which hopped and tried to escape, but to no avail.

The boy grabbed its head between finger and thumb. One flick, up and down, and the weight of the body cracked the neck.

While it shivered and fluttered in its death throes, Alan hummed quietly to himself and broke up a small stick. It was forked, and he snapped the two twigs away before thrusting the long stem into the ground. The pigeon was still now, and he laid it down with its neck resting in the fork to make it appear to be standing, before wandering back to his hiding-place. He enjoyed luring pigeons like this. One bird flapping on the ground was guaranteed to attract the attention of others flying past, which would be certain to investigate, thinking there must be food. And as each was shot and killed, then laid out as if pecking at the ground, still more would be tempted to join those enjoying such apparently rich pickings.

It was a good day. He'd seen seven birds so far, and this was the third he'd hit. If he carried on like this, he and his mother would be able to have a decent meal – and profit from the ones he would sell. He only wished he was more accurate with his sling.

When Jordan found him, Alan had increased his total by one, and he was crouched low waiting for another to come and land. It gently glided down, and Alan cautiously rose. He released the bullet, but his aim was poor, and the bird took off at speed. Alan grimaced, twirling the cords of his sling around his forefinger.

'How did you catch the lure?' Jordan asked.

'Birdlime,' answered Alan shortly. 'Made from the holm tree in the churchyard. I spread it on the elm one evening, and the next morning there was this pretty pigeon!'

'Will you keep it?'

'No, she's trapped enough others,' Alan said, and quickly wrung her neck, gathering up the other bodies happily. 'A good morning.'

Jordan nodded, staring at the birds hungrily. Each one was more meat than he and his family would usually eat in a fortnight. The rabbit his father had brought back the day that Herbert died had been unique, and delicious for that very reason, although there was some pleasure in knowing that he himself had shot it. He was going to take it home, and it was simply luck that Edmund had happened along the road at that moment.

That thought reminded him of the reason for his visit.

'Alan, do you think we ought to go to the manor and tell them about . . .'

'We've told them all we can.' His eyes were not on Jordan, but staring out across the field as his fingers deftly looped cords over the necks of the dead birds. The younger boy could feel his tension, but didn't know how to help him. It was Alan who had been caught by the priest, not Jordan, and the cruel lash-marks still hadn't faded.

'I *hate* him,' Jordan said aloud, and the virulence of his hatred surprised even himself. The priest had beaten them all – oh, many times – and yet he was the one who taught them to love their fellow man.

Alan glanced at him with a worried frown. 'We can't do anything, though. He's a priest. Who'd believe anything we said against him?'

'My dad would believe me – he's always said the priest is a bastard.'

'Your dad? Jordan, he's useless! Look at him, he's a drunk

who can't hold his place in the vill, and who's become a villein again.'

Jordan felt stung into defending his father. 'That wasn't his fault! It was the mistress, and—'

'You can't mean you think he's all right? After the way he's treated you?'

Jordan sulked. His thrashings were known all around Throwleigh, and his father's drinking had also gained him notoriety. He brushed angrily at a tear and sniffed. He wasn't going to let the older boy upset him again.

It happened all too often. Alan had the abilities of an older boy. His skills with bow and sling were cursed by several people in the area, and he couldn't help but look down upon Jordan sometimes, like a patronising elder brother. His tone could be quite scathing when he talked about Jordan's father; Jordan had a child's kindness and generosity of spirit, but he had more perspicacity than most adults, and he was sure that Alan's disapproving tone when talking about Edmund had something to do with the disappearance of his own father. It was a form of jealousy.

Alan shouldn't have been so sharp, he knew, but it was so tempting sometimes when Jordan whined on about things. His father was a waster – useless. Couldn't even fix the fence when it fell two years before, and that was why they had lost their pig and later most of their chickens: a fox had got in, and all the time Edmund was snoring, drunk, on his bed. His wife could do nothing, nor could the two children, both were too young. So because he was lazy, Edmund had squandered all his family's assets.

But it wasn't Jordan's fault, and Jordan was Alan's only friend here. They were renegades – almost outlaws. They and young Herbert had wandered far over the surrounding countryside, playing at the bartons, hunting each other over the moors . . . That thought reminded him that now there were only the two of them, not three.

It still seemed only a short while ago that there had been four of them, including Tom, his brother. But, because of Herbert, Tom was dead, or so Alan's mother said. Alan wasn't greatly exercised by questions of responsibility – he knew that people died, whatever their age. Even during his short life Alan had seen friends and acquaintances starve, many of them dying because of the famine.

His mother blamed Herbert for Tom's death. She was convinced that if only Herbert had called out, Tom could have been saved, but Alan couldn't feel any resentment towards Herbert for that; Herbert was too young. And now he too was gone.

'Alan, we could give them proof of what the priest's like,' Jordan said after a moment.

'How can we do that?' Alan wanted to know. 'He's a priest and everything – how can we show people what he's really like?'

'His shoe?'

Alan paused and his mouth fell open. 'You think we . . .'

'Why don't we go back and see if his sandal is still up there? If we can find it, people would have to believe us, wouldn't they?'

Baldwin stared in amazement as the monk stormed from the chapel. Stephen's contempt was all too plain, and it could only be because he had guessed that Baldwin had been a Knight Templar. It was the only explanation. Stephen had obviously heard the accusations – the ridiculous, trumped-up accusations pressed by government officials on behalf of the French King: allegations that Templar brothers underwent obscene initiation rituals, that they ate Christian babies, that they committed the heinous act of sodomy with each other, even that they spat on the Cross!

The knight sat back weakly, his hands on his knees. If the monk were to spread this news, Baldwin's position in the country would be hideously compromised. He had no protector, nor could he afford to buy off someone who threatened blackmail. If his career as a Templar monk should be bruited about, a priest or maybe even a bishop would hear, and they would be bound to try to have him arrested and put to the flames which he had escaped by so slight a margin before.

Baldwin forced himself to breathe slowly, to think rationally. He felt as if he had been punched in the guts, and there was a light dew of sweat on his brow as he feverishly recalled the monk's expression. Then he stopped, and his frown gradually faded.

It was impossible for the monk to have made the fabulous leap to the conclusion that Baldwin had been a member of the Poor Fellow Soldiers of Christ and the Temple of Solomon from the few words the knight had given. Yet the brother had drawn back as if repelled, and suddenly Baldwin recalled how he had put the question. In his nervousness and hesitation, he had phrased the query hypothetically, and the priest had obviously assumed the knight was accusing him of breaking *his own* vows.

With the relief this cogitation gave him, Baldwin could have laughed aloud. When he heard footsteps outside the door again, so great was his revival, he smiled broadly. The monk walked in and Baldwin greeted him warmly.

'Brother, my apologies! I fear I gave you entirely the wrong idea. I did not intend to imply that *you* had been guilty of anything. I am truly sorry if I alarmed you, but it was absolutely unintentional.'

'I am glad to hear it,' Stephen said coldly. Although Baldwin continued to offer fulsome apologies, the priest appeared only partly mollified, and it was only gradually that he allowed himself to be calmed. Eventually he sat down again, although not next to Baldwin this time, and closed his eyes as if exhausted. Opening them again, he gave Baldwin a keen look and settled himself. 'Come, tell me what is troubling you.'

This time Baldwin was careful to make himself understood. 'Brother, I once swore an oath, but the man in whom I put my trust proved faithless. He pursued me, without reason, and proved his own dishonour. Have I been right to recant my own vow?'

'I would have to know more, but if you are saying that you swore your honour and allegiance to a man, and that man subsequently betrayed your trust, I would think that his betrayal would be the defining issue. What I mean is, his lack of honour would release you from your vows to him. How did you recant?'

'I swore an oath to chastity, but now I have married.'

'Well, if you made an oath before God to marry a woman, God wouldn't punish you. Your wedding vows were holy, for God has instructed us to marry. Your vows to Him would carry precedence over any taken previously to a mere man.'

Baldwin thanked him, but frowned. The priest had said all he could to ease his mind, but it wasn't enough. Baldwin had given his vows to God when he had joined the Templars. 'Stephen, what would the position be with a monk who decided to give up his calling and take himself a wife? Would the oaths given at his wedding carry greater weight than that of chastity?'

'Why should you wish to know such a thing?' Stephen asked, and his voice had an angry edge to it once more. 'Are you trying to spread rumours about my brethren who may have fallen from the high ideals they should have embraced?'

'No, no, Brother. I am simply trying to clear the point in my mind.'

'Well, clear your mind of the point. It doesn't concern you.'

Baldwin could see that he had unwittingly overstepped the mark once more, and again he offered profuse apologies. Eventually the priest relented, and the small spots of anger on his cheeks faded.

Sitting quietly, Baldwin wasn't fully convinced by Stephen's argument. Absolute conviction could only come from explaining his difficulty in detail, ideally to a senior cleric, and that was impossible. The more important the man, the more likely he was to be ambitious, and the more likely he would be to inform the church hierarchy of a renegade Templar. That thought brought to mind other functionaries, and Baldwin found himself meditating once more on the steward of the house. 'I must ask, Brother, are you aware of any reason why Daniel should hate the farmer in Throwleigh, the one called Edmund?'

'*Him?* The tenant to be evicted?' Stephen asked, but Baldwin was sure he saw a flicker in the priest's eyes. 'What could a steward have against a man like him?'

'Nothing that I can understand,' Baldwin said honestly. 'Yet he appears to want to harry Edmund into an early grave. Was Daniel particularly fond of the young squire?'

The priest pursed his thin lips, as if debating whether to answer. When he spoke, it was with a certain caution, as if he was measuring his words with care. 'I doubt whether Daniel was any more fond of the child than I myself, and I was not. No doubt it is unkind to state the fact so baldly on the day of the child's burial, but I could not find it in me to like Master Herbert. He was wilful, disobedient, and often deceitful. I was regularly forced to chastise him. On the very day his father died, he . . . Well, perhaps I shouldn't say more.'

'Please tell me,' Baldwin said. 'I fail to understand what could have happened.'

'Very well. That same morning, young Master Herbert was found by his father trespassing in the orchard with two friends. When seen, Herbert helped his accomplices to escape, and then, when he was asked by his father who the two were, he lied, saying he'd seen no one. He subsequently proceeded to plead for them, when it was plain to all that they must be punished. The last command Squire Roger gave to me was that I should whip the child, and so I did. Children, Sir Baldwin, have to be trained, the same as any other animal. They must be taught to respect their elders, to tell the truth, and to behave honourably. I fear Master Herbert was not able to do these things. Perhaps in Sir Reginald of Hatherleigh's service the lad might have learned.'

'Perhaps,' Baldwin agreed, but he was secretly shocked at the priest's candid words. It was appalling, listening to the man who was to bury the child, talking about him like this.

'I think that was probably why the squire himself died.'

Baldwin looked up. 'Eh?'

'I only meant that since the squire fell dead from some imbalance in his bodily humours, they must have been caused by something. He left here in a tearing hurry to go hunting, but was delayed because he had to ride off to demand that the friends of his son should be punished. Thus logically I feel fairly sure that Master Herbert, although unwittingly, was himself a parricide.'

'You don't truly mean to say you believe that the child was guilty of his father's death?' Baldwin cried.

'Oh, it's all very well, Sir Baldwin, to wish to think the best of all the dead,' said Stephen huffily. 'But hypocrisy is not one of my faults. In any case, I am only telling you what others also think. Even the boy's mother blamed him.'

'Lady Katharine?' Baldwin burst out.

The priest nodded calmly. 'Yes, Sir Baldwin. I know you saw how she treated her son at her husband's grave. It was perfectly obvious, was it not? After that, I don't know if she felt anything more than loathing for her son. She had loved her husband, you see. And when her son caused him to die, I think she lost all feeling for him. Poor child.' He stared thoughtfully through the window. 'He was always unlucky.'

'In what way?'

Stephen threw him a surprised look, as if he had been musing to himself and had forgotten that Baldwin was present. 'Hmm? Oh, I only mean that he often got himself into scrapes – and then again he was ever a hapless child. For example, he was present when another local boy died, a little chap called Tom – only a toddler. He fell into a well, and young Master Herbert didn't fetch help. Usual sort of thing, often happens. But I don't think the parent ever truly forgave him.'

Baldwin kept the eagerness from his voice as he asked, 'Whose child was it who died?'

Stephen shrugged. 'A maid from the village who works here for Lady Katharine – I think because my Lady took pity on her.'

'Oh? Is she the wife of Edmund?' asked Baldwin, recalling Christiana's face and wondering whether she worked at the hall.

'Him? Good God, no!' For the first time Stephen gave a dry smile. 'No, Anney's husband was still more feckless than Edmund. Anney's man left her shortly after the birth of her second son, Tom. It was found that he was already married.'

Baldwin felt curiously deflated. He had hoped it might be Edmund. It could have explained much.

'There was no reason to think Anney would have tried to harm the boy, Sir Baldwin,' Stephen said sharply. 'She blamed him, certainly, but that's different from harbouring a lethal grudge. Her boy fell into the well – you know how dim these villein children can be. The only aspect of culpability was Master Herbert's inability to call for help, but he was only three years and a half at the time, and not many boys so young would have been able to do anything. The Church shows us that children are like lunatics – they don't act with free will because they can't distinguish between right and wrong. That's why children under fourteen aren't legally responsible for their actions. Anney wouldn't have hurt him, I am sure. No doubt she regretted he didn't call for help – but regret is a different emotion from that which demands the wreaking of vengeance. She's a good woman; she wouldn't bear ill-feeling towards Master Herbert.'

'What of her husband?'

'Ah, well, he's no longer here for us to ask him. I fear he shan't be seen in these parts again.' Stephen gave a thin smile. 'I arrived in Throwleigh a little before the drowning of her child and he was gone by then; I heard he went shortly after the birth of the second boy. Tom, the boy who died, wouldn't have known him. I understand Anney gave and received nuptial vows, but his promises weren't valid: he was already wedded. He left her to raise both boys as father-less bastards.'

'Where did he go?'

'Back to his first wife – somewhere down towards Exeter, I heard. Her brothers came and collected him.'

'This Anney must be lonely.'

Stephen looked at him with genuine surprise. 'Why should you think that? She has enough to keep her busy. She even has her own cottage in Throwleigh, although it looks ready to collapse.'

Baldwin thanked him, and soon after left the priest to prepare for the interment of the child. The knight walked thoughtfully down the stairs and out into the yard towards the stables, but every now and again his attention was drawn to the door of the storeroom, where Herbert's body waited for its burial – and on his face was fixed a puzzled frown.

Simon was surprised to find his friend outside. 'Thanks for leaving me with the repellent Thomas, old friend. I look forward to repaying the compliment. You'll be delighted to hear that the new lord of the manor has gone to prepare for his breakfast so we're safe from him for a while.'

'Thank the Lord God for that at least!'

Simon noticed his expression, and the movement of his eyes towards the storeroom's door. 'What's on your mind, Baldwin?'

Baldwin shook his head. 'I cannot help wondering . . . Simon, Herbert's body showed all the signs of having been run over, didn't it? Yet we only saw the corpse at night, in darkness, didn't we?' he added, as if to himself.

'Baldwin, are you thinking . . .?'

'Simon, his death was not viewed by all as a particularly sad occurrence. To his uncle it was an absolute godsend, because he could acquire this land; to Lady Katharine's maid it meant revenge, because Herbert saw her son drown without calling for help; Lady Katharine herself apparently blamed her son for the death of her husband. And then we have this steward enthusiastically advocating the arrest of the farmer, and it turns out that even the damned *priest* wasn't fond of him!'

'Don't suggest the priest was responsible,' the bailiff chuckled, but then his manner changed. 'You're right, Daniel *was* insistent this morning, wasn't he? You don't think he considers his new master could be guilty of killing his nephew, do you? That would explain why he was to keen to have us return.'

Baldwin didn't meet his eye. 'When we came here before, I told you I felt responsible because I should have seen the danger surrounding the child. Hearing that he had been run down and died by accident was a relief, but now I have to wonder whether I was right to assume that.'

'You saw the body – so did the Coroner,' Simon pointed out. 'The death has been recorded as an accident.'

'Yes, but what if the Coroner, like me, only saw the child in the dark of the storeroom?'

Simon gave a low sigh. 'What do you wish to do?'

'We have to see the body again, Simon. We *have* to.'

CHAPTER FOURTEEN

The Lady Katharine sat in the hall, at her side the maid whom Baldwin correctly assumed to be Anney. He had not studied her before, but did so now and liked what he saw. She had a broad, intelligent face with calm grey eyes, and looked the kind of woman who would be steady in an emergency.

Unfortunately they were not alone. Servants bustled about under the stern gaze of Daniel, who studiously ignored Baldwin; Thomas of Exeter stood near the fire, a smirk of contentment on his full features, sipping wine from a cup as he surveyed the room; James van Relenghes sat with his guard at a bench nearby. Then, as if there weren't already enough people, the priest came in. Baldwin felt exposed and unwelcome, making his request in front of so many, but he knew he must go ahead and do it.

'My Lady, may I ask for a moment of your time – perhaps in private?'

Lady Katharine wore a thin, gauzy veil over her eyes, and he couldn't read her expression from her thin, bloodless lips, but he could hear the petulance in her voice. 'Now, Sir Baldwin? Can't it wait a day? My son's dead and I have his funeral to think of. Leave me to my grief for this day at least!'

'I cannot, Lady,' Baldwin said quietly and regretfully. 'I have but one request to make. There are some facts which have come to my notice, and I would like to see your son's body again – in daylight.'

She seemed to stiffen. Her hand, still gripping a small swatch of cloth, froze into immobility by her face. 'Why?' she demanded agitatedly.

'Lady, I only saw his body in the dark, and now I have heard things which might mean . . .'

'You think he was murdered? That it wasn't an accident?' she said, her voice rising with an edge of hysteria.

Before Baldwin could answer, James van Relenghes approached, shaking his head sadly. 'This will not do, Sir Baldwin. It is not fair to discompose the lady on the day she is to bury her only child. There can be no excuse, sir, none. Do you really mean to say you think Herbert was murdered?'

'I do not know,' Baldwin said unhappily. As he spoke, the Fleming took Lady Katharine's hand and patted it comfortingly, as if she needed protection from Baldwin himself. The knight did not like being cast in the role of bully manipulating a poor widow, and he allowed a hint of truculence to seep into his voice. 'It is regrettable, but we have to make sure, as far as is practicably possible, that it was a mere accident that he died.'

'I won't have it!' Thomas cried suddenly. 'You are trying to make out that someone here had wanted to kill the boy, and that's not on. Think what people would say – especially the serfs.'

'Consider, Master Thomas, what people would say if you refused permission for us to inspect the body in daylight,' Simon said mildly.

Thomas gaped. 'What do you mean? Are you threatening me?'

'No,' Baldwin said suavely, 'but the good bailiff is quite right. What would people think if they heard that the man who prevented a proper inspection was the very man who benefited from the death of the heir?'

'If you put it like that . . .' Thomas said, suddenly pale. 'Maybe it – um – it would be better to allow you to carry on.'

'In God's name! Do as you wish!' Lady Katharine burst out. 'My husband is gone, and now so is my beloved son. All your vaunted skills cannot avail me. Do what you think necessary!' She turned on her heel and stalked off to the other side of the room.

And Baldwin noticed that James van Relenghes went immediately to her side.

Nicholas and two of his men respectfully carried Herbert from the storeroom, using an old door as a stretcher, and set the corpse down on a thick rug laid over the cobbles of the yard. Removing the door, they stood back quietly, waiting for Baldwin to carry out his inspection. The knight spent some minutes gathering together a small jury, and only then did he go to stand by the body.

There were several witnesses: Stephen was there, as was Godfrey – for the first time without his master, Simon noted. Baldwin had called several workers from their duties in the vill or the house to come and observe his inquest, for he was no Coroner, and wanted as many witnesses as possible.

When he was satisfied enough people were present, Baldwin crouched down and hesitantly touched the little figure's winding-cloth. It covered the boy's whole body, reaching down to his feet, where it was tied up. 'Poor fellow,' he muttered, and took the knife Nicholas held out to him, quickly slicing through the cord and pulling the linen away.

Simon, who knew the fragility of his own stomach, had already withdrawn. From a safe distance, he saw one of the jurymen suddenly whip his hand over his mouth and stumble backwards to vomit at the stable's wall. Another curled his lip at the smell, but the rest, evidently struck from a similar mould to Baldwin himself, craned their necks with fascination.

The child was flaccid and pale, except for the skin of his back, which had gone an odd, dark colour as if it was badly bruised, but Simon knew from long experience with Baldwin that this was normal, bearing in mind that the lad had been lying face uppermost for so long. Simon wasn't surprised to see how the boy's limbs moved so easily; he knew that after a day or more the stiffening of *rigor mortis* wore off. The sight of the body being rolled over and studied was all too familiar, and yet the fact that it was so small brought a lump to his throat, reminding him of his own beloved Peterkin.

Peterkin had been even younger than Herbert when he died. Simon swallowed, recalling the sense of frantic despair as he watched his only son slipping away so slowly. The boy

159

had been fractious for a few days, but then he caught a fever, and for a day and night he wouldn't eat or drink, while his bowels ran with diarrhoea. When at last the pitiable squalling became more feeble, and was finally stilled, Simon had almost felt relief to see that his boy's suffering was over – and yet that brought with it an immensity of guilt, as if he knew he was glad to have lost the constant irritation of a crying child.

Standing here now and witnessing another man's heir being subjected to this intense scrutiny filled Simon with shame, as if he was himself abusing the dead boy by his presence.

But Baldwin knew no such qualms as he touched the boy's chill flesh. His total concentration was on the body and the wounds; he had no time for sentiment. He removed the small wooden burial cross from the boy's chest and studied the figure, then began to look over each limb in turn. As his hands probed and prodded he kept up a continual commentary, speaking in a fast, low undertone.

'Ribs crushed. A long mark passes over them, just as if an iron-shod cartwheel had rolled over him – although spine appears whole. Left leg badly broken . . .' He peered closer. 'Could have been done by a sharp horseshoe. The skin looks as if it has been cut open cleanly. The other leg is whole, although well scratched . . .'

Daniel murmured, 'He was playing hide-and-seek up on the moorside with some of the lads from the village. Crawling around up there, the boys always get scratched by furze and brambles.'

'Thank you, Daniel. The left arm is fine: elbow is grazed, but it has had time to heal and form a scab – I think we can discount this, it is an honourable wound of the type that all boys wear. Right arm also undamaged. Face a little scratched, and left cheek has taken a glancing blow which has partly slashed the skin. At the boy's back we find . . .'

Suddenly Baldwin was silent, his hands moving over Herbert's head, touching the cranium softly, then he bent and stared more closely, pulling apart the scalp like a man searching for lice or fleas. Finally pulling away, the knight wiped his hands on a damp cloth and stood a while staring down at the corpse. Then he looked up with a firm resolution, and raised his hand. The crowd was silent, waiting expectantly.

'This boy has been run over by a wagon, but he was already dead. He was beaten about the head until there was scarcely a bone unbroken, probably with a lump of stone or a piece of wood. Whoever did this murdered the lad. He was not hit so harshly that the skin was greatly broken, but just enough to shatter the skull. The scratches and marks are there under his hair if you look.'

As he finished the jury shuffled unhappily. A murder meant a fine to be paid for breaking the King's Peace, and all in the vill would have to find the money.

While the men digested this unwelcome news, Thomas appeared in the doorway, and now he stared out, his lip curled in revulsion. 'Are you done yet?'

Simon stiffened. He glanced at Baldwin and gave a shrug as he accepted responsibility. This was Dartmoor, *his* territory. 'Yes, we have finished now, Thomas. Thank you all for coming to witness Sir Baldwin's examination of the corpse. I fear there is no doubt that Herbert of Throwleigh was murdered, and everyone in the manor must be attached. No one can leave the place until we have gained sureties from them and everyone must prepare to be questioned.'

There was a gasp from the small group, then Thomas spoke again. 'You can't! We're to hold the funeral today!'

Simon felt his belly churn as the wind altered, bringing to his nostrils the faint odour of putrefaction. 'Um, perhaps you're right. The Coroner can order an exhumation if he wants, but we've already examined the body. Provided Stephen writes down the details, I think the Coroner will be satisfied.' There was no point keeping the boy from his grave: he would soon become painfully odorous. 'Wrap him up again.'

Thomas stomped off to give his orders, and Simon rubbed his temples. 'What a mess!'

'Yes,' said Baldwin, but now he stared down at the body with a puzzled expression. 'Why should the killer have ruined his head like that?'

It was apparent that the other diners had awaited their return, and after Baldwin's announcement, the meal was a muted affair.

The table was set out up on the dais. There was no need for a second table; there were not enough mourners to justify more. Lady Katharine sat at the middle, with Stephen on her right, and Thomas on her left. Baldwin was installed with his wife at the end, where he would not even be able to meet Lady Katharine's eye, let alone talk to her. Simon and his wife were at the other end. James van Relenghes and his guard took their places opposite the lady.

With the fire roaring in the hearth, the atmosphere on this spring day was stifling. Simon was well aware that Baldwin was firmly opposed to the drinking of strong ale or wine too early in the day – he generally drank fruit juices and water – and yet this morning he gratefully polished off a pint and a half of weak ale. Simon ate heartily enough, as he usually did, but every so often he cast a glance at his friend. The knight occasionally spoke to his wife, and showed her the same courteous respect as always, but he seemed preoccupied, which was natural enough.

All had expected the day to be depressing, but this new turn, the suggestion that young Herbert's death was no accident, had affected the people there differently; from his vantage point at the end of the table, Baldwin found he could observe all their reactions.

Brother Stephen sat as though in deep shock, or perhaps, Baldwin thought, in guilty reflections on his unkind comments earlier that morning. At the other side of the large table, Thomas of Exeter ate with a furious speed, as though forcing food into himself was a means of displacing unpleasant musings. He hardly spoke a word, grunting at comments addressed to him, and rose from the table before anyone else, muttering about seeing to his horse.

In direct contrast, James van Relenghes was almost embarrassingly talkative. In different circumstances Baldwin would have thought he was trying to impress Lady Katharine. He was most attentive to her, talking of the courage and prowess of her dead husband, assuring his hostess that her son would have been no less brave. He went so far as to assert that Herbert could have felt nothing, that his death was swift, saying that he had seen so many dead men and children during his term as a soldier that he was personally convinced of the fact.

His words had no impact on the grieving woman. If anything, she was driven into a deeper despair by his constant chatter, and at last she raised a feeble hand to her temple and, pleading a severe headache, begged to be permitted to leave the company. Daniel leaped to her side and helped her to her feet.

It was almost a relief when she walked from the room with her maid Anney. All at once the others began to hurl questions at Baldwin, who deflected many, but couldn't hide the main facts.

'If he was killed, I am surprised I noticed nothing,' James van Relenghes said. 'I was out that way.'

'On your own?' Baldwin asked.

'Oh no, Godfrey was with me, as usual,' the Fleming said smoothly. 'I fear you must look for another suspect. Perhaps the priest here.'

'You were out there as well, Brother Stephen?'

The cleric gave an unhappy nod. 'Yes, but I was further up the hill. I had gone out for solitude – I had no wish to have Herbert for company.'

Baldwin's line of questioning killed off further conversation. It was as if he had accused all those present in the room of the murder. Now people avoided each other's eyes, as if each suspected the others, or each expected to be personally accused. Before long, all had finished their food and filed from the room.

Simon and Margaret followed Baldwin and Jeanne into the small enclosed arbour behind the stables. Here, in a quiet, secluded space designed as a private garden for the lady of the house, three apple trees and two pears stood, bent by the blast of wind from the tor behind, but the manor's stock of medicinal herbs grew tolerably strong and straight in well-regulated lines. A turf seat was set into the wall of the house, and the women sat here. In the lawn was cut a channel, and a small stream had been diverted to fill it and play musically as it fell over stones.

After the ladies had made themselves comfortable, Simon could hold his impatience no longer. 'What's the matter, Baldwin? You look like a man with piles anticipating a long day in the saddle.'

The knight gave a feeble grin. 'I wish it were something so simple. I was meditating on the miserable position of that poor lad. There he was, suddenly without a father, and everyone about him would have been happy if he had dropped dead in his turn. Well, now he has, and I can imagine that some people here will be gratified by this turn of events, no matter what their pious expressions might imply.'

'That's a dreadful thing to say,' Margaret protested. 'You surely can't think that poor Katharine isn't genuinely broken-hearted by the loss of her son?'

'Margaret, you are a kind and gentle woman: you have borne your husband several children, and you loved them all. You are a natural mother, and I know you grieved deeply when they died – but you didn't see the face of that woman when she was standing at her husband's grave. She wanted no part of her son; she wanted him away from her. Wouldn't any woman wish for the comfort of her child at a time like that? She did not: I saw her. She was *revolted* by the sight of her boy.'

Margaret shook her head. 'It may be that she had a perverse reaction; I have heard the squire was furious with Herbert on the day he died. As a wife she might have felt bitterness towards her son, but that's not the same as hating him and wishing him dead, Baldwin.'

'I may be entirely wrong, just as I have been over so many other aspects,' he admitted. 'It is my fault. I should have protected the boy.'

Jeanne could see his sadness and confusion. 'I find that hard to believe, husband. You could probably have done nothing to save him. It is enough for you to discover his killer.'

He took her hand, but stared out over the moor behind the house and didn't meet her eyes. 'If I had been here, it is possible I could have prevented his death.'

'Will you arrest the farmer?' Margaret asked.

Baldwin shook his head. 'There is no evidence that he was responsible for anything. Daniel pointed us to him – but then Stephen pointed me towards Lady Katharine, and Thomas had as clear a motive as Edmund.'

Suddenly his voice hardened. 'Enough! I will stop being directed by events. So far I have been blown by other people's winds of fancy – no more! Now I shall do what I should have done in the beginning, and investigate this damned affair properly. Simon, let's go and see where the body was found.'

CRAPTER FIFTEEN

It was Thomas who volunteered to take them to the spot. He was standing near the door with Stephen when Baldwin asked for a guide, and promised to lead them straight there.

'We won't need mounts – it's only a short walk from here,' he said importantly. 'Do you wish to go now?'

Simon glanced at Baldwin. 'There's no point in delay. The Evensong of the Dead is not for hours. We might as well see the place immediately.'

Baldwin reflected on that as they walked northwards from the manor. The Evensong for the Dead, the *Placebo*, was the first half of the funeral service, and after it there would be a vigil held over the body. Next morning the *Dirige* would be sung, and after that they would return to the graveyard so that Herbert could be buried next to the squire. Father and son had only been separated for a few days.

Some quarter of a mile north of the manor, Thomas stopped and the other two halted behind him. They were in a

167

typical, desolate part of the moor. The hill rose up on their left, and the land fell away to a small wood on their right; the road was narrow, only wide enough for smaller carts and wagons, and was holed and rutted, the peaty soil beneath soft and treacherous.

'When it rains, you know all about it up here,' Thomas commented.

Simon nodded grimly. 'It's a hard moor. If it's wet, you run the risk of bogs and mires, or a badly sprained ankle because of the mud. In the summer, the grass covers huge holes in the ground where the water has drained away and taken the soil with it. You can be riding over what looks like solid ground, only to fall into a massive pit. Usually it's only two or three feet in depth, but sometimes it can be worse.'

Baldwin eyed the landscape sourly. In the main it was heather and gorse, the stuff they called 'furze' here, which stood a mere foot and a half tall. Every now and again he could see twisted, stunted trees, or tall bushes. None was more than ten feet tall, giving the area an eerie, unpleasant feel.

'I wish you joy of your inheritance, Thomas,' he said, 'but I confess to a desire to see more trees.'

'Hah! Ignore this blasted, wind-scoured view, Sir Baldwin, and turn the other way. Look! Down in that valley is Throwleigh itself, and that little vill is worth pounds each year, even now after five years of poor harvest. The only trouble here was always my brother's softness with the villeins. What they need is a firm hand. Once they realise I know what I'm about, they'll knuckle under!'

Simon disregarded his boast. As bailiff he knew many of the landlords on the moors, and he was aware that Squire

Roger had not been an easy touch. In addition, the squire was ever polite, and greatly more courteous than his younger brother – and Simon was quietly confident that he would never have uttered so disloyal a comment about Thomas.

To Baldwin's faint surprise the land beneath them looked good. A small stream trickled by at their feet, its passage cheerful even out here. Below them the trees rose higher, protected from the fiercest blasts of the wind by their position at the foot of the great hill. Over their tops the knight could see thin wisps of smoke rising from the vill beyond. Men would be tending their coppices, setting aside the larger branches and boughs to dry, some to be burned to warm their homes over winter, others to be hewn into planks; women would be going about their business, grinding the last of their grains from last year's harvest into flour to make their hard, dry bread, then planting and weeding in their vegetable gardens; their children all out in the fields throwing stones at the pigeons and other birds which would try to steal their grain before it could throw out the tiniest shoot.

And Herbert would never see it again, he thought, his mood sombre again. 'His body was where?' he demanded.

'Here.'

The knight set off quickly, and Simon had to hurry to keep up with his friend.

There was nothing to show that a child had died here: any sign of where his body had lain had been obliterated by traffic over the last few days. Simon stared down at the mud and peat at his feet, shaking his head again. It was appalling that the boy should have been murdered and left where he had fallen. He was about to comment on this when he saw that Baldwin was not even glancing at the roadway.

They had come round a bend at the top of a slight rise. The hill on their left was steep, and the road formed a terrace, having eaten into the hillside. It had created a bank some three feet above road level, at the top of which was a thick mass of ferns. Baldwin's attention was divided: he kept peering through the ferns, then over to the verge at the other side of the road, his features sharp with speculation.

'The wagon would have come from there, Sir Baldwin,' Thomas said, pointing helpfully back down the road.

'Yes, but the child wouldn't. Herbert must have come from the bank there.'

Simon followed his pointing finger and realised the knight was considering a long track which had been gouged through the foliage. 'What is it?'

'If someone were to drag a body through the ferns, it would leave a long trail in the vegetation just like that, would it not?' Baldwin said. 'Broken fronds of fern, snapped stems of foxgloves, and even the occasional gorse bush has been overwhelmed!'

Thomas threw him a confused look. 'So?'

'So the child was murdered up there, and dragged all the way here, even hauled through gorse – not the kind of plant anyone would willingly crawl over.'

'But the lad was killed *here*, Sir Baldwin.'

'You think so?'

'Of course!' Thomas declared irritably. 'How else could the farmer have done it? I know where Daniel took you this morning. Edmund saw poor Herbert here in the road, decided to take his revenge, jumped on the boy, beat him to death, and then thrust his body under his cart to make it look like an accident.'

Baldwin considered him silently for a long time. Then: 'I had never expected you to be so imaginative, Master Thomas. What makes you think the farmer would behave in so foolish a manner?'

'He was seen here – Daniel told you!'

The knight clambered up the bank and crouched, searching the ground. 'He was indeed seen on this road. It is a busy route apparently – and that is what makes me believe that Edmund couldn't have committed this crime.' He stood suddenly, cutting off Thomas's shocked interruption. 'Look, the man wouldn't be mad enough to kill the child out in the open here, would he? He may be poor, but he doesn't strike me as mad. What if a rider should have come upon him in the act?'

'Well, then, that's why those tracks were left: he dragged Herbert up the bank, killed him there, and then threw his body back down,' Thomas hazarded.

Baldwin smiled. 'Almost, but if someone were to come across his wagon left here untended, they would suspect something was wrong. Why on earth should he take so great a risk?'

'Maybe he was overcome with anger, Baldwin,' Simon pointed out while his friend subjected the surrounding vegetation to a careful study. 'After all, we know he had reason enough to loathe the squire's family. Isn't it possible he saw the boy and became enraged? Here was the son of the woman who was bringing him back to villein status, the son of the man who'd decided to throw him from his home, enjoying a walk in the sunshine, not a care in the world. Edmund might have simply snapped. Or perhaps he accidentally hit the boy and knocked him down and injured him? He might have jumped down from the cart to see how he was, and then, realising it was Herbert, decided to finish him off. Then he got back on his wagon, and rode over him properly to make it look like an accident?'

'These are fascinating speculations,' Baldwin said patiently, 'but they don't cover the facts. First, this broad swathe of plants all flattened and pointing towards the road; second, there are no other tracks near here. If the farmer *had* dragged the child up this way to kill him, I'd expect to see the plants bent over in the other direction. Third, Edmund would hardly find the child here, bundle him up, carry him some distance up the hill there, murder him, and then haul him all the way back here, all the time hoping that no one else would see his cart parked.'

'Then who *did* kill my nephew?' Thomas challenged him.

Baldwin gave a dry smile and pointed to the track. 'When we find out where those marks come from, we may have a better idea.'

Thomas waved his hand, taking in the whole area. 'Utter nonsense! Look at that hill, there are numberless trails all over it – but they're caused by sheep, cattle, horses and other beasts. Just because of a few marks, probably made by a goat, you mean to tell me you'll ignore the farmer's guilt?'

His manner made Baldwin's temper rise. 'Is it better that I should leap to assuming a man's innocence or that you should assume his guilt, Thomas? You have suggested a weak story to explain this murder – I find it unconvincing and have told you why.'

'Oh, there's no reasoning with you! You've obviously made up your mind and won't be swayed. You may find that in Crediton your methods suit very well, Sir Baldwin, but I can assure you that here in the moors we consider action better than prating or foolish theorising. I'll have the man arrested.'

Baldwin gave a gasp of exasperation, but Thomas had already set off back to the manor, kicking at stones like a petulant child. 'Oh, the cretinous idiot!'

Simon grinned up at him where he stood on the bank. 'So what now, Sir Diplomatist?'

'Now we find out where this trail leads us.'

Godfrey had watched the knight and bailiff walk off with the master of the manor, and when Thomas returned alone, he shrugged himself from the wall where he had been leaning, and moved off to intercept him.

'Why, Master Thomas, have you mislaid the knight and his friend?'

Thomas gave a sour grimace, spitting, 'The man's mad! He prefers to go off on a wild goose chase rather than arrest the fellow who's guilty.'

It was good to have an audience, and on his way to the stableyard, Thomas fulminated about the foolishness of knights who had no knowledge of the stupidity of farmers and other lazy villeins. In between his curses and dark mutterings, Godfrey came to understand the course of his conversation with Baldwin. Leaving Thomas to fetch men to arrest the farmer, he walked out in front of the house, down to the little wood that lay before it. There, at a short distance from the stream, he found his client.

James van Relenghes had not enjoyed his morning. He had hoped to be able to get Lady Katharine on her own, so that he could press his attention on her. All the women he

173

had known had tended to enjoy someone with a strange accent paying court to them, as if it were a kind of additional compliment that a foreigner should exhibit interest, and although he dared not be too obvious, he knew he didn't have overlong to achieve his scheme. The Lady Katharine had shown little delight at his flattery so far, but although that was frustrating, he knew he must make allowances for her position. She'd only recently lost her man and her boy.

Yet it was disappointing that he had failed to even engage her in conversation. Every time he attempted to speak to her, her steward interposed himself. It was most frustrating. James van Relenghes had a specific ambition: he wished to make love to Lady Katharine, to take her, body and soul, and to do so speedily. He couldn't afford to wait while she overcame her better instincts. He didn't have time.

This was the problem which nagged at him now, while he spun his knife in his hand and hurled it, flashing in the sunlight, to the mark he had cut in the tree before him. As always, the blade struck where he wished, but weakly, hanging at an angle, the handle drooping towards the ground. He was standing contemplating it when Godfrey arrived.

'Sir, the knight has figured out that the boy was pulled through the ferns.'

Van Relenghes nodded slowly. 'How much has he discovered?'

'He has guessed that someone dragged him along there and dropped him down into the road. That drunken fool Thomas told me – he disagreed with the knight and came back here in a sulk. He's fetching men, and then he's off to Throwleigh to arrest the farmer.'

'Ah, good!' Van Relenghes rubbed his hands together, smiling thinly. 'If they arrest him, that should divert attention from anyone else who was on the moor that day.'

Godfrey shook his head slowly. 'I don't know what you plan, sir, but I'll not see an innocent man go to the rope. No matter what else, if the farmer looks close to being hanged, I'll tell the lady about you and Thomas.'

Van Relenghes glanced at him with honest surprise. 'Would you? But that would mean people asking what *you* were doing up there. Some might think you yourself could have killed the child.'

'No matter. I'll not see the farmer hanged for something he couldn't have done.'

'You'll do as you are told!'

Godfrey beamed. He stood motionless a moment, then his hand flew under his leather jack. When it reappeared, van Relenghes caught a glimpse of a flashing blade. Godfrey flicked it upwards, caught it and cast it in one fluid movement; it whirled past van Relenghes's ear, scything through the air, and he heard it strike his target a moment later.

'I'll not see an innocent Englishman murdered to suit the plans of a foreigner, whether he pays me or no,' Godfrey said, and now his grin was fixed, like a smile carved on ice. He walked past his master to retrieve his dagger.

Van Relenghes was tempted to reach for his sword – but better judgement prevailed. Godfrey was a master of defence, a man well-used to protecting himself. He had turned his back on van Relenghes, but that did not mean he was unprepared, and after witnessing the lighting speed of his movements, the Fleming wasn't convinced he could draw and be certain of killing him before Godfrey could reach his knife.

And van Relenghes was quite certain that if Godfrey did get to it, he could throw it before he, James, could unsheath his sword.

He did not move, watching as Godfrey grabbed the hilt of his knife, which was pinned securely in the tree, exactly perpendicular, the blade buried over an inch deep in the living wood. The force with which it had struck had knocked van Relenghes's own dagger loose, and it lay on the ground. Godfrey stooped and picked it up. He twirled it in the air three times, before catching it by the point of the blade, then studied it for a short while before passing it back. 'A good knife, sir – but not strong enough for fighting,' he commented. 'Not for fighting *me*, anyway.'

Van Relenghes watched him walk away, perfectly composed and relaxed, and as the Fleming thrust his dagger back into its sheath, he tried to control the painful thudding of his heart.

In Godfrey's eyes he had seen, just for a moment, his own death.

CHAPTER SIXTEEN

Petronilla brushed the rushes from the hall's floor, moving them into the screens, and thence out to the stableyard. They had not rotted yet, and with the bones, half-gnawed by the dogs and rats, and the damp patches where dogs and cats had defecated or pissed, they were heavy. It was hard work moving them to the yard, and once there she leaned and rested on her besom, staring drearily at the manure-heap so far away, over at the other side of the stables.

When she saw Hugh, she put a hand to her back, rubbing slowly, allowing her face to take on an expression of patient suffering.

Hugh hadn't seen her sudden collapse. As he approached, all he saw was a young girl with gleaming fair hair and slim body, who was in apparent pain.

Of the two servants, Edgar was more inclined to flirting. Hugh, a dour man at the best of times, was content with his own company. It was the way he had been brought up; the son of a farmer, as soon as he could fit stone to sling he had been sent out to protect the flocks from predators. By nature he was self-sufficient and comfortable; he admired women, and occasionally desired them, but the inns and alehouses could satisfy his needs, and he saw little point in the needless expense of a wife of his own.

His quietness in the presence of women was often construed as enormous shyness; it wasn't. He simply saw no sense in engaging in flattery to no end. But his master had ensured that he had learned to be polite in order that he should not embarrass Simon or Margaret when they visited well-born households and, although his gruff, 'Are you well, miss?' could have been spoken in a softer voice, the words themselves were enough to assure Petronilla that she was safe from having to carry the rushes over to the manure-heap.

As compensation, she was prepared to be friendly with this morose-looking fellow.

'You're the bailiff's servant, aren't you?' she asked.

'That's right, miss,' Hugh said, walking to the stable door where a large pitchfork rested. He returned and speared a large forkful of the rushes and walked to the manure-heap. 'I work for Master Simon Puttock, Bailiff of Lydford Castle under the Warden of the Stannaries, God bless him.'

'He must be keen to find poor Master Herbert's murderer,' Petronilla said sadly, thinking of the boy's ruined body. A long tress of hair had escaped from her cap, and she twirled it round her finger. Hugh didn't notice that she was able to stand upright with ease now, nor that she was able to follow him from rushes to dung-pile without pain. 'It must be a lot of responsibility, having to seek killers.'

'Yes, but he's good at it. There's never a murderer escapes my master,' said Hugh inaccurately.

'What, never a one?' she asked, pleasingly impressed.

He shrugged, but even Hugh could have his head turned a little by such approving adulation, and he swaggered as he returned to the rushes. Glancing at her from the corner of his eye, he thought to himself that she was a remarkably attractive girl, with her open, fresh features and high, clear brow, unmarked by the pox or wrinkles. He shoved his fork into the rushes and grunted as he lifted it.

'Never a one,' he repeated with satisfaction. 'Master and the knight always find their killers. It's not always easy, and not always safe, but they catch 'em all right.'

As he spoke Thomas emerged from the hall. At his side was Daniel, his staff of office under his arm, indignant and resentful at being ordered by Thomas, and ready to take out his pique on other servants. 'Petronilla!' he called bossily. 'What are you doing out here? Get inside and see to the hall, it's filthy!'

'That's what I am doing, Daniel.'

'Don't answer me back, wench!' the steward snapped. Then, almost to himself, 'Where *are* those damned stablemen?'

Hugh ignored the men as they stamped and bellowed, but when two grooms arrived, he leaned on his fork and listened. There was a quick bustle, horses were brought, saddled and made ready, and then with a shouting of orders, Thomas, Daniel and two others rode off furiously, heading towards the vill.

'What's their trouble?' asked Petronilla, returning to the yard once the men had disappeared.

'They think they've found the lad's murderer,' said Hugh conversationally.

She shot him a look. '"Think"? You don't sound convinced.'

'I'm not.'

'Why?'

Hugh bent back to his task. 'Because it's easy for someone to guess who might have done something like this, and easy to arrest someone who's poor. Until I hear my master say he thinks it was this man, I won't worry about it.'

James van Relenghes saw them talking. He had heard the clatter of hooves and had walked back to the road in time to see Daniel and Thomas with their men disappearing on the road to Throwleigh, their horses throwing up large clouds of dust and sods of turf as they sped over the verge rather than take the longer way on the road. Their destination was obvious.

Van Relenghes was content with the turn events were taking. He strolled back to the house and nodded to Hugh. Seeing the girl loitering about, he paused. Like Hugh, he admired her face, the way the sun shone golden in her hair where it had drifted from her cap, the sheer happiness in her smile as Hugh made some comment. Van Relenghes wandered over and asked her politely, if a little shortly, whether she could fetch him a large pot of wine. He would wait for it in the hall, he said, and waited pointedly until she flounced off to the buttery.

The hall was empty when he entered, and he drew a chair up to the fire, sitting before it while he waited for the girl to return.

She had looked very attractive out there, he reflected. Of course the widow was infinitely more desirable, with her money and her aura of elegance and . . . and her sheer independence, modulated with the vulnerability which her bereavements had conferred upon her. Her self-possession made her incredibly attractive to van Relenghes. He had known wealthy widows in other countries – quite a number – but this one would be even more enjoyable. Others had been easier, it was true, but the very lack of a challenge had made those victories less complete somehow, less perfect.

With Lady Katharine, her self-possession would make her surrender all the more delightful, he reckoned, and smiled to himself. Her composure would make her eventual submission sweeter still. The certainty of his success was in no doubt, for van Relenghes knew that his tall, dark good looks were magnetic to women. The fact had been proved to him time and time again. No, he entertained no doubts of his abilities to entice Widow Throwleigh into his bed. It would take time, but eventually he would be able to enjoy ruining her.

But for now there was little opportunity, not at the earliest until she had put her brat into his grave, and had given him time to rot. Not until she had recovered a little from that misery and the weak, womanly failing of grieving for her man, could he hope to be able to win her affection.

As he arrived at this conclusion, Petronilla came in and poured his drink. He was so deep in thought he hardly noticed.

He was reflecting happily that now his revenge was almost complete. The squire was dead, his heir likewise, and once

181

he had ruined Squire Roger's widow, James van Relenghes's curse would be fulfilled.

Petronilla left him, turning at the door and pulling a face at his back. She didn't like having to obey the whim of a foreigner; especially when they didn't even bother to acknowledge her when she put herself out to serve them.

Outside Hugh was still clearing her rushes, and she was about to go to him when Nicholas sauntered out from the stables. He glanced casually up and down the yard, and then smiled at her.

Petronilla wasn't in a mood to be polite to strangers, but at least this one was another servant, like herself. When Nicholas pulled a sad grimace and made a dumbshow of drinking, winking to her, she at first tutted to herself, but then tossed her head and flung her arms up dramatically before returning to the buttery and fetching a fresh pair of jugs, carrying them on a tray out to the stable.

Nicholas was sitting on a bale of hay, playing dice with a groom, and he looked up as she stood over him, pouring his wine.

He was edgy, as he should be after coming back to this place so far from civilisation. Although he had his men about him, he was anxious lest he should be discovered. Surely it was only luck so far that had saved him from discovery by Anney, but if that situation should change, he knew he was in danger unless his master should protect him.

Like many, Nicholas was a man of simple desires and urges. He was lonely and a little afraid, and at such times he turned to comfort from a woman, but the nearest tavern he dared use was a long way from here. It would be madness to try the one near Anney's home. He might still be recognised.

Looking up, he noticed that Petronilla, although she wore an air of bored sulkiness, from this angle bending over him, looked intensely desirable. She was frowning with concentration, ringlets of hair framing her pretty face. She had behaved quite coolly towards him since he arrived with Thomas, but he was sure that was only a front, after what he'd seen. He met her eye and gave her a broad, wolfish smile, his hand cupping her breast.

'Little maid, would you like to earn a silver piece?'

The sound of the jug smashing, the hissed curse and patter of feet made Hugh start. Godfrey had been resting at the door with a quart of ale, and the two men stared as Petronilla hurtled past, her cap awry, hair flying loose, tunic lifted to allow her to run, face red as a russet cloth. The men watched her shoot through the door and out of sight.

'What happened to her?' Godfrey asked with bemusement.

Hugh scowled as he caught sight of Nicholas standing in the doorway to the stable. 'I reckon he tried his luck.'

Godfrey nodded slowly, keeping his face fixed on Nicholas. 'He'd better be careful or his luck might run out.'

The trail led them straight up the hill. Every few yards Baldwin peered in among the ferns and furze at either side, looking for footprints, hoofprints, *anything*. Each time he had to shake his head with bafflement and carry on.

There was still only the one track, travelling in one direction. That was an easy inference: all the plants had been pushed or dragged over one way, down towards the road. Baldwin was puzzled. He would have expected to find a wide, trampled space where the boy had been caught and murdered; he would also have expected whoever had gone down here one way to have scurried back up again after the deed, but there was no sign of footprints, demonstrating that the killer, or killers, had kept concealed by crawling away after leaving the body at the roadside, and after a suitable pause had taken to their heels. The lack of any such evidence made him resolve to search the vegetation at the roadside again once they had completed this search.

Even as he cast about them, he could feel his aggravation growing.

'Simon, can you remember when the last rains fell?'

'Feeling a bit damp?' Simon laughed.

'*Damp!* My tunic is soaked from the hips down, my hose are wet through, and I am growing quite cold – and all this in the bright sunlight! Why hasn't the sun dried all these blasted plants?'

It wasn't only the damp that was getting on his nerves; he was also being assaulted by prickles from the gorse-bushes, which were penetrating his hose and shirt. The spines of these moorland shrubs appeared able to stab through even coarse material, and he muttered a curse against them as Simon spoke.

'The sun hardly reaches here; the top of the hill keeps all of this side in the shade at this time of year – and I expect you didn't notice it, you being recently wedded, but last night there was a heavy shower of rain.'

Baldwin ignored the comment; there were too many opportunities for coarse jokes at his expense now he was married, and the bailiff tried not to miss a single one. To change the subject, Baldwin pointed ahead with his chin. 'Will this hill never end? It feels as if we have been climbing for miles.'

'That,' said Simon, puffing as he stopped at Baldwin's side, 'is the trouble with the moors. Whichever direction you wish to take, you tend to have to go uphill.'

Baldwin gave a dry chuckle and set off once more. Now they were walking up the edge of a small valley. Below them, mostly hidden by the ubiquitous gorse and ferns, they could hear a fast-flowing stream. In the valley there were a few stunted trees, but here on the moors all was low-growing and dull, apart from the sweet, almond-smelling, bright yellow gorse. The hillside rose up before them, menacing in its height. Baldwin glanced behind them and whistled. The scene was spectacular, with a view over many miles. Southwards he could see more hills rising one after the other in succession, their flanks unspoiled by towns or villages, only a few stone walls and enclosures marking the smooth green plains. East the land was lower, and he could see gaps in the trees where farmsteads and bartons lay. Their smoke rose up calmly in the clear air.

'It is very peaceful here,' he murmured.

'It looks it, doesn't it?' Simon said glumly, sitting down on a lump of moorstone. 'Trouble is, that's just an illusion. The miners over the other side of this hill cause enough grief for me, God Himself only knows. Then the farmers are always coming to blows with everyone else, especially with the tin miners when the buggers move streams and leave whole areas completely dry while flooding others. Miners come and cut peat – well, they have the right to it, so that they can smelt their ore – but they always have to take chunks from prime pasture to upset the farmers, don't they?'

'Stop your moaning, and let's carry on.'

Simon eyed his friend surreptitiously as they climbed. The knight was still deeply troubled by what he viewed as his lapse, not that Simon looked at it in the same light. To the bailiff it was as plain as the nose on his face that occasionally boys would die. His own lad was not that long in his grave. It was possible that Herbert had died, as Baldwin suspected, because of a jealous adult seeking an inheritance, and if that was Herbert's fate, they had a duty to avenge him, but that was an end to the matter.

But Baldwin appeared to take this murder as a personal challenge, as if he were engaged in a private feud with the killer.

The bailiff knew his friend too well. Baldwin was inflexibly determined to see justice prevail. He had suffered at the hands of bigots and knew how it felt to be persecuted for no reason. It was because of this that he could be stubborn, pig-headed even, in his pursuit of criminals. Simon hoped that marriage would erode some of this obduracy, but it was a little much to expect that Baldwin would be cured so soon.

This case had gripped Baldwin more forcibly than previous ones. It was something to do with the knight's fervent desire for an heir of his own, Simon felt. The bailiff himself had much the same urge, although in his case, having buried one boy already, he was more committed to ensuring that his daughter was able to produce the family and grandchildren he and Margaret desired. In Baldwin's case there were no children.

Baldwin was losing heart. He still hoped to find some physical proof that the boy had been dragged down here – or some proof that a man had subsequently run *back* up here, trying to keep hidden from the road . . . but he was beginning to feel the first twinges of doubt. Could he be, literally, on the wrong track?

What was more, it was several days since poor Herbert's death, and with the rain which had fallen since then, there was no real likelihood of finding traces or clear evidence.

The track they were following was like a scar in the vegetation, circumventing the gorse, but going straight on through ferns. The direction of the path made little sense to Baldwin. It never appeared to take a straight line, like that made by a man walking, but rather it took an odd, curving route, broader than a sheep or a man.

'Here,' Simon said suddenly, 'what's this?'

Baldwin went to his side. There, off to the right, was another mud track, leading down into the valley of the river. A sheep or two had been along it, for their spoor could be clearly discerned, but their prints had not hidden the others – the human footprints.

The knight crouched and stared, trying to control his excitement. This trail was subtly different from that which they had so far followed. This second one was considerably thinner, and the brown fern fronds, where they had been broken off, were fresher, with fewer trampled into the mud. More important to him, though, were the four pairs of prints.

One was of a small pair of shoes or boots, and the owner had been walking away from the valley, moving towards the track Baldwin and Simon were following. The knight carefully stood and made a firm impression of his own boot alongside the path to gauge the size. His foot was considerably larger than the smaller prints by a good two inches, maybe two and a half in length, and wider by almost an inch, so it could have been the footprint of a woman.

The others looked more on a par with his own: the second set appeared recent, and headed away from Baldwin and Simon down into the valley ahead, while the third seemed identical with the second, and headed in the same direction.

But these were not the only ones. A fourth pair of footprints returned from the valley, and these were the oddest by far, because although the left foot was shod, the right was bare. The mark was smudged a little where animals had crossed the track, and every now and again it had been obliterated because of another footprint being superimposed upon it, but there were many images perfectly delineated of the whole foot, with each toe clearly displayed.

While he considered this, Simon touched his shoulder and pointed silently. Baldwin followed the bailiff's finger. The path down to the river took an easy line along the contours of the hill, dropping at a very shallow rate, but gradually going to the water itself, some forty yards or so below. At the bottom was a plateau of flat ground, with the broad curve of the stream sweeping around it. Standing in the middle of the grassy plain Baldwin saw the man who had caught his friend's attention.

At the base of the cliff was Stephen of York, but this was a very different man from the urbane cleric. He was kicking at ferns as if in a rage, pulling apart clumps of heather, peering beneath bushes of gorse. Now that the knight was aware of him, he could hear the priest's voice over the pleasant murmur of the water, and his eye went to the sets of prints. If one pair belonged to the priest, Baldwin was comfortably convinced that two others did as well. But why should the priest have returned from the water half-shod?

Stephen's voice was a continuous, low curse. It was as if he was damning the whole land, uttering impassioned oaths at every bush and blade of grass. At last he kicked at a low shrub, and missing it, overbalanced and fell hard on his rump, where he sat weeping.

'Should we go and see if we can help?' Simon asked.

Baldwin was silent for a moment, lost in thought. It was tempting to go and question the priest – they would have to at some stage – but something held him back. Stephen was a priest, and deserved cautious treatment. If he was guilty of anything, Baldwin and Simon had no jurisdiction over him, for Stephen, like any ecclesiastic, was not answerable to the secular authorities. He was responsible only to Canon Law.

If Stephen had anything to do with Herbert's death, questioning him now might only warn him of the need for an alibi. No, Baldwin reasoned, it would be better to see what they could find on the track, and then, if there were any solid facts to present to Stephen, they could gauge his reaction unwarned.

'God knows what he's up to there, but I want to see where this track goes,' he said, and ducking low, they made their way back over the brow of the hill before the wailing priest could see them.

CHAPTER SEVENTEEN

The two men had finally gone. Jordan squirmed along until he reached the lip of the cliff, from where he could look down on the plateau. Stephen had rolled over in the foetal position now, hands covering his face while he gave great shuddering sobs.

Feeling a tug at his heel, Jordan carefully pushed himself away and returned to Alan.

'Is he still searching for it?' Alan asked urgently.

'No, he's just blubbering,' Jordan said with contempt.

'That's good. We'd better get back then. The monk won't know we've got it, and we can keep it hidden until we want to use it.'

'But how can we use it?'

'We'll see. Maybe we won't need to. But if we do, and we show it, and say where we got it from, they'll realise what he did.'

Jordan glanced back doubtfully as Alan began to ascend the shallow incline. Stephen was a priest, a man who was supposed to be beyond any misbehaviour. He was appointed by God, supposed to be perfect and good. And yet Alan was right – they had seen through his front. Jordan had been taught that a man like Stephen was above any evil act, but that must have been wrong.

The man should have been incapable of sin, but Jordan and Alan had witnessed it.

Simon was dismayed when he looked up and saw how the clouds had gathered. 'Baldwin, we have to get back.'

'Why?'

'It's going to rain.'

'Simon, if you think I'm going to run back to the manor because of a slight drizzle, you are mistaken. Those clouds hardly look as if they could fill a small bucket.'

'You remain, then. I am going to get back to the house.'

Baldwin gave him a blank stare. 'But why?'

'You don't know the moors like I do. We're here with no cloaks or jacks. When that rain hits us, we'll be soaked in moments.'

'Oh, nonsense!'

Now Baldwin regretted his rashness. 'I am sorry, Simon. I thought you were simply picking on a pretext to go back. I had no idea how this rain could get through to the skin.'

Simon grunted, mopping his forehead with the hem of his tunic, then wringing it out again. They had made for home as soon as the downpour had set in in earnest, but by then, as the bailiff knew, it was too late. This Dartmoor rain had a curiously pervasive quality: it appeared only a thin mizzle yet it swiftly permeated all their clothing. The drops were flying almost horizontally. The only compensation for the bailiff was the expression of horrified disgust on Sir Baldwin's face as he felt the drips slithering down his skin.

The wind blew from behind them, but it whirled and howled in their ears, and Simon had to speak loudly for Baldwin to hear him. 'If we keep to the riverbank, we'll soon make it down to the road, and then all we have to do is turn right to follow it back to the manor.'

The knight nodded, and the two set off again, slithering in the black, peaty mud. Baldwin looked down with dismay. The track was a quagmire now, and every step he took thrust his ankle under the surface. His feet were wallowing in the stuff. He looked up, narrowing his eyes against the wind, and it was here that he fell.

He was some feet behind his friend; he placed his boot on what looked like a solid enough rock, but when he put his weight on it, it slid away. Suddenly he was off-balance and toppling backwards; he put out both hands, but his right thumb caught awkwardly on another stone, and the nail was ripped off.

At first he didn't notice. He sat, his backside throbbing where it had connected with another lump of rock, staring bleakly ahead, swearing quietly but with feeling. Then he stood up, furious with himself for his clumsiness, trying to brush off the worst of the mud and assorted plants, and generally besmearing the whole of his tunic. Glancing at the stone on which he had landed he was about to kick at it when he stopped dead.

The rock stood out in the peaty mud all about, but near where he had fallen there was a clear smudge next to the track, roughly circular in shape. It appeared to connect

Simon and Baldwin's path to another trail, a narrower one this time, that curled away up the hill. Baldwin gave it little attention, thinking it was merely a sheep-path. However, he noticed a cord sticking up from the mud, and he prodded at it with a foot. He suddenly realised it was a piece of leather, and knelt down to pull it free. Then, frowning, he studied the ground round about at closer quarters.

Simon returned, puffing and blowing up the hill on realising his friend had disappeared.

'Don't you think it's time we got back to a cup of wine and a warm fire? What are you up to now?' he demanded irascibly. But then a look of concern came to his face. Baldwin followed the direction of his eyes and swore when he saw the blood dripping from his thumbnail.

'Are you all right?'

'Simon, this is where the boy was killed!'

The bailiff stared down, then back at his friend. 'What on earth makes you say that?'

'Look,' said Baldwin, pointing carefully at the smeared patch of mud. 'He crawled up here, for some reason, but some-one met him and brought a stone down on his head. Perhaps the stone I just fell over was the very one that killed him.'

'Don't you think you're being a bit over-imaginative?' Simon asked disbelievingly. 'There's nothing to show he ever came near here.'

'We followed the track all the way from the road, so it is fair to reason that he might have come this way,' Baldwin said. 'But this is what makes me believe he was here. See this?' He held out what he had found: two narrow thongs tied to a stout patch of leather.

'A sling?' Simon said doubtfully.

'A typical boy's toy,' Baldwin agreed. 'I'd be prepared to gamble that he had it in his hand and let it fall when he was struck.'

'Farfetched!' Simon scoffed.

'Perhaps. But let's consider it as a possibility.'

'You say he crawled here. Why should he do that?'

'Perhaps he was playing up here, pretending to be a hunter or a man-at-arms.'

'Oh, really?' Simon asked sarcastically. 'And on what do you base that? It looks like a sheep-track to me.'

'Oh, Simon! Look at the way it curves round – when have you ever seen a sheep wander like that? Sheep go to great efforts to follow the contours of the hills they traverse, while this is descending steadily, down from that ledge . . .'

'You want to follow it, don't you?' Simon sighed. He glanced up at the sky. The rain had slowed now to a gentle drizzle, and the bailiff reminded himself that he was unlikely to get any wetter. He gave a long-suffering sigh. 'Oh, Christ's bones! Very well! Come on, then.'

'Shove the bastard in the storeroom!' Thomas said as he drew his mount to a halt in the court. He watched his grooms lead the dejected figure of Edmund away before he dropped from his horse, feeling that he had at least shown he could make decisions, which was more than that damned fool from Furnshill.

He left his horse standing and walked towards the stables. Nicholas stood in the dark a short way from the door.

'Well?' Thomas demanded.

'The Fleming went inside a while back, sir. I've not seen him since.' Nicholas forbore to mention his attempt at finding solace. Petronilla was unlikely to complain – she was only a servant. Not that his master would mind overmuch. The wench had better make up her mind to be more friendly in future. After all, Nicholas was his master's trusted steward and, now Thomas owned the Throwleigh demesne, if Petronilla wanted to keep her job she would have to look after Nicholas too.

The reflection made him grin, and he promised himself that he would renew his acquaintance with the maid as soon as he could.

Thomas kicked idly at a stone, sending it skipping over the dirt of the yard. 'What will he want now?'

'Sir?'

'That sodding Fleming. He's after something, but *what*?' Thomas was no fool, no matter how indiscreet he might be in a tavern. He knew men, and at this moment he was perturbed by James van Relenghes. 'He's banging on about purchasing a plot of land from me, but I don't believe he's really that bothered. If I had to guess, I'd say he was more interested in Lady Katharine than in any of my territory.'

'Maybe he wants a plot to settle on.'

'It's stupid – as if I'd sell some of the estate! I need every penny it brings. Even if there weren't an entail, I wouldn't sell to some foreigner with smarmy manners.'

'Perhaps he's after your sister-in-law. She's not bad-looking.'

'Be sensible, fool! The bitch isn't out of her widow's weeds, for God's sake.'

Nicholas said nothing, but gave his master a meaningful look.

'You think . . .' Thomas thrust his hands into his belt and stared thoughtfully out into the yard. His servant was better acquainted with the ways of women. Hadn't he been married twice himself? 'You really think he might be considering an attempt on her?'

'Look at the way he is with her: I've only seen them together out here in the yard, but he seems to be all over her like a cheap tunic. Call me old-fashioned, but I'd say he was showing all the classic signs of trying to get inside her drawers. He hangs on her every word, praises her work, defends her husband's memory . . .'

'Would a man after her do that?' Thomas asked doubtfully.

'Sir, if you want a woman to trust you, first you have to show you approve of her and her choices. Since she married your brother for love, only a complete idiot would suggest to her that the squire was a cretin with more brain between his legs than over his neck.'

'Hmm. And you think this foreigner's driven by what's between *his* legs? I can't see why. She doesn't possess much – her dower won't be a lot.'

'I doubt whether that's his aim. More likely he just fancies a tumble with her.'

Thomas nodded, and seeing the Fleming at the hall's door, he sent Nicholas away. Now he thought about it, van Relenghes's behaviour was easily explained away by this simple inference, and Thomas felt oddly put out, as though he had been slighted. There was a principle at stake here, and Thomas was Lady Katharine's legal guardian now that he was master of the lands. If this Low Country adventurer wanted to roll in the grass with her, he could cause plenty of embarrassment for Thomas.

Making a snap decision, Thomas crossed the yard.

James van Relenghes smiled and nodded his head with mild courtesy as Thomas approached, but Thomas barely acknowledged him, stating immediately: 'Sir, I am afraid I must decline your offer to buy the land north of here.'

'But I had hoped . . .'

'I know what you'd hoped. It has to do with my sister-in-law, and I tell you now, sir, it won't do! Not in my house. You would demean her and my family? I say, not in my house!'

Van Relenghes's face froze. 'Of what exactly am I being accused?'

Thomas opened his mouth, but before he could speak, he was aware of Godfrey standing behind his master. There was no weapon in his hand, yet he radiated preparedness. His master had lowered his brows until they were an unbroken line of frowning malice above his eyes.

'You don't scare me, Sir James!' Thomas lied. 'I'm aware of the advances you are attempting with my brother's widow, and it won't do! I won't sell you my land, so your business here is done.'

Like many cowardly men, van Relenghes enjoyed seeing fear in others, and bullying those weaker than himself. To him Thomas looked like a frightened little mouse, and he had to restrain the urge to laugh. Little mouse; little man. He was pathetic. 'I am here at the invitation of your sister-in-law, not you. You could, naturally, try to throw me from the premises, but then I would be within my rights to defend myself,' he said, and tapped his sword hilt meaningfully.

Thomas recoiled, almost tripping over the bottom step. 'You draw that, and I'll have you cut into pieces, you bastard!'

'You threaten me again, Thomas, and I'll challenge you. Would you like that?' van Relenghes said, slowly pacing after him as Thomas retreated. 'Well – would you? I was a soldier while you were still puking at your mother's breast; I fought for your King in France with your brother while you cried at scratching your knee; I could draw now and take off your head before you saw my sword leave its scabbard. I shall say this only once, Thomas: I am here to pay my respects to your sister, not you. I shall stay here as long as that lady requires my presence, as a matter of honour and courtesy, and if you or anyone else tries to evict me, I will – *I will* – protect myself and her.'

He watched as the merchant scuttled past and darted into the hall. Godfrey hadn't moved, and the Fleming walked past him, his face carefully blank, and into the hall after the manor's new master.

Only then did Godfrey shake his head, a puzzled expression on his face. 'Neatly done, Sir James. Now you've upset your host. What can that achieve?'

CHAPTER EIGHTEEN

Baldwin's thumb did not hurt, it was completely dead to all sensation, but as he surveyed the land ahead, he meditatively sucked at it, certain that it would start to throb before long.

They had gone all the way up to the top of the hill following this track, and now both were carefully studying the ground.

'Well, Baldwin?' Simon asked at last.

'I have no idea,' admitted the knight frankly. 'It looks like three separate paths through the ferns, which have met here, at this larger patch.'

The rain was now only a feeble reminder of the recent downpour, but it still trickled unmercifully down Baldwin's face from his soaked hair. He gave the heavens a black look. 'It's ridiculous to remain here guessing. Let's make our way back.'

He motioned down to the stream, and Simon nodded.

'And on the way,' Baldwin continued, waving his hand, 'I'll clean this up in the stream.'

Their path to the water was slippery down the steep slope, but at least it wasn't far. Soon they were at the bottom, and Baldwin saw that they had arrived back at the same plateau they had seen earlier.

'What are you doing here?' Brother Stephen demanded, getting up from his seat on a rock.

'Brother, I am glad to see you,' Baldwin said disingenuously. 'We were walking about here when the rain set in, and weren't sure which way to go, and then I fell and did this.'

The priest stared at him, and Baldwin was struck by his expression. The long, regular, feminine features were twisted, the brilliant eyes red and raw, while the cheeks were pale and scratched in places. He looked like a man who had peered into the pits of hell. However, as his gaze fell on Baldwin's thumb, a semblance of his normal self took over as he helped Baldwin to the bank of the stream and made him dip the thumb deep in the cool water.

Baldwin was grateful for his care, but couldn't help glancing speculatively down while the priest helped him, and then he found it very hard to drag his attention away from the two prints lying side-by-side on the damp soil: the prints of his shoe next to the nearly identical ones of the monk.

Alan and Jordan skirted round the outer wall of the orchard before they could at last stand up straight once more. They trotted off towards their village, and spoke not a word until they came to Edmund's house. Here Alan took the small bundle from the younger boy.

'I'll keep this at home in case he tries anything.'

Jordan nodded. His friend's face was pale in the gloomy light, and after what had happened to them over the last few days, that was no surprise. Now, with this evidence to prove the cleric's crime, at least they should be safe from his vengeance. Jordan had suffered beatings from many in the vill before, but no one had assaulted him with the same violence as Brother Stephen.

Jordan watched Alan scuff his way slowly through the dirt to the door of his cottage. It was late morning now, and Jordan's belly was rumbling.

Christiana would have his pottage ready: a bowl of cabbage and onion, garlic and leek, boiled with a few of the remaining dried peas from the last year's crop. Apart from the rabbit he'd shot, there had been no meat since Candlemas.

He had been fortunate – God, he was lucky! – on the day that the squire had dropped from his horse. Everyone had been so busy rushing around wondering what to do, no one had had time to execute Squire Roger's last expressed wish to see Jordan beaten.

At the time he had been out in the shaw behind the house trying to clean some of the mud from his knees and feet. He'd heard the noise of horses, then the rasping voice of the squire, and he'd quickly sneaked round to the front of the house. He'd immediately thought that his father was in trouble – about to be arrested.

The altercation that followed was terrifying. Here was the man whom the whole village went in fear of, the most powerful man any of them was ever likely to meet, and he was calling for him, Jordan, to be punished. Yet the boy could cope with that. A thrashing was only a momentary thing; a few rubs and the pain dissipated. No, worse was seeing his father struck senseless as the whipper-in obeyed the squire's command.

The boy did not idolise his father, but Edmund was his liege. It had been oddly galling to see him resorting to pleading with the squire, and worse to see him collapse as he was knocked aside.

Now Jordan was home. He paused at the door. His father had been drinking sulkily ever since that day, and the more he drank, the more the family suffered. Since the news of their pending eviction, he had taken to thrashing Christiana or the children at the slightest provocation.

Matters hadn't improved even with the news that the family could stay in their house, for being allowed to stay wasn't enough – not when they were to be made serfs again. His father was furious, bitter that his freedom had been taken from him. Edmund had come back from that meeting demanding ale, and then punched Christiana when she remonstrated that he was drinking too much and the family couldn't afford it.

These thoughts flashed through Jordan's mind as he stood with his hand on the wooden catch. There was no sound from within and the silence was intimidating. It was almost as if the house had been ransacked, and even now a man waited behind the door, ready to spring out at him. There was no reason why his father should have gone out, but he might have decided to visit another cottage where there was more ale. He did that sometimes when Christiana was brewing a fresh barrel.

Steeling himself, Jordan shoved the door wide. His mother sat murmuring a curse in a slow, steady monotone. There was no food bubbling in the pot, no welcoming scent of herbs and greens, and no sign of his father. Jordan's six-year-old sister Molly stood at Christiana's side, hugging herself in fear, not knowing how to calm or soothe their mother.

Jordan gazed about the room. 'Where's Dad, Mummy?'

'He's been taken.' Her voice was flat, but the boy felt suddenly weak with horror as she continued hollowly, 'They say he killed the squire's boy.'

Petronilla entered the screens warily. The shock of Nicholas's hand on her breast hadn't faded, nor had the disgust she had felt. He had assumed he could take her, that was what he had meant, and she felt demeaned; abused. She was determined never to allow herself to be left alone with him again.

She heard the Fleming and his man walk through the screens and decided to test her luck; she must clear the place before her mistress came down from her solar.

There was no sound from the hall, and she carefully peeped inside. To her relief she saw the place was empty, and she strode inside with confidence. The fresh rushes she had laid gave off a pleasant odour, and although the house was still and quiet, sunk in the gloom of the double mourning, the aroma of grass and meadows gave the place a slight hint of sunshine, of pleasant days to come.

The girl smiled, collecting the dirty bowls and plates, jugs and drinking pots. It was sad to think that the young boy was gone, but she was pragmatic. She had known three of her own brothers die at birth, and a sister, before her mother herself had passed on, exhausted, at the age of three-and-twenty. Life was continually ending – that was a simple fact. The sooner the house got back to normal the better, she felt.

On hearing steps in the yard, she gathered up all the remaining crocks onto her tray and hurried out to the buttery. There she paused. The argument between Thomas and van Relenghes was clearly audible, and she held her breath, convinced that there would be a fight – but when it all fizzled out, she regretfully set about her chores.

After some while there were voices in the hall, and she obeyed a call to serve Lady Katharine. Her mistress was accompanied by Jeanne and Margaret, and Petronilla was sent to fetch them wine.

It was later, when she was filling jugs, that she found the boy. Wat lay on his side beneath a barrel, his jug. On his face was fixed a broad smile of sheer delight while he snored softly, the empty pot rolling gently beside him.

At the sight, Petronilla sank down on a stool, her hand resting gently on her belly, and a small smile played at her mouth as she wondered what *her* child would look like at Wat's age.

It was then that she heard the low whistle. There at the doorway stood Nicholas, and Petronilla felt her previous good humour dissolve.

'Maid, I am sorry if I upset you earlier,' he said. 'I didn't realise you'd be offended.'

'How would you expect a woman to feel?'

Nicholas gave a self-deprecating simper. 'It didn't occur to me that—'

'That *I*'d care!' she hissed.

It was no good. He could see that nothing he could say would alter her feelings towards him. He had tried to soothe her, mainly, it had to be said, so that he could attempt to win her over, for she was very comely. But now he became irritated in his own right. He was here at great risk to himself, and that reflection made him impatient. 'Well, why don't we agree on a compromise?'

'What do you mean?'

'I could give you a penny for the night?' he asked hopefully, and then ran before the pot could hit his head.

Baldwin was not in the best of moods when the sodden trio arrived back at the manor. He stood a moment in the screens, arms held out at either side, watching the water stream from his sleeves, and gave a sigh of sheer frustration. It was not unknown for the weather to change suddenly for the worse, even in Crediton and Cadbury, but to have got so sodden so quickly was vile.

Rather than attempting to dry his clothing before the fire in the hall, Simon had hurried off to fetch a dry tunic and hose, while the priest went to his chapel for a clean robe. Baldwin copied them, donning a clean linen shirt and tunic – one his wife had made just before their wedding. Glancing at his sword-belt, he buckled it on once more, but his training took over, and he pulled the blade from its scabbard to check its condition before leaving the room. The rain-guard had worked well, the leather disc between hilt and blade preventing water from seeping into the scabbard and rusting the beautiful blue steel. He nodded happily, wiped it with an oiled cloth, and thrust it back in its sheath.

With his hair dried on a towel and combed straight, his new sword a comforting weight on his hip, and wearing a fresh tunic with richly embroidered neck and sleeves, he felt more like a knight again and less like an impoverished peasant.

When he entered the hall, his wife and Margaret were still sitting by the fire with Lady Katharine, all of them plying their needles. Jeanne smiled at him, but as he bent to kiss her, she noticed his thumb. 'My love, what have you done?'

'I fell and broke my thumbnail – nothing more.'

Lady Katharine raised her face, bleared and miserable from weeping, but still with that strength of character showing in her piercing grey eyes. 'You should be more careful, Sir Baldwin,' she said quietly. 'The moors are treacherous.'

'I learned that much today, Lady,' Baldwin said with an ironic smile.

His wife looked serious. She had lived at Liddinstone, a manor owned by the Abbot of Tavistock, and was only too well aware of how dangerous the moors could be. Her husband was no fool, and could protect himself against outlaws, but that was no guarantee that he would be equally secure against the elements. She was about to say so, when Simon entered. He walked over to Baldwin, a frown distorting his features.

'Thomas has arrested the farmer.'

Only a few minutes after the two men had hurried out, James van Relenghes and his guard came in.

Godfrey walked to the side of the fireplace and leaned against the wall. To Margaret he was the picture of cool self-possession. His composure was almost unnatural. He glanced at her, gave a brief smile, but then his attention flew to the door as he heard steps. Seeing Petronilla, he appeared to relax; his shoulders dropped and he slouched comfortably, as though, since there was no immediate threat to his master, he could afford to be at rest.

James didn't notice how wary his servant was on his behalf. Godfrey was being paid: he should be loyal, and that was an end to the matter. The Fleming strolled languidly to the fire, looking at the ladies' needlework as he passed, and complimenting Lady Katharine on hers, praising the fineness of her stitches, and taking a seat nearby where he could watch her. Unfortunately, his words had the opposite impact to that which he wished. She shuddered and called for her maidservant to fetch wine, rolling up her work and setting it on the floor at her side, composedly resting both hands in her lap, trying to hide the turmoil she felt.

She hadn't wished to hear the two men in the yard, but it had been almost impossible to miss their shouting match through her open window, and now everything van Relenghes said to her felt wrong, somehow – false. On the face of it, his words had appeared reasonable enough, for he had been a friend of her husband's, and yet . . . even that simple fact seemed odd now. Squire Roger had told his stories about fighting in France and Wales so often, Katharine felt she knew most of them by heart, and he had never once spoken of a Sir James van Relenghes. If she had been a young maiden, she might have thought, as Thomas clearly did, that the Fleming was courting her, and yet there was no hint of true affection in his manner, more a calculation.

But there was no point in his attempting to win her. If she had been a wealthy widow, one with lands or an enormous dowry, there could have been logic to it, but as matters stood, surely there was nothing she possessed which he could desire.

She daringly glanced in his direction, and felt her heart lurch as she saw his face light as if with love.

It made her feel physically sick.

CHAPTER NINETEEN

'Well, what of it?' Thomas demanded. 'I am lord of my own manor, you know!' He was walking up and down in the yard, and with every word he spoke, his fists clenched, as if expecting the knight to try to attack him.

Baldwin was surprised by his truculence but held up a hand soothingly. 'Thomas, I am not disputing your right. All I asked was, has he confessed to anything?'

'No, but I have spoken to his neighbours, and they are all agreed that he is an habitual criminal. He's been suspected of stealing food and chickens before now. He has a common fame in the vill.'

'It is a large leap from that to murder, surely?'

'Oh, these villeins stop at nothing. This one in particular is known to be lazy and a drunk – and beats his wife regularly. It could hardly be anybody else.'

Simon avoided Baldwin's eye as the knight gave an exasperated 'Pah!' of contempt. The bailiff knew how his friend felt about such statements. It was a simple fact that members of a village would often find a man guilty if he had been described as 'common' or 'notorious' in the indictment. If they had the slightest doubt as to the man's true honesty and integrity, they would convict him because otherwise they would all be held responsible for the supposed thief's good behaviour; if they had a shred of doubt as to whether he was guilty or not, this threat, of having a massive fine imposed should the man later get arrested for another crime, often made them find their neighbour guilty just so as not to run that risk!

However, instead of exploding, the knight merely said, 'Did anyone see him return to the village on the afternoon Herbert died?'

Thomas blinked, and for a moment stopped his restless pacing. 'How should I know? What a question! Who *cares* whether anyone saw him? He was on the road and killed the boy – that's all we need to know.'

'I suggest you ask people in the village whether they recall seeing him, and if they did, what was the state of his hose,' said Baldwin imperturbably.

'His hose?' Thomas gaped.

'If he walked up through all those ferns and furze, he'd have got his legs soaked, wouldn't he? It would be the final proof you need.'

Thomas gave him a cold look. First the damned Fleming, now this man telling him how to run his own affairs! 'I have all the proof I need.'

'Then that is fine. But I would suggest you send someone to check. You wouldn't want the bailiff here to demand that the man be freed just for want of one question, would you?

Why not ask at the houses next to his, and at the tavern, in case he dropped in before going home. And then, if you have no objection, I would like to speak to your prisoner.'

Thomas gave his agreement grudgingly and walked to the stables. Shortly afterwards they could hear him bellowing for a groom.

'I suppose you'll want to go back up to the moors later when it's dry?' Simon asked reluctantly.

'It would seem the right thing to do,' Baldwin agreed. He had not yet had a chance to tell his friend about the similarity between the cleric's footprint and the one up on the track, but he did so now.

Simon was dismissive. 'It's probably coincidence. How many men around here have feet the same size?'

In answer, Baldwin set his foot into a patch of dark mud. Grinning, Simon copied him, making his own mark along-side it. The two prints were similar, but there was a significant difference in width. The bailiff shrugged.

'See? I expect if you check the prints of the Fleming and his guard, not to mention the stablemen and gardeners, steward, Thomas, and others, you'll find that they'll all be about the same. That proves nothing.'

'You are probably right – still, it does suggest that two people might have been up there, and that together they might have been responsible for Herbert's death. And for the strangest possible reason, one of them was shod with only one shoe.'

'What I don't understand is why the prints disappeared,' Simon mused.

'Ah, that's the easiest part to explain,' Baldwin said. 'Think about it. Two people walk up that path – they meet the boy, kill him, and drag him to the road; as they walk, the body they are dragging will sweep away all their tracks. What baffles me is where they *then* disappeared to.'

Simon gave him a serious stare. 'You really believe the priest killed Herbert?'

'Not necessarily. Whoever dragged the body back did wipe out Stephen's prints, but that only tells us that the priest didn't go down that path after the body had passed by.'

'And those who dragged it down clearly didn't go back up the hill,' Simon agreed. They were standing at the gate, and they passed through and out to the clitter beyond, each selecting a rock on which to sit.

The bailiff narrowed his eyes and gazed along the road northwards, continuing slowly: 'Why should anyone *want* to hurry back up the hill? It would only lead them to the moor, and that'd be lunacy. There are miles of moor between here and the next household: surely whoever did kill the boy had reason to do so, and that means it was someone who knew him, not some wandering vagabond.'

'Absolutely. The killer was someone from the household, or from Throwleigh. A destitute outlaw will sometimes waylay a man for his purse, but would hardly think a five-year-old worth the risk of a rope. Whoever killed Herbert definitely had a motive.'

'Thomas would say that this farmer, Edmund, had motive enough.'

Baldwin grimaced. 'Yes, he probably would, but I still think Edmund is the least likely suspect. A drunk is rarely capable of killing and concealing his crime.'

'I have known alcoholics commit murder, especially when intoxicated,' Simon pointed out.

'Of course you have, but what we have here is a careful attempt to conceal the murder, to make it look like an accident – and a drunken man would find it hard to do that. For instance, could the farmer have dragged the body so far without leaving some trace to show he was there? A footprint, a . . .' His voice faded as he considered.

Simon picked up a handful of stones and began throwing them at a large black slug at the foot of a rock. 'I wonder how large Thomas's feet are.'

'A good question. Our new squire is the man with the best motive for killing the lad. He wanted the money and estate – he's never made any bones about that. But I also have to wonder about the length and shape of my Lady's feet.'

'Baldwin, for God's sake! Herbert was Lady Katharine's only son!'

'But she blamed him for causing the death of the squire. You didn't see the hatred on her face at her husband's graveside.'

'She's a woman, in Christ's name!'

'Forget chivalry for a moment, Simon, forget courtesy. Lady Katharine is an intelligent woman, one with a long life ahead of her – she can only be some five-and-twenty years old. Any man marrying her would always know that the main part of her dowry would be his only until her son grew to be of age – and any son of his own would be without an inheritance. Tell me, if you were in her shoes, wouldn't you wonder how much better your future prospects would be, without the burden of a readymade son?'

Simon stared aghast. 'You're asking me to believe that she adored her husband, but in the same breath you propose that she killed the only fruit of that union: I say that is unlikely. You suggest that she could not only plan to destroy her own son, but that she could participate in his end: I consider that improbable in the extreme. You then say she might be considering her future with another man, that she is already considering her next husband, yet that would presuppose that a suitable husband would wait for a year so that she could avoid any accusation of infamy for marrying before the end of her period of mourning. That is far too speculative.'

'Perhaps, but it is possible. Look at the way that the Fleming is trying to insinuate himself into her favour.'

'You think he is?' Simon asked doubtfully, then smiled with delight as he hit the slug. It fell from the stone leaving a yellow stain. 'Even if he were, surely it's unlikely that she'd countenance his advances. You can't doubt her feelings about her husband, can you?'

'No-o,' Baldwin agreed. 'No, her misery was all too plain after Roger's death. And yet van Relenghes appears to think he can win her over.'

'I reckon it's more likely that a band of marauding outlaws came past here, murdered the child, went up to the moors and were swallowed up by a mire, than that *she* could have been involved.'

Baldwin gave a grin at his friend's exasperated tone. 'Very well, then, Simon. So we have more to discover about the whole affair.' He looked up to see Nicholas cantering past on a pony, heading for the Throwleigh road. 'It seems Thomas has sent to check on Edmund's hose. Perhaps we should begin by questioning the man whom everyone assumes is guilty.'

*   *   *

When they arrived at the locked door of the small cell beneath the chapel, they found a sulky Wat waiting with Daniel and Thomas. The boy carried a tray of food, Baldwin was relieved to see: at least the farmer wasn't going to be starved while he awaited his appearance in the manor's court. The new lord of the manor said nothing, but gave a sharp gesture, and the steward shoved a massive key into the lock. It made a grinding noise as it turned, but then opened, and the men all entered. Baldwin was last, and when Simon turned, he saw the knight speak quietly to Wat before slipping inside.

The knight found himself in a simple cell some twelve feet square. It was not so terrible as some he had seen – his own little gaol in Crediton was worse, a mere hole in the ground – but this was dark and gloomy. The only light came through a grating high in the wall. To Baldwin the sunlight looked as if it had expended all its energy in breaking in, and having achieved that it was so enfeebled it had no ability to warm.

Edmund was seated on a bench in the corner. A toilet bucket had been provided, and from the stench he had already used it. Baldwin winced. Ever since his time in the Knights Templar, when he had spent many months in the Kingdom of Cyprus, he had appreciated cleanliness and fresh odours. Edmund was quite obviously terrified; he equated his arrest with his death – and not, as Baldwin thought privately, without good reason. It was evident that Thomas viewed him as the perfect scapegoat.

Baldwin took his seat on an old barrel and studied the farmer. Edmund had lost his previous swagger. Now he sat as one crushed by events too monstrous to defy. Every so often he gave a brief shiver, as if the cold had eaten into his bones, and he refused to look at his visitors.

Thomas swung a riding switch, which caught the farmer on his shoulder. He flinched and drew back as the new squire cried, 'Tell us what happened, fool, or you'll get worse than that!'

Simon said curtly, 'We want to know what happened on the day that Master Herbert died, Edmund. Don't worry that you'll get punished if you are innocent. I'll ensure you're safe.'

'Sir, I've done nothing – it wasn't my fault,' Edmund said, and for that moment his voice was strong and clear, but immediately his tone dropped and he began to snivel. 'He was dead when I got there. I didn't do anything that could have hurt him, he was beyond that already.'

'Tell us what happened.'

Edmund sniffed, his attention apparently fixed on his worn-out boots. 'I told you I'd been up to Oakhampton, and after I'd sold what I could, I'd gone to the tavern. God only knows, there wasn't much money, not from the few eggs and chickens I could sell, but I needed something to refresh me. The last few months have been so hard, sir, and what with being told that we were to be evicted, and then that I'm to be servile again . . . well, I needed a drink.

'I was there a while, long enough to swallow two quarts of strong ale, before setting off for home. I came down past the Sticklepath, and out onto the moor road, then cut through the woods to the lane where I could turn off to Throwleigh. That was when I saw Master Thomas on the road, and chose to walk this way instead.'

Simon glanced up at Thomas. The Master of Throwleigh gripped his switch tightly and took a short step forward.

'You dare to try to implicate *me*? By God's blood, I'll see you flayed for this!'

Baldwin took hold of his arm, remonstrating gently. 'There's little point in asking questions if you're going to thrash him when he gives you an answer. All right, Edmund – why did you decide to pass by the manor?'

Edmund looked exhausted. 'I told you the truth before, Sir Baldwin. I found a small cony, and wasn't going to leave it to the rooks, so I picked it up, but when I came to the fork, I saw Master Thomas on the road to Throwleigh, and thought I'd better not go past him; he might realise I had something with me.'

Thomas gave him a filthy look and spat at his foot. 'Liar!'

Simon and Baldwin ignored him. There was a silence for some moments, and then Thomas threw out his hand passionately. 'Look at him! I ask you! What would *I* have been doing down there, eh?' Emboldened by his own rhetoric, Thomas spun round to face Edmund. 'Well? What was I doing, then?'

Edmund sighed, and glanced hopelessly up at the grille in the window far above, paying no heed to Thomas, who hurled his crop away from him and began pacing up and down.

It was not the first time Baldwin had seen such a look on a man's face: it showed complete despair, the realisation that whatever Edmund might attempt, he was already doomed. That look of complete submission to fate was commonplace on the faces of men and women whom Baldwin had been forced to accuse in the past, especially when a Coroner was present and the court could demand the highest penalty; that of death. It invariably meant that the prisoner knew that the forces of authority had already decreed his end. Baldwin knew that he must remove Thomas if they were to discover more.

'You want food?' he asked, and when Edmund gave a surly shrug, he called Wat inside. Wat passed the tray to the prisoner, and then glanced at the knight.

Simon could have sworn that as Wat met his master's eye, Baldwin gave a fleeting wink. Wat nodded, and hurried from the room while Baldwin leaned both elbows on his knees and surveyed the farmer.

For his part, Edmund lifted the jug of ale and sniffed at the contents, then prodded his bread and dipped a finger into the bowl of pottage – but nothing excited his appetite.

'If you don't want to eat, put the tray aside,' Thomas snarled, and was about to kick it away when there came a loud shout from outside. 'What's that?'

Baldwin cocked an ear, an expression of vague surprise on his face. 'It sounds as if someone is calling for you, Thomas. It's all right – you go and we'll remain for a little longer.'

'I'm staying right here.'

Simon grinned broadly, but there was steel in his voice. 'Why's that, Master Thomas? Don't you trust us alone with your prisoner? I shouldn't worry – I am Bailiff for the Stannaries, after all.'

Thomas considered him irresolutely before glancing at Baldwin; he was rapidly coming to the conclusion that he loathed all knights. That damned Fleming had dared to stand against him and continued to pay court to Lady Katharine, and now Sir Baldwin was forcing him away so that Edmund could be questioned without him. This conjecture was reinforced by Thomas's certainty that the voice calling so loudly for him was that of Edgar, Baldwin's servant. 'Of course I trust you, Bailiff,' he growled untruthfully. 'But I'm not happy that a serf of mine should be interrogated in my absence.'

'I assure you I will not harm him,' Baldwin said, in a tone that made Thomas blanch with anger.

Meanwhile Simon had crossed his arms and leaned against the wall well within Thomas's field of vision. He was not close enough for Thomas to consider him threatening, but he was closer than was necessary, or strictly polite.

The knight sighed and held up both hands in a gesture of resignation. 'Do you wish us to leave our questioning and follow you? We may be able to discover something here which could have some bearing on the murder of your nephew, but if you really insist . . .'

'No . . . no, you remain here,' Thomas said, his manners returning at last. Casting a last suspicious glance at Simon, he walked from the room.

Instantly Baldwin was on his feet. He took the tray from the farmer's lap and passed it to Simon. 'Now listen very carefully, Edmund,' he said urgently. You are to be accused of murdering Master Herbert – you understand me? If that happens, you will be tried as a felon, and will almost certainly be found guilty. You comprehend your problem? You are a villein under the court of the Master of Throwleigh—'

'I'm no villein, I'm a free man,' Edmund declared, and there was real anger in his eyes, undimmed by fear of retribution.

It was true, he thought. He was a free man, with a certificate to prove it. His mistress might try to assert that she

219

owned his body, but his father had been given that crucial document by her husband – what right did she have to rescind it?

The response was enough to satisfy Baldwin, and he slapped the farmer's shoulder. 'Then behave like one! Now – did you see Thomas on the road that day?'

'Yes.'

'What was he doing?'

'He was searching for something – I don't know what.'

'Was he on his horse?'

'No, his mare was held by that man of his. Thomas was on his feet, prodding and poking with a stick in among the ferns and furze.'

Baldwin nodded. 'So you took this road, up past the manor?'

'Yes. I didn't want to meet up with that fat bastard again. He's never liked me, and I didn't fancy any more of his insults.'

Daniel stirred himself at last. 'Edmund, you be careful what you—'

'Be quiet, Steward!' Baldwin thundered. 'Hold your tongue or leave this room. I'll not have you prejudicing this man's evidence! Now, Edmund, Thomas wasn't yet your master, was he? You thought that your Lady Katharine was still the executor of Squire Roger's will, and the legal guardian of Master Herbert, didn't you?'

'Yes, sir, but there were rumours.' He leaned back, and his face took on a sneer. 'Like how Master Thomas was keen to be the next squire, like he wasn't happy to find that there was another one, Master Herbert, between him and his inheritance.'

Baldwin heard a gasp and swift intake of breath. Without turning, he knew from the expression on Daniel's face that Thomas was back. He made no sign that he had heard anything, but instead held Edmund's attention. The farmer looked back with a kind of arrogance. He had witnessed Thomas's return, Baldwin realised, and had made his statement with the intention of denouncing his new master.

There was a new courage flashing in his features. Baldwin had heard that some of his comrades, brother Templars, had been the same: they had accepted the most appalling accusations for a period, but when still more hideous allegations were added, they were finally stirred into defiance. Even the most broken, tortured men preferred to declare the truth; those who could have saved themselves by simply pronouncing one single lie chose to damn their tormentors instead.

'Did he see you?'

'Yes, Sir Baldwin. Both did. They looked up as I came near. I saw Master Thomas recognise me. He just stood there, while I took the right-hand fork to avoid him. Never said anything, just watched me until the bend of the road took me out of his sight.'

'What then?'

Edmund's gaze dropped, and Baldwin knew instinctively that this was the core of his evidence.

'I rode on for a few hundred yards, under the shade of the trees, and then came to the open moor again. I saw the other two men, the foreigners . . .'

'He means van Relenghes and his guard,' Daniel murmured.

'. . . and they both stared at me like I was some sort of outlaw or something,' Edmund continued bitterly. 'I'd never seen them before. I was worried; they both looked warlike, and the way they kept their eyes on me, I thought they might attack . . . and then, well . . .'

'The boy?'

'Yes, sir.' His eyes dropped, and his voice fell as if the matter was too grave to be spoken of loudly. 'I felt it more than anything. There was a crack, and the cart gave a sort of jump, and—'

Baldwin interrupted him. 'You saw nothing in the road before you hit him?'

'No, but I was looking over my shoulder. At those men.'

'And you did not hear Master Herbert cry out?'

Edmund shook his head with conviction, and Baldwin tried to envisage the scene in his mind. Having been to the place, it was easier to picture how it might have happened. The farmer, nervous on seeing the brother of his dead lord, rode on quickly, only to find himself confronted with two intimidating strangers a long way from any help. Would it be any wonder that the farmer would keep his eye on them rather more than on the road ahead? The horse could see where the potholes were, and it would be better for Edmund to make sure he was not about to be attacked from behind and robbed. Especially as he was about to pass under that slight bank, Baldwin reminded himself. The bank, only three or so feet high, but standing just at the corner of that curve in the road . . .

'When you had passed, was he on his face or his back?' he asked.

'His back, sir,' whispered Edmund, closing his eyes at the memory. It was a sight he would never be able to forget. 'He looked like my own lad, sir. I thought I'd killed Jordan.' A tear trickled down his face.

The prone figure had been so like his own son, he had scarcely been able to move, so great was his feeling of dread. Then he'd stopped the horse, taken several deep breaths before clambering shakily down from the cart and walking the few paces to the still body. Only then did he recognise who it was.

'I see,' Baldwin said, but he looked puzzled. 'To reiterate: you drove round the corner, out of sight of the two men, and over the child's body. There was no sound of him calling out, so far as you heard – and you definitely found him lying on his back?'

'That's right, sir. As God is my witness.'

'Did you run over his head?' Simon asked.

Edmund shuddered. 'His head? God's teeth, no, sir! The wheel went over his chest. The mud showed that plain enough.'

'Now, Edmund,' Simon continued, 'did you see anyone else on the moor that day?'

'Yes, sir. There was a carter who passed me a while before I got to the fork in the road.'

'That'd be the fishmonger?' Simon asked, glancing back at Daniel. And when the steward shrugged: 'Thomas, send someone to find this itinerant fish-seller and bring him to us as soon as possible.'

'I also saw Petronilla up on the hillside above the stream just before I saw the two men,' Edmund recalled, his face screwed up with concentration.

'The maid?' Simon asked. 'What would she have been doing up there?'

Daniel grunted. 'She often goes up that way to fetch eggs from the ducks. There are several up towards the big pool, and her mistress likes fresh duck-eggs sometimes.'

223

'Anybody else?'

'No,' lied Edmund stoutly.

'The very first question that'll occur to everyone will be, "So why didn't you immediately go to the manor and fetch help"?' Baldwin asked.

Edmund gave him a strange look, as if doubting the grave, dark-featured knight's intelligence. 'Why, sir? Because the manor knows me only too well, and I'd just been told I was to become a villein again. Would you have gone running back to a place where they'd be as likely to string you up as thank you?'

'Why should they?' Baldwin asked quietly.

'Because they'd think I'd run down the boy on purpose, of course! Wouldn't you?'

Baldwin considered him, head on one side. 'No, I wouldn't. You're a fool often enough, you brag about things when you're drunk, I have no doubt, and I can tell that you beat your wife, but as to killing a child for revenge – I doubt it. Especially since . . . How old is your horse?'

'Eh?' The man's face registered his surprise at the sudden question. 'Fifteen, I suppose, but so what?'

'How fast can he haul your cart?'

'I don't know, he gets me from Oakhampton fast enough.'

'Could he overtake a running dog?'

'Well, not with the cart, of course . . .'

'Could he overtake a running boy?'

Thomas thrust himself past Simon and went to stand between Baldwin and the prisoner. 'What in God's name has all this to do with anything? Are you making fun of my hospitality, Sir Knight?'

'*Out of my way*, Thomas!' Baldwin roared. Thomas blenched and fell back before the knight's enraged glare. Baldwin stood, glowering.

'You know perfectly well that this poor fool had nothing to do with the death of your nephew; he couldn't have run down a child on a cart pulled by a broken-down nag. This whole affair is a farce, and you have contrived to have an innocent man arrested – someone who couldn't possibly defend himself. You selected him carefully, didn't you?'

'He might have run over Herbert without the boy seeing him,' Thomas said.

Simon had no idea what the two men were talking about, but two factors weighed heavily with him: he had faith in Baldwin's judgement, and Thomas was showing signs of extreme anxiety.

'You know as well as I do that that's rubbish,' Baldwin said sharply. 'A lad lying on his back, and you suggest that he couldn't see what was coming towards him? Or perhaps you believe that he wished to remain there, and wanted to be run down?'

'Perhaps he was unconscious?' Thomas suggested with a slight frown, as if putting forward a novel new concept.

'Yes, and perhaps he was lying there because someone else had already killed him, eh? Master Thomas, you had your horse with you that afternoon, I believe?'

'Do you dare to suggest that *I*—'

'I suggest you should exercise your brain as to how to release this man without leaving a smear of any sort on his character – and at the earliest possible moment,' said Baldwin, and glanced towards the baffled farmer. 'Edmund,

225

you said the body reminded you of your son. Why was that? Was the boy wearing clothing like young Jordan's?'

The shaken farmer took a moment to consider the question. 'No, sir, it's only that my lad often used to play with Master Herbert. The last time I saw Squire Roger was when he came to complain about my son playing with Master Herbert in the orchard, I remembered Jordan saying he was going to play up at the manor, and automatically thought to myself that it must be him. That was all.'

'Well, all I can say is, I think you ran over a dead boy, farmer. Herbert was dead long before you hit him.'

'He might have been alive,' Thomas protested.

'If he was alive, he was unconscious and unaware of the cart heading towards him, which means the farmer was not responsible. The man who knocked the child down in the first place was responsible. *Wasn't he?*'

CHAPTER TWENTY

'This is becoming more confusing, not less,' fretted Simon as they walked into the bright sunlight again. 'How did you get Edgar to call for Thomas like that?'

'Oh, I had a little word with Wat before we went in. I knew we'd get nothing out of Edmund with Thomas throwing his weight about.'

Simon nodded, and sat on a bench by the hall's door. 'I wish to God this was only a simple accident as we first thought,' he sighed.

'So do I. We know that Thomas, the man who stood to gain most by Herbert's death, was in the area when the child was murdered. I have no affection for that poor, stupid farmer, but I think we can allow him the benefit of the doubt. If he lied, Thomas would have corrected him, but he didn't, which tends to make me believe Edmund's story.'

'So the child was already unconscious when he was run over,' Simon murmured.

'Alas, I fear that Herbert was in fact dead before Edmund ran over his body,' Baldwin said gravely. 'I am very suspicious of the head wounds found on the corpse. The bones at the back of his skull were shattered, which was surely not done by accident.'

'Someone wanted to make sure of the boy's death, I suppose.'

'Perhaps,' Baldwin said slowly. 'Someone who wanted to kill and then cover up the evidence – by making it look like an accident. That was why Herbert was placed on the road. I am certain that whoever killed the boy did it up on the hill, and then dragged the body down to the road. It is possible that his attacker was a man with only one shoe, who may have had an accomplice – a woman. And now we find that Thomas and his man were both in the area, as were the Fleming and his man. *And* Edmund said he saw Petronilla. We know the murderer or murderers didn't go back up the hill towards the moors, because we couldn't find any tracks. That may mean that they simply walked home along the road – which suggests they came from the hall itself.'

'That's the most sensible conclusion,' Simon said thoughtfully.

'And yet any guest wearing only one shoe would be remarked, would he not?' Baldwin frowned. 'Take Thomas as an example. If he came back here with one shoe only, people would comment.'

'Perhaps he lost it but then found it again before returning home.'

'You suggest that he lost it, chased up the hill, struck down the boy, dragged the body to the road, dumped it, then went all the way back to where he lost his shoe . . . A strange sequence of events!'

Simon had a sudden flash of inspiration. 'But what about the sling in the mud, if it *was* Herbert's!' he exclaimed. 'What do boys always do with slings?'

Baldwin gave him an appreciative smile. 'They fire at any target they like – especially people they *dis*like – and especially if they feel secure from retaliation, as the son of a squire would.'

'Herbert could have fired at Thomas or his horse; the horse bolted, and somehow the fellow lost his shoe. When he could, he took his horse back to the slope, found his attacker, struck out in rage, and realised too late that he'd killed him. He pulled the boy all the way back to the road, left him, and then had to go and find his shoe again.' Simon nodded contentedly. 'I think that covers all the facts.'

'Brilliant, my friend. Quite ingenious. Except – I hardly like to mention . . .'

'Come on – tell me.'

'What of the small prints, the ones we thought were a woman's? And what was the priest searching for today? Why did we find no sign of a horse's hoofprints near the trail through the undergrowth? Oh, and why did Herbert's head have that spectacular damage?'

'As to the last, perhaps Thomas hit him with a rock.'

'No, Simon.' Baldwin shook his head with an affectionate tolerance. 'We are not quite at the truth of the matter yet.'

But as he stared out over the vast hill behind the hall, Baldwin was aware of a sense that he was gradually advancing towards the truth – and when he got there, he would bring the murderer to justice.

*   *   *

The little procession was ready to leave for Throwleigh as the sun began to fall, heralding the onset of the long twilight. Baldwin had expected that the mourners would be riding to the church, but to his surprise the people gathered in the yard were all on foot.

On its bier, the body wrapped in its white shroud looked even smaller than Baldwin remembered. Four well-built young farmworkers had been instructed to carry the child to church, and they all stood quietly respectful, knowing that they might not receive the money promised if they were to misbehave. Thomas and Katharine were dressed in their best clothes, the lady with a dark veil to cover her face, and all the servants and guests were suitably sombre as the cortège got under way, the priest moving off before the dead boy, murmuring a dirgeful chant, his eyes downcast, as he slowly paced through the gate and out into the roadway.

Baldwin, Simon and their wives walked close behind Thomas and his sister-in-law. Thomas appeared nervous of the bailiff and knight, stunned with a personal misfortune that had nothing to do with his nephew's funeral. Baldwin would never wish to prematurely convict a man or make any false assumptions as to his guilt, but after all he had heard, he was growing ever more suspicious about the dead squire's brother. Thomas clearly stood to gain most by the death of Master Herbert; he was nearby at about the time the boy had been killed; he could quite easily have struck his nephew down and left him in the road.

And yet Baldwin was not convinced. He chewed his moustache, recalling what Edmund had said: that his son Jordan had been playing with Herbert that afternoon, and suddenly a whole new series of fascinating speculations arose in his mind.

If there had been *two* children there that afternoon, Herbert's friend might well have seen him being attacked by Thomas. Then Thomas would inevitably have tried to catch the other, to silence him. And if he was unable to lay hands on Jordan, what a perfect trap to lay for the boy's father instead!

But that was impossible, Baldwin realised. There was no way that Thomas could have realised that Edmund would be the next rider on the road; that would presuppose that Thomas enjoyed the protection of an ally – someone who would wait with Herbert's body, and as soon as he saw Edmund rattling along on his cart, could drop down into the road and position the corpse ready for the 'accident'.

Then he considered Nicholas. The steward had been there too, according to Edmund. How large were *his* feet? It was an intriguing notion, and Baldwin pondered it a while before moving on to another suspect: James van Relenghes. What had the Fleming been doing out on the moors that day with his guard, Godfrey? He would definitely have to speak to the two men.

Now, the party of mourners were already dropping down the gentle slope that led to Throwleigh itself, and soon the massive bulk of the church ahead became visible.

Simon and his wife were fully aware of the solemnity of the occasion, having buried their own young son only two years before. Poor Peterkin had been struck down over the space of a few hours, and from being a strong, pink, healthy boy-child, had suddenly become a sickly, squalling baby in the throes of fever and convulsions. His death had been quick, once the disease had taken hold, but Margaret and Simon had never really got over it, and now Simon sought his wife's hand and gripped it. She looked up at him and he could see the tears in her eyes, but she gave him a brave smile and squeezed his hand.

The service was no different from any other, and for Simon it went past in a meaningless series of tableaux: the incense wafting greasily as they entered the church; the boy lying now on the hearse, covered with its pall; the candles lighted, just as they had been for Herbert's father only a few days before; the priest with his mournful voice intoning the words of the service of Evensong, beginning with the *Placebo*. Simon bowed his head and said his own prayers for the soul of the boy, and as he did so, he asked for the continued protection of their poor dead Peterkin. He heard Margaret sob quietly, which brought the prickling of tears to his own eyes.

All too soon it was over. The priest left to see to the mourners, for quite a large number were to be paid to sit up with the corpse overnight; all the poorest of the vill had offered themselves for the vigil. There was often good money to be earned by staying at the side of a corpse during its last service in church.

Lady Katharine remained outwardly calm throughout the *Placebo*, but as soon as she was touched on the arm by Thomas to indicate that it was time to return home, she recoiled, and then began to shake her head convulsively, as if in desperate denial of her son's death.

Thomas's face went red with embarrassment. He was nonplussed in the presence of such despair, unsure how to react. As he reached to help her up from the pew, she gave a high, keening wail, and in her disordered state of mind struck at him, in the process knocking her hat from her head. Thomas was transfixed at the sight of her hysterical face, wide-eyed with horror and revulsion as she slapped at him.

And then she screamed: 'Murderer! Murderer! You killed him, didn't you? You killed my son to win our estate!'

Hugh puffed and blew as he rolled on to the heavy barrel into the buttery. Once there, he hoisted it on the table and wedged it. Taking the heavy mallet, he held the tap over the bung, pausing while he worked up the courage for the one, solid blow. Then he brought the mallet down swiftly and slammed the tap into the barrel, losing not a drop of wine.

Satisfied, he used a blunted bodkin to knock the spile out of the top of the barrel so that the wine could flow, and then, determined to ensure that the wine was of a good enough quality for the funeral party on their return, he most assiduously tested three cups in rapid succession.

Wat entered as he was emptying the last. 'Hugh, Edgar wants your help with setting out the tables in the hall.'

'Shouldn't Petronilla be doing that?' demanded Hugh and belched loudly. He gave a long, satisfied sigh. 'Aah! That's good wine.'

Wat looked from him to the barrel, and moved imperceptibly towards it. Instantly Hugh slammed a fresh spile in place to stop the wine flowing, and glared at the boy.

'Do you remember how you were on Sir Baldwin's wedding day? Eh?'

'That wasn't my fault! I just had a bit too much strong ale. I'm so thirsty, Hugh, can't I just have a small drop of—'

'No, you can't. You've had enough today already. Think what your master would say if we found you asleep under the barrels again. God's teeth! You're hardly ever sober these days.'

'But I'm thirsty!'

'The trough is outside,' Hugh stated implacably.

'Shouldn't you go and help Edgar?'

Hugh eyed him suspiciously. He credited the lad with the same deviousness as he had himself exercised when he was a young whipper-snapper and wished for wine. 'Why should he want me? Hasn't he got enough others to help him?'

'Like who? They're all at the funeral,' Wat said, sulkily surveying the barrels arrayed in their neat lines at the wall.

'What about Petronilla and the other serving girls?'

'She's gone off somewhere. Don't know where.'

'Well, maybe you could find her. And if you manage it quickly,' Hugh's voice dropped conspiratorially, 'you'll get a pint of something to warm you later, all right?'

With a happy grin, Wat nodded and shot through the door. Hugh sighed and patted the barrel regretfully before making his way out to the hall.

Wat tried shouting for Petronilla at the door to Lady Katharine's solar, but there was no answer. Outside in the yard he stopped, wondering where to search first. The orchard held the demesne's main flock, and it was possible that the maid was there, milking ewes, or she might be in the byre collecting the cows' milk – but then she might have completed both tasks and now be in the dairy, or maybe the kitchen. Choosing the dairy as the most likely place, he scampered off to the little building at the side of the byre, next to the stable.

He searched through all the farm buildings, and found no sign of the girl. In the dairy the cows were lowing mournfully; all, he noticed, had full udders. Obviously Petronilla hadn't been here yet. At the kitchen there was a shriek from the harassed cook telling him to clear off or he would get such a clout over the head he'd see stars at noon-time. It was as Wat left the orchard, glancing up towards the moors, that he saw her at last. She was hurrying back from the direction of the common where poor Herbert had been killed.

Wat tutted to himself after wasting so much time, and trotted to the gate to intercept her.

He was waiting patiently as she approached. 'Miss, the servants are in the hall, and would like your help to set out the tables for the party.'

Her face, he saw, was troubled, and she looked at him as though she didn't recognise him. 'The servants? Oh, they'll be setting out the hall, of course.'

'Edgar wasn't sure where your mistress would like the tables set,' Wat said helpfully.

'I can show him. Oh, but the cattle,' she said distractedly, and struck her forehead with her hand. 'I haven't milked them yet.'

'Miss? Miss, your hand's all dirty.'

She glanced down, and automatically wiped her hands on her apron. Her face was full of confusion. She kept glancing back the way she had come, then at the hall, then the byre, with a look so filled with worry that Wat felt quite anxious for her.

'Miss Petronilla, don't worry,' he said with a mature deci-sion. 'You go and rinse your hands in the trough, and I shall milk the cows.'

'Can you?'

235

Her evident gratitude made him swagger as he led the way through the gate. 'I'm the son of Sir Baldwin's cattleman; I was almost born in a byre,' he boasted, then reflected a moment. 'In fact, my mother said I should have been born in the pigsty, but I think she meant the byre.'

Petronilla gave a laugh and ruffled his hair. 'Oh Wat, you make me laugh, you clot! If you're sure, then I'd be very thankful if you could milk the cows and let them out to the field. It would give me some time to help your master's servant. Do that for me and I'll give you a pint of my mistress's best ale.'

He nodded happily and scuttled off, and Petronilla went hastily to the trough to wash, carefully scooping water over her face and rubbing away any sign of the peat from the moors.

She didn't want anyone to realise where she had been.

CHAPTER TWENTY-ONE

The mourners stood in a huddle at the church porch, united by their sense of guilt, as if their unintentional witnessing of the sudden lunacy of the lady of the manor conferred some form of complicity upon them. Jeanne and Margaret had gone to Katharine and sent Thomas packing into the churchyard. Now he stood in a corner at some distance from everyone else, staring out over the fields towards the manor house itself, lost in thought.

That look of hatred on his sister-in-law's face had shaken him to the core. Her features had been twisted with emotion so that she was almost unrecognisable. The recollection made him shudder.

He felt the weight of people's eyes on him, and their silent wonder. No one could have missed Katharine's words. In the secret fastness of his mind, he cursed her, the *bitch*, for denouncing him like that before all the others.

'Thomas?'

'Oh, it's you,' the fat man spat. 'I should've guessed you'd want to question me again, Sir Baldwin. I suppose you want to accuse me of Herbert's murder now, is that right?'

'Hardly. I wanted to make quite sure that you were all right,' Baldwin said gently. 'It must have been a great shock.'

Thomas gave him a searching look. The knight did have a quietly compassionate look about him. Feeling slightly mollified, the other gave a grunt. 'What does it matter? I am perfectly fine. The stupid bitch doesn't realise what a help I have been to her, but there's nothing new in a woman not appreciating a man's assistance.'

'Do you have any idea why she should have made such an accusation?' Baldwin probed. 'She had been fine until just now – why should she suddenly turn on you like that?'

'Damned woman. I wish I knew,' Thomas sighed. 'God's blood! Why did she have to have her fit in there – in public? The rumour of it will be all over Throwleigh and up as far as Oakhampton by morning, for God's sake. Christ's bones! It'll be all the news in Exeter by tomorrow night. What have I done to deserve this?'

'She must have heard something from someone,' said Simon. He had walked up quietly while the two were talking. 'Somebody must have made some allegation about you. Why else should she come out with this?'

'You could be right, Simon,' Baldwin said, and threw a glance over his shoulder at the crowd waiting near the door. Most of them were the people from the procession from the house: van Relenghes and Godfrey, Daniel, the four labourers who had acted as pall-bearers, and some of the poor who had been hoping for money. 'But when could they have spoken to her?'

Thomas sneered. 'Those two were alone with her almost all morning, and most of the afternoon. No doubt it suits Sir James to slander me to her, the bastard! I'll get even with him, somehow. I don't care how long it takes me, but I'll make him regret saying things about me behind my back.'

'What could he have said?' Baldwin asked mildly.

Thomas shot him a look. 'Never you mind, Sir Baldwin! Just remember this, that slimy bastard is after one thing, and one thing only: *her*! He says he was a friend of my brother's, yet none of the people here ever heard Roger mention him.'

'You think he is an impostor?'

'What do *you* think?'

'Did you see him up on the moors when Herbert was killed?'

'Oh, for God's sake! Why must you keep asking me about that!' Thomas cried, thrusting his arms out on either side as if in despair. Then, as though accepting that the knight had little choice after the display in the church: 'Oh, very well – what do you want to know?'

'Was van Relenghes out on the moor when you were up there and saw Edmund ride by?'

'Yes. I passed him when I was on my way out. He was there on horseback with that damned guard of his.'

'Where were you going?'

'I had seen Stephen walking off that way and I was looking for him,' Thomas lied. He didn't dare admit to the true reason for his journey out to the moor that day, not after the display in the church. 'I wanted to ask him some questions. He was always my brother's secretary and clerk, and after Roger's death I had been looking into his affairs to help my sister-in-law. There were some matters I wanted to check up on – things Daniel had been involved with.'

'What sort of things?' Simon asked.

'The man has been a trusted servant for many years, and I am sure he is honest, but some monies appear to have been mislaid. Daniel is the steward, and he was given the cash, according to the manor's beadle, but the cash seems to have disappeared. I wanted to ask Stephen about it.' Thomas shrugged, hoping they would swallow the story.

'A difficult question to ask such a longstanding servant,' Baldwin agreed, ignoring the obvious lie.

Simon nodded thoughtfully. 'But we've heard from Edmund that you were attacking the ferns. What were you doing?'

Thomas's face reddened and he forgot to dissemble. 'I'll tell you what I was doing! I was looking for the little bastard who'd lobbed a stone at me. I'd missed Stephen, and gave a good day to the Fleming and his man as I passed them, but nothing more than that, nothing more than common politeness required. Anyway, I rode as far as the road to Throwleigh, and decided to take that way back so as to avoid meeting the Fleming again. And, since I hadn't seen Stephen on the top road, I thought he might have walked back towards the church, but I had only gone a matter of a few yards when someone shot a stone at me and hit my arse. When Edmund saw me, I was trying to find the little sod.'

'Do you know what van Relenghes and his man were doing up there?' Baldwin asked.

'Oh, I think they were merely getting a breath of air.' His face took on a shrewd, keen expression. 'Why – do you think they might have had something to do with Herbert's death, then?'

Baldwin refrained from commenting, but thanked Thomas just as the chattering of the people before the porch was suddenly stilled.

Lady Katharine came out, assisted by Jeanne and Margaret. The crowd was struck dumb by her tragic appearance. Quietly the congregation parted to allow her to pass, and the three women moved down the line, Katharine with her head bowed, stumbling slightly as if she was unconscious of the lumps and bumps in the path. Margaret caught Simon's eye as the bailiff moved forward to assist, and gave him a faint shake of her head. He remained where he was, grateful to be relieved of the duty of aiding the woman in her grief – and wondering what could have ignited her misery. He could only assume that seeing her son's little body on the hearse had made her reason falter.

Van Relenghes and his man strode along behind as if prepared to guard Lady Katharine from any importunate guests.

One man did not hold back. As the three women passed, Daniel, the steward of Squire Roger's household for many years before Lady Katharine had arrived, stepped forward, and ignoring Margaret and Jeanne's quick frowns, he took his lady's arm. She glanced up at him once, and then seemed almost to melt into his embrace, grateful for a face she could recognise even through her misery.

Simon felt the pain of her suffering, but knew he could do nothing to help her. He glanced at his friend, but Baldwin wasn't watching Lady Katharine. As she passed by, his attention was fixed with a terrible concentration on the face of the Fleming.

James van Relenghes was watching Daniel with an expression of deep animosity, almost as if he was preparing to draw his knife and strike the steward down there and then.

Simon's eyes went automatically to Daniel and his lady. With his arm about her shoulder, holding her hand in his, resolutely keeping his attention fixed on the road before him and ignoring all about them, Daniel helped Lady Katharine back towards the manor.

Hugh upended his pot and held it out to Petronilla, belching softly. 'Thanks,' he said gruffly.

Petronilla chuckled to herself. She was comfortable in his company. Hugh was the sort of man she liked, strong and stolid, not the kind who would try to take liberties either, she thought with an angry toss of her head as she recalled that damned Nicholas. If he tried those tricks again, she would teach him a lesson he would never forget.

'It's good ale,' Hugh said, giving her an approving nod. 'Did you make it yourself?'

'Yes. I help with the brewing.'

'You do it well.'

She smiled, and at that moment Wat returned, happily announcing that the cows were all milked and the milk was in the dairy with the maid in charge.

'What have you been doing all that for?' Hugh asked.

'To help me,' Petronilla told him, and filled a good-sized pot with ale, handing it to the boy.

'Thanks,' he said, sitting and taking a goodly gulp. 'Ah! That's better.'

'Don't go drinking too much tonight,' Hugh grumbled. 'You know what strong ale does to you.'

'Oh, I'm all right usually. It's only when I have a bit too much . . .'

'You *always* have a bit too much – and then you snore and puke,' Hugh said.

'Well, after all he's done for me today, I don't mind,' Petronilla said with decision. 'He can sleep in here if he wishes, and if he's sick, I will clean up after him.'

'Don't encourage him,' said Hugh. 'He could vomit in his sleep and choke.'

'Well, you could stay here with him, Hugh.'

Petronilla was content with Hugh's company. Not because she felt any lust towards him – if anything, she felt the opposite – but she did understand him, and the fact that he seemed happy to sit with her in the buttery was a comfort. The pair found that they had quite a bit in common. She had been raised in Moretonhampstead, while he hailed from Drewsteignton; she had been daughter to a gooseherd, he was the son of a shepherd; she had been taken on by her master, Squire Roger, when she was sixteen, he by his first master when he was only fifteen.

It would be good to have Hugh sleeping here in the buttery – and if it caused talk, she didn't mind. Not now – in fact, it could be a useful diversion for gossips.

Wat held out his empty cup hopefully, and Petronilla refilled it. The lad was feeling on top of the world. This manor was very different from Sir Baldwin's household, but he liked the people here. Especially Petronilla. She was kind towards him, and he was aware of a moderately amorous attraction. To an extent, he was jealous of Hugh, who could sit back and listen while she prattled. Wat wanted her to talk to *him*, and it was to gain her attention that he cleared his throat and said, 'What were you doing up on the moors, Petronilla? Had you fallen over?'

She flushed. 'Fallen? Why, no, Wat. Why should you think that?'

'Because your hands were all dirty with mud. I just thought you must have tripped.'

Petronilla shot him a look, but the boy's face was innocence itself. Making a comment about the slipperiness of the moors, she added in an undertone to Hugh: 'The truth is, I had to get away for a while,' and told him about Nicholas's advances.

'So what did he actually say to you?' Hugh asked, his brow wrinkled with concentration.

'He offered me a coin to sleep with him. And put his hand here,' she said, touching her right breast.

'If he tries it again, you tell me or my master. We'll protect you. That foreign bastard can't go around assuming Devon girls are the same as his over there,' said Hugh stoutly.

'Thank you, Hugh,' she said gratefully, and tears sprang into her eyes again. It was so consoling to be able to share her problem with someone who would actually exert himself on her behalf to help and protect her.

Unlike her lover.

CHAPTER TWENTY-TWO

Sir Baldwin was determined to question the Fleming as soon as possible. The hospitality at Throwleigh was adequate, certainly, but unremarkable – which was quite understandable, given the recent tragic events – and yet van Relenghes seemed determined to remain even though the atmosphere should have been painful to anyone with a sense of courtesy. Baldwin was sure that the man had some ulterior motive, but he couldn't see what that motive might be. Unconsciously, he began walking faster as the mourners headed back to Throwleigh Manor, and soon drew level with Sir James. Simon, seeing the direction his feet were taking him in, smiled grimly to himself and increased his own speed to match the knight's.

'Sir,' Baldwin said, smiling in a friendly manner. 'Could I speak to you for a few minutes while we return to the manor?'

Godfrey glanced at his master. Van Relenghes scarcely acknowledged the knight, but nodded as Baldwin and his friend came level. Godfrey fell back a short distance, not from politeness to give them privacy, but to give himself room to unsheath his sword. He had no reason to distrust the knight, but he knew his place: he was paid to protect his master.

It was the knight who began. 'It is a pleasant part of Devonshire, this.'

Van Relenghes gave a dry chuckle. 'There are worse parts?'

'You should see the middle of the moors,' said Simon with feeling.

'If it is more desolate there than here, I have no wish to.'

'But you enjoy taking in the views, don't you?' Baldwin said. 'Like on the day poor Master Herbert died.'

Van Relenghes stiffened. 'What do you mean by that?'

'Nothing, sir. But I heard you were out on the moors that day. Was I wrongly informed?'

'No, I was there.' To Godfrey's ear his master's voice carried a faint trace of anxiety; only a hint, not enough for anyone to have noticed who didn't know the Fleming. 'But I do not like my movements to be tracked in this way. Why do you question people about me?'

'It is hardly surprising, is it, when a child of rank is murdered?'

'Do you suppose I had something to do with his death?'

Godfrey allowed himself to relax, taking his hand from his belt and flexing the fingers. His master sounded amused, nothing more.

'I would hardly think that without very convincing evidence. But I would be very glad to hear what you saw out there that day. I know that Thomas was in the area. Did you see him?'

'Oh, yes. The fellow rode past us once with that servant of his. He gave us a good day, and stopped to speak to us. After a while he carried on. We didn't see him again after that.'

'What did he want to talk about?'

Van Relenghes smiled beguilingly. 'I am not sure that I should tell you, Sir Baldwin. But lest you think the man is honourable, let me say that he was prepared to take my money in exchange for his promise to persuade his sister-in-law to sell me a portion of the estate. He made this offer to me in front of my servant here.'

Baldwin and Simon exchanged a glance. The bailiff could see that his friend was unsure how to proceed, and said, 'Did you and he agree on a deal?'

'Agree?' Van Relenghes frowned sternly at Simon. 'God's blood, no, Bailiff! Would you expect a soldier to try to deprive his comrade's widow of her livelihood? Of course not. I was disgusted by Thomas's bad faith and turned him down flat. He rode off in a passion – absolutely furious, he was.'

'Why should he have thought you would be interested in such a deal, I wonder?' Baldwin murmured.

'How can I tell?' van Relenghes shot back. 'All I know is that he is hard up for money. He speculated and lost, and now he needs cash badly.'

'You learned this before coming here?' Baldwin asked, surprised.

Van Relenghes spoke frankly. 'I heard of this man while in Exeter, and yes, I checked into his background. I wanted to know whether he was the brother of my old comrade. But I fear that when you ask for information, sometimes you are given more than you wish to hear.'

'Was there anyone else on the road that day?'

'We saw that drunken farmer, of course.'

Godfrey smiled. The man had been so obviously the worse for drink that he and his master had laughed uproariously once Edmund had passed them, sitting uncomfortably on his board, his eyes wide and fearful at seeing two such men out in the middle of nowhere. His fear was all too plain, and although he tried to be surreptitious about it, they could see him peering blearily over his shoulder at them as his cart creaked round the curve in the road. A thought suddenly struck Godfrey.

'Master, there was the other cart, the one with the fishman coming back from the manor,' he put in. 'He passed us a short while before the farmer, going the other way.'

'That must be the fish-seller Daniel mentioned,' Simon said.

'Yes, I'd forgotten him,' the Fleming said languidly.

'How did he look?' Simon pressed.

'Look?' asked van Relenghes. 'What sort of a question is that?'

'Was he scared? Alarmed? Upset?'

'I hardly know what some villein might look like while alarmed,' van Relenghes said dismissively.

'He was fine, sir,' Godfrey said. 'He came past us at a slow walk, whistling happily enough, gave us a good day, and carried on.'

'You see my reasoning, Baldwin?' said Simon, facing his friend. 'If he'd just ridden past – or over! – Herbert's body, he'd have shown it, wouldn't he? But he came by and greeted these gentlemen as if nothing had happened. I'd bet Herbert's body was put in the road *after* the fishmonger had passed by.'

Baldwin nodded, then: 'Did you *hear* anything as he approached, or perhaps after he'd gone past?'

'Such as?'

Baldwin's face hardened. 'A boy screaming, for example.'

Van Relenghes shook his head. 'I had other matters to consider at the time. The last thing on my mind was whether some fool of a farmer might take it into his head to kill my comrade's son.'

'Did you visit him often?'

The Fleming shook his head sadly. 'I fear not. I would have, but I have only recently come to this country. Until a few weeks ago I was serving in the castle in Bordeaux. Otherwise I would have been here before. Especially if I had known my old friend had so charming a wife!'

His eyes were narrowed with amusement. It was intolerable that a man should make such a comment about a woman who had been bereaved for so short a time. Even a friend and comrade shouldn't joke of such a thing. It smacked of impropriety.

Baldwin continued as if he hadn't noticed. 'You chose to come here to pay your respects after Squire Roger died.'

'When I heard what had happened, I thought it was only right that I should come and offer what comfort I could to his widow.'

'Where were you when you heard of his death?' Simon pressed.

'In Exeter,' van Relenghes admitted coolly.

'Ah, yes – Exeter. A place only a single hard ride from here, by coincidence. And it was by similar good fortune that you were here when the squire's son was killed.'

Godfrey could see van Relenghes growing edgy. Whether it was irritation at being questioned or nervousness at the line the questions were taking, the master of arms wasn't sure, and he listened with interest.

'Where did you fight?'

Van Relenghes waved a hand irritably. He felt as though the bailiff was studying him suspiciously, and tried to force an easiness into his manner. 'All over. We fought in Wales and Scotland for your King, spent time together in Flanders with—'

'If you'll pardon my saying so, you're a lot younger than the squire.'

'Only a little. He was almost fifty, and I am over forty.'

'He looked a lot older,' Simon said, and Godfrey thought he could detect a trace of sadness, as if for a friend who has died too early.

'He always looked old. He could behave like an old man as well.'

'In what way?'

Van Relenghes regretted his lapse and swore to himself. For a man discussing a friend who had only just died, it was scornful in the extreme. He quickly tried to change the tone from insult to praise.

'Oh, he was a stickler for discipline among the men-at-arms, would stop any nonsense with women and other camp-followers, that kind of thing. He was known to be harsh with soldiers who misbehaved or disobeyed his orders – but that's needed in an army. If your King had had more men like Roger, his armies would have conquered even faster.'

'Oh, I see,' Simon said, and Godfrey felt a grudging admiration for his master. He appeared to have lulled the bailiff.

The knight was silent for a while, walking along thoughtfully. 'You are quite sure you didn't hear the sound of a boy screaming or anything at all after the cart passed you?'

'No, there was nothing.'

'There was a cry, master,' said Godfrey, unable to withhold his evidence.

'What was that, Godfrey?' Baldwin asked.

'Before the cart came past us, sir. In fact, just after Thomas went off, I heard something upstream.'

'Whereabouts would this have been, exactly?'

'At the road there, where we were, is a small bridge, and up the hill I could swear I heard a shout. I don't know if it was a man, woman or child, but it was quite distinct to me.'

'You didn't hear this?' Baldwin demanded of the Fleming. Van Relenghes shook his head with mystification. 'If I had heard it I would have told you,' he said simply.

Baldwin glanced at Simon. 'That must be up the track, up near the side of the stream.'

'Yes,' Godfrey offered. 'Where the priest had been.'

'You saw *Stephen* up there?' Simon asked.

Van Relenghes interrupted before his guard could answer. 'Oh, yes. We saw *him*. We were talking, and as we looked up the hill, there he was, near the brow. When he saw us, he disappeared.'

Baldwin was decided at last. Stephen might be a priest with all the privileges his position entailed, but there were too many questions over his movements on the day Herbert died.

'I think we shall need to speak to this disappearing priest,' he said.

*   *   *

251

Their arrival was a sombre event. There were cold meats and salad vegetables laid out on a great trestle in the hall, the leaves slowly wilting in the warmth of the fire, but most people ignored the food, apart from Thomas, who appeared to have a healthy appetite.

Baldwin led his wife to a seat near the fire, taking two pots of wine from his servant and watching the other guests while Petronilla and Hugh served wine and ale to them.

'Is all well?' he asked.

Edgar gave him a short nod. 'Fine.'

'Where is Wat? He should be helping you.'

'Wat is asleep.'

'Wake him.'

'*Very* asleep.'

Baldwin groaned. 'You didn't let him near the buttery? Edgar, for the love of Christ, haven't you learned about him yet? You know how he was at our wedding!'

'Sir, I was assisting the cook in the kitchen. Wat was with Hugh, and I think he thought it would be amusing to test Wat's resolve.'

'God's blood!'

Jeanne stirred and gave Edgar a warm smile. 'Thank Hugh, would you? And tell him I shall remember his kindness to my servant boy at the *very first* opportunity.'

Edgar flashed her a grin and disappeared to serve another.

Jeanne shook her head. 'I think that man of Simon's has a rather unkind streak in him. He appears to enjoy ensuring that Wat feels miserable each morning.'

Her husband grunted, but his attention was taken by the priest, who had just entered. Baldwin knew he had stayed with the mourners who had been paid to keep the vigil, and would only now have managed to return.

Stephen of York stood at the doorway, and when he met Baldwin's eye, instantly looked away and licked his lips. After a moment's hesitation, he disappeared. Baldwin sipped at his wine. He could swear that the priest was scared of him. And it was clear enough that the man had been out on the hill where young Herbert had been killed.

The knight found himself looking forward to questioning the priest with a keen anticipation.

Petronilla hurried back to the buttery, and seeing Stephen sitting blankly on a stool, fell onto a barrel with a gasp.

'I couldn't face speaking to him,' Stephen said heavily. 'He knows. I'm sure he knows.'

Her brow wrinkled with worry. 'They can't know. No one saw us.'

'When I hit the boy, he screamed, and that bastard guard of the Fleming's saw me, I'm convinced of it.'

'If he was so certain, the bailiff would have arrested us.'

'It's the knight I fear. He's the clever one, the one people say can see inside a man's soul through his eyes.'

'Well, you're safe, anyway, Stephen. All they can do is force you to abjure the realm.'

He flinched at that. It was a hideous thought, having to run from all this. He hadn't ever dreamed that so soon he might be returning abroad, exiled for life, never to see his birthplace again. That was what abjuring involved: giving the oath to the Coroner at the church's gate, promising to leave the country by whatever road the Coroner selected, dressed as a penitent carrying a cross, and if an abjurer left the road for any reason whatever, his life was forfeit: he could be beheaded on the spot.

Benefit of clergy meant he wouldn't be executed, though, and that was something. Petronilla didn't have the same protection. Stephen patted her hand. 'Don't fear. You will be safe enough. Once they have me, they won't bother with you.'

She gave him an anxious look from the corner of her eye. 'I have done nothing to make me fear the rope. It's not that which worries at me. It's that man Nicholas.' It hadn't been possible to tell the priest before, but now she burst out with the sordid story. 'He grabbed me, *here*!' she cried, and her tears glistened as she remembered the scene. 'And now whenever I pass him, he leers at me.'

Stephen felt a rush of affection for her sweep through him. He took her hand and held it to his breast, and she saw the kindly smile touch his eyes. She bent her head and allowed him to gently kiss her hair. 'Be easy, child. You shall be safe; I shall see to it.'

'Safe from who?' Hugh demanded, marching into the buttery with two empty jugs of wine, and overhearing the priest's final words. Although he habitually wore a scowl, beneath it Hugh had a generous soul and a soft-natured heart, and he had taken a liking to this poor young girl.

The priest gave him a rather measuring look. 'My son, there are some men who insist on taking advantage of women, whether the women wish to comply or not.'

Hugh's dour features visibly darkened. 'Has that hench-man tried to muck about with you again?' he asked Petronilla.

She gave a sour laugh. 'No – since I've kept well out of his way.'

Stephen looked serious. 'You mustn't do anything against him, Hugh. You'll only get yourself into trouble. Leave him alone, but tell me if he tries something again so that I may rescue this poor girl.'

Hugh nodded. In silence he refilled his jugs and left the buttery to rejoin the guests in the hall.

But Stephen sat a while longer, holding Petronilla's hand in his own and staring at the ground as if on it were written the answers to all his confusions.

CHAPTER TWENTY-THREE

In his home at Throwleigh, Jordan sat quietly in the corner of the room, his dark eyes never leaving the rocking form of his mother.

Christiana sat before the little fire, her daughter Molly cuddled on her lap, her figure casting a terrible, crone-shaped shadow against the far wall. It looked like a witch, swaying from side to side as she cast a spell of doom on them, waiting to leap upon the family and bring disaster to them all.

And the disaster had happened. There was no protection for a family that had no means of support, and if his father was thought to have killed Herbert, he was guilty of treason. Jordan wasn't sure, but he thought his father could be burned alive for that. It was as vile an act as could be envisaged: it was still more wicked than 'petty treason', the murder by a wife of her spouse. Everyone knew that Edmund's manumission, his formal release from serfdom, had been revoked by Lady Katharine, and it followed that everyone would believe that he had killed her son in revenge. He could expect no mercy.

Jordan felt the sobs rising in his throat once more, and sniffed hard to quell them, wrapping himself tighter in his blanket. The fire was low, but they had little wood left to burn, and it was very chill at this time of night. It was normal for Jordan to shiver himself to sleep throughout the winter and well into spring, and if it was too cold even for that, he would climb into the bed with his parents and sister. Now, with the house silent in the absence of his father, he wanted to cuddle up with his mother. He felt a hole in his very soul at the sight of her misery, and longed to ease her fear, and make things better – but he didn't have the words. Somehow he knew that only another adult could do that.

He was hungry, but dared make no demand for food. There was none to be had, and asking for it would only set his mother off again into another frenzy of rage at her useless husband.

And it was all because his father had been arrested for running over Master Herbert, Jordan knew. His father – arrested, and for something *Jordan knew he couldn't have done*. Fortunately, he and his friend had the thing that could demonstrate the priest's guilt, and now he decided that there was no time to lose. He must go with Alan to see the knight, the man everyone said was so clever.

A shiver of fear upset his resolve. It was one thing to want to protect his father, to rescue him from prison, but to speak to a knight? When he was a lowly serf? It had been a shock for their family, to become slaves once more, but Jordan had speedily adapted to his new position. If anything, it had made his friendship with Alan even stronger – for now he was on the same footing as the older boy.

Jordan's spirit quailed within him at the thought of speaking to a knight – and a Keeper of the King's Peace at that. This Sir Baldwin was the most powerful person the boy had ever heard of, even superior to his old master, Squire Roger. Would he listen to a boy with a story such as his?

Baldwin and Jeanne joined the bailiff and his wife. They took their stand at some distance from the fire, nearer the trestles which were now being cleared of food.

Jeanne was struck by the change which had come over her husband. The quiet, introspective man she had married had gone, and in his place was this implacable stranger who had but one aim – to avenge the death of the young Master of Throwleigh. She had seen Baldwin at his work several times already, at Tavistock and in Crediton, but never before had he appeared to be so fired with grim determination.

He drank his pot off now, and held it out to Edgar to refill. 'This wine is good.'

'I am glad you like it, Sir Baldwin. It is from my last shipment from Bordeaux.' Thomas had appeared as if from nowhere, and stood now at Baldwin's elbow.

The knight nodded. 'From Bordeaux? That is where the Fleming says he came from.'

'Him?' Thomas snorted. He was feeling more himself now, and he gave van Relenghes a cold stare. 'I'd be surprised. He has more the look of a wandering mercenary than a soldier.'

A manservant dropped a bowl, which shattered, and Thomas gave a roar of anger, striding over to the man and slapping him on the face.

Baldwin and his wife exchanged a glance. 'He is not quite so calm as he would like us to think,' said Baldwin, and before Jeanne could respond, she saw his eyes light on the Fleming and his guard once more. 'Simon, we haven't managed to get that fellow Godfrey alone, and yet he is a prime witness as well,' he went on.

'Who, the weapons master? He's said all he's likely to, surely?'

'I wonder. What if we could get him away from his employer?'

'You'd need a polearm to separate the two of them,' Simon joked.

'Why, though?' Jeanne asked suddenly. 'I mean, why should the Fleming need to have a guard with him all the time even while he's here, safe in a hall? On a journey any man of sense will have a guard, particularly now with so many outlaws on all the highways, but why in here? Even Thomas has left all his men out in the stables.'

Baldwin looked down at her proudly. He loved his wife for her beauty and abilities, but never had he felt such an attraction purely for the value of her common-sense. 'My love, you have hit the nail perfectly.'

'But what is the answer?'

Simon drained his own pot. 'That's simple. A man only has such a guard when he's in danger, and the fact that he has Godfrey with him all the time is certain proof that he does not feel safe here in the hall.'

'No friend of the squire's would come to harm here,' Jeanne protested.

'No,' her husband agreed, 'and there is another explanation which Simon has missed, but . . .' Before he could say more, his attention was drawn to the little huddled figure near the fireplace: Lady Katharine.

She slowly rose to her feet, and Baldwin saw her close her eyes as if in prayer. Her veil had been raised so she could drink, and now she dropped it back over her face. With a cautious precision that proved her consumption of wine had been considerably higher than usual, she stepped away from the roaring fire towards a cooler seat.

At her side moved her faithful retainers: Daniel and the maidservant Anney. Then Lady Katharine stumbled, and Baldwin saw two things that intrigued him.

The first was that Daniel instantly reached out and took her arm, gripping it carefully above the elbow. She rested her other hand on his for a moment, looking up into his face with gratitude, before gently extricating herself and sitting.

The second and equally interesting part of the tableau was Anney's reaction to her mistress's near-fall. The woman made absolutely no move to save her lady from falling. It was as if she had no interest in whether her mistress hurt herself or not.

Anney watched the people in the room dully. There was no pleasure in being here. It was hard enough to be away from her son, and the Lord God Himself only knew what Alan would get up to tonight without her there to keep him under control. She didn't need the extra responsibility of looking after her lady while she received these men. Especially at this, the occasion of Herbert's funeral.

Anney glanced at her mistress and was unnerved to see that Lady Katharine was watching her.

'Are you thinking of Tom, Anney?'

Anney nodded shortly. What else would she be thinking of, she wondered angrily, with all these fine, noble people here to celebrate the little life of Master Herbert? And yet what was Herbert but a useless fool, a boy who had let her own child die?

Perhaps a little of her bitterness of spirit transmitted itself to Lady Katharine, because she blinked again, quickly, as though about to break into tears, and looked away.

That day was all too clear in Anney's memory: she supposed it always would be. The morning had been bright and fresh, without a hint of the wet weather that was to follow, and she had set off for her work with a light heart. Because of her bigamous husband, Anney had lived away from the manor, preferring to remain in the cottage in the village, even after his deceit was proven and her journey homewards became so difficult, if not dangerous. It was partly from the hope that he might return to her, and partly that she felt secluded from the pointing fingers and laughter of other servants if she had her home as a hiding-place.

The morning had begun like any other. She had risen before dawn, kicking Tom and Alan from her bed. Both boys knew their duties, and Alan had fetched the bucket and started his walk down to the stream, while Tom had collected two large faggots of sticks to make up the fire. While she was in their garden picking vegetables for their food, he had taken his flint and knife and begun to strike a spark to his tinder.

He had been sleepy, and his aim was poor, and when Anney came back inside, her skirts holding a small cabbage and onions, to find no fire burning in the grate, she angrily clipped Tom about the ear and shouted that he was pathetic.

Then, dropping the vegetables on the floor, she had taken the snivelling child's knife and struck a strong spark, from which she soon had a small fire lighted. The two bundles of wood would be enough for the day, and provided Alan and Tom kept an eye on the fire, the house should be warm enough at evening for them to have a hot drink before retiring to their bed.

Except her son, her Tom, would never sleep in bed with her again. That was the day he'd died in the black gloom, drowning in the slimy, weed-encrusted base of the well-shaft, and all because her master's boy hadn't the gumption to call for help.

On that last day she'd eaten a dry crust or two of bread, and so had her boys, and she had allowed them to eat an egg between them, a spare one which she had kept back from Daniel's beadle, before sending them off on their jobs. Alan then, as now, was a bird-scarer, and with his sling would keep crows and rooks from the crops, while Tom had been granted the position of playmate to Lady Katharine's child.

At the time his place, and the trust in him which it implied, had been a magnificent honour to Anney, but now it was the greatest regret of her life that her boy had been taken on. There was no point in receiving an honour if it wasn't possible to enjoy the fruits of it in later life, and the only result of this had been the ending of his life. If it hadn't been for the job, he would be alive now. But he had taken the job, he had played with Herbert, and he had fallen into the well – nobody knew why even now – and from that moment on, her life had been empty.

Lady Katharine met her gaze again, and the eyes of both women filled with tears.

'Anney, I'm so sorry about Tom. Only now can I truly understand how you must have felt.'

'My Lady,' Anney said, and grasped her hand. With difficulty she forced a certain sympathy into her voice. 'I would never have wanted to see Herbert die. Anything but this. It is so miserable to lose a son this way.'

'Any way in which one loses a son must be cruel,' Katharine said.

'At least he is with God,' Anney murmured. That was her sole comfort since Tom had died: at least he would be at peace now in Heaven. Mary would take in the youngster, Christ would treat him like a brother – wasn't that what the priests always said? It was only reflections like that which had kept her sane in the long, depressing evenings after her son had been taken from her.

Not that her lady had understood at the time, Anney reminded herself.

When she had found Herbert, he was standing at the edge of the well, peering over into the depths, and she had cried to him to come away, but he had said that he was waiting for his friend. Only then had Anney realised something was wrong. She had shouted down into the echoing depths, but when there was no answering call, nothing, she had gone to search other, more obvious places, first with annoyance, but soon with nervousness.

Tom was nowhere to be seen, and at last she called the steward – a cold, clammy panic setting in as Daniel and the men fetched ropes and dropped them down into the foul interior. One of them gingerly undertook the mission, a young-ish fellow, she recalled, Ralph, a groom with the arms and shoulders of a blacksmith, and a high brow. He returned with the child in his arms, both of them dripping green weeds and slime. Anney had managed one shrill scream before collapsing with horror.

Lady Katharine had not comprehended her distress: perhaps she thought serfs couldn't suffer much, perhaps she assumed that a mere servant couldn't feel the same pain as a highborn woman.

She understood it now, all right, Anney noted with a vicious sense of justice.

'Shall we find Stephen and question him now?' Simon asked.

'No,' said Baldwin thoughtfully. 'He has to prepare for the burial tomorrow.'

'There is another man we must see: Nicholas. At least he won't be so difficult to prise away from his master as Godfrey,' Simon said.

Baldwin agreed. 'I could do with a walk to cool my blood. A stroll in the fresh air would be most pleasant.'

Simon grinned to himself. There was a more pressing desire on his part, having now drunk the better part of two quarts of ale, but he decorously avoided mentioning it in front of Baldwin's bride. Instead he and Baldwin took their leave of their wives and went outside, Simon strolling to the heap of manure at the corner of the stables and relieving himself.

The evening was breezy, and the wind soughed and moaned about the yard, scattering straw in little whirls. Baldwin, gazing up at the numerous stars, stepped into a pile of hound's faeces and muttered a curse, making Simon chuckle as he straightened his hose.

Light from lanterns and braziers blazed cheerily in the open stable doorway. Peeping inside, Baldwin saw grooms and stablemen polishing harness and saddles, chattering happily like so many rooks preparing for the night.

At the other side of the long building were the five men Thomas had brought with him. Nicholas and his companions were seated on logs playing dice, and none looked up until the knight and bailiff were almost at their backs. Then the sudden silence as the leather-polishing stopped penetrated even to the five, and their game was halted.

Nicholas stood, grunting as his bones complained from resting too long on a cold, hard seat. 'Sirs? Can I help you?'

The stable workers slowly began to work again, but not so noisily as they all eavesdropped. Baldwin was sure that the manor's servants did not like Thomas's men.

'We would like to ask you some questions,' Simon said smoothly. 'You were with your master on the day the boy was killed, weren't you? Out towards the north.'

Nicholas licked his lips, but without visible concern. 'Yes, sir. Squire Thomas and I rode out in the afternoon.'

'Why did he take you with him?'

'My master knows this area – he grew up here,' Nicholas shrugged. 'So he knows that there are plenty of felons – and other dangers about. Or what if he was thrown from his horse on the moors?'

'You didn't go to the moors, though.'

'We went where the fancy took him.'

'Until you met the Fleming and his man.'

'What if we did?' His tone had altered, as had his stance. Now he stood as if ready to spring.

Baldwin edged to his left, Simon right, to defend themselves. The other four men also rose to their feet. None had reached for a weapon, but now the knight saw the fearsome war axe leaning against the wall, a heavy bill above it. Nicholas himself wore a heavy falchion, not a modern weapon, but a good, solid, battering blade that could be ferociously lethal in the right hands.

The grooms were silent. Nicholas was now their steward and they looked at each other, unsure whether to interrupt or ignore what was developing into a fight.

Baldwin threw a look at his friend, and Simon nodded, saying, 'Nicholas, we want to know what was said between your master and the Fleming that day.'

'It's nothing to do with you.'

'I'll be the judge of that . . .'

'No.'

'And we want to know what happened later, when you held Thomas's horse while he thrashed around in the undergrowth,' Simon continued. 'What was that all about?'

'I reckon you've been listening to stories. I don't remember anything like that,' Nicholas said, and laid his hand near the hilt of his sword.

As he did so, Baldwin saw one of Nicholas's colleagues reach out idly and grab the handle of his axe, while another, a truly disreputable-looking scoundrel with a cast in one eye and pox scars all over his face, thoughtfully tugged a long Welsh knife from its scabbard. The others stood, one making for the bill, the last, a one-eyed man pulled out a dagger.

Baldwin had never been the best of swordsmen, but he thanked his stars that his father had taught him how to defend himself against English fighters: 'Don't wait for the bastards to decide what to do! If you think you're close to a fight, hit the sods first.'

He whipped out his sword with an electric sparkle of blued steel and sprang forward even as he brought his left hand down to protect his belly. At his side he heard his friend drag his own blade from its scabbard, but his eyes were already on Nicholas.

The man gaped, not believing anyone would accept odds of five to two, but then he realised his own danger, and grabbed for his falchion. His blade was half out when Baldwin reached him. The new sword was a flash of blue, and Baldwin swept it right, smacking the flat against Nicholas's elbow and slamming his hand away from the falchion's hilt. Instantly Baldwin sidestepped Nicholas, and lashed out with his foot. His boot caught the back of Nicholas's knees, whose legs collapsed, and he crumpled as though pole-axed. Simon had already marched to him and as Nicholas stared up, Simon stamped his foot on his chest, the point of his sword at his throat. Simon smiled down at him, but Nicholas found no comfort in his expression. The bailiff's eyes were glittering with a cold anger.

Baldwin had moved some paces beyond the prone Nicholas, and now he stood facing the others, his sword steady in his hand, peering at them under the shining steel of his blade. He didn't like the look of the bill: no one could protect himself effectively against a weapon with such a long reach. If the man handling it had any skill, Baldwin knew he was lost.

'Well?' he demanded. 'Are you going to leave us alone to question your leader?'

The cruel head of the bill pointed towards him now, and he raised his left hand, evaluating likely manoeuvres that might give him some chance of success, but before he could attempt any, another force came to his rescue.

Behind his opponents the grooms had sat open-mouthed as the knight grabbed his sword, but now they had set aside their cloths and oils. Two had quarter-staffs in their hands, and they held them threateningly at the back of Thomas's men.

'Put your weapons down,' Baldwin commanded, and the men shamefacedly set the polearm and axe back against the wall. The grooms relaxed, and Baldwin let out a quiet sigh of relief.

Leaving the grooms guarding the men, who returned to their dice with complete insouciance, Baldwin stood over the recumbent steward. Simon removed his foot and ran his sword back into its scabbard, but Baldwin kept his out, and allowed the point to touch Nicholas's throat.

'What happened when your master met the Fleming?'

'It was nothing. The foreigner wanted to buy lands from the estate. He'd said so the night before, and my master was minded to help him, that's all.'

'It wasn't your master's to sell,' Simon growled.

'He was going to persuade Lady Katharine that she'd be better off without it.'

'You mean he was going to talk her into breaking up the place for his own profit?'

Nicholas eyed the blade resting on his neck with disgust. He wasn't used to being disarmed and beaten like this, and the ignominy of his position made his tone bitter. 'What do you expect? He needs the cash. His last ship foundered, and there's no other way to buy the wine he needs to keep his business trading.'

'It is curious,' said Baldwin, 'but the Fleming recalls the discussion going in a different direction. He thought it was your master who approached *him*. As an old comrade, he would hardly be likely to try to rob the squire's widow.'

'Him?' Nicholas spat contemptuously. 'My master was a better friend to the squire than van Relenghes ever was; the Fleming hated Squire Roger's guts! They fought for the King, but at one battle van Relenghes captured a wealthy French Duke and ransomed him.' He noticed Simon's baffled expression. 'Don't you know the law? All important prisoners must be sold to the King so he can personally ransom them. The Fleming was trying to keep all the profit for himself, and that was illegal. He could have had his head taken off for that, and when Squire Roger threatened to tell the King, van Relenghes had no choice but to hand over the prisoner; but he never forgot that it was the squire who had cost him all that money. The Fleming had to flee the army before his attempt at fraud could be discovered, and he blamed the squire for his loss. That's why he hated Squire Roger.'

'How can you be so sure?'

'Talk to Godfrey, the Fleming's guard,' Nicholas sneered. 'He used to be at war with the squire. Ask him what *he* knows about the man he's protecting.'

CHAPTER TWENTY-FOUR

Petronilla was up before daylight to do her morning chores. In the hall she found several other servants lying on benches above the rushes and garbage where the rats scurried, and she clicked her tongue irritably at the thought that she should be awake while they snored on. Making no effort to be quiet, she hauled a fresh pair of logs to the fire and dropped them near the still-warm ashes, setting small twigs and tinder above the hottest part and blowing on them until they caught, then setting more logs over the small flames. Soon the dry wood was glowing and spitting, and by then most of the other folk in the room were astir.

Edgar, as Baldwin's man, was first to his feet as usual; as soon as he had thrown his cloak from his shoulders he went out into the cold to shove his head under the water in the trough. Petronilla had no idea why he should do this – she thought it might be some kind of penance – but she did notice that he always returned looking a lot fresher.

Next to rise was Hugh, but in his case it was because he had been kicked awake by Edgar on his way past. Hugh woke slowly, his head coming up, eyes bleared, grumpily swinging his legs down from the bench upon which he lay, to survey the world through a yawn.

Normally, once Hugh was conscious, he would shake Wat into life, but today Hugh missed his morning routine, for Wat was absent from his patch on the floor next to Hugh's bench. While Petronilla hauled the hangings from the windows and unbarred the shutters to pull them back, letting in fresh air and a little light, she saw Hugh shuffle out to the buttery in search of the boy, and was rewarded a few moments later by the sight of him dragging Wat out to the yard to rinse him off. He had been sick during the night.

Edgar met them, shaking his head slowly. 'God's blood, Wat, you have to keep from trying to finish all the barrels at once. There will always be more to drink the next day. Why get yourself in this state each morning?'

The thirteen-year-old grinned shamefacedly, a faint tinge of green lightening his features. 'I didn't realise how strong it was.'

'Now you know,' said Hugh not unkindly, 'you can clear up the mess out there.' He passed the boy a bucket and old cloth he had found lying in the yard.

'He's not a bad fellow,' Edgar mused.

'No, he's going to be a fine lad. Likes his drink – but who doesn't?'

Edgar forbore to mention his own master's ambivalence to alcohol. He ran his fingers through his hair, caught a short yawn, and stretched himself like a cat. 'Time to go.'

Hugh nodded, but before Edgar walked back indoors, he stood a few minutes and watched as the sun lit the eastern sky. It was impressive, with deep purples and golds lighting the country all about them. Hugh knew that Edgar never failed to enjoy this hour of the day; the knight's servant was geared to early mornings. For Hugh himself, there was infinitely more pleasure in sleeping late and enjoying the night-time.

Still, as he turned and made his way back to the hall, he had to admit to himself that the morning was almost perfect. The birds chattered and sang in the trees, the rooks chuckling and calling as they preened and readied themselves for the day's excitement. A dog came out from the kennels, sniffed at a wall and cocked its leg before sauntering off to the kitchen, outside which it sat hopefully, scratching and throwing longing looks at the closed door every now and again.

Another dog barked, and there was the sound of horses stamping in their stalls in the stables. Hearing a door slam, Hugh sighed. The place was alive now, and he should get on with helping the other servants. The guests and household would be heading for the vill soon, to witness the *Dirige* and the burial of the boy.

'A fine morning, sir,' came a voice at his side, and Hugh found that Godfrey had joined him.

'Pleasant enough,' he replied cautiously. 'Your master still abed?'

'If he could, I think he'd remain there all day. Had too much to drink last night.'

Hugh nodded. The Fleming's face had become very flushed as he drank the strong red wine last night, and when it was time for him to retire, he had required his guard's help to negotiate the doorway. 'You worked for him long?'

Godfrey stretched his arms high over his head, then shook his head. He planted his feet a shoulder's width apart and began to sway first one way then the other, twisting his torso to and fro. 'He found me in town. Oh, good morning, Bailiff.'

'Don't stop on my account,' said Simon.

'Nay, Bailiff. I have work to be getting on with.'

'Protecting your master? But why does he need you at his side all the time? Isn't he safe enough in the hall?'

Godfrey's face broke into a broad grin. 'You haven't guessed, then? Ah, and I thought the Bailiff of Lydford was clever!' Chuckling, he made his way back to the door.

Hugh scowled after him. 'What's that supposed to mean, eh?'

'I wonder,' said Simon pensively. He was about to follow the man inside when a wholly ridiculous idea struck him, and he paused. 'No,' he muttered. 'That can't be right. No.' And still looking thoughtful, he went indoors.

Baldwin was sure he had never experienced a more doleful service than this. He stood with his wife and Simon and Margaret at the graveside, and watched the little shape being slowly lowered. Herbert's grave was right next to his father's, which made this morning's service even more poignant. Roger's grave was large, especially now it was filled, for the mound of soil at the top made it look even bigger, while the child's was tiny by comparison. One could almost imagine that Squire Roger was already in Heaven, but his son's dismal resting-place made Baldwin think of every story he had ever heard about Hell.

The little form reached the bottom. There was no coffin. He lay, a small figure wrapped in a linen winding sheet, and Baldwin saw his mother wince as the first shovelfuls were tossed on top of him, one striking the boy full in the face. Sobbing, she turned from the scene and stumbled away.

Daniel again was at one side of her, while Anney was at the other. Baldwin watched them walk the short distance to the churchyard gate, and thence to the road. When he turned, the priest was already slipping back inside his church. The knight was about to go after him when he decided to wait. It was too soon after the burial; surely it would be more considerate to leave the man with his thoughts for a while. He would be praying for the boy still.

'Oi! Get out of here, you little sod!'

Baldwin snapped around to see the furious Thomas hurling a stone at a lad a little taller than Wat. Fair-haired, and with that golden complexion so prevalent among the Saxons, Baldwin instantly registered his striking similarity to the servant, Anney. This must be Alan, her boy.

The missile struck the lad's chest with an audible thud, and Baldwin tutted to himself. He saw Thomas pick up another large stone, and called out, 'Hold on, Thomas. The lad's not here to make mischief, I'll be bound.'

'You don't know him,' Thomas shouted, taking aim.

'I doubt whether you do, either,' said Baldwin unruffled, as he took hold of Thomas's arm and held it there. 'You, boy. What are you doing here? Should I release my friend's arm and let him assault you?'

'I only wanted to see Herbert being buried, sir. I didn't want to upset anyone.'

'Come here.'

Alan was even more like his mother close to. His countenance was that of a child, but one who has aged prematurely:
his face was too thin for his age, his eyes too large for his
face. Baldwin had seen that look of pinched hunger before,
but not commonly here in Devon where even during the
abject misery of the famine people generally had been able
to produce enough to live.

'You are Anney's boy?'

'Yes, sir,' the boy said. Although he and Jordan had decided
to tell all to this knight, Alan had expected Jordan to be with
him. Now, alone with Baldwin, Alan was nervous of him.
Baldwin held such high authority; he was a Keeper, and a man
who could afford the best linen for his tablecloth and the finest
paindemaigne – bread made from purest white flour – to go on
it, instead of the heavy, rye-filled loaves that Alan and the
villagers had to eat. Alan decided to hold his tongue until he
could speak to Baldwin with Jordan to back up his tale.

'Herbert was your friend, wasn't he?' Baldwin confirmed,
and when Alan nodded, he glanced towards the gravedigger,
who was assiduously filling the small hole. 'It is a great
shame that he should have died so young.'

Alan felt his eyes brimming, and rubbed them on his
sleeve, sniffing loudly. 'It's not fair,' he declared.

'This is ridiculous, talking to a villein's son! What good
will it do, eh? A waste of time,' Thomas spat, hurling his
stone aside and stamping off to join the congregation at the
gate.

Baldwin ignored him and walked with the boy to the
wattle fence at the edge of the yard, leaning on it and staring
out over the trees to the massive hill beyond. 'What isn't fair,
Alan?'

'Him being killed like that. Herbert was a good friend to me and Jordan.'

'Jordan?'

'He's Edmund's son.'

'Oh, Edmund's boy,' said Baldwin thoughtfully. 'Is he as old as you?'

'No, he's quite a lot younger,' said Alan with the scathing contempt of a child for an adult making an obvious mistake. 'He's only nine: I'm nearly eleven.'

'I see,' said Baldwin, restraining a smile. 'And he was playing with you and Herbert when Herbert was killed?'

'We were all up on the hill playing hunters.'

Baldwin smiled. 'I used to play it myself when I was young.'

Alan looked up at him doubtfully, wondering whether the tall, grave man was making a joke.

'We used to play lots of games when I was a boy, before I was sent to be trained in warfare. Hunting was only one. I enjoyed all the shooting games – I used to be a good shot with a bow.'

'I haven't got a bow,' Alan said regretfully. 'It broke.'

'A sling is almost as useful.'

'Oh, I'm pretty good with mine,' Alan said complacently. 'But . . .' He was about to say more when Stephen of York came out of the church.

After the ceremony the priest had gone inside to settle the account with the paid mourners and to exchange his garments for travelling robes ready for the walk back to the manor. Now he stood in the yard, blinking in the bright sunlight. As soon as his eye lit upon the boy talking to Baldwin, the knight saw his expression change from one of melancholy to wrath.

Alan saw him too. With a noise that Baldwin could only describe as a bleat, Alan leaped the fence with a single bound and hared away. The knight watched the lad rush off until he was out of sight among some trees, a small frown wrinkling his brow.

'Has that young scoundrel been troubling you?' Stephen demanded.

Baldwin turned and gave him a smile. 'No, I was merely passing the time of day with him. He is very upset at his friend's death.'

'Him?' Stephen said scornfully. 'He's the best actor in the whole parish. Don't believe a word he says.'

Baldwin nodded, keeping the smile fixed to his face, but he was conscious of one thing: Alan had been terrified by the sight of the priest. As Stephen strode off to rejoin the rest of the congregation, Baldwin stared after him musingly.

Thomas was seething with fury as the procession began the journey back to the hall. It was plain stupid of Sir Baldwin to talk to that Alan! He was bound to lie, just like his father. The man had been a liar, a lecherous bigamist, and there was little doubt that the boy would follow in his father's footsteps. And he might tell Baldwin where Thomas had been on the day Herbert died. Thomas could live without that complication and that was why he now boiled with impotent anger.

'Are you recovered?' The soft, insinuating voice broke in upon his thoughts, and he almost jumped.

Van Relenghes gave a gentle laugh. 'I know *I* am suffering – I drank far more than usual last night. I gather your men drank a lot as well. Especially after they had spoken to the bailiff and his friend the knight.'

'What are you talking about?'

'Oh,' the Fleming chuckled. 'They forgot to mention it, did they? Well, never mind. I am sure they didn't tell the bailiff anything he didn't already know.'

'You bastard!' Thomas blustered. He was feeling bitter: the little scene with the boy just now had reinforced his feelings of being ignored and treated like some kind of untrustworthy felon. He wanted to lash out and hurt someone, but there was no one suitable, apart from this tall, sarcastic Fleming. 'You foreign buggers are all the same.'

'Oh – in what way?'

'You can't lose gracefully, can you? You wanted my brother's land, and now I won't let you have it you'll enjoy anything that discomforts me.'

'I only enjoy scenes which I have myself created.'

His calm words took a moment to sink in, but when he realised what the man had said, Thomas gasped and stopped dead in the road. 'You told her that I'd been negotiating with you? Is that why she made that scene in the church?'

Van Relenghes chuckled softly, then leaned forward until his face was only inches from Thomas's. '*Yes*, fool! If you had a brain to think with, you'd have realised that immediately. And now I have ruined your chances of settling down here, because she will make your life miserable in any way she can! That will be most pleasant for me to reflect upon when I return to my own hall.'

'You turd! You think you'll make it home? Why, I'll—'

Van Relenghes gave a massive yawn. 'Godfrey, I think Thomas is about to threaten me. Do prepare yourself to look fearful, won't you?'

He walked on, his guard laughing, and Thomas was left alone, clenching and unclenching his fists in the road.

'You whoreson bastard! I'll see to it you regret that! I'll make you bloody eat your words!'

CHAPTER TWENTY-FIVE

Baldwin and Simon were walking with their wives a few yards in front of this hushed dispute, and thus saw nothing of Thomas's rage or the Fleming's delight.

Simon could see that his friend was frustrated, but could think of no way to relieve his mood. Baldwin, he knew, would worry at the problem until a solution presented itself to him, and only then would he be able to relax.

'Did you learn anything from that boy?' he asked.

'Nothing – no. If I had been able to speak to him a little longer, I might have done, and yet perhaps I did find out something,' he said thoughtfully. 'The lad is plainly terrified of the priest.'

'Well, of course he is. Many people are,' said Margaret. 'The parish priest is the only man of any learning that a villein will ever meet. He's the one who officiates at every critical ceremony in their lives.'

'Especially in a small place like this,' said Jeanne. 'Here Stephen is the only man who can read: he's the one who will tell them whether it is a fasting day or a meat one, which day of the week it is, and so on.'

Baldwin smiled at her. 'I know the people here are peasants, but even my own villeins know what the day is,' he said in a tone of mild reproof. It was all too common for those in a higher station of life to assume that serfs were little more intelligent than the oxen which they used to pull their wagons.

Jeanne shook her head, amused by his presumption. 'I do not speak from idle foolishness, Baldwin. You forget that I have lived as Lady of a manor similar to this one. I know these people. They have no time for speculation, no time to play or enjoy leisure. Their lives are hard, geared to the weather and to the hours of daylight rather than some arbitrary notion such as a day's name. It's different for you and your peasants, living up at Cadbury, where the weather is warmer, and where the rain runs away rather than sinking into the ground to form mires, where trees grow straight and tall rather than bent and warped.'

'Perhaps, but I do not know whether young Alan was scared of the figure of authority, or of Brother Stephen the man.'

Simon agreed. 'In that case we need to find out more about this mysterious cleric, don't we?'

Nicholas was in the courtyard when the procession returned from the church. He had ordered the other men to remain in the stable out of the widow's sight, from respect for her feelings; he himself stood quietly near a rain-butt. He had been sharpening his knife, but he set his whetstone and dagger aside when the mourning party slowly made their way to the hall.

When the mistress was out of the way, he picked up his blade once more and tested it with the ball of his thumb. Still blunt – it was taking an age to put an edge on this one. He was about to bend to his task again when he became aware of his master hurrying towards him.

'Nicholas? Come here. Listen to me, I have a job for you.'

Hugh had been waiting at the door. Seeing the party approach, he walked quickly inside to stir the warmed wine in the jugs by the fire. As he crouched there, Lady Katharine entered. She acknowledged him with a pale shadow of a smile, and gratefully took a large mug from him.

Hugh politely offered Anney a cup, but she refused with a quick shake of her head, and Daniel took it in her stead.

Then the guests were filing in, and Hugh was having to serve faster than he could manage. When the jugs had all been emptied, he hurried from the room and into the buttery, where he found Wat, mercifully sober.

'Quick! Fill this lot,' Hugh ordered and sat on a barrel. 'Where's Petronilla? She ought to be helping.'

'I suppose she's gone for another walk.'

'Don't talk rubbish!'

'I still don't understand why she had such filthy hands yesterday,' Wat frowned.

'What are you on about?' Hugh demanded, and listened with surprise as Wat told how he had seen her the day before, all mucky with black soil smeared over her hands. Hugh was no fool and, after being servant to the bailiff for so long, he was able to make quick inferences, but for the present he only muttered grumpily, 'Never mind her, you get more jugs filled, lad. The party in there will be dying of thirst soon.'

As soon as the jugs of warmed wine were ready, he took them into the hall and began topping up people's pots and mugs; the flow of conversation, muted at first, became louder. Shortly after this, Petronilla came in. She too carried jugs, and she took her station near her mistress, although with many a confused glance at Thomas. Hugh could understand her feelings: she knew her master was Thomas now, and although she was still loyal to her mistress, she had no wish to damage her position with him.

Hugh pursed his lips and went to his master's side. 'Sir?'

Simon listened, his expression unchanging as his servant told him about the girl and how she had returned from the moors with her hands covered in peaty soil. 'Interesting,' he murmured at last. 'Well done, Hugh.'

At the other side of the hall, Baldwin had been trying to get closer to the priest, but each time he made his way through the throng, Stephen moved on. Eventually Baldwin fetched up against a pillar, and he stood there, testily staring at the tonsured figure for some while before he realised someone was speaking to him.

'Anney, my apologies, my mind was elsewhere.'

The maidservant gave him a mocking curtsey. 'So kind of you to apologise to a poor villein like me.'

Baldwin thought she was an attractive-looking woman. Her face, although marked by channels of grief, some for the loss of her husband, some for the loss of her son, was still fresh and youthful, and she had a glowing complexion that many ladies of position would have given much of their wealth for.

283

'A woman with your looks will always be able to force a poor, innocent knight to apologise,' he riposted.

'Thank you again, Sir Baldwin. I don't know what I could have done to merit such compliments.'

'Come, lady, you can hardly be unaware of your attractions.'

She gave a low, throaty chuckle, but there was little humour in it. 'You mean to a man like my husband?'

'Anney, I am sorry. I never intended to remind you of him.'

'Why shouldn't you? He was the only husband I ever knew. I don't hate him. How could I, when he gave me my two boys? I believe you are hoping to speak to the priest?'

Baldwin nodded. Stephen was now at the opposite end of the room, deep in conversation with Thomas.

'I thought so. You'll find it difficult, Sir Baldwin. He doesn't want to talk to you.'

'Why?'

'Perhaps he's scared you'll discover something.'

'Such as?'

'Such as how he disliked the squire's son,' she said coolly.

'What could he have had against so young a child? Herbert was only five or six.'

'Five, but rowdy with it. He never attended to Stephen's lessons, wouldn't obey his sternest orders, and treated the priest like a figure of fun. Herbert also used to shoot at him with his sling whenever he could, and for that Stephen would give him a good hiding.'

'Did Herbert's parents realise what was going on?'

Anney gave a short laugh. 'Squire Roger had won his son a place with Sir Reginald of Hatherleigh. What more could he ask but that his cleric should teach the boy the same way he'd already taught the sons of Sir Reginald? There was no difficulty there, I assure you.'

Her tone interested Baldwin. 'You think he *wanted* to beat the child?'

'Of course he did. He hates children – not only the squire's son, all children. It wasn't just Herbert he thrashed: my own boy was often whipped or punched by him, and never for any real misdemeanour, only because it pleased him to do so. Look at him! He has such a soft, womanly appearance, and yet he has a heart of flint!'

Baldwin followed her gaze. The priest was still chatting to Thomas, his face animated. That same hint of femininity that he had seen on first meeting the priest caught the knight's attention once more. If it was not for the tonsure, Baldwin could have thought him a woman from this distance. It was hard to believe that such a person could enjoy hurting children, and yet that was clearly Anney's belief.

'Are you sure he wasn't merely trying to teach them obedience?' he hazarded.

'Master Herbert was a pleasant, well-spoken child, and my own boy is very well-behaved. He has to be, seeing as how he's had to learn to fend for himself without a father. What a lad like him needs is the gentle hand of someone who appreciates him, not bullying from one who should know better. And as for poor Jordan . . .'

Baldwin expressed polite interest but the woman shook her head. 'No, I'll leave it to you to speak to him. Make up your own mind.'

'What do you think of the Fleming?' Baldwin asked after a moment.

'Him? Haven't you realised yet?' she asked, and then gave a long sigh. 'Look at him! Ever at my lady's side, always there with a flattering word, a generous compliment. It's like watching a knight courting a lady, isn't it? The man wants her. He knows she won't inherit all the estates, although I think that was a shock to him at first because he was hoping that he might be able to master the whole manor with luck, but he still hopes to win her and whatever Master Thomas thinks fit to endow her with.'

'*What?*' Baldwin demanded, startled. 'But the woman has only just buried her man. She can't remarry – it would leave her open to the charge of unchastity! She could be accused of lasciviousness – or of being guilty of infidelity while married!'

'In short, she would be suspected of infamy,' agreed the maid unabashed. 'Yes, she would, but would the Fleming care? Next time you talk to him, look deep into his eyes, Sir Knight, especially when he smiles, because the smile never touches them. He is cold and unfeeling, no matter what his words might be. Watch him carefully, Sir Knight. He's not what he appears to be.'

When Jordan met Alan out at the fields near the manor, he could see that his friend had already heard the news about Edmund.

'Are you all right?' Alan asked him quietly.

Jordan nodded. His eyes were red from weeping all the long night, and he felt utterly miserable, but he said nothing. He couldn't rely on his voice, and didn't want to scare the quarry.

Thirty feet away three pigeons were feeding from four tiny mounds of grain. Others were circling, unaware of the two boys. A fourth and a fifth gradually felt the desire for food overcome their fears, and plummeted downwards. When mere inches from the ground, they stretched their wings, halting their mad plunge, and landed gently. In a few minutes there were eight there, and only then did Alan spring his trap. He pulled quickly at a hempen string before him; the knot at the far end slipped free, and the framed net fell swiftly onto the eating birds, only two managing to make off.

Flapping, the six remaining pigeons could not escape, and the boys laughed with delight as they ran to the net, sitting down and wringing their necks before beginning to pluck and draw them.

'Have you seen your dad yet?' Alan asked.

'No, he's up at the manor, in their gaol there. I'll go and see him later. We'll need to take him food, I suppose. Alan, we must tell them about the shoe. Otherwise my dad might be hanged, and he had nothing to do with it.'

Alan appeared not to hear him. 'I talked to that knight this morning.'

Jordan waited expectantly.

'He seemed quite all right, really,' Alan continued thoughtfully. 'Didn't seem to look down on me just 'cos I'm a villager or anything, but listened to what I thought.'

Jordan watched as his friend pulled a grass shoot and sucked the sweet, pale end.

'Maybe we should explain about the shoe,' Alan murmured.

'You think we should take it into the manor?'

Alan nodded slowly. 'I think we should tell him about the priest.'

*　　*　　*

Hugh gratefully handed his jug to Edgar and walked through to the buttery. There he drew off a large pot of ale for himself and carried it outside for a breather.

The early promise of the bright morning had been false, and now thick white clouds smothered the sky like a blanket over the whole world. Hugh took a deep breath and let it out contentedly. This was his country, for he had been born and brought up on a farm outside Drewsteignton, and he knew the moors and their weather as well as he knew himself and his own moods.

Especially around here, the north-eastern part of the moors, he could recognise the way that the weather was likely to develop. The hill behind the manor led up to another, still more massive, and this one, Cosdon he had been able to see from his father's farm when he was out with his sling and his staff protecting the family flocks from beasts of all kinds.

It was a comforting scene. At the other side of the yard he saw four or five men, the ones from Thomas's party. They watched him narrowly as he came out, visibly relaxing as they recognised who he was. Hugh gave them an interested look. They had the appearance of a set of outlaws setting an ambush, but they scarcely took any notice of him, and Hugh sat on a moorstone block, comfortably certain that they were no threat to him. Soon he began to nod.

CHAPTER TWENTY-SIX

Inside, Baldwin was still digesting Anney's words about Brother Stephen's hatred of children when he once more found himself being addressed. He apologised automatically. 'I am sincerely sorry, but I was miles away.'

'So I could see,' Thomas said, smiling thinly. 'I thought you looked lonely over here, and decided I would come and make sure you weren't upset or over-full of wine, eh?' And with that remark he would have prodded the knight's belly, had he not caught a glimpse of Baldwin's expression.

Thomas was feeling more at ease with himself now. He was still unhappy about his sister-in-law's denunciation in the church, in the midst of all their friends – and before the altar, in Christ's name! – but that was mere indignation compared with his blind fury at the man who had caused the outburst: the Fleming. However, Nicholas would soon make the slimy git regret his remarks to Lady Katharine, whatever they may have been.

'Have you heard whether Edmund's hose were damp?' Baldwin asked unkindly.

'No one appears to have seen him that evening,' Thomas replied warily.

'No matter. I trust you will shortly be releasing Edmund. It was kind of you to seek me out to tell me,' Baldwin said distantly, eyeing the pot in Thomas's hand. The new master of the manor had evidently made himself free with the wine.

'No trouble, none at all,' Thomas said, and belched. 'And you enjoyed your chat to Anney? She's a good enough woman, I daresay, though her son Alan is an unholy terror.'

'I have found that if you treat a dog like a wild beast, it will reward your patience by behaving like one.'

'Eh? Oh, I daresay. But her brat really is a pest. Of course, his mother can't see it, or won't. As far as she's concerned, the sun shines out of his arse.'

Baldwin was annoyed that the man should demean the woman while he was drunk. 'I found her intelligent and quickwitted, unlike some. If a woman finds little fault with her offspring, that is hardly cause for censure. Especially if she has already lost one boy, as Anney has.'

'Oh, I see she's convinced you. She's a clever spark, I'll give her that, but as for her lad, he'll end up on the gallows, you mark my words.'

'Why do you say so? I spoke to him, and found him sharp, but not villainous, just as I would expect from his mother.'

'Be careful of what he says to you. If you don't believe me, ask the priest.'

Baldwin felt his interest stirring again. 'I saw Stephen talking to you just now,' he said. 'Was that something to do with this young Master Alan?'

'Oh, no. No, he wanted to ask my advice on a private matter, that was all,' said Thomas, but he could not help looking complacent. It was quite an honour to have been confided in by the priest. He still didn't like Stephen, but at least the man had confessed, and that made a lot of difference to Thomas. He was the respected master of a big hall now, as Stephen had proved. If a cleric could feel so sure of his integrity that he would dare confess such a thing, then Thomas must be wonderfully important in the eyes of those around him.

To Baldwin's mind he looked puffed up with his own pride.

'May I ask what the matter was?' he enquired, carefully setting his voice at a low, flattering level, as though he was keen to know why Thomas's advice had been sought instead of his own.

'It was a matter of some delicacy, I fear, and I couldn't possibly tell you what it concerned, Sir Baldwin. Under confidence, you understand. Strictest confidence.'

As the man tapped his nose knowingly, Baldwin was tempted to laugh at his blundering stupidity, but managed to keep a straight face. 'Ah, of course.'

'But these boys,' Thomas added solemnly with a grimace and shake of his head, 'they're the most unholy nuisances. They shout and run when they shouldn't, they play practical jokes in the churchyard and carry on as if there were no authority that could hold them.'

'Ah, yes.'

'They shoot their damned slings at anything that takes their fancy. Often out poaching, so I'm told. And they fire at people when they want to, knowing they can run off and hide. That's what ... Anyway, they shoot at folks for no reason, just to make them jump or fall from their horse. They have no respect for anyone. I'll tell you this, if they're not taught a lesson soon, they'll be fodder for the gibbet, and nothing more.'

Baldwin wasn't listening, and missed his lapse. The knight was quite certain that he could never learn anything of any use from the bone-headed Master of Throwleigh, so he merely nodded and made understanding noises while watching the rest of the guests. He could see that Simon and their wives were enjoying a story from Edgar, who had a store of jokes and tales suitable for occasions even as sad as this. Behind them, sitting on her large chair, was Lady Katharine.

The knight watched her for a moment. At her side was the maid Anney, holding her mistress's drinking vessel, and even as Baldwin watched, she passed it to her lady, hardly glancing at her as she put it into Katharine's hand. Baldwin was convinced there was a lingering resentment between maid and mistress, but he was not convinced that it could have sparked the fuse that led to the murder.

The mother herself was an enigma. Had Baldwin only seen her reaction at her husband's funeral, when the woman had recoiled from her own son as if in revulsion, he would have believed her more than capable of hating Herbert enough to kill him. And yet now, having witnessed her despair at the funeral, he found it hard to dispute Simon's outrage at the suggestion. It was unthinkable that a woman should knowingly murder her own boy.

As he considered her, Daniel touched her shoulder and bent to whisper in her ear.

There it was again, he thought. Glancing at Jeanne, he saw her quick nod, and he grinned to himself. She had seen it too – the hand resting on the shoulder just a moment too long, with that hint of a certain special affinity accepted by both sides.

It was then that he noticed van Relenghes again. The Fleming was standing unconcernedly sipping at his wine, alone for a moment; his servant had gone to refill a jug.

Baldwin studied him dispassionately, recalling the way Anney had described him. James van Relenghes had the look of someone set apart from the group within the hall. It was not because he was foreign, because that would imply isolation caused by incomprehension, either of language or customs; no, this was a different sort of otherness. He was aloof, separate. He smiled pleasantly enough at people who spoke to him or passed by, yet Baldwin watched the eyes, as he had been commanded by Anney, and sure enough, they reflected an inner coldness. The eyes displayed calculation; the potential for shallow deceit.

As if aware he was the subject of a close scrutiny, van Relenghes glanced up and met Baldwin's gaze boldly. He raised his goblet cheerily, then bowed slightly and sauntered from the room.

'I think someone needs to teach you a lesson,' Baldwin murmured, his attention flitting to Lady Katharine. 'Whatever your game is, I hope you get your come-uppance.'

Godfrey had not noticed his master's departure. A moment later he returned to where van Relenghes had been standing, his jug in his hand, and looked round casually, expecting to see his master. Soon his search became more keen, and he walked around the room, earnestly seeking van Relenghes, before stopping dead, head cocked to one side, listening to something outside. He ran from the room with every appearance of agitation.

Baldwin had no idea his wish was already being granted.

Hugh was dozing on his stool of moorland stone when van Relenghes came out.

'You – fetch me a horse,' he commanded. 'I wish to ride.'

'You need a groom for that, sir,' Hugh yawned. 'They're over there.'

'Fetch me a horse, drunken sot!' van Relenghes hissed, kicking Hugh's pot, which shattered into a hundred pieces.

Hugh looked at the shards, then leaned back.

'Did you hear me? I want a horse, now!' van Relenghes said.

'Nothing to do with me,' Hugh said, insolently closing his eyes.

'You had better do as you are bid, serf, or—'

Suddenly van Relenghes became aware that they weren't alone. The men who had been waiting at the other side of the yard had silently walked up and now formed a close circle about them.

Nicholas smiled. 'We've been asked to have a word with you, Fleming.'

Van Relenghes went pale as he realised he was trapped. He kept his hand from his sword – he would have had three men grab his arm before he could pull it two inches from its scabbard – and tried to be calm. 'What do you want?'

'You've wronged our master, haven't you? He wants us to explain that he doesn't like people telling villainous lies about him.'

'This is something I should discuss with your master. Now, if you—'

'Oh no, sir. He asked us to speak to you, most particular like,' said Nicholas, and moved to stand directly in front of the Fleming as he attempted to sidle away.

'I have to speak to the Lady Katharine.'

'No need. This is my master's hall, isn't it?' said Nicholas conversationally. He nodded, and one of his companions, a heavy man with a wall-eye, took hold of van Relenghes's sleeve.

'Keep away from me! Leave go, scum, or I'll—'

Hugh watched impassively as Nicholas reached for his dagger. A second man grabbed the Fleming's free arm, and he was held still. With that Hugh's expression changed.

'Here, you can't do that! Give him room to swing his blade.'

Nicholas pushed him away with his free hand. 'Go back inside if you don't want to see a man punished.'

'Fight him fairly, or leave him alone,' Hugh stated. 'This is no better than an outlaw's trick. Let him get his sword out.'

'Piss off, serf, unless you want to join him!' hissed the walleyed man, and Hugh stood stock-still a moment.

He gazed at their faces. Mostly bearded, two of them scarred, one with a single eye and a damp, empty socket where the other should have been. All had the same animal lust to inflict pain. They would attack Hugh too, unarmed as he was, if they had the slightest provocation. Resigned, he took a cautious step backwards, then another.

'Now, Master Fleming,' said Nicholas comfortably.

'*Godfrey!*' van Relenghes screamed, wide-eyed with terror, as the blade moved towards his face.

*   *   *

Hugh bolted inside, colliding with someone running out. It was Godfrey. The master-of-arms tripped over Hugh's foot, and fell headlong into the wall, striking it with a dull thud and collapsing. Hugh had stumbled as well, but he went over Godfrey, who cushioned his fall. Rising quickly, he hurried into the hall, making straight for Daniel.

'Thanks,' he said, and before the astonished steward could stop him, he snatched Daniel's staff of office and sped back outside.

The Fleming's face was a bloody mask, and Nicholas, laughing, was about to make a second long slash, when Hugh exploded into their midst.

His first blow caught the man on van Relenghes's left, and he crumpled without a sound. Before he had fallen, Hugh had whipped his weapon into the quarter-staff fighting position, and swept it down on Nicholas's knife hand. The man gave a shriek, more of surprise than actual pain, dropping his blade, and while the group remained frozen with surprise, Hugh had time to thrust at Wall-eye: the point of the stave hit him high in the belly, and he fell, gasping loudly as he tried to catch his breath. Then Hugh could face the others.

There were three remaining, and Hugh was comfortable with the odds. Nicholas had drawn his sword, a single-edge falchion which had seen better days; one of the others had a heavy Danish axe, while the third had a bill. He was Hugh's main problem: a man with a weapon of the same length and reach.

He saw the bill move to his left, and dropped the point of the staff to parry, immediately trying a stab to the gut which was knocked aside with ease. The man knew how to handle his weapon, Hugh noted glumly. The bill swung low, aiming at his legs, and Hugh withdrew his left foot as the blade passed, immediately stepping forward to attack the man's open flank, but as he did so, Nicholas slashed at him, and Hugh had to swing away, retreating before the sword. The axe swung in a mean arc, and Hugh took another pace back.

There were voices now, people shouting, one man egging on Hugh's opponents, the rest calling for peace, but Hugh kept his eyes on the three men before him. They had sorted themselves out now: the sword was on Hugh's left, axe right, and bill before him.

Making a quick decision, Hugh sprang to his right, feinted with his staff, making the axeman swing to defend his right, and then reversed his grip, sending the butt smashing into the side of the man's head.

As the axeman grunted and fell, his axe hit the bill of the man behind. Hugh quickly took advantage, and swung the top of the staff into his throat. With a hideous gurgling scream that sent a hot thrill of excitement into Hugh's blood, he dropped his bill and fell to his knees, grabbing at his throat as he fought for air. Hugh sent the pole's point at his head above the ear and he fell without another sound. Walleye was breathing stertorously, resting on all fours, so Hugh casually dropped him with a short cut of the staff at the back of his neck.

But all the time his attention was fixed on Nicholas. Hugh walked around the fallen men, his staff pointing at the wary survivor, who gripped his sword with both hands, staring in fascination at the point of the stave as it moved slowly, from side to side, then up and down, at no time more than a few feet from his own neck.

297

Nicholas had been in many fights, but never had he been foolish enough to stand against a man with a staff when he only had a sword. A wooden pole was of little use in the hands of someone who had no idea how to use it, but a man who was skilled with a pole was always at an advantage against a man with a sword. As the iron-shod point of the thick oaken stick darted to his left, Nicholas instinctively moved the blade to guard his side. The jarring shock of the two weapons colliding was enough to make him wince.

All at once the point swung low, aiming at his knees, and he had to leap back, away from his men. He had hoped that one would get up and help him, or that this furious little servant would stumble on one of them, but now even that vain hope was taken from him. Nicholas knew he was going to lose, and when he did, he would have no defence unless his master admitted ordering him to attack.

'It was my master!' he shouted. 'I was ordered to wound the Fleming because of what he said about my master.'

'So what?' demanded Hugh, and poked the stick forward again, this time aiming at Nicholas's chest. The blow was badly timed, and easily blocked, but with a weapon of little more than two feet long, Nicholas couldn't take the advantage, not against a staff of nearly six feet. It was hopeless.

Hugh had his measure, and he began to strike faster: first at his left, then his right; up towards Nicholas's head, down at his ankles; back towards his shoulders, down to thrust at his belly, all the time pressing forward, never allowing Nicholas time to relax from a blow before the next was in motion, never allowing him a moment to catch his breath, constantly seeking an opening, shoving forward.

It wasn't that Hugh had a desire to hurt the man, but since he had become involved in a fight which was not of his making, Hugh was determined to win it.

The end was not long in coming. Nicholas saw the attack at his head, saw the pole move from right to left as if Hugh was going to swing at the other side of his head at the last moment, moved his sword, and then, just too late, saw that the staff wasn't where it should have been: instead it was coming straight towards his face.

CHAPTER TWENTY-SEVEN

As the stave struck Nicholas's nose and the man jerked backwards to lie unconscious on the ground, Simon gave a loud guffaw and applauded vigorously. He strode to his servant's side, clapping him on the back as he stood glowering breathlessly at his victims. 'Well done, Hugh!'

The bailiff and Baldwin had been among the first to rush from the hall to see what Hugh meant by his seizure of the staff, and they had witnessed almost the whole fight. When Baldwin had put his hand to his own sword, Simon had shaken his head; he had seen Hugh fighting against larger numbers before now, and the sight of his man knocking over all the fellows from Thomas's entourage was no surprise to him. An English farmer's son soon learned to protect himself from all predators.

Baldwin glanced about him at the men lying all around, one or two groaning, Nicholas snuffling and shaking his head, still stupefied by his broken nose. 'Yes, you fought well – but what was it all about?'

Hugh leaned on his borrowed staff, trying to catch his breath. 'They were holding the Fleming so he couldn't fight back, and that's not right, sir. When I tried to get them to free him, they threatened me, and shoved me away, so I got angry.' He gazed about him, his spirits sinking a little as he realised how many witnesses there had been to his fight. At Sir Baldwin's side was his wife, and Hugh saw Jeanne was staring at him with open-eyed astonishment. 'Well, they shouldn't have pushed me,' he said grumpily.

'The steward said his master had ordered him to attack van Relenghes, didn't he?' said Simon.

Thomas stood listening at the step to the hall, his features strained and pale. His face told the story only too well: he had never conceived that the Fleming could have survived. Of course, van Relenghes had his guard, but Godfrey was a mercenary, not someone who'd risk his neck against over-whelming odds like this. Thomas had assumed the Fleming would lose.

'It was nothing to do with me. The man was lying.'

'Your servant, Thomas?' Simon said disbelievingly. 'He'd tell such a lie against you?'

'Of course he did! Probably wanted to rob the Fleming,' said Thomas.

'What did you tell your man to do?' Simon asked him. He had walked nearer, and now stood staring down at the Fleming. Van Relenghes's face was covered in gore, and Simon glanced at Petronilla, who gave a shiver, but nodded, and went to the trough to fill a bucket. She began cleaning his wound, a long gash from ear to nostril.

Thomas felt a stab of satisfaction. Nicholas had done his job well, no matter that he had given the game away afterwards. Thomas had insisted that his man should ruin the Fleming's good looks, and that scar alone would succeed. Many women like their men to have marks on their faces, but this one would permanently damage his handsome features. Thomas heard the bailiff speak again, and glanced up.

'I said, what did you order your man to do?' Simon demanded. 'Look at him! Why did you order him to wound a guest in this house?'

'I can answer that, I think, Bailiff.' Lady Katharine descended the steps, her finger pointed accusingly at her brother-in-law.

'This was how Thomas, my dear brother, tried to honour the memory of my husband and my son. He ordered the punishment of this man on the day of my son's funeral just so he could have his revenge on the one who betrayed his secret to me.'

Thomas made a feeble little gesture, which vaguely indicated the people about him. 'My lady, surely – um – we should talk about this in private. There's no need to discuss family affairs in the open with servants and villeins to witness it all.'

'Why should we not discuss it here? This is my home, Thomas!' she snapped.

'No, Lady. It is *mine*! And I choose not to speak of such matters in the court like a serf begging alms. If you wish to talk to me, I shall be inside.'

So saying, Thomas gathered his pride to him like a man trying to wrap himself up in a tattered and shredded cloak. He gave Simon a cold glance, up and down, and strode up the stairs, past the lady and into the hall. A second or two later Godfrey appeared, blinking and rubbing an ugly bruise on his temple.

As if in general agreement that the entertainment was over, the crowd began to disperse, some laughing, many winking and grinning at Hugh, who suddenly realised he was still gripping Daniel's staff of office. He shamefacedly lowered his head, walked to the steward and passed it to him with a mumbled word of regret for taking it so rudely.

'Don't dare to apologise,' Daniel said, struggling not to laugh. 'After what I've seen today, you're welcome to it whenever you need it. What a fight! I swear I haven't seen such a staff-fight since the Welsh wars!' He clapped Hugh on the back. 'And for protecting the manor's guest, whatever the greasy little bugger may be like, you deserve the thanks of all of us here. Come inside and drink wine with me, friend. I'd hate to think you were my enemy, after all!'

But before returning to the hall, Hugh went to Petronilla, still squatting at the side of the Fleming. Godfrey was assisting her, holding a damp cloth to the bloody cut, while the girl gently wiped at the clots on the man's face. He lay quite still, his face a perfect mask of pain.

'Thanks,' Godfrey said simply. 'I'm only sorry I missed seeing your defence of him.'

Hugh shrugged. 'He'll need that wound stitched.'

'Yes, well, someone can do it later. It's not a hard job,' said Godfrey easily.

Hugh turned away. Baldwin and Simon were already on the steps which led back to the hall, and Hugh was about to follow them when Godfrey touched his arm.

'I threatened you, when you were trying to serve drinks in the hall. I'm sorry about that. After you protected my master I can't help feeling we owe you something in return.'

Hugh stared at his feet. He wasn't used to accepting gratitude from others, and didn't know how to respond.

Godfrey grinned crookedly. 'Don't worry, I can't promise you money . . .' Hugh's morose expression deteriorated, '. . . it's only this: I know your master and the knight have been trying to find out what happened that day . . .'

'If you know something, you should tell them. I'll only get it all mucked up.'

'Very well.' Godfrey glanced down at his master. 'How is he, Miss?'

'He'll live.'

'Let's see your master now, then.'

Hugh nodded, and shouted to two stablemen at the other side of the yard. They ran over and, under Hugh's supervision, dragged or assisted his assailants to the barn before taking a door off its hinges and lifting the Fleming onto it. Godfrey stopped them carrying him into the hall. 'I doubt whether the Lady wants to see him like that. Take him to the kitchen, it's warm enough, and he can't come to any harm.'

Hugh walked slowly back to the hall. Strangely, although he was aware of a sense of pleasure at having beaten so many men, a satisfaction which was made more intense by the fact that he had done so to protect a man who would loathe owing him a favour, Hugh felt something else as he walked over the threshold.

It was a feeling of profound sadness, as if some doom was about to be laid upon the house and all who dwelt within it, and as he passed into the hall, Hugh shuddered with the premonition of evil.

Margaret crossed the floor with Simon, and stood a little to the side of Lady Katharine. The bailiff's wife couldn't help noticing that the latter was strangely animated, and although the red-rimmed eyes and bright nose gave her a feverish look, her posture was regal, especially in her disdainful treatment of Thomas, who sat near the fire with another cup of wine in his hands.

When Hugh came back in, Margaret took a jug and filled a pot, handing it to him, smiling. 'Well done!' she said warmly. Hugh shrugged ungraciously, but with real pleasure, while Simon filled more pots and passed them around to all those assembled.

'I ask you all to drink to Hugh,' he boomed, 'a hero among servants! Hugh!'

Margaret returned to the side of Lady Katharine and poured wine for her. The bereaved woman drank deeply, holding the cup with both hands to steady it. She needed to steel her nerves for the inevitable confrontation with Thomas, Margaret thought, and it was only when she had refilled Lady Katherine's pot that she allowed her attention to wander around the room again.

Anney was nowhere to be seen. She had been out with the others to witness the fight, but still hadn't returned, and Margaret clicked her tongue at such dereliction. It was especially important that she should look after her mistress on a day like this, when she had not only buried her child but had also endured the shame of a fight between guests at the funeral party. Margaret tut-tutted silently. She would have to speak to the steward about Anney.

*　　　*　　　*

The priest huddled at the back of the hall near the door, even more pale than usual, his eyes dull and listless. Catching Margaret's eye, Brother Stephen gave her a ghastly smile.

Scarcely knowing what he was doing, he raised his drinking pot to his lips and took a deep draught. It felt as if the walls of the room were closing in on him; the place was stifling with all these people! He knew he was in enormous danger still, even though Petronilla had gone and destroyed some of the evidence. There were too many who had seen him up on the moors that day . . . and he was unpleasantly aware of Godfrey's cool gaze on him. Then Godfrey looked away, and with a freezing feeling in his bowels, Stephen saw him look from Sir Baldwin to the bailiff.

Simon was insisting that Hugh should drink all his wine and have another cup to wash it down. In the midst of his delight it was some time before he noticed the grave-looking servant standing behind Hugh. 'Are you all right, Godfrey?' he cried bluffly. 'Your master'll recover from his scratch, never fear! I've seen much worse.'

'So have I, Bailiff. Many times,' said Godfrey drily. 'That wasn't why I was quiet. I wish to make a statement in front of the whole company, but am not sure how to begin.'

The Lady Katharine had returned to her seat by the fire; her steward stood behind her, gripping his staff once more. Her expression was one of deep shock, as if after burying her husband and her child, and then witnessing the small battle at the very entrance to her hall, she was close to collapse.

Stephen saw the vacuity of her expression and walked to her side. He touched the cross at his waist, his face filled with compassion, then reached out towards her, but his hand hovered a few inches from her shoulder, as if he did not dare interrupt her thoughts.

Simon felt that in that simple, humble gesture, Stephen had given him more of an insight into his character than all the sermons he had heard the cleric give or the conversations he had held with the man. The priest might appear cold and unfeeling, even perhaps cruel sometimes, but he was still a man, and perhaps, Simon thought, watching him from the corner of his eye, perhaps he was a man with the same desires as any other, no matter what his oaths implied. For there was a hint of reverence in his way of standing there next to his mistress, like a knight who has been overwhelmed by the beauty of a lady.

Lady Katharine looked up at last, noticing the silence that had gradually fallen all about her. Seeing Godfrey at its centre, ready to make some sort of announcement, she gave a small frown and waved her hand. 'Do you wish to speak, Master Godfrey? Please go ahead.'

'If you are sure, Madam,' he said, and shot a look at Thomas.

'I doubt whether there is anything you could say which would surprise me. Is it about Thomas trying to make me sell off parts of my land?'

The merchant was sitting upright now, and had fixed him with a piercing – no, Godfrey amended, a *threatening* stare – but one in which the fear of personal discovery was all too evident. 'I've got nothing to hide,' Thomas said gruffly.

'On the day your son died, my Lady, this man arranged to meet my master. Sir James demanded that I should be present, in case of any risk to himself, and I thus overheard their entire discussion. I think Sir James has already told you the general tenor of what they discussed.'

She nodded, with a contemptuous glance in her brother-in-law's direction. 'Yes. Thomas demanded money in order to persuade me to sell parts of my land to van Relenghes. My brother-in-law was prepared to sell his nephew's birthright for his own gain.'

'That's right, my Lady,' Godfrey acknowledged, and lowered his head. 'And I confess that I held my tongue about it, and for that I beg your pardon. There were two reasons, my Lady: first was the consideration that I was paid by my master, and for a man like me that consideration must carry weight; but second was my belief that something odd was being planned by my master. If I were to leave his service I could not have discovered what he intended.'

'Which was?' Simon interrupted.

'Nothing more than the ravishing of Squire Roger's wife.'

There was a shocked intake of breath from the gathering. Simon was quiet with anger. 'You mean this?'

'Oh yes, sir. James van Relenghes is a conceited fool who believes that no woman can reject his advances. You see, he wanted revenge on the squire. My master once captured a hostage and ransomed him, allowing him to go free. The prisoner was a French Duke, and the squire – your husband, my Lady – heard of this and forced the Fleming to repay all the money he had won. All hostages of rank were to have been sold to the King in order that he could ransom them himself, and he paid a reasonable rate, but van Relenghes was greedy. He wanted the lot. Squire Roger got the money and gave the Fleming some time to escape before he told the

King – thus in van Relenghes's mind Squire Roger cost him a king's ransom *and* his career.'

'So he was motivated by revenge?' Simon said.

'Yes, sir. The Fleming hated the squire, and wanted to mete out punishment on his wife and child. Well, I think he thought the best way to ruin the Lady Katharine was to show she was guilty of infamy, taking another man soon after her husband's death. And he thought he could make her take him. I don't think he wanted to merely damage her reputation. No, I reckon he thought that by showing her to be unfaithful to her husband's memory, he could also hint that she was adulterous during the squire's life, that he was cuckolded. That way the Fleming would get back at the man he really hated.'

'And you chose to keep this secret?'

'I remained at his side all the time to ensure my Lady was safe. Perhaps I was wrong, but if I had told of the scheme, my master must have found out that someone had spoken. It would not be hard to guess that I had opened my mouth. And I thought it better to remain with him, to see what else he would attempt. Especially since I had my own debt of honour to repay. I used to fight with the squire – oh, many years ago. So did another man with whom I have spoken.' He saw no reason to say that the man who had given him much of his information was Thomas's own servant, Nicholas.

Lady Katharine gave him another nod, slower this time.

'And now, my Lady, allow me to make amends to you for my secrecy. Here and now, I accuse your brother-in-law of murdering Herbert, your son.'

309

CHAPTER TWENTY-EIGHT

'You've been here all the time?'

In the stable, Nicholas winced as Anney wiped some of the blood from his nose. 'Yes,' he mumbled, his voice nasal and thick with pain. 'I couldn't go and see you, though, could I? What would you have done?'

'Probably hit you, you bastard,' she said evenly. It was true: she would have been happy to hit him if he was standing – but not now, not like this. Nicholas was a picture of dejection, sitting on the stool with his head tilted back so the blood wouldn't flow down his shirt any more and would have an opportunity to clot. 'I don't think I'd have managed to get you so well as this, though.'

Nicholas wheezed through his open mouth. There was a dull ache between his eyes, and he had a desperate urge to scratch his ruined nose, but he daren't touch it, not yet. 'I'll get the sod back for doing this.'

'You think so? After he put four of your friends down and then you as well, you really think you'd have a chance against him?' She patted away another dribble of blood from the tender, shattered skin, and felt him flinch as her damp cloth touched him, but not as much as when she said, 'What happened to your wife?'

'What of her? She left me.'

'Left you?'

He curled his lip. 'She got upset when she found me in bed with a strumpet.'

Anney leaned back and surveyed him. There was truth in his face; he wasn't of a temper to lie, not now, and Anney, for the first time in the ten years since he had been taken from her, realised how lucky her escape had been. Nicholas was no more than a brute who would drink himself into oblivion whenever he had an opportunity, then beat his wife for any one of a number of imagined slights, and turn to a pox-ridden whore at the first opportunity to prove his virility.

It was hard to believe that she had spent so long pining after him, wishing he hadn't been taken back to his first, legal wife. But he was still the father of her children, and Anney was content to look after his wounds because he was also the only man who had ever held her heart. And although she had no wish to discuss the affair with him, it gave her some comfort to know that the father of her dead boy was with her.

The boy whose death had been caused by that spoilt brat Herbert.

'Eh? What's that? You say you think I . . . The man's mad!' Thomas spluttered, puce in the face.

Godfrey ignored him and went on with his statement. 'My evidence is this, Lady: he and his servant left us because he saw your maid Petronilla approaching and didn't want to be overheard by her, or so he said. She came ambling idly along, and my master, who thought she might be able to give him information about you, tried to hold her up and talk. I had no wish to listen to his flattery and lies, so I took my horse a few yards away and left them to it.

'Then there was a cry up on the hill, away near the top. When I looked up, I saw the priest thrashing about him with a stick at the furze, shouting out in the most unholy fashion about boys generally, but your son, and his friend Alan in particular. I had no idea why at the time, but I heard the priest shout something about slings. Now I think I understand why.'

Simon moved a little, so he could glance at the priest. Stephen did not look up, but kept his head bowed as if in prayer, and the bailiff was convinced he was hiding something. And yet perhaps it was only this, that he *had* been near the scene of the boy's death. He was thought to be a child-hater, so maybe he had decided to keep quiet in case he could be suspected.

Godfrey continued, 'At the time, Thomas and his man were near the fork in the road, and I saw them stop there and glance back, so they obviously heard the shouting too. Petronilla did as well, and she scampered straight off up the hill to pacify the priest. I saw her. Just afterwards, Thomas and Nicholas carried on their way, but soon after they had disappeared around the curve in the road, I saw a figure dart across it. It was a boy.'

'Was it Herbert?' Baldwin asked immediately.

Godfrey gave a slight shrug. He wasn't absolutely certain. 'I'm no father; one boy looks much like another to me, especially when he's been rolling in mud, which this one had, by the look of him.'

'He always liked that. It was one of their games up on the hill,' said Lady Katharine softly. There was a catch in her voice, and Stephen rested his hand reassuringly on her shoulder. 'Chasing each other through the bushes and squirming their way through the peat all over the common. I used to scold him and smack him when . . .' She buried her face in her hands.

'My Lady, do you want me to be still?' Godfrey asked.

After a moment, she lifted her head. 'No, please tell us the rest.'

'You don't believe what this man says, do you? He's only a whoreson mercenary!' Thomas shouted suddenly. 'Look at him! Would you trust his honour?'

Godfrey ignored his outburst. 'The figure ran over the road, then I saw him dive into the bushes at the other side and disappear. I thought nothing of it at first. Oh, I assumed the lad must have done something to the priest up the hill there, but that was as far as I got. Beyond that, I had no thought for him. Then I heard the bellow of rage from *him*,' he said, and pointed to Thomas.

Thomas flinched as the finger stabbed towards him, but then met Godfrey's stare with a resolute fury as Godfrey finished his story.

'Thomas screamed and I think I heard his man laugh, but then Thomas must have dismounted from his horse because I turned and saw him running towards me. As soon as he saw me, he demanded whether I had seen a lad coming my way.

313

Well, I shook my head, wondering what on earth all this fuss was about, and he said: "The little bastard shot me with a sling and if I catch him, I'll wring his insolent neck!" Then he swore and went back the way he had come.'

Godfrey paused and stared down, as if debating whether to continue. 'My Lady, I also have to tell you that this man has no money. He needed the inheritance to save his finances. I think he ensured your son was put out of the way.'

Simon gazed at the miserable Thomas. 'Well? What do you have to say for yourself?'

'Me?' Thomas sneered feebly. 'What could *I* say, Bailiff? You've made up your mind already, haven't you? "Oh, the evil creature, he's prepared to try to get himself a few pennies from his brother's estate" – a brother, you'll recall, who has left me nothing, *nothing*! And the estate would all have been mine if he hadn't taken that *dam* to wife so he could start breeding. Why shouldn't I have got something out of it? It should have been mine anyway, and why on earth the law allows a puling brat to take a man's lands, I don't understand.'

'You know full well that the law is there to protect the weak, like poor Herbert,' Baldwin stated sternly.

'Oh, spare me the lesson on the law! The weak, you say? What exactly am I supposed to have done? Eh, Sir Knight?'

'You've been accused of murder,' said Simon sternly. 'And as bailiff, I have to tell you that I am inclined to believe the accusation. You admit to your lust for the estate, you confess your dislike of the boy, and you knew that he was the only person standing between you and your greed. All you needed to do was kill him, and you could possess the lands you always hankered after.'

'I . . . That's rubbish!' Thomas spat, rising to his feet. Edgar was close by, and took a step nearer, but Baldwin gave a slight shake of his head, and his servant remained where he was.

'Rubbish, I say – you suggest I killed my own nephew, forsooth! In God's name, it would have been easy enough, but I never even saw the little devil. He wasn't there!'

'Then who did you see?' Baldwin asked, and seated himself at a bench. Simon sat at his side, and the two of them stared at the disconcerted man.

By that simple action, they had altered the whole tone; Thomas now felt he was truly the subject of a legal court, the suspected felon in this heinous crime. He swallowed. Suddenly he was sober, and fearful. He felt his legs quiver, and stared from one to the other, hoping to see a sign of sympathy in their eyes, but there was nothing. When he allowed his gaze to wander about the room, he saw contempt on all the faces, except Katharine's: hers radiated pure hatred.

'Well?' Simon asked. 'Who was it down there? We've heard from another that you were off your horse, beating among the bushes, and now we learn that you had run back and called out to Godfrey. Who was the boy if it wasn't Herbert?'

'I think it was that cretinous son of a villein, Alan,' Thomas muttered. 'The little shit has hit people before. Ask Stephen about him, he'll tell you – go on, ask the priest! The sod sits in the bushes and when he sees a rider coming past, he tries to tickle up the horses by hitting them with a stone from his sling. He got me instead of my horse that day, hit me right on the thigh, and painful it was, too – that was why

Godfrey heard me shout. Anyone would have cried out, hit by a bullet like that.'

'What did you do then?' Simon pressed.

'Like Godfrey said, I went in search of the brat; I was going to give him a sound thrashing if I had the chance, but I couldn't find him, and from what Godfrey said, the sod hadn't gone back that way. Thinking that he must be hiding down the slope or out on the road to Throwleigh, I made off back the way I had come to head him off. When I still couldn't spot him, I started searching for him in and among the bushes.'

'And then you heard a cart coming your way?' Baldwin asked.

'Yes, but not Edmund's. The one I heard was the fishmonger's cart coming back from the manor. I looked up when that thing came rumbling along, and had a good look at it in case Alan was clinging on beneath, but I couldn't see him, so I went back to the bushes again.'

Simon frowned, and jerked his thumb towards Godfrey. 'You said you remained up there. What else did you see?'

'Sir, after Thomas went off in a rage, I sat there laughing awhile, and didn't notice much. When I did look about me again, I saw that Petronilla had disappeared. She was going to pacify the priest before he could hurt the boys – well, that's what my master thought . . .'

Lady Katharine stirred. 'Bailiff, she knew my feelings towards the priest. Stephen always resorted to the cane at the slightest provocation, and I had a fear that one day his zeal would overcome him. Petronilla would have gone to protect my boy if the priest had caught him so far from home.'

'Which means that Stephen and Petronilla both thought that Herbert was up the hill with them,' Baldwin pointed out.

He too glanced at Godfrey. 'What makes you think that Thomas captured and killed him?'

'This, Sir Baldwin. Only a little while later, my master and I were about to ride back to the manor when we heard a short cry and a bellow of anger, and then a few minutes later a boy hared over the road going back up the hill towards the priest. By this time Stephen had gone quiet, and I reckoned the girl had persuaded him to leave well alone, but a few moments later up came Thomas, puffing and blowing like a spent nag, pointed up the hill, and was away, over the road and into the bushes.

'At the time it all seemed so ludicrous I was ready only to laugh, but then I thought to myself, if the brat likes taking shots at horses and riders, maybe the best place for me is beyond reach of his sling – and so I rode away.'

'So your evidence is,' Baldwin concluded, 'that the lad was alive then, that Thomas was enraged and could have done the boy harm – although you say he was still on foot?' Godfrey nodded, and Baldwin gave Thomas a puzzled frown.

Simon set his head on one side. 'Did you ride straight back to the manor then?'

'No, sir. We were about to, but I persuaded my master not to take the direct route within range of his pebbles.'

'Why?'

Godfrey grinned. 'Sir, like I said, I thought the boy was up there with a sling. I didn't fancy being his target on my ride home! Sir James agreed to take the longer route homewards, and as we were about to turn and go off, we saw the other carter, the local man.'

'Edmund,' Simon nodded.

'Yes, sir. He was drunk, that was obvious. He was reeling on the seat every time he hit a pebble on the track. He looked mightily fearful of us too: two strangers, well-accoutred, armed and obviously not local. He hunched his head down into his shoulders like a snail, and tried to avoid meeting our gaze. We just stared at him, for fun, you understand, and he rode on by. But when he got some few yards from us, I saw him turn and stare back at us.'

Baldwin looked at Thomas. 'We heard that Thomas was down at the other road when Edmund passed, yet you say Thomas ran over the road before the cart came into view?'

Daniel interrupted. 'Edmund must have been lying!'

'I don't think so, Daniel,' said Simon. 'The distance Thomas had to run was only short, yet Edmund would have seen him up to a half-mile away from the fork. I daresay Edmund saw him, chose to take the other road, and then Thomas set off after his assailant, running up to the higher road and over it before Edmund got there.'

'That would explain it,' Baldwin agreed. 'So then, Godfrey. After witnessing all this excitement, you rode away from the scene with your master.'

'Yes, sir. We went straight down through the bushes to the Throwleigh road, and came back that way.'

'What of you, Thomas?'

The sagging figure eyed him bleakly. 'I went after the sod, I admit, but he escaped. I couldn't catch him – I never even saw his face.' He stopped and stared about him, then burst out, 'You have to believe me, I wouldn't have killed him! He was my nephew, for God's sake! I wouldn't have hurt him.'

Katharine rose shakily to her feet and, without glancing at anyone else, crossed the floor to him. She stood before him, holding his gaze, and suddenly her hand whipped out and struck his cheek. Bunching a fist, she hit him again, and then she flailed at his chest with both hands, and shrieked, 'You killed him! You murdered my Herbert, my poor, darling Herbert! Murderer!'

Daniel rushed to her side and caught her wrists. Speaking softly and soothingly, he forced her to turn from the ashen Thomas, and led the sobbing woman from the room. A few yards behind them strode Stephen, his face troubled, hands fiddling with his rosary.

Thomas suddenly shouted, 'Where's Anney? Get that bitch in here! Get her to tell you what *she* was doing up there!'

CHAPTER TWENTY-NINE

Jordan stood before the imposing gates and stared up, awestruck. If it weren't for the stoic friend at his side, he would have turned and fled from the place. As it was, his feet felt as if they were rooted to the spot.

It wasn't only that this gate and the buildings beyond represented power and money, it was also the recent history of his family. The lord of this demesne had been going to evict them from their house; they weren't only going to lose it, but were claimed to be villeins, too, their freedom gone for ever, and Jordan couldn't help but feel a qualm at the sight of the studded oak gates which loomed so menacingly above them.

Yet he had his duty to perform. His father was here, in his prison, probably starving, almost certainly beaten for no good reason, just because the Lady hated him and his family. That thought made him swallow nervously, aware that she might order his own punishment, but it also fired a contrary determination to do whatever he must, to suffer beatings or whippings if need be, to get his father released.

Alan took a deep, shuddering breath – proof that he was not quite so bold as he had tried to make out. He felt the peril of the imposing gates as well.

It made Jordan sorry for the older boy. He knew Alan wanted to be the leader in their escapades, and yet here he was, fearful, while Jordan's own anxiety was leaving him, to be replaced with a wish to get the dreaded interview over and done with.

'Come on, Alan. We might as well get on with it,' he said, and took his friend's free hand, the one that didn't bear the little parcel.

Edgar found Anney gently bathing Nicholas's wounds. She agreed to return with him when he said that the bailiff wished to speak to her.

'Bailiff?' she asked tentatively, looking about her. Those who met her eye soon glanced away, and she experienced a quickening of her heartbeat. Edgar took her into the hall and led her forward until she was standing before the bailiff and the knight, who studied her in silence a moment. Thomas, who was swiftly becoming drunk, sat on a small stool nearer the fire. Every now and again he lifted his pot and supped noisily, and when the cup was down, his breath snored almost as if he was asleep.

'Anney, we have heard you were up on the hillside on the day Herbert was murdered,' Simon said. 'What were you doing up there?'

'Who says I was?'

'Thomas says he saw you there.'

321

'Me?' Anney demanded. 'What has he accused me of, the devil?'

Her voice was little more than a squeak, and she knew her face must be deathly white. There was no way she could hide her stupefying terror at being examined here, in the room where her husband had been taken from her, the room where her boy's body had been exposed to the gaze of all those in the village who despised her. This hall had been a place of horror to her for so long, and now it held the threat of the rope. She could almost sense the creaking, swaying gibbet.

She felt a swimming sensation, as though the walls were moving around her. It was so like that time, when she had been called before the old squire, to stand here and be questioned and harassed by officials so that they could formally decide what all knew, that she had been taken in by that ne'er-do-well outside, who had stolen her virginity when he was already wedded to another.

Simon saw her tottering, and hurried over to help her to a bench. 'Edgar, could you fetch some wine?'

'No, sir, I'm all right,' she protested, sitting quietly. 'I felt a little weak, no more.' However, Simon passed her the pot when it arrived, and she drank from it thirstily. 'Thank you, sir.'

Once he had returned to his seat, the bailiff glanced from Thomas to the maid. 'Thomas says you were also up there on the moors, Anney. Could you tell us what you were doing?'

She lifted her head coolly: her boy needed her. How could Alan survive without a mother? He didn't even know Nicholas, his father. She met Simon's serious stare. 'Yes, sir. I was following the priest.'

Baldwin lifted his head, surprised. 'Why?'

'Because I knew he was there to satisfy his lusts.'

Many of the onlookers gasped, and the bailiff and his friend exchanged bewildered glances. Simon blinked and asked, 'What evidence do you have for this?' He was relieved that the cleric was not present to hear the accusation.

'I have the evidence of my eyes, sir. What more do I need? You ask others around here, and see what they say!' she declared hotly.

Baldwin tried to calm her. Her face had been pallid, but now it shone with a feverish glow, and he wasn't sure of the strength of her mind. 'Anney, priests take oaths of chastity, but if Stephen of York failed to maintain the high standard expected, I fear he is not alone . . .' he said soothingly.

'What do you think he's doing, telling people like me that I am a sinner, when *he* can satisfy his every carnal whim, eh?'

Baldwin and his friend had no need to look at each other. Both had the same thought: Anney had admitted a misdemeanour in the confessional, probably to carnal knowledge of the bigamist who had fathered her children, before discovering that the priest was guilty of similar lecherous acts. She wanted revenge on a man she thought was a hypocrite; showing that the priest himself was as guilty as she.

'What did you see on that day?' Simon asked.

She stared at him, breathing quickly. 'I'll tell you what I saw! I saw Stephen grab my son, and beat him with his stick. Alan was lucky, he twisted out of Stephen's hand and managed to escape – but what happened then, eh? Stephen tried to catch Alan again, running up the hill and searching through the bushes, until he gave up and went back down to the stream. I was about to return to the manor when I heard this dreadful shout, and suddenly the priest appeared, coming up the slope again towards me. But he didn't see me, his eyes were fixed on the boy.'

'*Your* boy?' Simon asked in the sudden hush.

'Oh, no. Alan was too quick for the priest. No, the boy I saw was Herbert. The poor mite was pelting along as fast as he could, up towards me, with his sling in his hand. He'd only been playing a prank, I think, but the joke fell flat. Brother Stephen wanted his revenge, and he took it . . .'

'What sort of prank? We must understand exactly what happened,' Simon said with a trace of weariness.

'What do you think? What do boys usually do? Herbert had his sling in his hand and probably fired a bullet from it at the priest's arse, just in jest – and no more would have been said or done if Stephen was an ordinary man.'

Baldwin leaned back with an exasperated sigh. 'Anney, you like to hint at things, but please come to the point. You say he's no ordinary man, but what do you mean by it?'

She sat up exultantly. 'You ask me what sort of man he is, and I'll tell you: he's a sodomite, a pederast! He likes little boys, he likes to—'

Simon held up his hand and talked over her even as her face became flushed with a fierce kind of joy at relating the accusation she had heard with such horror such a short time ago.

'Anney, be silent! This is a very serious allegation indeed, you realise? If you are inventing this, if you have no proof, you could be in very grave danger for accusing a man in holy orders. Think, woman! If this is mere villainous gossip, hold your tongue! Don't force us to record your thoughts if they are based on nothing more than speculation.'

'*Speculation!*' she spat. 'Do you think it is speculation when your own son comes home crying because a cleric has beaten him black and blue in the street? Is it guesswork when you witness the man thrashing a five-year-old in his chapel? I saw him – the day the squire died, I saw Stephen beating Herbert in his chapel, before his altar! This priest is evil! He has unnatural lusts, and tries to force the boys of the vill to give themselves to him. He beats them because it satisfies a wicked desire in him!'

There was no doubting the sincerity of her tone. She had leaned forward in her desperate desire to convince, and her eyes met Baldwin's with an almost frightening intensity.

He didn't know what to believe. That the woman was quite sure in her own mind that this was true he had no doubt, but that was different from knowing that her apparently wild denunciations were correct. She was picking at the sleeves of her tunic, worrying at the hems, trying to pull a thread free, and when it was, tugging at another. Her face looked careworn, he thought, and her body, although wide and strong-looking, was too thin. In her face the eyes stood out with unnatural brightness, as if all the power of the body were held within them.

It was the face of a woman pursuing her enemy: a man who had threatened her remaining child. She would accuse Brother Stephen of anything to protect her boy. Baldwin hadn't noticed her singlemindedness before, and he blamed himself for that. The two deaths in Lady Katharine's family had forced him to concentrate on the poor woman who sat in front of Anney now rather than the maid herself.

He concentrated on Anney, and was not reassured by what he saw. Her eagerness to see the priest ruined before his whole congregation, and her desire to convince Simon and him of the priest's guilt, were quite hideous.

Seeing his musing stare, she suddenly stood and faced him.

'Don't trust to my word: *ask* him! Make him swear on his Bible, make him come and question *him*,' she demanded. 'Let him try to preserve his reputation! Make the pervert stand up to someone who dares confront him with his evil sins!'

The object of their enquiry was at that moment kneeling solemnly before the altar in his little chapel. He finished praying, rose, kissed the cross which adorned his stole, and removed it. He was filled with a feeling of melancholy.

His despondency had started on the day that the master had died. It had begun badly, when that young devil Herbert had so wilfully misbehaved, but from then things had grown steadily worse. Petronilla had been waiting for him after he had beaten the boy here in the chapel, and he had been surprised at the expression of horror on her face, and of course he hadn't the faintest idea why at the time. He'd explained that he had been instructed to thrash the child, but that hadn't helped.

And when Anney with her pinched, suspicious face had appeared, leading Herbert away and demanding Stephen's presence in the hall, Petronilla had quietly insisted on arranging a tryst. Her doggedness had first alarmed, and then positively scared him. God knew what the bitch might get up to if he didn't, so he'd agreed, and they had arranged a day to meet up near the stream where they had gone so often before. That was the day Master Herbert had died . . .

Stephen thrust his alb and stole into his chest and shut the lid, his lips pursed. He knew it was wrong of him to have felt such loathing for the boy, even if he only acknowledged it in the privacy of his own mind, but he couldn't help but despise Herbert. Especially after what he'd done to the priest that day.

Just because the boy had died, Stephen was prepared to pray for him, as his mother desired, but he had no intention of keeping his own feelings hidden from his God. The child had caused the death of his father – of that Stephen was quite convinced – and had deserved his end, the barbarous little villain!

Squire Roger may not have been the ideal, God-fearing, learned and cultured lord that Stephen could have wished for, but for all his faults he was a kindly and generous man. Now, all because of that mendacious little swine, he was dead, and it was unlikely, from what Stephen had seen of Thomas, that his services would be required for much longer. Soon he would be forced to move to Exeter, or perhaps further afield.

He closed his eyes, and slowly sank onto his wooden chest, breathing deeply to control the anxiety he felt at this reflection. It was so hard, to be forced to find a new situation at his age. God only knew how far he would have to travel to find himself somewhere to live. And it was all because of that damned Herbert!

He was about to go to his private chamber and sit in quiet meditation when he heard a light tapping at his door. On opening it, he was surprised to see the knight's servant.

'Sir, would you come with me to the hall, please?'

*   *   *

Alan was as scared as Jordan, but he swallowed hard and carried on walking towards the hall. The bustle all about them was unnerving, especially when men leading horses walked past swearing at them, or riders cursed at them for wandering so slowly. This was a busy, working manor, and people had too much to do to want to stand aside for youngsters.

Jordan saw one groom staring at them suspiciously, and was glad that he'd left his sling behind. He was sure he recognised the man as one of his targets from the week before, and averted his gaze quickly. It would be humiliating to be captured and beaten now, just when they were trying to hand in the evidence that would destroy their enemy.

There was no doubt in either of their minds as to where they must go. They had to see the bailiff and give him their evidence, and that meant going to the hall. They had been there often enough; it was the place where their master, Squire Roger, had held all his celebrations, as well as his courts. Their lord had given feasts for Christmas, for harvest, for sheep-shearing, and all the other festivals, religious and otherwise, which punctuated the year.

On their way to the hall they had to pass a large gathering of workers who lounged at the door to the kitchen. Here another face caught Jordan's attention. It was an ageing farmer, a freeman, but one of those who rented land from the manor and who had to pay his annual due of labour to the demesne. Like the others, he was here to collect his wages in food and ale.

'Ho, there, young Jordan! What are you doing here? And you, Alan, you little devil. Have you both been called to the lord's court?'

His friends all laughed at his sally. Alan in particular was well known to all the men in the area, and though some could laugh at his mischief, several eyed him sourly, recalling times when they had caught him running through their gardens or trying to shoot squirrels on their land.

'Sir, we're here to see the knight and the bailiff.'

The old farmer's smile dimmed. 'And why do you think the knight and the bailiff would want to see you two, eh? Go on, boys, clear off and play on the moors. Don't interrupt men like them when they're about their business.'

'But we have to – we have proof of who murdered the squire's son!'

CHAPTER THIRTY

Simon gave a distracted 'tut' when he was told that there were two boys outside to see him. He was about to snap at the obsequious old farmer that he had better things to do than act as nursemaid to a pair of children, when Baldwin put his hand on the bailiff's arm. Something in the farmer's anxious features made him think that this was important.

'Hugh, go with this man and take the lads into the buttery. No doubt Wat is there. Leave them in his tender care, and we'll see them later, once we've heard what the priest has to say for himself.'

Hugh finished his pot of wine and slouched through the door. It was only a short time later that Edgar returned, the sorry-looking priest behind him.

'Sir Baldwin? I understand you wish to see me.'

'Not I alone, I am afraid, Brother Stephen,' he said quietly.

Anney leaped to her feet. 'Sodomite! Murderer! I accuse you—'

'Anney, if you can't hold your tongue, you'll have to leave the hall!' Simon felt his anger rising. 'Let me remind you that this man is a priest, and that this is not a court. Even if it were, only an ecclesiastical one could charge Stephen. You have no right to pursue him, and I have no power to convict him.'

Stephen listened with every sign of bewilderment. On entering he had walked straight to a chair, and now stood in front of it, his face registering astonishment. He stared, first at Anney, then at Simon and Baldwin. 'I don't understand, Bailiff – what is this? I thought there was a need for my help, but you say I have been accused of something?'

'Of the murder of your charge – of Herbert of Throwleigh,' Baldwin intoned solemnly.

Stephen dropped heavily into his chair. 'Is . . . is this a joke? I can't believe anyone would accuse me of something so heinous as murder.'

Baldwin was studying him closely. The sudden collapse looked very contrived, and the man's expression did not carry the same conviction as Anney's.

He shot her a look. She was glaring furiously at the priest, her look as venomous as a viper's bite. The knight did not understand why she should loathe the man so much, but then reflected that for her, the only person in her life who amounted to anything was her son, and if Stephen had often beaten him, and that unfairly, she might well harbour a grudge. Then again, if she seriously believed that he was a perverted man, who might prey on children to satisfy his sexual proclivity, would it be any surprise that she would wish to see him ruined, destroyed as utterly as she thought he had destroyed young Herbert?

Simon was speaking again.

'We have heard quite a lot about the day that Herbert died, Stephen. Witnesses state that you were seen up near the stream. Many saw you there, and several saw you attacking Anney's boy, and Anney herself says she saw you chasing after Herbert and trying to thrash him. She says you murdered Herbert – did you?'

Stephen sat up on his seat. As the bailiff had said, he was safe here. There was no court which had jurisdiction over him other than a correctly constituted church one. Stephen glanced at Anney and allowed a little of his contempt to show. 'No, of course not. The woman's deranged.'

'Me! I'll—'

She would have rushed at him, had not Edgar stepped forward and blocked her path. The priest shook his head sadly.

'Bailiff, this woman has been deluded for many months now – in fact, I believe she has been thus ever since her first boy died. He drowned in the old well in the yard, you know. What with that and the discovery that her husband was no more than a lascivious fellow who would swear marriage vows to any woman whose bed he wanted to invade . . . well, you will comprehend why this poor woman has a fixation about all men, not just me.'

'That's a lie!'

'All I can say is, I *didn't* kill my young master Herbert – why on earth should I? And as for the other, er, wild allegations . . . well, I am prepared to forgive them. She clearly doesn't realise what she is saying.'

All this was said so coolly that Simon almost thanked him. But then he recalled the other evidence. 'So you say you didn't see him up there?'

Before the priest could respond, Baldwin rested his elbow on his knee, cupping his chin in the palm of his hand and gazing at the cleric with a distracted air. 'Stephen, we have heard that you grabbed this woman's son, Alan. Why was that?'

'Why?' Too late, Stephen realised that he should have instantly denied seeing Alan. He shrugged. 'He was up there spying on me. I get bored with the boys constantly following me everywhere. It becomes thoroughly tedious after a while, and when I found him doing it again, I sought to convince him that continuing to do so would only result in pain for him.'

'So you caught him and beat him?'

'I tried to, yes. But the boy twisted away, and escaped.'

'And you chased after him?'

Stephen assented.

'What did you do then, Brother Stephen?'

'I . . . I went to the stream to sit and contemplate. I like it up there, it's peaceful and pleasant.'

'What about Petronilla?' asked Baldwin.

'She spoke to me for a few minutes before I went to the stream, but please don't ask me what about – it was a matter of the confessional, you understand.'

Simon nodded. He knew as well as anyone that the secrecy of the confessional could not be breached. 'And she left you?'

'Yes.'

'A little later you were seen chasing after and catching Herbert. Why?'

Stephen's face hardened. 'The little devil fired a stone at me. It hurt. I dare to suggest that if someone had done such

333

a thing to you, Bailiff, you too would have tried to punish the perpetrator.'

'Quite possibly. But I wouldn't have killed him.'

'Do you suggest that I did?'

Baldwin spoke softly. 'Tell us what happened.'

'He shot me. I got up and couldn't see anyone, but I heard a rustling and laughter, and chased off towards it. When I got there, Herbert jumped to his feet and ran away. I am fairly fleet of foot, but he was too fast for me.'

'What then?'

'Then?' Stephen blinked, unsure what additional evidence the knight needed. 'Why, I returned to the stream.'

'What had you lost there?'

Stephen froze, but then licked his lips and gave a feeble smile. 'What makes you think I had lost anything?'

'We saw you searching on the day it rained. You had gone back to seek something, and were looking most assiduously under bushes, so I assume that whatever it was must have been valuable.'

'No, it was merely a small trifle, nothing much.'

'You mean to tell me that you went back there a few days later and started fumbling all over the place on your hands and knees trying to find an insignificant trifle? What would you have done for something valuable?'

'I do not think I need to remain here to be harangued,' said Stephen with dignity. 'If that is all, I . . .'

'It was not that you were searching for a shoe, Brother?'

Stephen paled, and his voice dropped to a hushed whisper. 'No!'

'You are lying: you *were* looking for a shoe. On the day Herbert died you had been struck by a pebble and took off

334

after your attacker, and as you pelted after him, your shoe fell off. You caught the boy, struck him in your rage and fury, and went back to find your shoe without realising how severely you had hit Herbert. Later, when you decided to return home and passed by the same place, you found the boy's body . . .'

'No, no, that's not true,' Stephen said, shaking his head.

'. . . and in a panic, not knowing what to do, you hauled his body to the road, waiting until a cart arrived, at which time you thrust the boy down onto the road itself. Then you came back home.'

'No . . . *no*,' Stephen kept repeating, his face full of an astonished horror.

Simon scratched his ear. 'Tell us the truth, then. You can see how convincing the evidence is – convince us. What is the truth?'

Alan sat idly on a barrel, swinging his legs while he surveyed the room with wistful longing. There was so much food and drink in here; it would take him and his mother all year just to consume the dead game hanging on the walls, let alone drink the barrels of wine. Such wealth, he thought. To own all this would mean never being hungry again. The concept was wonderful – but impossible. He couldn't conceive of such fortune.

For Jordan it was still more fabulous; he simply gaped all around.

Hugh had stirred the snoring Wat, and the lad had brought Hugh more wine. Wat was older than Alan by some two years, but there was a certain mutual understanding between them: both had been brought up to work on estates, and both found the opulence of their halls more or less intimidating, although Wat was less overawed. Having grown up to run errands and help serve within the hall itself, he was naturally more attuned to the ways of a great manor. It was natural, just as it was natural that he should treat the other boys with a faintly distant politeness, as if to emphasise the slight difference that existed between them.

Once he was happy that the lads would not begin to have a vulgar brawl among the jugs and barrels, Hugh allowed his curiosity to get the better of him and he went through the screens to the hall, sitting on a bench towards the back.

'What's happening in there?' Alan asked once the figure of Authority, as represented by Hugh, had left them to their own devices.

'They're trying to sort out who could have killed the young master.' Wat eyed the jugs jealously. His head was heavy from the previous night and this morning's drinking, and he was sorely tempted to try some more wine, if only to ease the gentle pounding at his temples.

Jordan was experimentally tracing the inner surface of an earthenware bowl. He had never possessed anything quite like it, and his mother had nothing remotely so fine. It had a wonderful smoothness which he found irresistible, and he couldn't help but keep testing it with his finger to find a rough section.

He looked up as he heard voices raised, some angrily. 'Alan, isn't that your mum?'

It did sound like Anney. Alan dropped from his seat and padded to the door.

Wat told him not to stray out to the screens, for Hugh had made him promise to keep the lads inside, and Alan was content to obey. The door to the buttery didn't open opposite the main door from the hall, so Alan couldn't see who was talking, but that also meant no one could see that he was eavesdropping. As he listened to Stephen talk, his face fell, and he gazed fearfully towards the yard. Then he heard the cleric's explanation and the contemptuous way he dealt with Anney, and Alan glowered angrily. His mouth became a thin line.

He was more determined than ever to tell his story.

Simon tried to keep the disbelief from his voice. 'So what you're saying is, you were there up on the hill, but although you caught Alan and beat him, he escaped. Shortly afterwards, Petronilla arrived and tried to calm you down, and you went to sit alone by the stream to collect your thoughts, but Herbert hit you with a stone, and because of that you hared off back up the hill to deal with him, but you never—'

'I never caught him. I tried, but he escaped from me, and I finally came back here.'

Baldwin had closed his eyes while he considered this. 'Did he make any sound as you tried to get him?'

'No, I don't think so.'

'Because several people have said that they heard a boy cry out.'

'I . . . perhaps it was me they heard, when that damned child hit me.'

Simon could hear Godfrey chuckle at this suggestion, and when he glanced around at the master-of-arms, he saw the weapons expert shaking his head.

Only one person in the room appeared to be happy with the evidence being given, and that was Thomas. He nodded repeatedly as the priest spoke, and now he turned to Baldwin.

'You see? The boy I chased after couldn't have been Herbert – that poor child was further up the hill being attacked by Brother Stephen here. I think that is fair proof of my innocence.'

Simon and Baldwin exchanged a glance, and the bailiff spoke after a moment. 'It is clear that, for the moment, there is not enough evidence against any one person. However, it is also certain that the boy *was* murdered, so someone has been lying. When we know who, we shall proceed against them. In the meantime, I suppose there is little point in continuing for now.'

There was a moment's silence, and then people began to filter from the room. Anney collapsed on a seat and burst into tears; the priest looked at her with loathing, which Simon could well understand, after her vehement attack on him. Stephen gave the bailiff a curt nod of his head, and left the room. Shortly afterwards, Godfrey made a remark about seeing how his master was faring, and wandered out to the kitchen.

Thomas stood before Simon and his friend, arms akimbo. 'Well, Sir Baldwin? Bailiff? Do you have anything to say to me before I demand that you leave my house at once? It's bad enough that you allow your servants to fight in a vulgar display in my yard, but when you also have the bald nerve to accuse me of murdering my own nephew – in front of witnesses, too! Can you think of any reason why I should not throw you from my household this instant?'

Baldwin looked up at him mildly. 'Several, actually, yes. First is, we still aren't sure who *did* commit this murder, and should you throw us out, we shall naturally have to suspect your motives and wonder again at any involvement you yourself may have had in the killing. Second, you would be intentionally jeopardising our investigation, which my friend the bailiff here might look upon as an illegal act – and since his area is the moor, it would be within his jurisdiction, so he could arrest you. Finally, there is the simple fact that we have accused you of nothing. We helped show that other people were equally capable of committing this act, and by so doing we demonstrated that it was unjust to accuse you. I think you should be offering us your thanks.'

'*Thanks!* I would prefer, Sir Baldwin, to see you bound and dragged from this place behind a wild pony!'

Baldwin raised his eyebrow in a mild and amused rebuke, but his equanimity seemed to infuriate Thomas. The man was almost shouting now, he was so angry.

'To be treated in this way, in my own damned hall, before my own servants and sister-in-law – it is an outrage, and don't think that I won't be making a formal complaint, Sir Baldwin. I have heard often enough of the corruption of our King's officials, but never before have I experienced anything like this. It is a disgrace! To think that you, a Keeper of the King's Peace, could participate in such a charade! And as for you, Bailiff, I shall be seeing your Warden as soon as possible, and demanding that you be removed from your office. Such a way to carry on!'

'Have you finished? Only we do have much to do,' Simon asked neutrally.

'You think all this is in jest, don't you? Let me tell you—'

'Thomas, be still!' Baldwin said. 'Your bluster is foolish, and nothing more. As you have so politely noted, you are in the presence of one King's officer and one Stannary Bailiff. We have every right to remain here as long as we consider fitting in order to investigate this crime, and here we shall remain until our investigation is complete. If you have any difficulties with that, you should contact whoever you think fit. Otherwise be silent! Now, Edgar, what did you do with those boys?'

CHAPTER THIRTY-ONE

Jordan felt dwarfed by the size of the hall. It opened out before him, larger by far than the little church in the village, and when he glanced upwards, into the soaring height of the ceiling, he was so lost in wonder that he actually stopped dead, staring aloft.

'Is it the first time you have been inside here, boy?' he heard one of the seated men ask, and he snapped his head back to them, his face reddening as he realised how foolish he must have looked.

'No, sir,' he said. It was the dark-haired, bearded one who had spoken. He added, 'But I've never looked up before.'

'A good answer,' Baldwin laughed, and glanced up himself. The ceiling was fabulously ornate, much more so than his own in Furnshill, with rich carving on some of the beams. It reflected the wealth and prestige of the dead squire. 'It is worth studying, is it not?'

Alan recognised his voice. It was the man he had spoken to outside the church, the knight. He had a kind voice, Alan thought, not what he would have expected from a soldier.

'Come on, boys. We don't have all day.'

This was the other man, the bailiff. Alan nodded cautiously, and walked towards them both, Jordan behind him, too overwhelmed by the presence of such magnificent men to be able to think clearly, let alone speak.

'Sir,' Alan began, his eyes fixed on Baldwin, 'I haven't known what to do since the day our friend died. We were playing with him up on the hill, and I don't know, but we thought it would be better if we kept quiet about what we saw up there.'

'What are you doing here?' Anney demanded on seeing her son.

Baldwin cast her a look. He was not content with her evidence, nor with her behaviour. Something rang false to him. For now he curtly ordered her to be silent, before turning to the boys.

Baldwin smiled encouragingly and motioned to him to continue.

'Well, sir. We were up there that day. I'd got my sling, and so had Herbert, and we tried to get some birds, but we got bored, and all three of us started playing. Usually we play wars or something else, like hunting a wolf. That day I was the wolf, anyway, and Herbert and Jordan were trying to find me. Before they could, the priest caught me, and tried to beat me, but I got away.'

'Do you know why he wanted to hit you?' Simon asked.

'No, sir,' said Alan with a shrug. 'He often thrashes me for no reason. This time, I ran and ran because he looked so angry, and I went down the hill and over the road. And while I was there, I—'

'Shot me, you little sod!' snarled Thomas.

Alan spun round and stared. He hadn't seen Thomas sitting over near the fire.

Baldwin smiled at the almost comical expression of fear on the lad's face. 'You are safe in here, and I am sure that Master Thomas will not harm you. He wishes us to find out who killed your friend.'

'Well, then yes, I admit it, sir,' Alan said courageously. 'Master Thomas was riding past, and I didn't think he'd know where the stone came from.'

'I used to be a boy, you know! I can tell where a stone comes from. I myself have fired . . .' Thomas realised that confessing to shooting adults when he was a boy might not be fitting, and he suddenly shut his mouth with an almost audible snap.

Baldwin made no effort to conceal his smile. 'So, Alan, after that, you went back up the hill again, and what then?'

'I met Jordan and told him what had happened. Jordan and Herbert had been together up at the stream, and I asked where Herbert was. Jordan told me Herbert had gone to see what the priest was doing up there.'

Alan sniffed and rubbed his eyes with the heel of his palm. 'Sir, Herbert was very brave, he always had been, and never minded shooting the priest. I used to try to stop him, because I was scared of Brother Stephen, but he just laughed and carried on. Me and Jordan were worried, though, so we decided we'd go and get Herbert back before he could do something silly. We went up the hill.'

Simon looked at Baldwin. 'This would be after Thomas had chased the lad who shot *him*.'

'Oh, he tried to catch me,' said Alan dismissively, 'but I left him far behind. We got to the top of a bit of the hill, and down there by the stream, I saw the Brother. He was standing, staring into the water. Then I spotted Herbert. He was hiding behind a bush, his sling ready, and then he let it fly! He caught the priest right on the arse, and my, didn't he jump! But when he turned, Herbert hadn't hidden fast enough, sir, and the priest saw him, and ran after him. Well, I can outrun him, see, but Herbert wasn't as quick as me. He was caught, and the priest pulled him down and began beating him with his stick, and when he broke that, with his hand.'

To Simon's ears the boy was slowing in his speech. The bailiff thought at first that it was because he was coming to the end of his tale, but then he realised that Alan had more to say, but didn't relish the telling.

'Sir, then I saw the priest cuddle Herbert.'

'Cuddle him?' Baldwin narrowed his eyes. 'What do you mean?'

Alan's face had grown pale as he blinked at Baldwin. 'I know what happens, sir. I've seen men from the village with their girls down in the meadows often enough. And at the inn I've seen men with women. It's the same as a stallion covering a mare, or a dog with a bitch. The priest had taken off his shoes and robe, but to do that to Herbert . . .'

The knight swallowed, nodded, and said harshly, 'What then, Alan?'

'Poor Herbert was crying. I didn't like it, but I didn't know what to do. I didn't know what I could say to him. Me and Jordan came away, thinking we'd go home. It wasn't right, sir! Only as we went back up the hill, we heard Herbert give a sort of cry, and I thought he must have fallen. Jordan and me went back, sir, but we couldn't see either of them. They'd gone. All that was left was this, sir.'

And so saying, he brought out Brother Stephen's missing shoe.

Simon and Baldwin ordered their horses to be saddled, as well as mounts for Godfrey and Thomas. Simon felt it was only sensible for them to have as many witnesses as possible. While outside Simon told the grooms not to allow Stephen to have a horse. On foot the man wouldn't be able to get far if he attempted to escape. The bailiff almost wished the cleric would commit suicide before they could return.

He carried the shoe carefully, wrapped up in a cloth and thrust beneath his tunic. He was unhappy about this journey – it seemed to him as though he was participating in a peculiarly unwholesome enquiry, and it was one he would be glad to finish. Simon had been raised in the shadow of the growing Crediton Canonical church as it was being built, and he had an awe for men of the cloth. He rarely allowed it to alter his feelings towards clerics as men – he didn't like some, while others he counted as particular friends, such as Peter Clifford, Dean of Crediton – and yet he could not help but revere them because of their unique position as God's own representatives.

And now, he mused, as they trotted gently off towards the stream where the footprints lay, here he was trying to confirm the guilt of a priest, a man who was supposed to be their spiritual leader.

Baldwin's thoughts ran along the same lines, but he was less concerned with proving the cleric's guilt, and more with his own feelings. He was aware of a growing sense of the *rightness* of the matter as everything pointed more and more steadily towards the priest. It was almost as if he wanted the priest to be guilty of the murder, and that, he felt instinctively, was wrong.

He thought about his feelings for some while. It all stemmed from his treatment while he was a Templar, he knew, and that experience of injustice had influenced all his life from that point. He had trusted in the Pope and the Church, and both had betrayed him, the first from motives of personal greed, the second from an unthinking allegiance, assuming that whatever the Pontiff might decide had the force of a decision from God.

But Baldwin now had a great doubt. He had been prepared to accept every piece of evidence as pointing to the guilt of the cleric because he had *wanted* it to. It would satisfy his own desire for a personal form of revenge: visiting justice on one priest as the surrogate of the Church itself. And yet what if, by so doing, he was duplicating the injustice? A bitter irony, that: in trying to avenge the unfairness of his own treatment, he might himself be guilty of prejudice against another innocent party.

To reassure himself, he enumerated the indications of guilt to himself. There were many signs, from all that the witnesses had said. Anney, Godfrey, van Relenghes and Thomas had all seen the priest up on the hill. There was no doubt of his presence, and he did not deny being there. He admitted to grabbing Alan, and clearly he was already angry at that stage. It would hardly be surprising if, on being used as a target once more, he should really lose his temper.

But enough to engage in the homosexual rape – of a young child? Such things were not unknown, Baldwin knew that well enough. There had been cases in Cyprus, where the Eastern ways held some sway, and it had been hinted at within the Templars. Sometimes particular knights would disappear from preceptories; likewise priests were often suspected. Baldwin sourly accepted that he could all too easily believe it of the slender, feminine cleric.

The boy's death would surely have been accidental; perhaps the priest was as horrified as anyone else would have been when Herbert fell dead. Maybe that was it, the knight thought: Stephen swung a blow, not with the intention of killing, but with the aim of showing his anger. When he realised the boy was dead, he didn't know what to do.

What then? Of course he dragged the body down towards the road, and dropped it over the edge of the bank . . . after the fishman's cart had passed, but before Edmund came by.

Baldwin scratched at his beard. It seemed a little curious to him, but that was the evidence so far. There were the footprints, of course, and they showed that the priest must have been furious: not many men would have run up the hill with one foot bare. He must have been almost mad with anger.

No, there was definitely something wrong. Baldwin sucked at his moustache, his forehead creased with effort as he considered, but for the life of him he could not see where the chain of evidence, so strongly forged, could break down.

Wat was pleased to see Petronilla when she wandered into the buttery, glancing about her, picking up an earthenware jug with a man's face moulded to its front, and a glazed drinking horn, then filling the jug from the wine barrel. The two boys had been left in the hall with Hugh and Edgar, and Wat was lonely. Petronilla was fun – she treated him like an adult, unlike the others.

'How is the Fleming?' Wat asked.

Petronilla sighed, shaking her head. 'He's very quiet, but he'll live. The cut went deep, though, and he'll be in a lot of pain for some time to come.' She ran a hand over her brow, tucking a few hairs under her cap, feeling her exhaustion. Van Relenghes was deeply shocked by his attack. She had a shrewd suspicion that for all his tales of warfare and the life of a soldier, he had never been in danger of his life before, and being gripped and stabbed by Nicholas had terrified him. That, she thought, was why he had collapsed after the first slashing cut, not because he was so badly hurt, but because he was so petrified.

'Where is everyone?' she asked. 'I heard them riding off.'

'They've gone back to see where the boy was found,' Wat said off-handedly.

'Why? They've been there before, haven't they? That day when they got so wet.'

'Oh yes, but now they've been told what happened, and they're going to see the footprints.'

'Told what happened? What do you mean? Have they discovered something new?'

'Yes, miss. They've found the priest's shoe.'

Petronilla set the jug down carefully, concealing her horror as best she could. 'Where did they find it?'

'Two boys found it, and the bailiff and Sir Baldwin have gone to match it to the prints in the mud up there.'

She nodded, trying to control the pounding of her heart. It felt so strong she was surprised the lad couldn't hear it.

Thank God she'd been up there and raked the soil clear, so at least the men wouldn't be able to fit the shoe to the print.

But Petronilla had to know what the knight and the bailiff had been told. There was no one else to question, for if she were to go into the hall, surely the two men there would become suspicious as to why she was so interested.

She fixed a smile to her face, and winked at Wat. 'I'll tell you what, I could do with some wine after all the things that have happened today – would you like some too?'

The track was as distinct as before, although sheep had begun to use it, and they had cut through from one place to another, so that the trail which had been so precise now had the appearance of a tree, with branches spreading in all directions.

Baldwin and Simon led the way, riding to the left side of the path. It stood out in the late afternoon sun, the light striking the top of the bushes and leaving the track in shadow, and the knight walked his horse up, the feeling that he had missed something still niggling at him.

The boys' explanation had covered most aspects of the matter which had confused him before: the strange paths, meeting and diverging up on the hill, were obviously where the lads had been wont to play. Likewise, the trail leading back to the road was clearly where Herbert's body had been dragged.

They dismounted and tethered their beasts to a bush near the spot where they had found the marks.

Simon stared, then paced further down towards the stream. 'Some bastard's raked the place over!'

Baldwin climbed from his horse and gazed about him, baffled. 'But why? Did the priest come here to do this? When did he have the time? He's been busy conducting Herbert's funeral. And if *he* didn't – who in God's name did?'

'Do you know what Hugh told me about Petronilla?' Simon rasped.

CHAPTER THIRTY-TWO

Petronilla left the room with her belly churning. In the screens she stopped, uncertain where to go, staring about her with confusion. Only when Stephen called a second time did she hear him. Even with the revulsion she felt for him now, she couldn't refuse his pleading expression.

'They've gone to see the footprints, haven't they?' he asked.

She nodded. His gaunt features were almost corpselike. 'You're safe. They won't find anything. I cleared it all.'

'Pet, you're an angel,' he said, taking her hand. She instinctively drew away. 'Come, forgive me! You know the truth. I may not be a good priest, but I am not a bad man. Ah, well, God will give me strength. Petronilla, you have to tell the bailiff that you left me. Don't worry about protecting me, because I am safe already. I have immunity from the bailiff or the Warden. You must tell them you left me before I went down to the stream – that way you will be safe as well.'

'Safe?' she demanded, the tears springing back to her eyes.

'You will live, girl!'

'Petronilla?'

She turned at the voice of one of the grooms. Stephen stepped back to conceal himself in the doorway to the pantry. 'Yes?' she asked.

'That damned Fleming needs his cut stitched, but no one's about to help. Would you come?'

'Give me a moment.'

He turned and wandered back to the kitchen, and Petronilla was about to follow him when Stephen grabbed her arm.

'Don't forget, Pet! If anyone asks you, tell them you left me *before* I went to the stream. You're safe enough then.'

Hugh grew bored with answering questions from the two boys about his fighting skills and where he had learned to use half- and quarter-staffs. The lads were keen to know all about him at first, but the taciturn servant fitted no boy's dream of the ideal soldier, especially since he didn't even own a sword, a fact they ascertained early on, and soon they were demanding details of Edgar's life and weapons training, a fact for which Hugh's gratitude was roughly matched by Edgar's annoyance.

It was in an attempt to get some peace that Edgar went to the buttery. Petronilla had left some minutes before, and now Wat sat alone on an empty ale barrel. Edgar didn't notice that Wat's face was a little flushed, nor that his smile was slightly fixed. To the servant's mind, he had found a young boy, someone who would be the perfect playmate for the two pests in the hall. Nodding to himself, he went back to the hall, and smiled thinly at the boys as they began to bombard him with even more questions.

'I have to prepare my master's room now, so I shall leave you two with Wat,' he said, leading them through to the buttery. 'Don't wander. My master will probably want to speak to you again when he comes back.'

Wat beamed at them. He felt wonderful again. The half pint of wine which Petronilla had given him was coursing through his veins like liquid fire, and he felt more alive and awake now than he had all day. He wanted to run and laugh and tell jokes and play – but no one else was about to enjoy the sport with him. Petronilla was fun: he should go and find her, maybe persuade her to drink some more wine with him. But he wasn't sure where she had gone. It was sad, especially since he was expected to sit with these two children and look after them when he wanted to go and find other adults like himself.

Alan sat quietly on a stool near the door. Jordan remained standing by the door, staring awkwardly down at the paved floor. To Wat, both looked filled with trepidation, and he felt sorry for them. It wasn't fair that he should be complaining about having to entertain them, not when they had obviously been through so much.

Wat was a generous lad. He felt much better after trying the best wine in the buttery: it had cheered him no end, and he was filled with the conviction that the same cure could be worked on the two boys. He glanced at them, wondering, and swiftly arrived at the conclusion that the only means of testing his hypothesis was to try it out.

He let himself down from his barrel and went to the door. Peeping out, he could see no one, and grinned to himself.

'Feeling thirsty?' he asked the two visitors.

Baldwin dropped lightly from his horse as a groom took the bridle. 'Simon, something about all we have heard rings false. I want to speak to the girl Petronilla.'

In the kitchen, Petronilla cleaned the weeping fluid from the wound, while a groom threaded a borrowed needle. Kneeling at van Relenghes's side, he gave the Fleming a grin to try to reassure him, but as he stood poised, van Relenghes looked over at Petronilla.

'Pretty maid, I beg that you do me this service. Your touch must be softer than a groom's, and I hope your hand will be steadier.'

The groom gave her the needle, and she stood indecisively, staring down at him. Then, with a little sigh, and while the groom resignedly took hold of van Relenghes's legs to stop him thrashing around too much, she knelt and pinched the two flaps of skin together, stabbing the needle through and tying the thread.

It was hideous. She could feel the glittering, almost insane stare of his eyes, fixed on her with an awful concentration; each time she jabbed through his flesh, she saw his fists tighten at his side, although he made no sound and no other movement. The only sign of his torment was the sweat which appeared first like a fine dew on his brow, and then ran together into small streams that flowed over his temples; it was reflected by her own, which she had to keep wiping away with her sleeve.

When it was over, she rested back on her haunches. Van Relenghes closed his eyes, once, and opened them to smile at her with gratitude. Then, almost instantly, his eyes closed again, and he was unconscious. While the groom smeared egg-white over the inflamed scar, she walked weakly from the room, and stood leaning against the doorpost, a bilious roiling in her belly. She was sure she would never forget the sight or feel of the needle puncturing his skin.

'Are you all right?'

Looking up, she saw the serious knight. 'Oh, I am all right, Sir Baldwin. I have just been helping that Fleming, stitching his wound. But now I think I have to speak to you.'

'Ah, good. I was hoping you would have decided to help us.'

He led her into the hall. There, to Petronilla's secret fear, she found herself walking into what looked like a court of law. Baldwin took his seat next to his friend Simon. Flanking them on one side were Thomas, sulking, and Godfrey, while on the other were Daniel and the bailiff's wife. When she glanced around, she saw Hugh sitting behind her, near the door.

'Petronilla, we have not spoken to you before about the events on the day Herbert, your master, died. We have heard that you were out on the road that day, and that you spoke to van Relenghes and to his man here – do you remember that?'

'Yes, sir.'

'What did you talk to them about?'

'It was nothing, sir. This man's master was just chatting. Well, I suppose he was trying to find out anything he could about my Lady, but I told him nothing.'

'You ran off up the hill when you heard something?'

'Yes, sir. There was a shout, and when I looked up the slope I saw Stephen there, trying to beat a boy – Anney's lad, Alan. Well, I know what Stephen's temper can be like, so I hurried up there as quickly as I could.'

'Why? Did you think he could hurt the boy?'

Petronilla gave him a nervous look. 'I don't know – Stephen can be quite severe when he thinks a boy has been making fun of him. I just wanted to make sure that Alan was all right.'

'What did you find when you got up there?'

'Alan had escaped. Stephen was very irritated, and if he'd caught the lad, I think he'd have given him the thrashing of his life. So I talked to him and calmed him.'

'After you had spoken to him, as you say,' Baldwin interrupted, 'how did he appear to you?'

'He was fine, Sir Baldwin,' Petronilla smiled. 'Quiet and calm again.'

'How long were you with him?'

'Not long.'

'And then he went on down to the stream?' Baldwin pressed.

'I . . . I suppose so. He said he wanted to think . . .' she said. She held Baldwin's gaze as she felt the colour rise to her cheeks.

'Did he say what about?'

'It was something I had told him,' she said with spirit. 'A secret.'

'Ah yes,' Baldwin said. 'A confession, I understand. It strikes me as being very convenient.'

'What do you mean?'

'Petronilla,' Baldwin said, and leaned forward to stare. 'You expect us to believe that you went up there to protect a lad from the violent rage of this priest, and yet when you arrived, you calmed him in a moment? He can hardly have been over-fearsome if you could cool his passion so swiftly. I think it is more likely to have been the case that you told him something so terrible that it forced his mind from retribution on this child.'

She paled under the onslaught of his logic. 'No, it was nothing like that!' she protested. 'I just managed to cool him – I can, I know him well.'

'*How* do you know him so well?'

His eyes were horrible, she decided. All black now, as if there was nothing but a void behind them. Petronilla tried to pull her gaze away, but couldn't. His frowning stare was compelling, and she found herself shaking her head as if in response to some unspoken question.

Simon wasn't sure what chord the knight had struck with the girl, but it was clear that she was scared, and that led the bailiff to the obvious conclusion. 'Petronilla, did you see Stephen murder your young master?'

She shook her head emphatically. '*No!*'

Baldwin leaned back. 'But do you *think* he murdered Herbert, Petronilla? Because I am sure you do.'

'No, sir, oh, no!' she declared, and the tears sprang from her eyes at last.

It had been so hard, so terribly hard, to keep it hidden all this time. To think that any man could stoop to so heinous a crime as the murder of a little child was revolting, but that it should have been done only a few yards from her, was awful! She saw that none of them believed her. Condemnation was on every face ranged before her; they had all, she could tell, convicted her in their own minds for keeping quiet about the murder of her own master.

'No, sir, it's not that!' she said with a sudden passion, her head shaking from side to side. 'He couldn't have; really, he couldn't!'

But it was obvious that, however impassioned, her denial was of no use. Baldwin and Simon conferred quietly, occasionally nodding towards Petronilla. She longed to tell them the truth, but daren't. Stephen had explained to her so many times, hadn't he? She must remain silent about their love. There was no danger to him, for even a full ecclesiastical court could only force a cleric to abjure the realm, banishing him for life – and that, Stephen had said, would only be for the most heinous of crimes . . . but Petronilla could be in real danger. She would be looked upon as a prostitute: no more than a common whore. But that was before Herbert had been murdered.

'Bring Brother Stephen here,' Simon said, and Hugh went quickly from the room.

Petronilla felt Jeanne touch her arm, and the maid followed her to a bench where she was given a space to seat herself. She wiped her nose and eyes on her apron, and then gave herself up to her grief, weeping quietly as they awaited the arrival of the priest.

CHAPTER THIRTY-THREE

'What is all this, Sir Baldwin? If you are prosecuting someone for the murder of my Lady's son, I think she has the right to be present.'

Anney stood in the doorway, her mistress behind her. Lady Katharine looked as if she would be happier to have remained in her room, especially after the scene earlier with Thomas, but her maid was filled with indignation at the very idea that her lady might have been deprived of hearing any of the details of her son's death.

Simon stood. 'My apologies, Lady Katharine. I saw no need to distress you further, and I had thought that when you left us here, it was so that you could be spared the details.'

'Have you found my son's murderer?'

The bailiff motioned to a seat. 'Perhaps you should sit while we talk to your priest, my Lady.'

'Why? What possible help could that fool of a preacher be to you?' Lady Katharine asked in genuine surprise. She had never had much regard for Stephen of York. His skills as an orator were those of a man who had never learned his letters.

'Perhaps Stephen himself can let us know,' Baldwin said, and as he spoke, Stephen walked in, but this was a very different man from the solemn and confident priest who had so recently buried his master in the churchyard. He strode in with Edgar and Hugh behind him, wrathfully staring around him at all the people in the room.

'Under whose orders am I detained here?' he burst out. 'I have services to conduct in the church, and am being kept here against my will and against the teachings of Christ! Who dares to think he has the right to hold me here?'

Baldwin nodded to Edgar, and his man swung a chair forward, putting it down behind the priest.

Stephen turned and kicked it over, shouting, '*Don't* set out chairs for me as if I am some kind of invalid! Answer my question: who is responsible for delaying me from the service in Throwleigh? Whoever it is shall be reported to the Bishop of Exeter.'

'Be silent!' Simon roared. His sudden bellow made even Stephen gape.

'That is better,' he continued, but with a controlled aggression lying beneath his words, and he stood and walked slowly towards the priest. 'Because we want to keep our tempers, don't we? Otherwise, when we lose our tempers, we can forget ourselves, can't we? And then we can strike out at whoever is nearest, isn't that so? Even a young lad of eleven whose only offence was shooting his sling at you. You nearly killed Alan, didn't you? He thought he was about to die, and so did others, like Petronilla here. That was why she ran up towards you so swiftly, so that she could protect

Anney's child. And Anney herself had followed you up the hill, because she was worried about you.

'But even though Petronilla calmed you, after she went away another boy did the same thing, didn't he? He fired another bullet at you, and that meant you were brought to the boiling point again. You were wild as an angry boar! You had to find the brat, and teach him a lesson he would never forget. So up the hill you went, and you didn't stop until you'd caught the perpetrator – and when you had, by God you laid into him, didn't you?'

'No! Look – I couldn't have killed him.'

Baldwin observed all this with interest. A man's reaction to the impact of an accusation was often more revealing and gave him more of a clue about their guilt than what they might say.

This priest showed no hint of shame; he didn't have the appearance of a man who feared any form of conviction. He was simply filled with wrath. Stephen radiated blind passion, as if he might even leap over the floor and strike Simon where he stood.

His attitude made Baldwin reflect again on the evidence he had heard so far. Surely there was little chance that he could truly be innocent, not after the words of all the witnesses? And there was the matter of the footprints in the mud: those of a woman and a half-shod man.

'Stephen, please take off your right shoe.'

The priest turned to him and drew in a deep breath to blast him, but as he did so, Edgar went to his side. 'What in God's name for?' he managed.

'At the scene of the murder a shoe was found,' Baldwin said quietly. 'We think it was yours. If you refuse to try it on and let us see how it matches your other ones, we shall have to wonder why.'

But the priest's face had fallen. 'You found it?' he repeated. 'Where?'

'Where you had been looking for it,' Simon told him. 'Down near the stream.'

'I knew it must be there,' Stephen said, and slowly he sighed, picked up his chair, and sat in it. 'Very well. I admit the shoe is mine.'

'You confess to the murder?' Simon asked.

'Good God, *no*! I caught Herbert all right, and gave him a good thrashing, but that was all. He ran off crying.'

'Why did you beat him yet again?' Lady Katharine asked, her voice strained.

'He attacked me with a sling, Lady.'

'And you killed him,' Simon said.

'Of course not!'

'You were the last person to be seen with the boy, and you were alone.'

'I deny killing him.'

'Why did you take off your shoe?'

'Bailiff, I was making love,' he admitted quietly, shame-facedly avoiding the faces ranged about him which stared at him with such disgust. There was no sympathy in any of their eyes, only contempt, unutterable contempt. The priest began to feel a creeping anxiety.

It was Thomas who broke the silence. 'Bailiff, he admits his guilt. You don't have jurisdiction, but the victim was my nephew. I demand the right to seek justice my own way. Why do you not leave us? I will see to his punishment, and no one need ever know.'

Stephen stared. 'I am a priest! If you harm me, you will be damned for eternity!'

'You think so? I think you are already accursed. When your soul leaves you, it will roast for ever, and I see no need to delay it.'

'Bailiff, I look to you for protection!'

Simon refused to meet his urgent stare, and Stephen threw up his hands. 'Very well, I admit it! My Lady, I am sorry, but I have to confess my guilt. I apologise, it's not something I should have wished to have to tell you, but I have no choice now. It isn't my fault; the temptation has always been there, and God knows, I have struggled against it! But there are times when even a priest is weak, and for me it is when there is a pretty face and an open, enquiring mind. I can refuse most things, but not the two attractions together.'

'You admit it?' Simon burst out.

'I can't see how I can avoid it; Thomas will murder me from ignorance, else.'

'You confess to killing Herbert?' Simon confirmed.

'What? Of course not!'

'You deny the murder, then?' Simon demanded. 'You admit to being a pederast, but flinch at—'

The priest's face underwent a strange transformation. It went oddly pale, almost a greenish-white, before taking on a bright puce tint, so strong it was almost purple.

'*What?* You dare to . . . You have the . . . You accuse me of something like . . . You accuse me of *buggery*? Of sodomy, you devil? Are you prepared to try me with a sword, you obnoxious *bastard*? Give me a sword, you shit, and I'll put you to trial with a man, by God's own power. With His help I'll teach you to . . .'

Baldwin held up his hand and stared at the spitting priest. 'If you deny it, who were you talking about? You said you were prey to an attraction – who was it?'

'It was *me*, sir!' said Petronilla, and she burst into tears all over again.

There was utter silence. Petronilla had thrown her arm around her face, and now sobbed into her elbow; Lady Katharine was weeping silently, the tears streaming down her cheeks; Anney had her hand over her brow to conceal her tears; even Jeanne felt the drops falling from some kind of sympathetic reaction. The men simply stared at each other.

The exception was the priest, who stood glaring balefully at the bailiff, then gave a quick gesture as of disgust and fell back into his seat.

Baldwin was the first to recover. 'So it was Petronilla who walked with you down to the stream?'

'Yes. And while we were there, I am afraid I took advantage of her again. It was wrong, but I couldn't help myself. I have asked God for His forgiveness many times since then.'

'And after Petronilla had left you, Herbert fired at you?'

Stephen didn't answer for a moment, merely staring at Baldwin with a kind of frozen, angry coldness. 'I was not alone when he fired at me. He hit me on the arse.'

'You weren't alone?' Simon repeated slowly. He coughed and turned away as the implications of the priest's bitter tone came home to him. 'And you were hit on the backside. Ah, I see!'

'What would you have done, Bailiff? Just the same as me, I expect. I leaped up, pulled down my robe and tried to find the little bastard. That was why I was barefoot, because I had taken my shoes off while I was . . . with Petronilla. I fastened them on again in a hurry, and one came off as I chased after him.'

Lady Katharine felt her face harden as she became aware of the suppressed laughter all about her. She had an over-powering urge to scream at them; they weren't there for enjoyment, they were there to find the murderer of her boy!

'What happened then?' probed Baldwin. Alone of the men in the room he displayed no signs of amusement, to the lady's appreciation. He knew how painful this interview must be for her and wished to treat it with as much dignity as possible for her sake.

She looked back to her 'priest'. The title, one supposedly of honour, made her curl her lip.

Stephen lifted a hand and let it fall as if in sorrow. 'I caught up with him where the track leads down to the road. There was a large branch lying nearby, and I bent Herbert over a rock and whacked him with it. I told him that if he ever did something like that to me again, I'd see to it that he wouldn't be able to sit for a week. That was all.'

'What, you left him there?' Simon asked.

'Bailiff, my woman was back down at the stream. I wanted to make sure she was all right, for God's sake!'

Lady Katharine saw Sir Baldwin gaze at Petronilla.

'It's true,' she said. 'I have been seeing Stephen for months, and I wanted to talk to him because I have discovered that I am with child. But then his passion overwhelmed me, and I—'

'I think we understand that,' Baldwin interrupted smoothly. 'But how long was he gone, and how was he when he returned?'

'He was gone long enough for me to stand and pull my clothes back,' she asserted defiantly. 'I heard the boy cry out when he was caught, and saw Stephen strike him, and I could hear him crying still when Stephen came back to me.'

Lady Katharine had to swallow to keep the sob from bursting out of her. The talk of her boy being beaten, his punishment being spoken of so casually, made her feel physically sick with longing to see him again, to have a last opportunity to cradle him in her arms and soothe his hurts.

'And you both left together?' Baldwin asked.

'Yes,' Petronilla said.

'But why didn't you search for your shoe?' Simon asked.

'I couldn't find it,' Stephen said. 'I did go back briefly to seek it, but I was unsuccessful.'

'So you walked back to the manor without a shoe?'

'I thought it had to be a punishment from God for forgetting my vow of chastity,' Stephen said stiffly. 'I returned for a better look as soon as I had a chance, as you saw, but there was still no sign of it.'

Lady Katharine averted her face from the man. As he spoke, he had glanced towards her as if hoping to see some sign of forgiveness – but how could he expect *her* of all people to give him that comfort; it was an insult to her son's memory. However, the bailiff's next words caught her attention, and she slowly turned to face him.

'But Anney's son said . . .' Simon stumbled, and then was silent as he saw Lady Katharine's face.

She stared at the bailiff and the knight, who had caught his sleeve with an urgent warning, but too late. 'Anney's son . . .' she repeated, and looked at her maid with horror.

Anney met her gaze with an almost amused sneer. She had thought Simon would accuse someone else – she'd hoped the bailiff would find the priest guilty – but now her last hope was gone and there was no further alternative. With a loud sniff, Anney stepped forward with a dignified mien. 'What of it? Why shouldn't a son protect his mother?'

'What are you saying, Anney?' asked Baldwin quietly.

Lady Katharine saw Anney smile. It looked like a mask of pure evil. Her face was as white as that of a witch or a ghost. The heart beat twice as fast in Lady Katharine's breast as she heard her maid gleefully announce, 'I'm saying that I killed Herbert! And I'd do it again.'

And then Lady Katharine screamed once, and fell senseless.

CHAPTER THIRTY-FOUR

Instantly all was bustle as the women went to the lady's side to try to assist, and the men stood fidgeting, wondering what should be done. Daniel pushed through them all and picked his mistress up, lifting her as easily as if she were a mere child herself. Saying nothing, he turned and walked to a large bench near the fire, laying her down gently.

'Petronilla?' Baldwin called. 'Fetch feathers.' The girl gave an understanding nod. Burning feathers beneath a fainting person's nose would waken them. Only when she had gone did Baldwin look for Anney.

She stood at the back of those who crowded around, the smile still fixed to her face, as if she was pleased with the result of her words. Seeing him watching, she raised an eyebrow in polite enquiry, and gestured towards the door. Nodding, Baldwin followed her out and into the yard behind, Edgar at his side.

'You know why, of course,' she began. 'It was because the fool allowed my son to drown.'

'I had heard of that,' he agreed. 'But why should you demand his life as well? He was no more than a baby of three years old when that happened. Wasn't it enough that you had seen one child killed unnecessarily, without demanding the death of another?'

'If he had called out, done anything, my Tom would be alive now,' she hissed. 'You expect me to forget that? To be grateful that I have a position here in the manor, looking after her who gave birth to the boy who killed my son?'

'This murder won't bring your boy back.'

'No, but the revenge warms me, Sir Knight! Haven't you ever wanted to hurt someone, or even kill them, to avenge an awful wrong?'

He couldn't meet her eyes; he was himself tainted with a murder he had committed as retribution against one of those who had destroyed his Order.

'I see you have,' she crowed. 'Well, then, don't condemn me, Sir Knight, for doing the same.'

'But why wait so long? Why kill the child now, so soon after his father died?'

She faltered for a moment, but then the cold sparkle returned. 'I had lost my husband when my boy died. Why should *she* be protected when I had lost everything, eh?'

'You had not,' he reminded her. 'You may have lost a husband and a son, but you had Alan still. He was there to care for you, and yet you killed Lady Katharine's child just when she was at her most defenceless. That was truly wicked.'

'Perhaps – but he killed my Tom, and I could never forgive him that. Why should I? Herbert deserved his death.'

369

'How can you suggest such a thing? He was a boy, not a murderer or felon, just five years old!'

'Well, I see I shan't convince you,' she said with a shrug. 'But remember, I was prepared to kill to avenge my boy, and I'd be happy to do it again.'

He nodded. There didn't seem much more to say. He told Edgar to take Anney to the storeroom and to lock her inside. As an afterthought, he instructed Edgar to release Edmund, and to bring the farmer to the hall. Then, sighing, and with a sense of deep despondency, Baldwin made his way back indoors.

Edmund was sunk in a gloomy reverie when he heard the steps approach, and the door rattled to the sound of the bolts being shot back. The night had been hellish. He had only been given a jug of ale, no more, with his pottage, and he hadn't slept well. Tired, fearful, his mind filled with visions of what might await him, he cringed as the door opened to show only Edgar and Anney.

'Come on, Edmund – out. You're free.'

He gaped at them while Anney gave him a mocking smile. 'What, Ed, you want to stay here in my place?'

'*Your* place?'

Edgar sighed irritably. 'This woman has confessed to killing Herbert. That means you are released, all right? If you wish, I can lock you back in here, but if I do, I won't be in a hurry to let you out next time. Come on! *Out!*'

Edmund stumbled forward, but as he passed Anney, he stopped and stared. He couldn't understand it. She hadn't been there on the moor, she'd just set out on the road as he approached the manor.

'Go on, fool! Anney said quietly. 'Get out while you still can!'

He walked slowly and feebly through the sunlight. The yard was filled with noise. A cart had arrived and butts of fresh and salted fish were being unloaded and dropped onto the paved court before being rolled noisily to the storage sheds near his cell. Horses trotted past, their shoes ringing loudly on the stone, men marched with a regular snapping sound as their leather soles struck the ground, and all around people shouted, sang, or whistled as they got on with the day's work.

It was disorientating, and suddenly the man couldn't go any further. He stood in the midst of the bustle and stared about him with an almost panicked air.

Edgar saw his perplexity, and although he didn't know what caused it, he knew a spell in a gaol could be disorientating. He took the farmer's arm, and gently led him up to the hall. 'Come along. We'll get you a quart of strong ale before you go home. You need some form of compensation for your stay in the cell.'

Edmund obediently followed where Edgar took him, although at the door to the hall, he stopped, and stared at Edgar with a witless fear in his eyes.

Edgar smiled reassuringly, although he was rapidly becoming impatient, and helped the farmer through the door and into the buttery.

'Oh, no!' Edgar said despairingly. Draped over one of the smaller barrels he saw Wat. Nearby was Alan, who snored quietly on the floor, a broken pot at his side; Jordan lay near the wall, a broad smile on his face.

Edgar walked in and kicked the cattleman's boy. Wat gave a short, hiccuping cry, flailed at the air, and disappeared over the other side of the barrel. Alan instantly snapped awake with a snort and a shake of his head. Jordan remained blissfully asleep.

'Up, Wat! And find me some good ale, if you don't want a cuff round your head!'

'Ow, that hurt,' said the boy, reappearing rubbing at his head. He burped and sulkily fetched a jug, filling it from the butt he had been sleeping on.

Edgar shook his head in disgust, passed the jug to Edmund and led Wat from the room. Once outside, he took Wat by the sideburn and pulled up, twisting it, until the boy was on his tiptoes. 'You are not to enter that room again, understood? I can't trust you, and I won't have you embarrassing your master with your drunkenness. You won't go inside the buttery again while we are here.'

'Oh – ow! All right, sir, I won't go in there.'

'Now get into the hall and wait!'

'Yes, sir.'

'And take your drunken friends with you.'

So saying, Edgar hauled Alan to his feet and shoved him out, and then went to Jordan and pulled the semi-comatose lad up. Jordan opened his eyes blearily and smiled inanely at his father. 'You're free!' he blurted, and hiccuped.

Edgar thought Edmund looked like an ox patiently waiting for the goad. He stood quietly, apparently oblivious to the presence of his son. His imprisonment, even for so short a time, had affected him badly, and now he shuffled slowly and aimlessly gazed about him like a dazed old man with fuddled wits.

Jordan belched winey fumes in Edgar's face, and the servant winced in disgust. He thrust the boy towards Wat and

Alan, who each took an arm and half-carried, half-dragged their friend to the hall. Meanwhile Edgar refilled Edmund's jug and asked the farmer to follow him again.

Jordan blinked and gazed about him with the dull-witted slowness of an old man. After the relative gloom of the buttery, this hall, with its sconces and candles and roaring fire, was almost painful on his eyes. All he wanted to do was sit next to his dad in a dimly-lit corner and doze again, but he daren't. Not with the people in here.

Baldwin had returned, and now sat next to the fire with his wife, holding her hand. His friend Simon was standing in front of the fire, and his face was gloomy, like Baldwin's, although he looked positively cheerful compared with Thomas, the new master. He sat by himself, avoiding everybody.

Daniel wasn't about, which was some relief. Jordan knew that the steward wielded vast power, and he was always scared of him. He was also secretly glad to see that the mistress was nowhere to be seen. Then he went cold as he saw Petronilla sitting on a bench, her face held in her hands, and Stephen behind her, his hand on her shoulder.

Wat quietly walked with his charges over to a bench and all three sat just as Edgar and the farmer entered.

Baldwin glanced up; Jordan thought he looked exhausted. It was odd to see a rich man showing that kind of fatigue. Usually it was only their staff who looked tired, at least in Jordan's experience. While the peasants all toiled and slaved to keep the lands fruitful and the store-rooms filled, Squire Roger for instance had spent his time in pleasurable pursuits: hunting, riding, playing with his weapons.

373

But Jordan's attention was soon diverted to his father. Edmund stumbled in like an old man. His face was pale and drawn, as though he had been incarcerated for years, and Jordan felt the drunkenness fall away as his fear rose. He didn't realise his father was freed; to the boy it looked as if the knight and bailiff were about to pronounce sentence upon him.

The knight glanced up. 'Ah, Edmund, please come here, near the fire. You must be cold.' He watched as the farmer slowly shuffled forwards and held his hands out to the flames. 'Edmund, I am sorry that you have been so ill-served,' he continued. 'I can only hope that in future your life will become easier.'

It was at this moment that Daniel appeared in the doorway. At his side was a thin, smiling, ruddy-faced man, with a face much scarred by the pox, who glanced about him with a casual interest.

'Sir Baldwin,' Daniel said. 'You wanted to speak to the fishcarter.'

'You are the carter who was here on the day that Master Herbert died?' Baldwin asked.

'Yes, sir. I was here that day.'

'You know that the boy was killed and his body dumped on the road. Did you see him?'

The carter gave him a pitying look. 'Sir, if I'd seen the lad lying hurt or dead I'd have put him on my cart and brought him back here. I have a boy his age myself, and wouldn't expect a man to leave my boy in the road.'

'Did you see anyone else that day?' Simon asked.

'Him, sir,' he said, pointing at Edmund. 'He was on his cart riding over here, although he was some ways back. I saw two gentlemen on horses, out near the stream – oh, and Anney, of course.'

'Where was she – up on the hill?'

He glanced at the bailiff. 'On the hill? No, she was on the road, some way from the house here.'

Baldwin's head snapped around, and his face had lost its dark scowl. He peered closely at the fishmonger. 'Are you quite sure? We thought that by the time you passed along the road, she must already have left the track to go up the hill.'

'I don't know about that, sir – all I can say is, she was on the road, and I passed her within a few minutes of leaving the manor. Just after that I started to drop down the hill and saw the two gentlemen on their horses at the bottom. I passed by them, and a little way on I saw Thomas here, and his man.'

'Did you see anyone else?'

'Up there? Only a boy, staring out at me. That one,' he said, pointing at Alan.

'Alan, Jordan – come here,' Baldwin said, and the two slowly climbed to their feet and, exchanging a glance, went forward.

'We have had someone confess to the murder of your friend,' said the knight. 'I am sorry, Alan, but your mother admits it.'

The boy gaped, then stared at Jordan. 'But she wasn't even up there!'

'No, but you and I know who was, don't we?' said Baldwin. He gave Alan a steady look, and Simon felt a cold horror wash down his spine even before Baldwin spoke.

'Everyone here should study these two. There can be no doubt what happened, I think. I have gone over it time and time again in my mind, and I can see no other solution. Anney was *nowhere near the scene of the crime* when

375

Herbert died; when she confessed, it was because she wanted to protect the true murderers. Edmund knew nothing about the killing either. At first perhaps he honestly did think that he might have run the boy down, and the shock was made all the more hideous for him because he truly believed for a moment that he had killed his own son.

'Then we have poor Petronilla. I can conceive of no woman less likely to be able to murder than one who is just about to become a mother for the first time, especially one who feels so alone and desperate as this girl, with no man she can legally claim as husband. As for the priest, Stephen, who was so keen to thrash his charge at every opportunity, and who received a stinging shot on his backside while he was . . . busy – well, he caught Herbert and beat him – but murder? If Stephen had murdered the child, surely he would have beaten him to death then and there – only he didn't, because Petronilla was with him, and she declared that he returned to her, and that she heard Herbert when Stephen had rejoined her.

'Then we have Thomas, who was down at the road. Yet how could one think that *he* might have captured a boy? He is not fleet of foot. Nor is there anything to suggest that the Fleming or his servant rode away from the place where they had been for so long. Edmund saw them, still lounging, probably waiting for Thomas to return so that they could go back to their negotiations, only he never reappeared. Instead they were passed by a fishmonger, and then by a carter going home after the market. They became bored and went home the longer way, hoping again to pass Thomas.

'But two fellows were always up there, unaccounted for: Alan and Jordan. Two who always appeared to be above suspicion because they are young, and because so many others had good reasons to want to see Herbert dead.

'We can assume that Herbert saw the priest making love with Petronilla, that Herbert's sense of fun made him shoot Stephen in a painful and unfortunate part of his anatomy, but Jordan and Alan had no idea Petronilla was there. That was why they felt safe in fabricating the priest's rape of their friend. They had no idea that he had an alibi – and I have to say, it was most fortunate that he saw fit to own up to it.

'What reason could these two have for killing the boy, eh? One had the same motive as his mother, didn't you, Alan? You wanted to avenge the death of your brother. What of you, though, Jordan? Why did you want him dead?'

Jordan flinched as the knight's eyes met his. It felt as if Sir Baldwin was boring into him. 'Sir, I—'

'Shut up, you fool! Remember what I told you!' Alan hissed.

Jordan blinked, then screwed his eyes tight shut with the effort of not crying.

Baldwin walked to him and took hold of his shoulders, softly pulling the unwilling boy towards him. He put a hand under Jordan's chin and raised his head. 'Look at me, child. You will not risk the rope if you tell me what happened.'

'It's not fair!' Jordan snivelled. His alcohol-induced confidence had fled, and now he knew he was found out. 'We thought the priest would never dare confess to covering Petronilla – he always said it was a sin, so how could he admit to that? He shouldn't have told you. We'd be all right if he hadn't told you!'

Edmund stood staring open-mouthed, and now he strode forward. 'Jordan, tell him you had nothing to do with it. Go on, *tell* him!'

'I didn't want to, sir,' Jordan said, sniffing. 'He wasn't supposed to die. It just happened.'

'What did?' pressed the knight.

'Sir, Alan and me found him, and he was all cross with Alan, because it was Alan who fired at the priest . . .'

'No, I didn't, it was *you*!' Alan protested aghast.

'. . . but Herbert wasn't as good as us at hiding in the bushes, and the priest saw Herbert and beat him instead. And when Herbert saw us, he was crying, and said he'd tell his mother and make sure the priest knew, and then Alan would get lashed as well, and Alan told him he'd kill him if he did, and—'

Alan kicked Jordan, and the knight had to sweep the younger lad out of the way while Edgar took Alan's arm and pulled him aside. The boy pointed at Jordan and sneered: 'He's lying. Or maybe it's because he's drunk. He's been drinking all the ale in the buttery.'

'Alan,' Simon said quietly. 'Your mother has admitted to killing Herbert. Either she is telling the truth and must be burned at the stake for petty treason, or she is lying – lying to protect someone.'

The youth stared at him with fury. 'He's going to say it was all me, but it wasn't! He hit Herbert too. I wasn't alone up there, and it was Jordan who held him down while I hit his head with the rock.'

'Is this true?' Baldwin asked the boy in his arms.

Jordan no longer cared. The last few days had been a nightmare. Knowing his father was innocent, but unable to get him freed without admitting his own guilt; realising that the shoe, the one lost by the priest while he made love to his woman, would be enough to ensure that the hated man should be blamed instead – this had given him hope for a while, but then the plan had gone wrong, and now here they all were, and he had admitted what he had done. Jordan broke down and wept, even as Alan at his side sniffed and wiped the tears from his eyes.

How could he explain? They had to hit him to make him shut up, but the harder they hit, the louder he cried. Finally, only when he was silent, did they realise their crime.

And then they heard Lady Katharine's shrill voice from the doorway.

'Is this true?'

CHAPTER THIRTY-FIVE

Lady Katharine had been left on her bed when Daniel went out to the yard to accost the fish-seller, but she had soon recovered. The faint had left her weak and shaky, but she had managed to rise, and looked at her reflection in a mirror.

It was no longer the face of a happily married woman and mother, nor of the successful wife of a powerful squire. Her face had become a mask of horror. All that she loved had been destroyed. Even the woman in whom she had placed all her trust had betrayed her. Lady Katharine could hardly believe all that she had heard, and yet she must.

Staggering a little, she made her way back to the hall and there, while she leaned on the doorway, she heard the boys and Baldwin.

She could not absorb it. There was a scream rising inside her, which felt as if it might snuff out her very life if she allowed it to escape. It was composed of all her agony, all her sorrow at what she had lost. If it left her body, it must take her soul with it.

'Is it true?' she whispered.

Daniel made to move towards her, but she held out a hand without speaking, and he stopped, frozen with despair.

Baldwin closed his eyes for a moment, then said compassionately: 'My Lady, I am so sorry. You should not have heard this. But I fear these boys are at last telling the truth of it. They murdered your son.'

Lady Katharine nodded once. She bowed her head, turned, and left.

'Go with her, Daniel,' said Baldwin gruffly and the steward hurried from the room.

Baldwin glanced at Edmund. The farmer stood staring at his boy, an expression of complete disbelief on his face. 'You *killed* the boy?'

'Dad, we didn't mean to! We were just punishing him. It was like a game at first, but then I made him bleed, and he kept going on at us, saying he'd tell his mother. We wanted him to shut up, that was all, and then he tried to get away, and we had to stop him, and he tried to shout, so I held him, and . . .' Under the appalled stare of his father, Jordan slowly ground to a halt. Crying, he covered his face with both hands.

'It was mainly me, sir,' Alan said, after giving his friend an ugly look. 'If you want to hang me, I am ready.'

Baldwin snapped, 'Oh, be silent, boy! You've done enough damage for a lifetime.'

'What will happen to them?' Edmund managed after a few minutes.

'They are too young to be accused. They don't know the meaning of good or bad, right or wrong,' Baldwin said.

'They cannot be treated like adults. They will have to be taken away to be looked after by someone else. Either the Church or a lord will have to take responsibility for them both. But not together, I fear – they should not be left together in case they lead each other to new felonies.'

'Sir Baldwin!'

'What is it, Daniel?' the knight demanded irritably.

The steward pointed with a shaking finger. 'It's Lady Katharine, sir. She has locked herself in her solar, and I can't get her to speak to me. Oh God, I think she may try to kill herself!'

It was evil, this whole place. Only a few weeks ago she would have thought that it was blessed, because then she had her husband and her child, but now she knew it was cursed. How else could a boy, another mere child, have murdered her son? She glanced up at the tapestries lining the walls, at the magnificent bed with its straw mattress lying on its mesh of ropes. In that bed she had lain with her husband; beside it she had given birth to her son. Yet now everything about this hall, even this room, was hateful; defiled by the ending of her son's life.

With a kind of wonder she stared at the guttering candle in her hand. It flickered and shone, bright and beautiful. Fire! Fire could cleanse the most evil of spirits; that was why witches were burned, so that their malevolence died with them. Fire destroyed and left only wholesome, fresh emptiness. Burned stubble left clean fields; burned trees left soil ready for ploughing; burned wood warmed the soul and the body together. Fire was good.

Lady Katharine slowly stared about her, then lifted the flame to the hanging serge curtains that draped the bed.

They took light in an instant, and soon the bedding too was ablaze.

Thick, greenish-yellow smoke from the straw of the mattress began to fill the room, mixed with repellent fumes as the uncarded wool in the pillows smouldered, and all at once Lady Katharine felt an awful fear rise in her.

Heat gushed, and she staggered backwards as if in a trance. The bedcurtains had become sheets of flame, and now they released themselves, the thin material converted into fine ash that danced in the fire like demons. When a gust of air blew in through the window, the flames glowed white for an instant.

Suddenly she wanted to be free from here. She no longer wanted to see this house ruined and laid waste; she simply wished to escape. But there was no door any more, only a ring of flaming cloth all about her as the tapestries burned. She could feel the skin on her face and hands beginning to scorch; the hair of her brows and the tiny, fine ones on her cheeks were curling.

She turned this way and that, but the door was hidden. With a scream of terror, she felt the flames climb higher.

When Simon reached the window, she had collapsed, and he clambered inside as quickly as he could, grabbing her and throwing her over his shoulder before hurrying out once more.

The manor was destroyed in a matter of hours.

The magnificent hall in which the squire had entertained his numerous friends was gutted, a mere blackened, smoking shell. Stray cinders had lodged in the straw roofing of the stables and the kitchen, and it was only the diligence of the

383

grooms that had saved the animals from burning alive. Fortunately they were all released in time, but not a single building escaped from the devastating effect of the fire. Daniel had attempted to rescue some of the stores, but had been forced to give up when barrels began to explode, and he had sent the men to the lines of those trying to douse the flames with buckets of water.

In one way, Daniel thought, as he stared at the ruin of his home, it was the death of Anney's young Tom which had led to the end of it all. Until he had fallen into it, the manor had possessed a well in the yard, a good, deep one, which would have made ferrying water that much easier and quicker; since his death, the well had been filled in, for a well that killed was destroyed, just as was a man, and the squire had never got around to digging a new one, so all the water had had to be brought up from the stream, away down the hill.

He glanced about him again, taking in the men and women standing in little groups. One figure stood out: the knight, Sir Baldwin.

Baldwin walked up to meet the steward. 'It must be the first time I have seen you without your staff, apart from when Hugh snatched it from you,' he said gently.

'It was in the hall,' Daniel told him sadly. 'There seemed little point in grabbing it – not when there were more important things to rescue.'

'Was anyone killed?' Baldwin asked, gazing at the people all about.

'I don't think so. Even van Relenghes was saved. A couple of grooms got him out before the flames took hold of the kitchen. Oh, God's teeth, what a mess!'

Baldwin eyed him sympathetically. 'You cannot blame your mistress. She was under a great deal of pressure, poor woman.'

'Oh, I know. And I am glad in a way, too, for I don't think I would have been able to bear serving Thomas of Exeter,' Daniel confided. 'But to think that the manor that my squire built and established is gone! It's terrible.'

And he clearly felt the misery. His eyes couldn't meet Baldwin's, but instead ranged over the wrecked area with a fevered misery, as if he couldn't quite take it all in. Baldwin shook his head sadly, but he had a question he must ask. 'Daniel, tell me, why did you demand that Simon and I should return to investigate the boy's death? Everyone was content that it had been an accident.'

'I never thought it was. The lad could have outrun most carts, so why should he suddenly fall before one like that? I was convinced his death was murder.'

'So you really believed that Edmund was the killer, because of his treatment by the squire and your lady?'

'Ed? God's bowels, no! He's too weak and brainless to think of something of that nature. No, but he did give me a pretext to call you back. For *her*.'

'I see,' said Baldwin, and he really did, at last. It was not uncommon for a widowed woman to later remarry the man who had been her dead husband's steward, and the reason was all too prosaic: while knights and squires must spend time travelling from estate to estate, or going to war, their steward would remain at home – as would the wife. Often an understanding could spring up between them. Proximity could lead to affection. In Daniel's case he wanted to do all he could to alleviate his lady's suffering, and to his mind that included having her son's death properly investigated.

'My Lady – where is she?' he asked now.

'I will show you,' Baldwin said, and picked his way down the slope.

A few sheets and blankets had been saved, and these had been strung together over poles to create a shelter and give some protection from the cold and rain. Baldwin led the way there, and through the open side they saw Jeanne and Margaret tending to Katharine. Daniel hurried to her, and knelt at her side, burying his head in the sheets that covered her.

'How is she?' Baldwin asked his wife.

'She'll be fine. She got quite warm when the room went up, of course, but she received few burns, mercifully, and the coughing should go soon. The main thing is, we have to get her to a house so that she doesn't catch a chill.'

Baldwin glanced enquiringly at Daniel, who said: 'There's a farm not far from here. I'll send a man to tell the farmer we're on our way.'

The knight nodded and left the makeshift tent, walking slowly to the hill where Simon waited, standing guard over the two boys with Hugh.

'How is she?'

'She'll live. But God knows if her mind will recover,' Baldwin sighed.

'She'll be fine,' said a voice behind him, and he spun around to face Thomas.

The master of the ruins waved a large jug. 'I'd offer you some wine, gentlemen, but this is all I have remaining, and I think I'd like to enjoy what I can.'

'You still have your life,' said Baldwin.

'My life? I depended on this,' said the other, gesturing at the smoking remains, 'to fund my business. Now, even if the land brings in fifteen or sixteen pounds a year, I am still left with nothing right now. I'm ruined. I'll lose my house.'

'Return down here and rebuild, then,' said Simon. 'It wouldn't take long to put up a good-sized house; maybe not as large as your brother's place, but enough to support you and a family.'

'Here? Never!' Thomas declared, staring about him scornfully. 'What should I want with a place like this?'

Simon speculatively eyed the village nestling in the valley before them. 'Well, nothing I can say will change your mind, of course, but there are many places around here where the owners of villages have set up markets and fairs; they take a good toll of all goods for sale, and make money from taxing the villagers for the rooms they rent out.'

'Fairs! Markets!' Thomas said scornfully. He sneered and sipped his wine, but slowly, and he glanced towards Throwleigh with a pensive frown. 'Mind you, the roads here are quite good, aren't they . . .?'

CHAPTER THIRTY-SIX

When it began to drizzle, Baldwin called Edgar to his side; between them, the two bullied and threatened the traumatised victims of the fire into some semblance of order, organising a stretcher for Lady Katharine, who appeared unable to think for herself; kicking James van Relenghes to his feet; setting Hugh and others to guard the two boys.

Anney stood weeping. She had been rescued from her cell by Edgar, but she seemed to have no will left. Baldwin was surprised to see Thomas's man Nicholas go to her side and put his arm about her slim shoulders while he offered her comforting words. The knight was about to pull the man away, thinking he was merely trying to take advantage of the woman for his sexual gratification, when he saw how Anney reacted. She was gripping the man's hand and leaning on his shoulder like a lover, and the confused knight was left with the distinct impression that Anney was greatly soothed by Nicholas's presence.

He left her and went to make sure that the horses and cattle were being kept together before they could wander and be lost. Luckily Wat had recovered a little from his excesses of three or four hours before, and had been enlisted to assist the cattleman and stablehands. He saw his master, and waved cheerfully, preparing to set off with the animals to an enclosed field between the manor and the village.

All in all Baldwin was reasonably happy that things were as well as could be expected after such a disastrous day, and as the cavalcade began to make its way to the village to commandeer stables and buildings for all the people, he felt that all which could be done had been. He strode along the line to the front of the procession.

Seeing him, Jeanne glanced up at the door on which Lady Katharine lay, carried by four stalwarts from the stableyard. Jeanne had set out beside the stretcher thinking that she might be able to offer some companionship and help soothe the woman, but Lady Katharine was unable to speak coherently. She rambled, talking now as though her little son were at her side, now as if her husband were there; there was no sense to be had from her, and although Jeanne felt appalled for the lady, it was obvious that she served no useful purpose in being there, so she lifted her skirts and hurried to join her husband.

As they left the moors and followed the road down between tall trees on either side, he was talking quietly to Simon; behind them walked Alan and Jordan, heads hanging low, hands loosely bound and attached to a long thong onto which Hugh grimly held.

'What will happen to them?' she asked softly.

'That will be in the hands of Sir Reginald of Hatherleigh,' Baldwin replied. 'He may take them into his own household where he can keep an eye on them, but it's more likely he'll send them to a decent monastery, one where they can be taught how evil their act was. They'll need to pay a severe price for their crime, but at least they won't be hanged. They are saved that by virtue of their age.'

'You are sure it was them?' she asked doubtfully. 'I mean, what with Anney claiming she'd done it, and then there's the priest as well . . .'

'Stephen?' Baldwin asked, and grinned. 'No, that daft bugger didn't lie. I think he even admitted his bad behaviour to Thomas – maybe he thought Thomas would keep him on if the priest showed he had the same sensibilities, those of a rake. No, Stephen only had the one sin to worry him: his behaviour with Petronilla. I should have realised it before, especially since I managed to offend him so much when I spoke to him in the chapel . . . but it's so easy to think the worst of someone like him. He looks so effeminate, so thin and womanly; I thought that the first time I saw him, and because I didn't want to be prejudiced, I refused to see any bad in him. That was stupid, and not a mistake I shall make again.'

'But he used to beat the boys so badly.'

'Yes, I am afraid that some men will; but a beating never made a child turn into a murderer, any more than it made the man who performed it become some sort of monster. I was beaten when I was young, and it never affected me; nor did my father turn into an ogre because he clouted me when I misbehaved.'

'That's fair enough, but what of Anney?'

'Anney, I think, realised before any of us who was responsible for Herbert's death. She is no fool, that woman;

although she wanted to make quite sure that she wasn't wrong, and waited until the last possible moment, I think she knew that her boy was involved. Of course, it *could* have been a woman . . .'

'What makes you say that?' she asked.

Baldwin smiled. 'It was one of the first things I found puzzling when Thomas suggested that Edmund had been the murderer: a farmer like him, even one who looks fairly unfit and badly nourished, can lift much greater weights than a light boy like Herbert. If Edmund *had* killed Herbert, he'd have thrown the lad over his shoulder and carried him to the road; in the same way, the priest would have been able to pick up Herbert's corpse – if Petronilla had been an accomplice, so much the better, and easier, for him. But the body was dragged. That meant it had surely to be someone who was not strong – either a partic- ularly feeble man, a light-framed woman – or perhaps a child.'

'Then why didn't you arrest them immediately?'

'Because all these things occur to me now I can look at the case retrospectively, but it's only when the whole matter is tied up and complete that I realise how each individual aspect relates.'

'And it was hard to believe that children could have been responsible,' said Simon soberly.

'True,' said Baldwin. 'It was the last thing I expected. I came to this matter with a conviction that I was myself culpable for not seeing Herbert's danger, and I burned with the desire to see him avenged, but having seen one innocent child harmed, I didn't want to believe that another boy could have been responsible.'

'And there were so many people with motives, let alone the ability,' commented Simon. 'Almost everyone on the hill had time and the opportunity to murder the boy.'

'But what I don't understand,' said Jeanne more quietly, casting a look at the two woebegone killers, 'is *why*. They both claim that Herbert was their friend, and yet they murdered him. Why?'

Baldwin was silent, and it was left to Simon to answer. 'Boys this young can't always understand what is right and wrong. Neither of these lads is stupid, but they don't necessarily comprehend what death is, or perhaps more important, how precious life is. One of them said something about Herbert complaining, threatening them with exposure, because he hadn't fired the bullet that hit the priest. I daresay that was the crucial comment. Herbert was the son of Alan and Jordan's master, and now he himself was their master – and he knew it. If he felt hard done by, maybe he felt justified in exposing them – after all, he had suffered on the day his father died, hadn't he? All because the boys had been playing together. Maybe he was sick of taking the blame for everything they did as a trio and wanted to see them pay as well.'

'Sir, we didn't mean to kill him!' Jordan said plaintively.

'Was that what happened?' Jeanne asked him.

Jordan let his head hang again. 'He kept saying he'd see we got thrashed as well, and that we'd regret treating him so badly when he grew because he'd make us suffer then.'

Alan continued, 'We didn't mean to kill him, we only wanted to stop him threatening us, but then we saw we'd hurt him badly, and we got sort of panicked, because we knew we'd be in trouble if anyone saw what we'd done, so we thought we'd better make him quiet, so we hit him again, and then he stopped moving, and we didn't know what to do.'

'So you threw him in front of the first cart that came by?'

Jordan scowled angrily. 'It wasn't fair! We were just too late to throw him in front of the fishmonger's wagon. I'd not have shoved him in front of Dad if I'd known he was coming, but we left Herbert there once we'd chucked him down. We didn't want to be seen, not on the road with his dead body.'

'So what did you do? Wait to see what would happen?' Simon demanded.

Alan glanced at Jordan. 'No, sir, we went back along the road to see if anyone was coming, and then we saw Jordan's dad. And he saw us, too. The Fleming and his man had already ridden away, and Edmund turned back to the road ahead and saw Jordan. Bellowed what the hell was he doing up on the moor so late, and jumped down and grabbed him, catching him a right ding over the ear, so we both ran off before he could do anything else. That was why he rode over Herbert, I suppose, because he was still looking for us and not at the road.'

'It makes sense,' Baldwin said. 'But didn't you realise you shouldn't kill another boy?'

'Of course we did, but we didn't mean to!' Jordan protested. 'We never wanted to hurt him, we only wanted to make him stop threatening us, but when we hit him he kept crying that he'd tell his mother, and then we'd suffer. All we wanted to do was shut him up.'

At home in Exeter once more, Thomas of Throwleigh dropped from his horse and threw the reins at the groom, then stood glowering at the men unloading the packhorses, shouting occasionally at the ones who seemed least careful about their cargo.

Not that there was much, he reflected gloomily. Since that mad bitch had burned his inheritance to the ground, there was little enough to bring home to Exeter. He shook his head, a small gesture of dissatisfied acceptance, and made his way inside.

The shutters were all wide, and the din from the street outside was deafening. Thomas filled a pint tankard with wine and wandered to the window, staring out with a bemused eye. Why did the noise irritate him so? It hadn't bothered him before. Perhaps it was the contrast between the countryside about Throwleigh compared to Exeter, he thought, and kicked the nearest shutter closed.

'Nick! I . . .' He stopped. There was no point calling for him. Thomas found his resentment increasing. No hall, no money, and now no Nicholas; his whole life had been turned upside-down, on the promise of a manor with its huge hall and vast lands. Instead, here he was with his old place, mortgaged to the hilt and beyond, and without his best servant.

He fell backwards into his chair and drummed his fingers on the arm while he glared about the room with the embittered conviction that he had lost everything. There was nothing to be retrieved; no way to make an income.

'Bring me my secretary!'

Unless, of course, he could make Throwleigh pay for itself . . .

His clerk entered.

'Sit down, man. I want you to write a letter for me, to Sir Reginald of Hatherleigh. Something along the lines of, "Sir, you will know that my brother's house has sadly been destroyed in a great fire. It is impossible for me to be able to pay the usual tallage because all the taxes I impose on my villeins must be used to rebuild the house. However, I think it may be possible to pay the normal dues if you would consider permitting me to hold a small fair at my village of Throwleigh . . ."'

CHAPTER THIRTY-SEVEN

Godfrey winced at the sight of the fellow's stance. 'No, you hold the swordpoint *up* like this, for the outside guard. When it is held directly before you, the weapon is in the medium guard, like *this*. Have you never been in a fight?'

It was always the same, he sighed. Modern folk had no interest in learning real and effective methods of self-defence; they were too keen on chasing women and drinking all night. Especially those who fancied themselves as ladies' men.

That was the problem with James van Relenghes, he thought. The man was a fool, with his brain in his hose. He believed he could pull the wool over a man's eyes and could cuckold any husband, just because he sometimes had a certain charm, and there was nothing anyone could do to persuade him that he was wrong. Since the foolish attempt on the squire's wife, he had tried to win the affection of another woman, this time one who was still unfortunately in

396

possession of a husband. As far as Godfrey's informants went, she had not refused his advances, not by any means! However, the husband had heard of their secret assignations, and even now was searching for van Relenghes.

Godfrey stepped back, held his sword out once more, and allowed his opponent to swing at his head; ducking, Godfrey moved under his arm, gripped his wrist, and yanked backwards, pulling the arm up until the other had to drop his sword.

It was quite funny, really, he mused. Even those who disliked him intensely were sometimes forced to make use of his services.

'Now do you believe me?' he asked politely. 'If you want to learn how to use your sword properly, you have to learn the basic positions; if you get the stance wrong, anyone can get in underneath and get straight to you.'

'Very well,' said Sir James van Relenghes. 'I believe you. Er, could you release my arm now?'

As she walked into her house, Anney stood a moment and stared. The packed earth of the floor had been swept clean, and where the dismal remains of the previous night's ashes had been there was now a cheerful fire, which lighted the whole room with red-gold flickering warmth.

'Where are you?' she called, and hearing a voice behind the cottage, walked through to the yard. There she found Nicholas resting happily on his axe contemplating a stack of logs under the eaves.

'That elm was about to fall anyway,' he said defensively. 'I just helped it. And then I thought I might as well tidy up a bit; and then I thought the tree looked a mess, so I cut it up.'

She stood looking at him, then at the garden. He was right, the elm had menaced the cottage with the threat of collapse, but she'd never been able to get the help to bring it down safely and didn't dare attempt it on her own. There would be enough logs to keep them warm all though the winter with that lot.

'I thought you might like some help about the place,' he said off-handedly. 'You know, just for a while. Especially now you're alone.'

'Maybe. I don't know how I'll be able to feed the pair of us, though.'

'I spoke to the innkeeper. He's all alone there, and could do with some help. Usually he'd look to a girl, but he's getting old, and he fears being robbed. He reckoned I could help him, being able to protect him as well as serve.'

'What of your wife?' she demanded caustically.

He grinned. 'Ah. One is gone, but there's this other I know who gave me her vows.'

She stared at him without speaking while the thoughts whirled in her head. He was untrustworthy, dishonest, a bigamist, liar and bully. But he had always liked her, could keep a house clean, and already had a job to bring in money, which was more than she had now.

'Come here,' she said.

Later, in bed, when she had drawn their cloaks and some skins over them for warmth, she found herself weeping, but this time, and for the first time since Tom had died, her sadness was leavened with pleasure.

Less than a quarter of a mile away, Edmund sat before his fire and stared at the small flames while he moodily drank from his large pot. Standing, he stumbled to the barrel, lifted it and poured the contents into his mug. Only a small dribble remained, and he looked down in disbelief: he had only just bought this barrel from the alewife in the village, it *couldn't* be empty yet.

Filled with a sudden wrath, he hefted the barrel and hurled it across the room. It bounced against the wall, then fell back, smashing an earthenware pot.

It was one of Christiana's favourites, but that hardly mattered any more. She had gone, almost as soon as the news of their son's crime had become common knowledge, simply disappearing one day while he was out trying to sell his services to a farmer at Week. When Edmund had got home, there was no food, no fire, no daughter Molly, and no wife. All were gone. He'd run from the place, shouting for her, and hared off up the road to the north, desperately seeking her. She didn't have a horse, so she must be easy to find, but he'd seen no sign of her.

A passing tranter had found him asleep in the ditch at the side of the road the next day, and although it was several miles out of his way, the man had kindly taken him home, lighting his fire and warming him in front of it, wrapping him in an old cloak before leaving.

He had seen no one from the village since she had gone. Folks here seemed to want to avoid him, ever since the tales of his lad's horrible act had circulated.

But Edmund was happy; he didn't need anyone. There was nobody he could really trust, not even his own boy. He'd tried to raise the lad properly, but he'd gone to the bad; his wife was probably the reason, she would mollycoddle the sod.

At least the estate had agreed that his certificate of manu-mission was valid. That evil witch, Lady Katharine, had gone and Thomas had no need of Edmund's services. That was what the bailiff had said, wasn't it? That Edmund was free now, to seek his own employment and find a new life.

New life? Edmund's thoughts fractured like the smashed jug as he gazed about the empty, noisome room with dull, miserable eyes.

This was his life.

Baldwin walked from his front door and sat on the bench he had installed overlooking the view. From this point he could see the sweep of the south of Devonshire, and in the clear, bright sunshine of a late spring morning, the low sun lent an almost golden glow to the verdant lands. Small clouds floated past, their shadows giving texture to the scenery.

'Are you all right, my husband?'

Baldwin smiled. Jeanne came to sit at his side. She called and Edgar brought a tray on which were two pots and a jug. When she nodded, he left them, and Jeanne herself poured.

'It's a beautiful morning,' he said.

'Yes.' She glanced up at the sound of a hound baying.

'She'll live,' Baldwin said. His mastiff was still wounded that Baldwin should have deserted him for so long while he was at Throwleigh, and was still more anxious to see him for every minute of every day as a result.

Jeanne passed him his wine, and he gratefully drank half of it at a single gulp. 'That's good!'

'What do you think will happen to her?'

Baldwin sadly shook his head. 'I wish I knew, Jeanne. The Lady Katharine always looked so strong and independent, but I fear that the shock of losing her family, and then hearing her most favoured maid, the one in whom she had always placed her trust, assert that she herself had murdered the lady's son, toppled her reason. She will be well looked after in the nuns' convent, but whether she will ever truly recover, or will remain there, bound up for the rest of her days like a wild beast, is hard to tell. All I can say is, after so many horrors, perhaps it would be better if she never regained her faculties, for all that would mean is that she could once more appreciate her misery.'

It was an appalling state for the young woman to have fallen into. Baldwin and Jeanne had seen Lady Katharine before they returned to Furnshill, and the sight was awful. She had lain on her palliasse, dribbling and moaning, gazing about her with unseeing eyes and for all the world dead. It was a hideous scene.

'Ah well,' Jeanne said with a sigh. 'At least there will soon be the pattering of little feet to help us forget all about the incident.'

'Wonderful!' Baldwin agreed sarcastically. 'We'll have another drunken brat about the place, just like Wat. Another puling, mewling sod determined to eat up everything in sight and then bringing it all back.'

'Don't be so scathing, Baldwin. Wasn't it always you who said you wanted a baby?'

Baldwin gave her a long look. 'You know perfectly well that I meant one of my own. I didn't mean another man's.'

'At least he was a priest.'

'I don't honestly feel that is any compensation, Jeanne.'

'We couldn't have left her there all on her own, my love.'

'I suppose not, but I must confess that when you demanded your own maid, I didn't realise you meant you wanted a page as well. We could have bought one – there was no need to hire a maid with her own brood ready to pod!'

'Keep your voice down, Baldwin! I don't want Petronilla to overhear you saying things like that; she might get upset, and that's not good for a mother.'

'Oh, very well, but all I can say is, I hope she will find time to look after you between feeds.'

Glancing around, Baldwin saw that there was no one watching them. He grabbed Jeanne, picked her up, squeaking, and set her on his lap before kissing her thoroughly. The priest Stephen had not managed to settle his mind about his vow to chastity, but in a strange way, the death of Herbert himself had. Somehow Baldwin felt sure that it was right that he should love this woman, almost as if he had a duty to replace the lad.

He was content.

It was warm in the hall, and the boy had to pause before he could enter, it was so hot compared with the relative cool of the air outside. Also the sight of his master's guest made him hesitate.

'Hah! Jordan! Bring the wine here.'

Sir Reginald wasn't unkind, as Jordan had been led to expect, but he did require his servants to obey him speedily. The first thrashing Jordan had received after arriving here at Hatherleigh was caused purely by his being a little too slow in bringing the jug of wine when called. It had been a painful experience, and now he was prone to leap forward with alacrity when summoned, and as a result Sir

Reginald appeared to have taken to him with a degree of fondness.

The work wasn't too arduous either. Jordan was expected to help about the hall, assisting the steward with whatever he thought needed doing, tidying the buttery, restocking the storerooms, fetching and carrying trays and jugs and pots.

He brought the wine to his master and set it on the table silently.

Simon watched him with a curious smile twisting the edge of his mouth. 'How do you find your new home, Jordan?'

'It's fine, sir. I'm very happy here.'

'You wouldn't want to go home to your father?'

'To him, sir?' Jordan asked, his face blank.

'Your mother has left him, lad. I thought if you were to go home again, you might be able to help him keep his land going.'

Jordan sniffed and wiped his eye. 'I don't think so, sir. I don't think I could help him. He never listens to anyone – not Mum, not me, not anyone. If I went back, he'd beat me for no reason, just like he always used to.'

Simon smiled understandingly, and Sir Reginald waved the boy away.

When he had left the hall, the knight glanced at the bailiff. 'Well? He gave you a good enough answer, didn't he?'

'Oh yes, Sir Reginald. I never doubted he would. He's filling out nicely, too. You're feeding him too much.'

'Not me, bailiff, it's the damned women of the place. They all insist on giving him candy and extra portions of ale. Daft buggers! When I was a boy, servants were lucky if they were allowed maslin. Rye and wheat was good enough for the animals, my old father used to say, so it was damned well good enough for the slaves as well!'

Simon smiled thinly. 'Yes, I have no doubt. The main thing is, he appears happy enough, and I am sure he will flourish under your benevolent eye. What of the other one?'

'Alan? He appears to have an excellent aim with a sling and bullet, so I've sent him off to help watch the flocks north of here. I'm sure he'll "flourish" too! Hah!' The knight began to laugh rustily, like an old man who was dry of throat.

Jordan heard the men moving on to talk about the knight's lands nearer the moors, and this held no interest for him, so he silently walked out to the buttery, putting the tray down and setting a jug to fill under the wine butt.

The place was easy enough; certainly the work here was less arduous than it had been at home. There he'd always been up before dawn to do his chores in the house before setting off for the fields. Now he need rise only when he heard others already about their duties, and when he did go to the hall, there was food for him. He messed with the second shift of workers in this busy manor. There were so many staff that there wasn't space for all to eat at the same time, and even if there had been, someone must fetch the food and drink and serve the servants. So they ate in shifts, the knight with the first, and Jordan helped wait upon him before eating with the second.

No, Jordan was pleased with his new position. It was quite a stroke of luck. He hadn't expected to be able to live as well as this, not after he had confessed to killing Master Herbert.

But he was no fool, and knew that if he were to put a foot wrong, he might find life much more difficult. That was why he was so cautious. He kept his mouth shut, just as he always had. He was taking no risks. A word out of place could lead to severe punishment, and he had no wish for that.

Mind, Jordan had a feeling that he could control his life. There were not many men of his age who had killed, who knew the surge of power at ending another human's life. He turned off the wine tap, setting the jug on the tray once more.

No, not many people of his age had killed. Herbert had been a genuine, panicky mistake, but for all that, his death had been necessary, purely to prevent his telling Stephen and then his mother about Jordan and Alan hurting him. He'd been going to tell the priest immediately, and Jordan couldn't allow him to do that. As Herbert turned to run towards the stream, Jordan had already fitted the pebble to his sling, and a moment later his prey was down, whimpering.

After that they had no choice. They couldn't let Herbert go then, not after what they'd done. And when they were finished, they'd dragged his body to the road, to drop in front of the next wagon.

It was all very logical.

He wasn't sure why he was so determined never to go home again. Perhaps it was because of the treats he kept being given here. He'd never known so much food. After all, he'd been prepared to risk everything for his father, hadn't he? And only very recently, too, when Squire Roger had come to visit.

Jordan grinned to himself. He could feel the sling in the waistband of his hose, a comforting, protective little weight. It was odd, he thought, walking back to the hall; everyone had always thought that Alan was a good shot with a sling, and yet even Alan wouldn't have been able to hit the old squire on the head from that range . . .

He idly wondered to himself, while pouring wine for the knight and the bailiff, whether any boys as young as himself had committed *two* murders before the age of ten.

It was quite a thought.

Michael Jecks
The Oath

Amid the turmoil of war, nobody's life is safe...

In a land riven with conflict, knight and peasant alike find their lives turned upside down by the warring factions of Edward II, with his hated favourite, Hugh le Despenser, and Edward's estranged queen Isabella and her lover, Sir Roger Mortimer.

Even in such times the brutal slaughter of an entire family, right down to a babe in arms, still has the power to shock. Three further murders follow, and bailiff Simon Puttock is drawn into a web of intrigue, vengeance, power and greed as Roger Mortimer charges him to investigate the killings.

Michael Jecks brilliantly evokes the turmoil of fourteenth-century England, as his well-loved characters Simon Puttock and Sir Baldwin de Furnshill strive to maintain the principles of loyalty and truth.

Paperback ISBN 978-1-84983-082-9
Ebook ISBN 978-1-84737-901-6

Michael Jecks
City of Fiends

It's 1327 and England is in turmoil. King Edward II has been removed from the throne and his son installed in his place. The old man's rule had proved a disaster for the realm and many hope that his removal may mean the return of peace to England's cities.

Keeper of the King's Peace Sir Baldwin de Furnshill and his friend Bailiff Simon Puttock had been tasked with guarding Edward II, but they have failed in their task and now ride fast to Exeter to inform the sheriff of the old king's escape.
In Exeter, the sheriff has problems of his own. Overnight the body of a young maid has been discovered, lying bloodied and abandoned in a dirty alleyway. The city's gates had been shut against the lawlessness outside, so the perpetrator must still lie within the sanctuary of the town.

When Baldwin de Furnshill arrives, along with Sir Richard de Welles, a companion of old, he is tasked with uncovering the truth behind this gruesome murder. But, in a city where every man hides a secret, his task will be far from easy...

Paperback ISBN: 978-0-85720-523-0
Ebook ISBN: 978-0-85720-524-7

Michael Jecks
Templar's Acre

The Holy Land, 1291.

A war has been raging across these lands for decades. The forces of the Crusaders have been pushed back again and again by the Muslims and now just one city remains in Crusader control. That one city stands between the past and the future. One city which must be defended at all costs. That city is Acre.

Into this battle where men will fight to the death to defend their city comes a young boy. Green and scared, he has never seen battle before. But he is on the run from a dark past and he has no choice but to stay. And to stay means to fight. That boy is Baldwin de Furnshill.

This is the story of the siege of Acre, and of the moment Baldwin first charged into battle.

This is just the beginning. The rest is history.

Hardback ISBN 978-0-85720-517-9
Ebook ISBN 978-0-85720-520-9